Kudos for
Endangered

Like feel of story. Vivid characters. Intriguing setting. Beautiful prolog. Excellent fire-fighting scene and good sex scene.
> – Linda Lee Barclay, Literary Agent

Story sounds well-paced and imaginative.
> – Jacqueline Cantor, Editor

Landscape descriptions are beautifully painted. Good tale.
> – Betty Carpenter, Writer

What an exciting and suspenseful book you've written. I was especially taken by the extensive research you've done, not only about the logger-head turtles, but the flora and fauna of the barrier islands, their function, their aura, and their significant history.
> – Mildred Barger Herschler, Author of *The Darkest Corner* and
> *The Walk into Morning*

Combination of ecological and historical interest coupled with commercial story line is a fine idea.
> – Dawn Seferian, Editor

Story is unusual and setting intriguing.
> – John Sterling, Editor

I loved reading *Endangered*! Good job with the suspense and with making Melanie a sympathetic character.
> – Gloria Underwood, former English Professor,
> Savannah College of Art & Design

ALSO BY MARY HELEN AND SHUFORD SMITH

Nonfiction

Winning Wines: Medal Winners for $12 or Less

Winning Wines: Medal Winners for $10 or Less

101 Secrets for a Great Retirement

The Retirement Sourcebook

Camp the US for $5 or Less: Eastern and Midwestern States

Camp the US for $5 or Less: Western States

Photography

Focus on the Foothills

Children's Literature

ABC All-American Riddles

To Richard & Catherine —

Endangered

With Love,
Mary Helen "Lara"
Shuford "Food"

Mary Helen and Shuford Smith

Smithwrights

Tryon, NC

2010

Mary Helen and Shuford Smith
253 Judge Road
Tryon, NC 28782
(828) 859-9504
maraford@windstream.net

Library of Congress Control Number: 2010909025

This is a work of fiction. Names, characters, places, and incidents
either are the product of the authors' imagination or are used
fictitiously. Any resemblance to actual persons, living or dead,
events, or locales is entirely coincidental.

To our daughter, Cassandra

Caretta

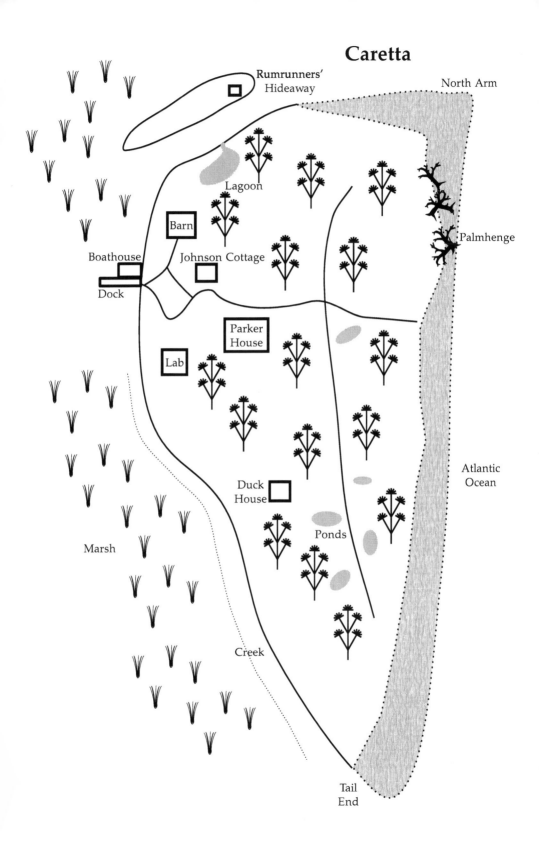

PROLOG

500,000 years ago

The large sea turtle nosed above the crashing breakers into the warm night air. Her powerful flippers touched the wet island sands and she crawled toward the drier high-water mark. Every few pulls, she paused and placed her neck flat on the sand to check the temperature. With great labor, she continued to drag her three-hundred-pound hulk across the beach. When she ran into a half-buried tree stump, the cumbersome turtle turned and returned to the sea.

As she regained the power of her appendages, she swam with grace in the current. For a while, she floated beneath the surface. Instinct told her: This island was the place to lay her eggs. Again, she heaved her body toward the appointed place. This time, no obstacle blocked her course. She reached dry warm sand and cleared away the overlying reeds.

With her two hind flippers, she dug a bulbous hole. Into the well-prepared nest, she laid one hundred forty-two-round white eggs. Once begun, no creature or distraction interrupted this elemental process, performed under the heavy, dark blanket of night. Finished, she shoveled damp sand into the cavity then packed it hard and smooth.

Tears coursed her leathery, sandy cheeks as she crawled back into the sea.

CHAPTER 1

6:30 p.m., Wednesday, July 22, 1987
New York, NY

The New York cityscape flashed by the windows of the BMW sedan cruising down the FDR expressway. Five occupants chatted as the well-dressed male driver maneuvered through traffic. Flowing from the stereo speakers, a soft violin concerto almost covered the monotony of road sound and cacophony of city noise. The smell of leather mingled with the two women's perfume as the hazy late afternoon sun illuminated the interior.

A blue car cut abruptly in front of the BMW. The driver's expression switched to one of incredulity as he mouthed a short expletive. The thirtyish-year-old woman beside him and the older couple, flanking a young boy in the rear seat, swung their heads toward him in silent disbelief.

The metallic-silver automobile began a slow slide to the right, striking the guard rail. Rebounding and crossing three lanes, the vehicle spun like an oversized top. Tires howled in protest as the auto careened out of control. A large sign standard stood in the way. Impact reversed the spin. A lone body flew from a sprung door.

Other traffic braked and swerved to avoid the unpredictable movements. Honking horns, squealing tires, and agonizing screams laced with breaking glass and grinding metal.

The sedan flipped and skidded, shooting sparks before smashing into a concrete bridge abutment. The car rocked and rested for a moment before it erupted into a fierce orange fireball.

Cautious motorists stopped their cars and stared at the conflagration. One bold person rushed to the body lying in the median.

In the departing blue car, the driver grinned into his rear-view mirror.

* * *

7:30 p.m., Wednesday, July 22, 1987
New York, NY

Ashley Parker took a generous sip of the rich red Italian Chianti. Swirling the liquid in the tulip-shaped glass, he observed the wine's legs form then run. "Quality costs — but it's worth it," he mused. Strains of an aria swelled in his ears. Glancing toward the gilded, mirrored wall of the expensive Northern Italian restaurant, Ashley approved of his reflected image. The jacket cut broadened the shoulders of his wiry, six-foot frame. His new hairstylist had sculpted his blond hair to emphasize his strong cheekbones. He savored this self-indulgent minute at the end of a long day. All too soon, the private booth would be crowded with the rest of the Parker family to celebrate his thirty-fifth birthday.

"More bread?" the waiter intoned, interrupting this bit of narcissism.

"Yes, of course," replied Ashley, flashing a practiced smile. In his mind he reflected, "Soon, I'll be getting everything I desire and deserve. It's been quite a haul to get this Parker to the top of the heap where he belongs."

Like so many people born into competitive situations, Ashley still felt the childish stings of inferiority. To him, his life had been a constant battle to prove himself. His competent, dynamic father, who still ran the family's shipping business under strict control, had made it all the more difficult. The harder Ashley tried, the less approval he thought he received. "Grow-up, Ashley." "You can do better, Ashley." "When are you going to settle down, Ashley?" That cycle had been interminable with first his parents then his wife. To Dad, he was still an impulsive kid. To his former wife, he was minor league — never quite enough. Now he had set his goals on a bigger arena.

"Excuse me, Mr. Parker. You have an important call," the waiter disrupted his contemplation a second time.

"Damn, not ever a minute to myself," Ashley grimaced as the waiter plugged in the phone at the table. Officiously, Ashley picked up the receiver and announced, "Ashley Parker here."

"Mr. Parker, do you know a Courtland and Margaret Parker, a Gregory and Melanie Evans?"

"Naturally, they're my parents, my sister, and her husband. Say..., who is this? What's this about?"

"I'm Sergeant Young with the New York Police Department. There's been an accident."

"Involving my parents and sister? Wh...what are you talking about? Where were they? What were they doing? You must be mistaken."

As if reading from a form, the officer monotoned, "The four adults and one juvenile were riding in a BMW that went out of control on FDR Drive. All occupants were taken to Bellevue Hospital. Do you know the young boy's name?"

"Parker Evans," supplied a subdued Ashley. He blurted, "Is anyone seriously hurt?"

"I'm sorry. But, I can give you no additional information, Mr. Parker. Perhaps the hospital can tell you their status. We found a charred invitation to your birthday dinner near the car, so we took a chance on contacting you at the restaurant."

"I'm on my way," Ashley murmured as he slowly replaced the receiver.

For several moments he stared straight ahead. While the aria built to a climax, dishes clattered. Ashley came to his senses and called, "Waiter!"

"Yes, Mr. Parker."

"Get me a taxi to Bellevue Hospital! This party's been canceled."

The drive to the hospital allowed Ashley an opportunity to regroup. How and why had all five been in Greg's BMW? His "perfect" brother-in-law had said he'd be late for the party. "Easy on the cynicism, Ashley," he lectured himself. The guy's been in an accident. Anyway, Greg was supposed to have a last-minute finance meeting with the head of Parker Transworld's Latin America operations since Marco de Costa was scheduled to return to Brazil in the morning. The other four family members were to ride in Dad's Mercedes to the restaurant. Something had changed their plans. What? Why were all five of them together?

Approaching the Municipal Yacht Basin, the taxi turned into the emergency entrance of the imposing medical institution. He groaned, "God, I hate hospitals."

The nurses' station in the emergency room was running at a hectic pace. Behind the counter, a white-uniformed woman seemed oblivious to the obnoxious noises, sights, and smells around her. She rapidly checked charts and computer screens. Ashley pulled himself together to give his name to the nurse. Moments passed before she acknowledged his presence. She pushed a button and Ashley was surprised with immediate results. A somber doctor appeared, ushered him into an examination area, and pulled the curtains along the track to provide a sense of privacy.

The doctor leaned against the bed, "I'm truly sorry, but there was nothing we could do. Only your sister was alive when the ambulance arrived. She's unconscious with weak but steady vital signs. We have her in X-ray now."

"What are you saying? Dad... Mom...?"

The doctor nodded.

"Greg... little Parker... they're all dead?"

The doctor nodded again.

"But, you think Melanie'll make it?"

"We think she'll survive."

Ashley sank into the plastic chair and stared at the cold white tile floor beneath his feet. Antiseptic smells and harsh fluorescent lights washed over him.

On the other side of the cubicle's curtains, a rush of footsteps, the wheels of a gurney, a flurry of excited voices filled the air as the tinny intercom called "Code Blue, Code Blue."

"Oh, God. Mom. Dad. Parker. Oh, Melanie, Melanie," Ashley whispered as he slunk lower into the seat.

* * *

8:45 p.m., Wednesday, July 22, 1987
Caretta Island, GA

Patrice Parker's wrinkled finger traced the scripted words so laboriously written many years ago, "The vessel broke up in a freak, late summer storm." The ink seemed to dissolve on the ancient parchment as she imagined....

Through the dark, wet night, monster waves swept the boat from one towering white crest, through a deep watery canyon, before lifting it into more wind-whipped foam. Lightning split the sky while thunder roared. Rain sheeted the deck as seawater flowed over the gunwales and under a loosened hatch cover. In the hold, cargo shifted and floated.

I shouted orders. Crew members wrestled the sails. The boat rolled wildly to port, throwing us broadside into the next mountainous wall of water. I fought the wheel, using all my strength to bring the bow into the force of the wave. Oh, my God! We're not going to make it!

The library door squeaked open.

Patrice Parker jumped, then snapped shut the yellowed, leather-bound book. For a second, her sixty-year-old face resembled a child's caught in the middle of a forbidden act. She whisked her bifocals from her nose and looked at the dark, full figure in the doorway.

"Miz Patrice? You be all right?"

"Yes, Louisa. What is it?"

"I knock, but you didn' hear. Dere's a call fo' you. I don' know who."

"Oh, thank you, Louisa," smiled the faded woman, nestled between the protective arms of the comfortable Queen Anne chair.

Reluctantly, Patrice bade her sea adventure good-bye as she put down one of the Parker family journals. She headed for the radio-telephone, the sole means of communication between the isolated island of Caretta and the Georgia mainland. A steady beat of raindrops echoed from the porch roof outside the window.

Pressing the lever on the rectangular box, she spoke into its transmitter, "This is Patrice Parker. I'm talking over a radio-telephone, capable of one-way speech. You can hear me when I push the handle; I can hear you when I release it. Can you hear me?"

She lifted her fingers from the control bar. In an instant, a sonorous bass voice boomed from the speaker. "Patrice, this is Roger Morrison in New York."

Recognizing the name of the Parker family lawyer, Patrice frowned. Never before had he called. Indeed, he rarely spoke to her at the family business meetings. A premonition of dreadful news hit her. "Mr. Morrison, why are you calling? Is something wrong?" wavered her thin voice.

"Patrice, there has been an accident — a tragic accident. Your brother Courtland and his wife Margaret have been killed — along with their son-in-law and grandson."

"Killed? No! How?" The exclamations tumbled out of Patrice's mouth, but she had forgotten to press down the control.

The voice continued on its own. "Their car struck a bridge abutment on FDR Drive. They were killed instantly. All except Melanie."

"Only Melanie?" breathed an incredulous Patrice.

"She was thrown from the car. She is in a coma at Bellevue Hospital."

Morrison's voice droned details as Patrice clutched the edge of the table. In her mind, she visualized pleasant scenes of Courtland and herself as children, of Courtland's wedding to Margaret, of them and their children vacationing here on the island. Memories flooded the woman's mind and tears of grief flowed down her cheeks.

"How about Ashley? What about Ashley?" interrupted the tearful woman as she stabbed the push-to-talk lever.

"He is fine, Patrice. He was not in the car. In fact, they were on their way to his birthday celebration. It seems ironic, does it not?"

"Ironic, yes. But, why? How?"

"Witnesses say a car cut in front of them and Greg lost control of his car."

"How malicious. Was the driver caught and charged? What are we to do?"

Papers rustled above the static of the transmission before the male voice continued, "I have offered to assist Ashley with the funeral arrangements and I'm preparing to notify the three regional directors of Parker Transworld."

"Three regional directors? Who are you talking about?" replied the dazed Patrice.

"Remember Kanjiro Fujiwara recently opened our Tokyo office. Now Marco happens to be in New York. But Emilio is at home in Lisbon."

"I can't take in all this. Oh, Emilio must be told immediately. He's practically family. I recall Melanie and Greg spent their honeymoon at his villa...." As she uttered Greg's name, a surge of despair filled her. "What about their child?"

"Parker was killed, too," the lawyer sighed with resignation.

"No..., no..., I can't take this all in. Why? Why?" She took a deep breath, "I'm sorry, Roger, I'm blathering and keeping you from your duties. Rest assured, I'll hold up this end."

After the phone call ended, Patrice allowed Louisa to help her return to her wing chair in the library. Patrice leaned on the ample woman and questioned her, "What will happen now?"

"I don' know, Miz Patrice, but de Lord'll take care of us."

Louisa's steadfast beliefs reinforced Patrice's resolve not to blubber. She sat in the chair and composed herself. "Go tell Jim and Grant. Let them know. We need to talk."

Louisa slipped out of the house to carry the news to Jim, her husband of fifty-five years, and to Grant, the Australian researcher living on the island.

* * *

12:00 p.m., Thursday, July 23, 1987
Savannah, GA

"What's your pleasure, my dear? A champagne lunch on the yacht or a quickie at a motel."

"How about rolling seas with all the extras?" she replied. "We have a business item to discuss and, besides, my body needs a lot of stroking."

"Hmm..., sounds promising," Adam Gardner murmured as he pictured his hand stroking Susannah's sleek, naked body. He relished the moment. Turning the car toward the boat basin, he relived in his mind the first time he had seduced her. Or had she seduced him? Life felt good. He knew he cut a swashbuckling figure with his dark good looks and natural, yet calculated, charm. The image served him well with the ladies. Adam especially savored the ones who expected him to dash in and out of their lives, as a pirate raiding for treasure before leaving for other conquests.

Adam glanced at the striking, dyed blonde divorcée who sat in the passenger seat of his navy blue Porsche. He had met Susannah Harris at a Savannah paper mill executive's dinner party. They had struck up a convenient sexual liaison that was fulfilling for both. He enjoyed being with her in private and in public. She was exciting in bed, not in the least bit shy about her lusty sexuality or his. She turned heads when she entered a room. She was a member of a prominent, old Savannah family whose connections proved useful in his real estate development business. There was no love in their association. They used each other for personal pleasure and gain. He felt complacent yet unembarrassed about their relationship from beginning to end. End? Were they nearing the end already?

Susannah contemplated Adam from behind her designer sunglasses and floppy brim straw hat, her disguise for hiding her long hair when she and Adam rendezvoused for their secret moments of pleasure. Again, she wondered where he had acquired the money to take over "The Hammock." She had learned all too well that a large real estate development took lots of capital to buy the land, grade it, install the water and sewer lines, and build the expensive homes and condominiums. The game worked only when the selling kept pace. She knew from her own experience — the dire straits where her father had left her and her mother.

Adam Gardner offered no clues to his life before he moved to Savannah. Any time she asked about his family or schooling, Adam evaded her questions with ease. He had learned his way around — geographically, professionally, and socially. His contacts proved valuable even to her in her fashion business. High profit demanded low-cost workshops filled with low-wage laborers. Adam had lined up both in two short weeks. And, he had proved his usefulness in other ways, she decided.

The music stopped playing and the radio announcer's voice filled the silence. "At the top of the news this hour, WSAV has learned that

Courtland Parker, the Chief Executive Officer of Parker Transworld Shipping and the owner of nearby Caretta Island, died in a traffic accident yesterday in New York City. Also killed were Mr. Parker's wife, Margaret, his son-in-law, Greg Evans, and his grandson, Parker Evans. The Parkers' daughter, Melanie Evans, has survived the automobile crash. Stay tuned to WSAV for more information as we learn the details."

Susannah turned pale and exclaimed, "Poor Melanie..., not only her husband but her child and her parents? Mercy!"

"How well did you know them?" queried a curious Adam.

"From my childhood — I went out to the island often." She could still see the elaborate sand sculptures that she and Melanie had created on the beach. "My mother and Patrice Parker — Melanie's aunt, Courtland's sister...," she groped to explain. "They're best friends." She was silent for a few moments. "What a combo. My dear, charming, conniving Mum," and a first-class bitch Susannah added silently, "best friends with an old maid recluse — strange bedfellows, so to speak.... Anyway, whenever they got together, Mum dragged me along. I saw Melanie a lot when we were little. We became good friends before she moved to New York."

"Oh, I had no idea," replied Adam as he glanced at the upset woman in the passenger seat. "I'm sorry, Susannah." Calmly he switched off the Porsche radio and continued, "I guess this changes our plans, doesn't it?" In the resulting quiet, he considered how this event and Susannah's personal relationship might prove valuable to him. Once again, he was astounded at the close intertwinings of a Southern town, similar to a nest of vipers. He had to be careful.

Adam focused on the possibilities. His companion could be a key in persuading the remaining Parkers to sell him Caretta Island. For years he had admired the piece of property and its profit potential. Last fall, he had approached Courtland Parker about the family selling to him. He had been rebuffed, rather rudely, he remembered. Now this accident changed the major players. The more he contemplated gaining control of the island, the more he considered the usefulness of his continued intimacy with Susannah Harris.

* * *

1:00 p.m., Thursday, July 23, 1987
Savannah, GA

"I'm very sorry to drop you as a Sea Island supporter, especially at this critical point for the loggerhead turtles. I hope this will be a temporary situation."

Rebecca summoned all her self-control and managed not to slam down the telephone receiver. She spat out, "Begging! All I do is plead for hand-outs from a bunch of greedy big shots. Most of those so-called executives never did anything to deserve their positions anyway, except play up to the right people."

The twenty-eight-year-old redhead glanced around her data-cluttered office, half-afraid to see someone who had overheard her unprofessional outburst.

Man, it's easy to get cynical, she concluded. I've got to find money for the sea turtle tagging project. I need to hire a couple more staff members so I can get out of the day-to-day operations and publish some articles. Publish, hell, I can't even find the time to write. No publication, no recognition. Pretty soon this "bright, up-and-coming marine biologist" will fade from the scene to become just another hack administrator stuck in a small museum. But, this big-business, anti-environment mindset and those pro-military idiots in Congress doom every worthwhile research endeavor. If an effort is unrelated to "national security" or "providing new jobs," then the bigwigs in charge consider it worthless — particularly if it involves protecting the environment. Maybe I should write a letter to the Department of Defense suggesting the sea turtle as a weapon, she chuckled, then I might get a grant. Perhaps strap a small, tactical nuclear missile on the shell, a torpedo on the belly — the latest in inexpensive, low-maintenance, organic submarines. The idea was not that far-fetched. The Navy had already trained seals, dolphins, and even whales for classified military operations.

She stared at the photograph of herself with the huge loggerhead turtle. Taken last summer, the electronic flash had helped capture her tired but happy smile and a glint in her blue eyes. The turtle's barnacle-covered shell, a small piece missing near its head, reminded her of the antiquity of these reptiles. Symbolic of the turtles' patterns evolved over millions of years, the shell contrasted sharply with her own face, the young research director.

"We're so ignorant," she muttered. "We put the bulk of our money and talent into turning a profit or killing other people. Why can't we have as strong a commitment to understanding the world around us?"

A knock on the door interrupted her chain of thoughts, "Excuse me, Rebecca, but you have a phone call holding on line two."

She smiled at her summer assistant. "Do you know who it is, Daniel?"

"I think it's Grant Yeats."

"Please stay and listen. This call could affect you, too."

She picked up the receiver and turned on the external speaker for Daniel, "Rebecca Woody speaking."

"Rebecca, Grant here. Can you hear me?" his Australian accent crackled. "This ancient radio-telephone seems to be acting up again."

Rebecca conjured up an image of the sandy-haired, sun-freckled engineer. In spite of their opposite work shifts, she had seen him often this summer. To her great pleasure, he proved quite aware of the island's ecological concerns — and of Rebecca Woody.

"Go ahead, Grant. Daniel and I are all ears. We hear you just fine. I hope you're going to tell me of an inexhaustible source for funds."

"Afraid not, my dear. In fact, I'm the bearer of most disturbing news. Courtland and Margaret Parker, Caretta's owners, have died in an automobile accident in New York."

"Oh no," Rebecca whispered. "They're so vital to my project." Immediately she experienced remorse for her selfish response to the couple's unexpected death.

"I'm not finished, Becca. Also, their son-in-law Greg Evans was killed. He was, if you recall, the Financial Director of Parker Transworld. Plus, their little grandson Parker died. Only their daughter Melanie survived — and she's in a coma."

As the horror settled into Rebecca's mind, an image began to form, replaying her last meeting with Courtland. She had been pushing for a formal contract that would detail the turtle project's right to unrestricted use of Caretta Island's beach. His comment, "Nothing to worry about, Ms. Woody. You've got a free rein as long as I'm around." And now, he's not around. Rebecca voiced, "Grant, how are their deaths going to affect us? I don't have a written agreement. Do you?"

"Worst-case scenario would be: We both lose our access to the island. Best-case scenario would be: We experience no change in the status quo. There are a hell of a lot of variables. So, it's all supposition at this point. I'm unsure what will happen here, Becca. Patrice is most distraught. I'll call again tomorrow."

"Of course. Any time."

"When do you intend to come back to the island?"

"Soon, Grant, soon. I'll let you know."

This time, Rebecca replaced the phone gently in its cradle as she tried to grasp her dilemma. Now in addition to a major funding loss, death had intervened. The essential family members, who allowed her project to gather loggerhead nesting data on their privately-held island, had been killed.

Self-consciously, Daniel shifted his weight from one foot to the other as he spoke softly, "Rebecca, are you all right?"

She looked at the young graduate student with sad eyes, "We've got a lot to do, Daniel. We've got to finish inputting the data into the computer so we can get to the island. And, we must focus on some long-range planning."

* * *

10:25 a.m., Thursday, September 3, 1987
New York, NY

Melanie's eyes opened with difficulty. Her eyelashes seemed glued together. Raising her right hand to brush the sleep from her right eye, she realized plastic tubes were inserted in her arm. Puzzled, Melanie let the limb drop onto the bed. The stiff sheet irritated her dry, hypersensitive skin. She blinked her eyes hard to clear the crusty, collected matter.

She looked around.

She was lying in a small room, painted a misty institutional green. Near the ceiling, a television was mounted on the wall. Its blank, gray screen reflected light from a curtained window behind her bed. Melanie moved her head to the right and saw plastic tubing connect her arm to an IV bottle on a metal stand. Other tubes and wires crisscrossed and plugged into rectangular metal boxes with lighted digital readouts.

At that moment, the door to the room opened. Slowly Melanie turned her head to the left and watched a white uniformed nurse approach her bed.

"Well, it's about time you woke up. Your brother will be so relieved," the nurse spoke in a cheerful voice.

"What? Where am I?" Melanie croaked. Her mouth felt dry, as if it had been packed in cotton.

"You're in Bellevue Hospital. You've been here since the car accident."

"Car accident?"

The nurse assumed a curt professional manner, checked Melanie's eyes then took her pulse.

While the nurse penciled notations on a clipboard, Melanie pleaded, "Water? Please, may I have a drink of water?"

"Of course. You're thirsty, aren't you? You haven't had a drink in over six weeks except for that IV."

Melanie's mind tried to register time. "Six weeks?" she asked.

The nurse nodded as she poured a glass of water from a pitcher. Then, she helped Melanie raise her head to drink the water from an elbow straw.

It hurt to lift her head. After a couple of sips, she felt tired and drowsy.

As she fell asleep, she dreamed she heard the nurse say she would call her doctor or brother.

The next time Melanie awoke, a bright bouquet of flowers blossomed in her line of vision. She forced her eyes to focus on the flowers then on the face behind them. Her sleep-fogged mind fought for recognition.

"Gre... Ashley," Melanie murmured. It was her brother standing next to her bed, not her husband. She stammered, "Where's Greg?"

"You've gained consciousness," ventured Ashley as his hand pushed the call button that lay beside Melanie on the bed.

Melanie worked hard at phrasing her questions. "Ashley, what's happened? Where's Greg? Where's...?"

"Shhh, Melanie," soothed Ashley.

A nurse poked her head into the room to see if she were needed.

Ashley asked, "Would you please notify Dr. Anders that Mrs. Evans is conscious?"

"Certainly, Mr. Parker," bustled the efficient nurse.

Ashley returned his attention to the watchful, confused Melanie. "The doctor will be here in a moment. He'll explain everything to you."

"Can't you tell me?"

"Yes, but I want the doctor here, too."

"The nurse mentioned a car accident. Is that right?" her voice slurred.

"Yes."

"Six weeks ago?" she questioned.

"That's right, too."

"What's today?"

"It's Saturday." He paused then added, "September 3."

"When? The accident?" she breathed.

"July 22."

"Your birthday?"

"Yes."

Melanie digested the information then her eyes widened. With what seemed an immense effort to her, she warily asked, "Ashley, where are Greg and Parker? What about Mom and Dad? Were they in the accident? Are they in the hospital, too?"

Miles Anders, the Parker family physician, strode into the tiny room. The distinguished, large-framed doctor dominated most rooms and situations.

"Melanie! The nurse said you had gained consciousness this afternoon. I hoped you'd come back around before I left the hospital today." Dr. Anders patted her hand warmly.

"Dr. Anders, Melanie was asking about our mother and father, her husband and son."

Melanie saw the strain on both faces and an unsaid message flicker between them. She tensed before the doctor replied, "I'm sorry, Melanie. They're dead."

She squeezed her eyes shut and willed herself dead, too. She waited. The air conditioning clicked and hissed. The television in the next room droned. She heard Ashley and Dr. Anders draw breaths. She refused to breathe.

Lying still, she waited. She waited for one of them to say something different. She waited for the world to stop. She waited for her own death.

No one said anything. The air conditioning and television continued to perform. She sighed. Nothing changed.

CHAPTER 2

9:30 a.m., Saturday, January 9, 1988
Caretta Island, GA

Caretta Island could be the crowning glory of eastern seaboard development, if Adam Gardner played the game properly. Assuredly, he knew how to play the game.

A sharp wind blew off the Atlantic and bit through Adam's coat as he guided his launch toward the unspoiled island of Caretta. He maneuvered into the narrow salt marsh creek channel and viewed the wooded expanse, not as pristine beauty, but as an opportunity.

Since that day when he and Susannah Harris had heard the radio announcement of the car wreck, he had brainstormed possibilities for this island. Adam knew change must come, thanks to the inheritance tax system. He also knew with the proper timing, he might benefit. He had marked a date on his calendar. Yesterday his sagacity had been confirmed with the receipt of the New York probate court's docket. It was time to take action.

Five months had passed, an adequate interval since the tragedy to present a business proposition to one of the survivors. Besides, another set of holidays was over. It was time for the family to turn attention to the business of a new year — and life.

He cut the engine and secured the craft to the dock. As he walked the crushed oyster shell road to Parker House, he rehearsed his approach to this talk with Patrice Parker, the lone family member who chose to live on Caretta. Susannah had supplied him valuable background information, detailing how Patrice had exiled herself to the island after her fiancé's death in World War II. He knew Patrice wasn't the decision-maker in the family, but he wanted her on his side. Besides, she was the one Parker on the island now.

Turning a bend in the road, he gazed at the Spanish villa in front of him. It was more imposing than he had imagined. Adam stood in the middle of the road and evaluated the edifice. He visualized the Big House, as many of the old plantation houses were called, as a clubhouse. In his mind, he drew an elaborate script logo for *The Villa* in gold ink.

The dull thud of wood hitting wood, caused him to notice two men unloading a cart of cut and split fireplace logs. One man was a wizened, old black; the other appeared to be a middle-aged, sandy-haired chap. When Adam continued up the road past them, he heard the younger man mutter, "bloody developer."

Adam debated issuing a challenge when a movement at the house diverted his attention. He discerned a thin woman behind the protective screening placed in the porch archways. He couldn't fathom any emotion on her face. He wondered, how long she had been watching him?

She called out a greeting, "Please come into the parlor, Mr. Gardner. It's quite chilly today."

Patrice Parker motioned Adam across the porch, through heavy doors, into the foyer. There stood a large black woman in a floral cotton print dress topped with a crisp, white apron. For a moment, Adam sensed suspicion in the dark woman's eyes. Her voice, however, sounded warm as she offered to take his coat.

Adam adjusted his tie and unbuttoned his sportcoat as Patrice led him into the parlor. He sat in a matching wing chair opposite the woman who appeared older and frailer than he had anticipated. He heard the small fire crackling in the fireplace. The housekeeper returned and offered him a steaming cup of coffee that he gladly accepted.

"Mr. Gardner, did you know only seventy-five years ago, the trip from Savannah to Caretta took six or more hours of hard rowing, if the tide were right?"

"No, Miss Parker, I didn't," an off-balance Adam responded. "That's an interesting tidbit of history."

"Now, sir, as I told you on the phone, I enjoy visitors. However, I am puzzled. What really brings you to Caretta on a wintry day to visit an old woman?"

Sipping his coffee and employing his most soothing voice, Adam replied, "Miss Parker, you do yourself disservice. And, I would greatly appreciate your calling me Adam."

She smiled and nodded.

Adam continued, "I wanted to see you after I heard the news about the tragic event that happened to your family — to offer my condolences — and my help." He realized his explanation for being here sounded weak, even to his own ears.

"That's very kind of you," Patrice replied with Southern graciousness. "It's difficult for me to believe it's been almost six months."

"Uh, yes." Adam rushed on, "Susannah Harris and her mother, Katherine, told me how much you and your brother have loved this place. He was most fortunate to have you here in charge. The consequences of this unfortunate accident must present immense legal and financial complications for you to maintain the island."

"What are you trying to say, Mr. Gardner, uh... Adam?"

Despite the woman's fragile appearance and her remarks about the past, her mind functioned quickly. Setting down his coffee cup, he turned to face her. "Forgive my awkwardness. But, I assume you enjoy Caretta for what it has been as well as for what it is today?" Adam questioned, recasting his net for her favor.

"Why yes, of course."

"And, you would like to continue living here, enjoying those benefits?"

"Decidedly."

Adam sighed, "Family islands such as Caretta are becoming a rarity these days because of federal tax laws. Many interests desire them. On one side, there are groups that feel no individual or family should own them. They believe such land should be under the total control of a governmental bureaucracy. I'm sure you'd hate to watch some faceless committee in Washington deciding Caretta's future."

He paused, noticing her nod in agreement before continuing, "On the other side, there are greedy people who want to carve the land into small parcels and sell them to the highest bidder. Such an auction-block mentality creates the tall concrete monstrosities paving so many of our beaches today. Neither case maintains the essence of Caretta, as you know and love it."

Perceiving Patrice's eyes take on a glazed look, he realized the need for specific examples. "I'm sure you've seen Wassaw and Tybee islands.

Wassaw has been turned over to the government and currently Tybee has become a monument to non-planning."

"You paint a bleak picture, Adam."

"I've become a realist over the years, Miss Parker. Naturally, I like to think the majority of people try to do what's right, but nothing works without planning. I've found to achieve what's best, one has to be there at the appropriate time with a good idea."

"Adam, I must confess. Courtland always handled this kind of decision. I have no idea where to begin."

"I understand completely. I have no ready answers for you, Miss Parker. But, I do want you to know I'm available to help. I'm a friend of friends of the family and I'm concerned about what's best for you and for your island. I'm relatively new to Savannah. If you check with Susannah Harris or her mother, you'll find out more about me.

"However, rest assured that I've had dealings with all types of special interest groups and I know you can maintain what you love about Caretta. I want you to consider me as a stand-in for your brother, implementing his and your wishes. No matter what, call me and I'll do all I can to insure you and the island maintain a special relationship. Just to be sure, I'll let your nephew and niece in New York know of my availability, also."

"I appreciate your offer, Adam. By the way, how are Susannah and her mother?"

"They're fine. They send their love," Adam said as he stood and offered his hand to the thin, older lady. "When change occurs, we can insure it's a good change, not a travesty to the memory of your brother. I greatly appreciate your seeing me today." He withdrew his hand from hers and reached inside the breast pocket of his sports jacket, extracted a leather case then a business card. "Here's my card. Call me any time. Remember: I'm available to help with any problem, no matter how small."

"Adam, you've been most perceptive. I'm glad you came today. I was worried about this meeting, but in a way, you remind me of James. He and I.... Well, that was forty years ago. From now on, please call me Patrice."

"With pleasure, Patrice. Please, don't get up from your warm chair to see me out. And, don't forget to call me if you need anything — anything at all."

The housekeeper was waiting in the foyer with his heavy coat. As he shrugged into his coat, again he sensed her distrust. He chose to disregard it. How much influence could this woman possibly have over Patrice or on the decision for the island?

Making his way to the dock and boat, he reviewed the conversation. He felt good about it. The awkward beginning had actually worked to his advantage. He had gained Patrice Parker's sympathies then approval. What luck that he, Adam Gardner, resembled her dead fiancé. She was nibbling at the bait, protecting her way of life.

* * *

11:00 a.m., Sunday, April 3, 1988
New York, NY

On this cold April morning, Melanie and Ashley sat in her Sutton Place co-operative apartment and looked down on the dreary city. The weather and the buildings merged to form a gray maze with no outlet. Below her, the East River appeared sluggish, going nowhere. The view matched her mood. She saw no place for herself in New York City.

During the past nine months, she had tried to reconstruct her life without her husband, child, mother, and father. Her brother had been attentive, but Ashley was undergoing numerous adjustments himself. He was shouldering full responsibility for Parker Transworld Shipping as well as accepting the family loss.

Many people, including the doctors and therapists, had told her how lucky she was to be alive. Physically and mentally intact, she had awakened from the coma. No bones had been broken; the accident itself was the only missing memory. But lucky? She had decided that opinion depended on one's viewpoint. Others could not fully understand, she believed. They had not lost a husband, son, and parents. She was the one who had to endure the endless void, the all-consuming grief.

Although she no longer preferred death, the misery of the past year made her ache for a new direction in her lonely life.

Remembering a recent purse-snatching, humiliation twisted inside her. Melanie could still hear the young boy's cry, "Let go, you rich, old bitch!" She didn't feel old. Yet, she had been unable to protect herself from that kid. He had pulled her purse out of her grasp then he had outrun her on the street. To add insult, no one had tried to help her. Melanie perceived a lot of dissonance — the physical inability to defend herself, the other pedestrians' unwillingness to get involved, the mental inability to put it all away. Something must change.

Melanie stared at her coffee. She swirled the last of the hot liquid in her cup. The once-treasured Zabar's special blend now tasted flat and metallic. Was it because Greg was not here to enjoy life with her? For about two months before the accident, they had not been getting along. They had been planning a short vacation for the two of them. She had hoped that time together would have allowed them to sort out their problems. Now she felt cheated. Would they have been able to repair their relationship? Now his sudden and total absence left a gaping hole in her life.

She missed Parker, their rambunctious nine-year-old. He would be ten now. He no longer had to be cautioned not to run in the building nor helped with his multiplication or division tables. Of course, she had not been the perfect parent, but she longed for his sloppy wet kisses, warm impulsive hugs, presents of dandelions or violets from the park.

Her focus shifted to her father and mother and special days they all enjoyed together. Now, holidays — Thanksgiving, Christmas, Valentine's Day — were disasters, as far as she was concerned. Her mind and body ached for the touching, hugging, and kissing that indicated she loved and was loved by her husband, son, mother, and father. On those particular days, she acutely missed the exchange of cards, flowers, gifts and, most of all, the shared moments.

Often, she seemed whipsawed by her own emotions as she remembered the good times, then, the not-so-good times. All she had were memories now. She knew these people had not been perfect, and she wasn't trying to make them perfect in her mind. She was trying to remember them exactly as they had been — complete with their quirks and flaws.

Though her father was regarded by all as a great success, she knew there were moments he had regretted a decision or had lost his temper. On one occasion, she saw him throw an unreliable computer terminal out a window. Courtland had expected the best performance from his staff and demanded it from his equipment. She wondered if he ever wanted to treat his staff with the same rash behavior he had shown the computer.

Her mother had accepted her roles of encouraging wife and nurturing mother. She had implemented most societal messages of her day about a woman's place being in the home and had expected her daughter to do the same. She questioned the need for the women's liberation movement and disliked the idea of women filling "men's" positions in the workplace. All of Melanie's life, Margaret had never desired a career. Consequently, her mother did not understand Melanie's desire to work at Parker Transworld when there was no monetary need for her to do so. Margaret's only activity outside the family had been volunteer work at the New York Botanical Gardens. Melanie and everyone else at Parker Transworld knew Margaret Parker always hid in her purse a romance novel, discreetly wrapped with chintz to cover the bodice-ripped heroine. That was in case she was caught somewhere with a moment to spare.

Melanie found her mother's decisions different from ones she would make under similar circumstances. Long ago, Melanie had decided it best to accept her mother's choices and to focus on what was positive, such as her mother's organizational abilities.

Now, after the accident, Melanie's own well-organized daily routines were upset — at home, at play, at work. For the past few months, she had ventured into Parker Transworld to attend meetings at Ashley's and her therapist's insistence. There, she discovered her talented assistant had everything under control. She felt she was unneeded. And, she, Melanie Parker Evans, could not arouse herself to find any interest in the family business.

She experienced the same apathy for her civic and social activities. Many of her friends and associates had stopped calling. It was just as well; most acted as if they were afraid to say what they were thinking.

She felt no reason to be. It was as if she were a hollow shell, emptied of her vitality, the forces that had driven her life. She wondered if she were the same woman she had once thought she was.

Looking at the gray scene outside the window then at her brother sitting across from her, Melanie wiped away a tear, straightened up in her chair, and spoke carefully, "I'm going to Caretta for a while. I need a change from New York."

Ashley ran a hand through his hair then glanced at the ceiling for a moment before responding, "I know you're upset after the car accident, the purse snatching, and all. But, what you need is to immerse yourself in work. Getting really involved will strengthen your outlook faster than running away."

"I'm not ready to work — or run away," she protested. "I simply need a change. I need time to regroup. My psychiatrist approves of my going. Others think it's a good idea, too. Besides, I've already started preparations."

"Come on," he pushed his advantage. "You've always been good at your work, even now. Besides, I need you, Melanie."

"Thanks, Ashley, but I have to go. Parker Transworld is performing better than expected. Daddy and Greg's idea to have Kanjiro Fujiwara open the Tokyo office has been profitable. That's amazing in its first year." She noticed Ashley bristle to the reference and quickly added, "And, you're doing an exceptional job, too. You really don't need me now while I'm a liability instead of an asset. I have to go."

"Melanie, I know it's tough," he responded in a deliberate manner, "and I understand, well... partially understand, what you're going through. Trust me now. A steady work routine will help you far more than weeks alone with that crazy aunt of ours."

"Why do you think Patrice is crazy? I imagine she simply likes her solitude. That's all."

"Give me a break. The old biddy's been alone so long she's forgotten how to relate to anyone. How's that supposed to be good for you?"

Melanie sighed. She knew her brother was trying to help. She realized, however, that though he had lost Mom and Dad, he had not experienced the death of a spouse and child. Too, she also knew from experience, Ashley's answer to difficulties involved working harder, achieving more, outdistancing the problem. She knew part of her housed that same competitive spirit — to be smarter or richer or better-known than someone else. What troubled her was Ashley's inability to balance that driving force with a peaceful, sharing approach to life, the very kind of nurturing her psyche now demanded. Patrice might be a loner and Caretta was definitely isolated, but an inner voice kept insisting she seek time to herself. Besides, Louisa and Jim were there. When she had been growing up, they had provided the kind of acceptance she wanted now.

Slowly she shook her head from side to side. Obviously, Ashley did not need what she needed. She wondered why. "Ashley, we could argue this all day. But, getting out of the city and trying a quiet perspective on the island seems healthy to me. Besides, it will help us decide what to do with Caretta and how to take care of our aunt, the staff, and the research activities."

"I understand, little sister, those are pending decisions, but they're actually quite simple. If you're looking for a change in perspective, the company has offices in other cities. You could work in any of them — Tokyo, Sydney, Lisbon, San Francisco. You're a big-city woman. The worst possible move for you is to go to that hot little sandspit. You'll dry up and blow away. When I talked with Patrice, she felt the same way."

Melanie puzzled, "That's strange. Last night she told me my coming would be wonderful."

"Don't expect me to explain her behavior," Ashley scoffed.

Melanie wondered if her aunt were being agreeable only because of the accident. Was she placing herself in another uncomfortable situation — next to someone being less-than-honest, partially senile, or crazy as her brother described her? Yet, Melanie knew she had nothing to gain by staying in New York, this memory-triggering location. The island of Caretta pulled her. Ashley's insistent badgering that work was the only answer was not for her. His single prescription for all ills was becoming irritating. He was denying her feelings. Besides, she sensed an emotional pull to the island.

"I'm going," she replied quietly. More firmly, she added, "I'll come into work to send out memos and make phone calls to let all our business associates know to contact either you or my personal assistant. I'll return when I feel I'm ready."

"Just remember you're not the financial genius Greg was. Nor, is the IRS going to wait forever for us to decide how to pay the inheritance tax on that hunk of prime coastal real estate," Ashley cautioned her as he stood and put on his coat. When he reached the door, he turned to face Melanie for one last shot, "Something tells me that you're making a big mistake."

* * *

A thousand miles south, a buzz of the telephone was answered with a terse, "Yes?"

"We've got a change in interference patterns," began a distorted voice.

"Wait a minute — what change?"

"Relax. It's not that big a deal."

"I thought we were running normal routine the next four weeks."

"This is only a slight complication. But, you may have to provide some special handling," continued the voice.

"Whoa! What kind of complication? What kind of special handling?"

"A new arrival. She's an unknown quantity. For now, just keep close tabs on her movements."

"How about some reinforcements from your end?"

"Handle her from there," the voice commanded and disappeared.

The conversation ended abruptly. Uttering an expletive, the figure hung up the phone and looked out the window at the marsh grasses, bending with gusts of wind and currents in the tide. A idea emerged: The true test of survival is how quickly one adapts to change.

CHAPTER 3

2:00 p.m., Monday, April 11, 1988
Approaching Savannah, GA

The plane's vibration rattled the melting ice cubes in the glass on Melanie's lap tray. A voice intruded on her mental space, "Would you like a refill?"

"No, I'm fine. Thanks," she politely dismissed the stewardess.

Yes, she was fine — just "peachy" — she reflected with sarcasm.

Once the drone of the engines would have put her to sleep; today it kept her awake. She looked at the middle-aged lady dozing beside her, then studied the painted-on expressions of the rest of her fellow passengers. Was she in a Norman Rockwell painting of thirty-five years ago? This unreal picture made her feel as if she had taken one of the psychiatrist's prescribed tranquilizers. With an urge to bolt from her seat and shake up the sedate passengers, she wanted to scream, "Anybody else on this plane lose their family?" As quickly as it had come, the bitter feeling passed.

Faces, smells, and lights blended with others in her consciousness. Even now, with her body recovered from the crash, her mind refused to acknowledge all the anonymous faces hovering in dim memory. She knew those figures no better than the characters on this plane.

She stared at the untouched meal on the tray, then let her eyes roam to the window and the storm clouds building above the gray-green, watery surface. Would her life regain its balance? Where were the upbeat emotions that once filled her existence? Would she ever adjust to life without her family?

After nine months, she could accept the deaths of her parents. Older people were supposed to die first, weren't they? Yet she still could not accept the deaths of her husband and child. While Greg's was appalling, Parker's death was the most horrifying incident that had ever happened to her.

Parker had been created from the love between her and Greg. Her son had grown in her body for nine months. They had watched him develop into a spirited young boy. He wasn't supposed to die. At least, he wasn't supposed to die until after she did. It was a loss of precious life. Other people, especially her brother, could not seem to fathom that the death of a child was the worst experience a mother could endure, even worse than losing a husband. It was overwhelming to comprehend that not only had she lost her parents, she had lost her husband and child.

And still, she couldn't remember the accident.

Life was unfair, cruel, capricious — a bitch. Reality had drilled that lesson into her these past months; she grasped it perfectly. Rationally, she knew she was grieving, experiencing depression. Awakening from the coma, she had cried until her body was wracked with new pains. In privacy, she had wailed; she had flailed at the facts; she had railed at God, then, the fates.

Nothing had changed. Yet, she knew that wasn't exactly true.

When she had gained consciousness, she had been filled with great anger. All of them — Greg, Parker, Mom and Dad — had left her behind. If they were dead, she wanted to be dead, too. However, she loved them too much to stay angry at them. Her anger shifted to God, fate, life. Then she recognized that these concepts were too great, too intangible. Her anger had changed — to apathy.

All those magazine self-help articles failed to address this new feeling of anomie, this sense of no identity or purpose she perceived without her husband, child, and parents. Other people's experiences didn't help. When they said that time would heal these deep wounds of sorrow and depression, she considered these people to be fools. There seemed no cure for what ailed her.

Thank goodness, the departure from her New York City haunts produced no pain. Only Ashley believed she was making a poor decision. Certainly, he wasn't bashful being vocal about it. Melanie knew she had choices to make, needs to meet. Right now, she defined her need as regaining control over her life — correction — what was left of her life. Melanie closed her eyes, tried to will her mind into a peaceful blankness.

The airliner hit a series of bumps. An almost-asleep Melanie felt the slide like a Tilt-A-Whirl carnival ride and would have sworn she heard a gasp, then crashing glass, and then... a chiming voice, "We are now making our final approach to Savannah. The captain requests...." She shook her head, tried to achieve a clearer focus, and pushed the button to raise her seat.

The instant she tightened her seatbelt, the plane dropped, flexed, and creaked. Shrill squeals filled the cabin. White knuckles grabbed the armrests. The seatbelt sign flashed its warning. The cabin lights flickered. The captain's voice, terse and tense, sounded tinny over the loudspeaker. They were entering an area of heavy turbulence.

The plane dropped again in a stomach-churning fall as it hit a wind sheer. Then, it lurched skyward and rotated to the right. The whole plane vibrated as if it were shaking itself apart. The engines whined a high-pitched screech.

Looking out the window, Melanie saw the ground quickly approaching, then, blur as the plane slid violently to the right, rose, and fell. Again, the plane tilted to the right.

Melanie's mind cried out, "We're going to crash!" A child's voice cried out the same fear.

"Abort! Abort, you fool!" she wanted to scream to the captain. "Go around! Try again! Land at a different airport! Go back to New York!" Melanie wondered if there were enough fuel.

She realized: "I don't want to die. I really don't. I know I've been wishing for death. But, I don't want it. I don't. I want to live! I need to live. I have to find myself. I want to make a life without Parker and Greg."

The intercom warned, "I'm sorry, ladies and gentlemen. But, I'm afraid we're going to experience a rough landing." The captain advised, "Please make sure your seat belts are securely fastened."

Melanie jerked in her seat when the hydraulics of the landing gear started to lower the wheels. The gear thumped loudly as it locked solidly in place. The lowering flaps made the plane shudder as it tried to slow. The plane gained altitude, then again, dropped suddenly.

Another wind gust hit the plane, tipping it crazily. The tension in the cabin was pierced by the hysterical crying of a little girl.

The woman next to her patted Melanie's hand reassuringly. At first she considered the gesture trite, but the contact of a human hand felt warm and welcome. My mother would have done that, she concluded.

The plane smashed onto the asphalt in a bone-crushing slam. Reverse thrusters roared. The passengers were thrown about in their seats.

The screeching tires could be heard above the roar of the engines. A right side tire blew. The plane swerved and skidded down the runway. A left side tire blew. The plane continued its skid. After what seemed an eternity to the passengers, the huge airliner came to a halt.

A collective sigh of relief escaped the grateful passengers; they had landed intact.

When the passengers had regained some resemblance of calm, her seat companion inquired, "Are you visiting Savannah for the first time?"

Melanie looked at the ashen-faced woman and was stunned by her apparent composure after they had almost died in mangled wreckage and fiery flame. She wondered how to reply to this innocuous question, so similar again to what her mother would have asked. She swallowed, then answered, "No, I lived in Savannah as a child. I still have family and friends here."

Those years seemed lifetimes ago. Would she find her life again or at least a different one here on the coast?

Inside the Savannah airport, she was relieved to see a trim, middle-aged black man dressed in white nautical pants and a navy blue polo shirt standing at the gate and holding a sign with her name. With smooth dispatch, he arranged to pick up her luggage before meeting her in front of the terminal. When he drove up in a white Cadillac, she exited the glass-front building. A strong, irritating smell overpowered the balmy air. The casually dressed chauffeur whisked her into the open back door.

"Whew, what's that?" she asked.

The man looked puzzled, then smiled, "Oh, that's just the paper mill. You'll get used to it."

When she was comfortably settled into the rear seat, the car pulled away from the sand-colored terminal and proceeded past World War II military barracks. As they continued, Melanie appreciated the wide avenues, the sparse traffic, and the open feeling around Savannah, this sea-level city on the Savannah River. They traversed extensive grassy marshlands before entering the guard gate of The Hammock, an exclusive riverfront development.

Melanie caught herself mentally describing the contemporary homes of cedar facades and glass walls mixed with Spanish colonials in the distinctive tabby finish of seashell and lime.

The chauffeur pulled the limousine between two wooden posts with brass lanterns and onto a curving driveway. A modern house peeked from behind aged, moss-draped live oaks. As the chauffeur parked the car between the garage and dock, Melanie noted a yacht and a runabout.

A tall, dark-haired, deeply-tanned man opened the limousine door. As he helped Melanie out of the plush interior, he introduced himself, "Mrs. Evans, I'm Adam Gardner. Your aunt requested I meet you at the airport and deliver you to Caretta."

Melanie caught her breath as she met his brown-eyed gaze. She was emotionally unprepared for dealing with his masculinity. She felt embarrassed, but remained impassive. "Thank you, Mr. Gardner."

"Adam, please. Would you like to relax and enjoy a drink or continue your journey to Caretta?"

"Call me Melanie and I'll take a raincheck on the drink. I'm eager to get to the island. I hope you understand." Melanie tried to smile as she explained.

"Of course. How long has it been since you were there?"

The small talk continued as Adam helped her aboard the runabout that was bobbing up and down with the waves. After he and the chauffeur loaded her luggage, Adam took the wheel of the boat, fired the powerful engines. With ease, the chauffeur jumped aboard the craft and stood next to Adam at the wheel. "Mr. Gardner, I think I'd better take you and the lady across."

"That isn't necessary, Junior."

"Mr. Gardner, a storm is coming." With his head he indicated the darkening clouds brooding in the east and the waves building in the channel. "I know these waters like the back of my hand. It could get bad out there. And, if you don't mind me saying so, I have more experience with boats — especially, if it gets rough."

Adam studied Junior's face, the sky, the water. Looking at Melanie, he said, "I can handle it, Junior. Thanks."

Junior shrugged his disapproval. He went to one of the seats, lifted it, took out a bright orange lifejacket. Approaching Melanie, he offered, "Let me help you into this."

"Is it necessary?"

"Always a good idea when the weather is changing. It isn't elegant, but it could save your life."

Melanie turned pale. "Is it dangerous to cross now?" Melanie didn't want to place herself in danger a second time in one day.

Junior adjusted the straps and said, "Just a precaution."

Following orders, Adam's assistant jumped onto the dock and untied the boat. He watched the runabout enter the choppier water of the channel. These weren't the best sea conditions for a boatman like Adam Gardner. The storm could build any minute. The man might be a high-powered real-estate developer but, in no one's wildest imagination, could he be called a seasoned seaman.

Once out in the wide channel, Adam became a bit more confident of the weather. He anticipated he could beat the oncoming storm to the island. Whenever he could, Adam studied Melanie Evans as she breathed in the mingled salts of marsh and ocean air. She was average height, a little thin for his taste — perhaps from a recent weight loss, naturally blonde, no wrinkles on her fair skin, and those green-gold eyes — so similar to the marsh grasses. Melanie Evans was an attractive woman except for that sad, dispirited look in her eyes.

Despite the overwhelming tiredness from her trip and the lingering numbness from her grief, Melanie recognized Adam's strong male interest. She was displeased and flattered at the same time. Melanie conceded his extraordinary good looks and manners as well as his apparent wealth, but, again, she couldn't make herself care. After Greg died, she had lost all interest in men. She was glad the wind precluded any conversation other than an occasional yell and gesture.

Behind the canopy's windscreen, Melanie gazed across the vast Georgia salt marshes, scanned the horizon intently and searched for the live oak trees of Caretta Island. There they were, dark gray in this weather and far off in the distance. How she yearned to return to their familiar protection.

The humpbacked, turtle-shaped island had been a second childhood home. The Parker family had come here for Christmases, Easters, and summer vacations. As a rule, her father had returned to work after a week, but her mother had stayed with Melanie and Ashley for as long as they liked. Caretta had been one big sandbox for the two of them and their playmates. Her favorite friend had been named Susannah Harris whose mother was her aunt's best friend. Of course, her father's unmarried sister Patrice, who no one dared call "Aunt Patty," had always been there. On occasion, one of her mother's brothers or sisters and their families joined them for a week or two. The caretaker and housekeeper, Jim and Louisa, had taught the youngsters to swim in the ocean, fish, bog for crabs....

The Parker family had owned this island since the Civil War. During the reconstruction of the South, her great-grandfather had come South and established the family in the Savannah area. When Melanie and her brother Ashley were children, the family had relocated in New York to meet the demands of the growing multinational shipping line. Patrice had been the sole family member to remain within the comfortable confines of the familiar island.

Melanie remembered the last occasion she had been on Caretta with her husband and son. It had been a Christmas to remember. Mother and Father had gathered Ashley, Melanie, and their families to the island again for the first time in years. The week-long festivities had provided a grand holiday. The nieces and nephews had reveled in the same activities their parents had loved: beachcombing, riding horses, being scared by huge alligators in the ponds, tracking deer, birdwatching, oystering.... Pine branches and holly had festooned Big House. Fires had roared in the fireplaces keeping them warm. The men had triumphantly hunted canvasback duck for Christmas dinner. Louisa had prepared meal after sumptuous meal.

Chestnuts roasting on an open fire — wait a minute, Melanie caught herself as a large wave rocked the boat. First, the Norman Rockwell scene on the plane and, now, a Norman Rockwell Christmas on the island? I'm creating fairy tales. Those times did produce wonderful memories, but the people were just people, and all was not perfect. And, most importantly, four of them were dead.

Still, she found herself half-expecting to see all of them standing on the shore ready to greet her. What tricks was her mind playing on her? She had to stop imagining a reality that could never exist. Just because she could think it, didn't mean it would happen. All was different now. Ashley had divorced his wife. Since then, he'd seemed to have developed a harder edge. Now Melanie saw little of her niece and nephew. Her own child and husband as well as her mother and father were dead. They wouldn't be joining her here.

A flood of tears engulfed her vision. Grasping the boat's rail, she fought the feeling of the world dropping away beneath her. Shaking her head, she focused her attention outward — toward her future and the approaching land.

Tail End came and went. The southern island tip was named after the turtle's anatomical counterpart. In fact, the whole island was named after the turtle. The Latin word *caretta* meant turtle; in scientific nomenclature, the species *Caretta caretta* referred to the gigantic loggerhead turtles who laid their eggs in the island sands each summer.

As the runabout entered the sea island's protection from the coming storm, it skimmed through gray-green tidewater, filling the channel and snaking among the marsh grasses. Here and there, a silvery fish jumped and graceful white birds flew away as the boat made its way to the estate dock. The blustery breeze promised seafood treasures. After the windy, choppy ride through the channel, Melanie was glad to see these calmer scenes.

The boat engine whined at a higher pitch as Adam reversed gears to sidle the craft alongside the dock. Melanie shifted her gaze to him. He looks as if he's an actor doing a TV commercial, she reflected.

An anxious Melanie diverted her attention to the island. What was she expecting? Why was she coming here? She had told Ashley she was going to help decide what to do about the island. But, she sensed it was greater than that. What was driving her like a loggerhead turtle to return to Caretta? Melanie stopped herself again — allusions to animals and visions of dead people? How about some black magic, too? She had always been the kid who had asked why. Her notions hadn't been so fantastic or sarcastic since she was a teenager.

At the end of the dock near the boathouse, the island jeep awaited her and her luggage. Further north, hulked a barn that served as the jeep's garage. Also on the left, along the white crushed shell road, stood a small house located in its own clearing. In Melanie's memory, the caretaker's cottage had always served as Louisa and Jim's home. Actually, Jim's ancestors had lived on this island before the Parkers had owned it. Now hurrying down the dock was Jim, welcoming her as he had so many times before.

"Welcum home, Mellie-Baby," crooned Jim. His expression could have been for an eight-year-old Melanie; his eyes, full of sadness, told her the words were for the grown-up Melanie who had lost her family. They clung to one another. Each drew comfort from the embrace.

"Louisa's waitin' fo' you up at de Big House," Jim gestured toward the hidden house.

Melanie was amazed how rapidly her ear adjusted to the soft yet guttural tones of Jim's Gullah dialect. Its slow cadence seemed appropriate to the island's soothing rhythms as the harsh New York sounds reflected the hard edges and hectic paces of the city.

Jim helped her into the jeep. When Adam climbed into the rear, Melanie gave Jim a questioning look. Adam's going to the Big House, too? She had presumed he was delivering her to the island as a favor to her aunt. Maybe he wanted to wait out the oncoming storm here?

Jim shrugged, suggesting he didn't understand Adam's behavior either. A sleek black cat leapt into the jeep beside Melanie's feet. Jim did offer an explanation of the newest passenger, "Dat's Ali Cat," pronouncing Ali as in Mohammed Ali. "He be no harm."

As they drove the winding white way to Parker House, Ali Cat settled into Melanie's lap and purred. The cat's purring helped relax her.

Absentmindedly, Melanie petted the cat as, avidly, she absorbed the details of her new surroundings. Wavering pines and rustling palm trees obscured the house from the road and dock. As they drove closer, she noted strands of gray Spanish moss and purple wisteria blossoms swaying with the wind gusts. The house itself stood impressive. It was a two-story, cream-colored tabby structure with a terracotta tile roof and matching painted shutters. Large lavender-flowered azaleas surrounded the foundation; wide-spreading live oak trees and tall, glossy magnolias shaded the lawn.

Jim halted the jeep at the steps leading to the screened porch. At the heavily-carved, wooden front door stood Louisa, the only housekeeper Melanie remembered at Parker House. Louisa must be seventy years old now. This woman she loved as a second mother was as plump and jovial as ever, but now her graying hair contrasted with her ebony skin.

Louisa hurried down the steps and wrapped Melanie into her arms. "Welcum home," Louisa breathed into Melanie's ear as she hugged her. Without any additional talk, Louisa conveyed her heartfelt concern and sympathy.

With soft breasts and strong arms around her, Melanie felt nurtured, as if she were truly home. For a long moment, she rested in Louisa's arms, basking in the motherly scent of the big woman.

"Yes, welcome back to Caretta," a reedy voice intruded from the sitting room adjacent to the foyer. Patrice Parker stood in the archway of the foyer. The years had been unkind to Melanie's aunt. Once-blonde hair had grayed; peach complexion had wrinkled; blue eyes reflected regret. Melanie hugged the stiff form of her aunt and planted the obligatory kiss on her powdered cheek. The smell of talc was stifling.

Melanie had never grown close to her aunt during past visits to Caretta. Patrice maintained an air of propriety, a rigidity that did not lend itself to warm confidences. It seemed to Melanie that life had passed by her aunt. Fleetingly, Melanie wondered if Ashley were correct. Would she feel comfortable with this woman for any length of time?

Patrice, ever-mindful of social position and manners, turned to Adam Gardner, "Thank you, Adam, for escorting Melanie home to the island."

Melanie experienced hope. Patrice had said "home."

"I meant it when I told you to feel free to rely on me for anything you need, Patrice."

"I hope you plan to dine with us. Your place has been set at the table and Louisa has prepared an elaborate Southern-style dinner in honor of Melanie's arrival," Patrice coaxed.

Melanie mused, they're on a first-name basis and, like a typical Southerner, Patrice is insisting he stay for dinner. Melanie almost missed Adam's affirmative reply.

"Good," replied Patrice. "Louisa and Jim will settle Melanie into her room. Let me offer you a drink in the parlor while we wait for dinner. Will Grant be dining with us, Louisa?"

"Yez, Miz Patrice. I done tol' him dinner's at seven."

"Melanie, join Adam and me when you're ready. Louisa, when Grant arrives, please tell him to join Adam and me." With that, Patrice commandeered Adam's arm and marched him into the formal receiving room opposite the foyer.

Melanie noticed Louisa's frown as she watched Patrice with Adam.

Slowly, the large, black woman turned and smiled at Melanie. "I'll show you yo' room, Miz Mellie," Louisa offered. She ushered Melanie up the curved, dark oak staircase; Jim followed them with Melanie's suitcases.

"That's OK, Louisa. I know the way," Melanie protested.

"Miz Patrice sez you deserve the mastuh room now you're miztress of Caretta," informed Louisa.

At once, Melanie understood. Louisa was trying to make things easier for her. She allowed Louisa to lead the way up the stairs to the room at the top. Jim brought in the luggage then gave Melanie another hug. He left her with a reminder, "You know where I be, if you need me."

Louisa took charge of the suitcases and Melanie, "You jus' lay down a minute while I hang up your clothes. Den you fix up yourself while I put dinner on de table."

Gladly, Melanie turned over all responsibilities to Louisa and lay down on the double bed. Allowing herself to relax, she watched Louisa move with slow grace around the room. It was so easy to let Louisa do things for her. This woman had always seemed to know what Melanie needed or wanted. Melanie pondered Louisa's nurturing instinct. She tended to the people she loved, her garden, this island, her God. What a difference between Louisa and her own mother, Margaret who had evolved into a socialite in New York where events and titles took precedence over people. Melanie marveled at how easily she slipped into

Louisa and Jim's "lowcountryisms" — their quiet way of doing things, their language.... Melanie had fallen asleep when Ali Cat joined her on the bed, purring as he snuggled against her.

* * *

The Parker House roof line was sharply outlined in the last glow of twilight. A screen door slammed and a gull cried in the distance as the strong breeze rustled palm fronds.

Slight movement came from the barely discernible form of a single person slipping among the shadows. Progress was slow as great care was taken not to disturb the fallen, dried palmetto fronds and live oak leaves. A noise from the interior of the house caused the figure to slide into the dark cover of the undergrowth.

A minute passed. Nothing moved. Again, the form emerged from the dark. It edged forward, staying away from the open spaces. Only the most careful scrutiny revealed an object being tossed underneath the wooden steps at the rear of the house. Then, the figure dissolved into the dusk. All was still once again.

* * *

"Wake up, Miz Mellie. Wake up. It's time you dress fo' dinner." Louisa gently shook Melanie.

Looking around the unfamiliar room, Melanie took in the fact all her clothes had been put away. "Thanks, Louisa. I'll be down in a few minutes."

When Louisa turned to leave, Melanie continued, "Louisa, why did Patrice invite this Adam Gardner to dinner?"

The old lady shook her head, "I dunno. She be juky these past months."

"Juky?"

"Dat's Gullah, Miz Mellie. It mean Miz Patrice not herself — not since Mistuh Courtland and Miz Margaret pass on."

After Louisa left, she explored the dresser drawers and the closet then chose a periwinkle blue dress that draped across her bust, making her weight loss less noticeable. For a brief moment, she wished for the same room she had occupied as a child and admitted her preference for a quiet meal. She realized, however, other people were involved with their wants and desires. Of course, the two older women wanted a big meal to celebrate her arrival — that was very Southern. Some things change; others stay the same. Southern manners and traditions never seem to change. Melanie decided to make the best of the situation.

From what she had seen so far, Patrice appeared in control of her faculties, unlike her brother Ashley's innuendoes and Louisa's concerns. Melanie wondered, though, at Patrice's decision to put her in the master bedroom. Did this action reveal that Patrice refused to take more responsibility within the Parker family or on the island? Did Patrice not want to accept change in her personal life due to her brother and his family's deaths? Indeed, why had Patrice chosen to live out her life in this secluded location? What circumstances had brought her to the island? All Melanie knew was that Patrice's fiancé had died in World War II. What satisfaction had Patrice found here alone? Was her aunt's lifelong seclusion a form of "running away?" Melanie had a lot of questions to ask: Would history repeat itself? Would she end up like her aunt? Was Melanie looking at her own future?

"Certainly, that Adam Gardner met the qualifications for a smooth operator — too smooth. What was this engaging man trying to accomplish? Why was he being so nice to Patrice and herself?" Melanie sighed. "The man must be after something. What? Was Louisa correct to be suspicious of this man?" She sighed again. Over the years, Louisa had been a good judge of character. So much of her own thinking still seemed muddled.

At least, Melanie was looking forward to meeting Grant Yeats. Her father had invested so much time and money in the Australian engineer. At Parker Transworld Board of Directors' meetings, Courtland had defended the allotment of funds to Yeats' desalination research as a commercially viable interest. If successful, the project would produce huge profits, not to mention benefits to the inhabitants of islands where water was scarce or nonexistent. Just the income from Middle East countries alone would be immense. She knew nothing, however, about the man in charge of the project. Was Grant Yeats young? old? handsome? bookish? adventuresome?

Her musings wandered to her father. So independent and competent, he had forced the company to keep pace with technological change. Melanie had envied his ability to adapt and to profit from most situations. Had she inherited that same talent? Would she adjust and find a new course for her life?

Until Parker Transworld's needs had dictated the family's move to New York, the Parkers had considered themselves Southerners. The city of Savannah did, too. The family members were as accepted as the old plantation families. Her parents had been considered society's darlings; the couple's picture and name had appeared often on the pages of the *Savannah News*. When they moved to New York, the social climate had been different, but her parents had adjusted and so had she and her brother.

Melanie remembered other aspects of her parents — how her mother's gentle demeanor had tempered her father's forcefulness, how easily Greg had fit into the family as her husband then into the business as an executive....

Melanie heard a peal of thunder then pelts of rain on the roof. She stopped herself from remembering. Of course, memories would exist here, too. She must find other people and ideas to fill her time, that yawning maw. She suppressed a giggle at this visual — her future as a big mouth or stomach through which she must pass. She must be hungry. Melanie brushed her hair vigorously and freshened her make-up. Then, accompanied by the cat, she descended the stairs with greater determination to adapt to current circumstances.

"Ah, here's Melanie. Grant, meet my niece from New York, Melanie Evans. She'll be with us for several weeks," Patrice explained.

A lean man offered his hand in a direct manner. "I'm Grant Yeats. It's an honor to meet you although I wish circumstances were different. Your family's deaths affected me deeply."

As Melanie accepted his hand, she looked into his clear blue eyes. All she could think to ask was, "Their deaths affected *you* deeply?" She realized, however, that he meant what he was saying. Controlling her sarcasm, she replied, "I, too, wish the circumstances were different. While I'm here, I hope you'll show me your research activities. My father was impressed with your ideas and their potential."

Melanie studied the man. Grant Yeats was in his thirties. His bronzed yet freckled face complemented his sandy, light-brown hair and spare frame. He nodded his head then smiled, "Again, I'm honored."

Adam Gardner looked as if he were about to interject a comment when Louisa bustled into the parlor and announced, "Dinnuh's served."

The interruption allowed Adam to practice a Tyrone Power move he thought might impress Patrice. He crooked his arm and offered it to her to escort her to the dining table. Following Adam's example, Grant accompanied Melanie to her place at the other end of the table and pulled out her chair for her. He sat to her right.

The table was loaded with fried chicken, baked ham, yellow squash, lima beans, turnip greens, sliced tomatoes and cucumbers, chow-chow relish, and Louisa's secret-recipe, beaten biscuits. The foursome served their plates. Conversation flowed. They discussed the storm and how weather influenced the island. Adam talked about various upcoming Savannah events.

Again, Melanie found she had to control her tongue. Her impulse was to present issues raised by her encounters with death. Death. Death. Death and its consequences were the pressing topics on her mind. This polite table talk with its coastal flair was all so familiar and all so unfulfilling, so bland, so meaningless. But, she knew these people meant well. Her dark topics would only alienate them. She decided the decent thing to do was to keep her mouth shut.

For dessert, Louisa served a rich, boiled custard. As the unlikely foursome finished the last bite, the sounds of wind and rain lessened.

The small group left the dining room and entered the foyer; Adam guided Melanie to one side of the hall. "Melanie, your aunt and I have been talking about the future of the island — after the government takes its share in taxes. I'd like to talk to you about it sometime soon."

"A bit premature, wouldn't you say Mr. Gardner?" spoke an indignant Grant who had overhead Adam's proposal.

"Actually, I think not," continued a slightly ruffled Adam, mimicking the Australian's accent while redirecting his attention to Melanie. "I would like to take you for an excursion on my boat and show you some of my ideas at work."

Ah, Melanie reflected. This man wastes no time, or moves, when it comes to business. Adam Gardner might be a charming, handsome man, but Melanie was seeing something in him she disliked — something ruthless and cunning.

The indignation shown by the Australian told Melanie that Grant didn't trust the man. She was intrigued by the way he had stood up to Adam's obvious self interests.

Before Melanie could reply, Patrice interjected, "Going out on Adam's yacht would be a pleasant diversion, Melanie. I imagine that an outing around Caretta would be good for you."

Adam smiled at Patrice, silently thanking her for her help. Bolstered by her approval, he smiled at Melanie with all the charisma he could muster. "Then I'll come the next warm, sunny day I'm free." Bowing slightly to Melanie's aunt, he intoned politely, "Patrice, thank you for a delicious dinner. Please convey my compliments to Louisa. The storm has passed. So, I'll be off." Adam glared at Grant; a glower was returned with equal intensity.

Walking down the oyster shell road to the dock, Adam avoided puddles. He shook aside his irritation toward Grant and reassessed his position. He sensed he had won Patrice's confidence despite their awkward first meeting in January, perhaps because he reminded her of her long-lost fiancé, James. He congratulated himself that his quick study of social mores of the thirties and forties had paid off with Patrice at dinner tonight. Now, he must gain Melanie's approval. Adam concentrated on the blonde heiress. She'd be far more difficult. He would need a solid performance to win her over. That irritating Australian could have a strong influence on Melanie. Too, he observed that Grant was attracted to her. He would have to make sure that Melanie became infatuated with him and not the Aussie. He started reviewing his options.

CHAPTER 4

5:30 a.m., Tuesday, April 26, 1988

Day broke over the island. A huge orange sun eased from its dark blue blanket of ocean. It gilded the sandy shores and lit the treetops of Caretta Island. Sunlight filtered through the sheer curtains into Melanie's bedroom. Warmed, Melanie and her feline companion stirred.

Feeling a sense of relief to wake without the insistent, blaring buzz of the alarm clock, Melanie lay in bed and contemplated the pleasure of watching the dawn. In New York, the darkness of night simply grayed into day. Tall buildings and pollution hid any spectacular sunrises and sunsets. Sadly, there were numerous New Yorkers who regularly missed seeing the sun rise or set over a natural horizon.

Melanie forced herself to get up and into a pair of shorts with a coordinated top. She covered both with a sweat suit, located a pair of socks, then, her jogging shoes. In the city, she could never bring herself to exercise in the skyscraper-walled canyons or what she considered the dangerous, manmade environment of Central Park. The city dwellers considered the park to be natural. To her, it was wild only in the sense that one would be safer in many untamed parts of the world. Predators lurked in the park — people like that purse-snatching boy.

"No, I won't worry about those things!" Melanie exclaimed out loud. The cat gazed at her questioningly. Her psychiatrist would not have approved of her negative thoughts; the psychiatrist would approve of her determination to start an exercise program. According to the doctor, exercise dispelled depression. Melanie was eager to be rid of the lethargy, this suffocating feeling that reminded her of a never-ending case of the flu.

With Ali Cat at her heels, she quietly slipped down the stairs and out the front door. She paused to savor the early morning tranquility of the island. The sunrays wove through pine and palm branches as if they were white oak splits in a basket. Resembling freshwater pearls, delicate dew drops sparkled as they precariously balanced on blades of grass.

Melanie stretched; the cat mimicked her. She marveled at the wholeness of her arms and legs. Again, she hoped this island interlude would bring a similar healthiness to her attitude. Jogging slowly, she started down the path to Crossroad, which cut a swath through the maritime forest from house to beach. When she entered the woods, to her surprise, Ali Cat sat down to wait for her return.

About three-quarters of a mile from the house, she crossed Backbone Road. It ran the length of the five-mile island from North Arm to Tail End. At its widest point, the island measured only a mile and a half. To her knowledge, the only other paths were overgrown hunting trails from her grandfather's era.

Picking up the pace, her legs carried her swiftly along Crossroad through the cool dimness of the woods. Here the palms, pines, bays, yellow jessamine, and tender tendrils of grapevines surrounded still, freshwater ponds. The forest was home to innumerable birds, deer, and other small mammals. This morning, she took little time to admire plants or animals as she hurried toward the beach. Melanie hungered to see the ocean and Caretta's sweep of uninterrupted sands.

At the shore, she took a few moments to catch her breath and rest her out-of-shape muscles. Looking around, she observed the beach extended as far as she could see to the north and south. She decided to jog south. The already bright sun beat on her face and shimmered off the waves. A soft, ocean breeze played with her hair as she jogged. Melanie breathed deeply of the restorative ocean air: in-out, left-right, in-out, left-right. Soon, she began to sweat. She stripped to her shorts outfit, leaving the sweats on the beach to retrieve on her return to Parker House.

As she continued her jog, she noticed how the ocean had been adding to the beach at Tail End. When she reached its tip, she surveyed the marsh grasses extending along Caretta's Tail End and neighboring Crab Key and Osprey Island. Turning, Melanie viewed the bluffs where ancient dunes met the marsh. Here, she and Ashley had spent many childhood hours searching for Indian pottery shards and arrowheads. The bluffs appeared untouched by the intervening years.

Walking back toward Crossroad, Melanie hugged the waterline. With the change of the tide, the breakers now moved toward her, rose, fell and hissed as they foamed and dumped treasures and trash: dead horseshoe crabs, sea shells, empty plastic soft drink liters, a canvas shoe... an endless array of ocean and human effects that excited and depressed Melanie. Humans made such a mess of an environment. She created a mental note to talk to Jim about how to clean the beach of the human debris.

From the scattered accumulation, she selected for closer examination a flat sand dollar, an intricately lettered olive, a whorled whelk, and a magenta seawhip. Next time she jogged, she planned to inspect North Arm. Another time she'd explore the freshwater ponds. She stopped in surprise — she was making plans for the future. It felt good to be here on this beach, to jog again, to make plans. All seemed well.

She picked up her sweatsuit and headed for Parker House. She had not let anyone know where she was going. She hoped no one had missed her. When she entered the family compound, Melanie did not notice five pairs of curious eyes observing her.

Grant shielded his eyes from the morning sun as he watched Melanie walk across the lawn. Knowing she had not yet discerned him standing near the lab, he stared intently at her approach. The damp tendrils of her shoulder-length hair highlighted the flushed skin of her lithe body. He imagined her green eyes from the previous evening.

He questioned his unsettled feelings about her. Here was a bright, pretty woman, probably emotionally vulnerable, but nothing to make him so uneasy.

Suddenly, he knew — indeed how could he ever forget Karen, the calculating, deceitful woman who had happily taught him about lust, then, cruelly taught him the meaning of betrayal?

She opened his office door and laughed, "Someone to see you."

He resisted the temptation to have Karen tell the person he was busy. He wanted to lock the door and make love to her right there on the desk. Those sparkling eyes and that supple skin had permeated his senses the last few months. He had never been happier.

Oh well, business calls. He stood as Andy, his unimaginative but opportunistic supervisor, entered and closed the door behind him.

Without preliminaries he opened, "Grant, I understand you've finished testing the prototype of the new actuator. What are the results?"

"It yields a thirty-percent improvement in efficiency over current models and it's fifty-percent simpler to build. And, I'm fine and dandy. How are you?" he added with a pointed note of sarcasm.

"I'm glad to hear that since I've received unfortunate budgetary news. Our division is cutting back. So, I'm taking over your project. Your position has been terminated."

"Wait a minute. Is this a joke, Andy?" Even as he asked, Grant read the harsh truth in the other man's eyes and realized what had happened. "I won't let you have it. I did most of that research in graduate school on my own. The work is mine! I only agreed to come here for a percentage of the royalties. There's too much of my life in those ideas. Sorry, Andy. No way."

"You have no choice. The models are already in my lab and you have no patent. Karen should be finished moving the files by now."

"Karen? She wouldn't...."

"My poor boy, she's my secret weapon. Did you assume she was actually interested in your body? You're pathetic, Grant."

Grant launched himself toward the smaller man. Simultaneously, the door opened and in strode two large security guards.

"Escort Mr. Yeats to his car, gentlemen."

Through the open door, Grant could see Karen packing the files into a box. A smirk defiled her lips.

Andy sneered at the frustrated, angry Grant, "We'll ship your personal effects to you. Thanks for helping me with my next promotion."

"Oh, there you are, Grant."

With a shake of his head the Australian realized the voice belonged to Melanie. Forcing a silly grin, he responded, "You caught me daydreaming. I see you've been jogging."

Her affirmative reply was lost in his amazement of how her physical similarities to Karen had triggered the vivid recall of the mortifying and maddening incident. He became cautious. The previous pain and disappointment were enough to last him a lifetime. He could never go through that again. Melanie was holding out her handful of shells for him to admire.

She prompted him, "Ready to show me your research?"

"You want to see my work?"

"Sure, if this is a good moment for you," Melanie smiled.

Blimey! Her smile reminded him even more of Karen.

"Let's start here. This building has been turned into my laboratory. Do you know much about the project?"

"A little, but act as if I know nothing at all," she replied.

At first, Grant provided short descriptions about each piece of equipment — the saltwater tanks, the solar collectors.... Before long, he found himself warming to her interest. His comments turned into obvious enthusiasm for his work. While they talked, he became more and more animated.

"My bias has always been toward engineering super-efficient products. So many solutions are nothing but bigger, more powerful machines that, in my opinion, often waste energy sources. I feel it's time to consider small and clever. For instance, your father and I had this dream of practical, low-cost desalination — powered by the sun."

Melanie interrupted, "Wait. Why use solar power? Aren't there conventional methods to take care of the process?"

"You're correct," agreed Grant. "There are big, power-hungry, expensive pieces of equipment available to desalt water. But, stop and think for a minute. Suppose we perfect an inexpensive gadget that runs on solar power. Imagine the effect on people who live in thousands of remote locations. Consider coastal cultures becoming independent of filthy cisterns or fortuitous Artesian wells for their water. Sailors might have fresh water whenever needed. The equipment could be made small enough for sailboats."

Seeing the possibilities held her attention, he relaxed a bit before continuing, "It's not a new dream. Alexander Graham Bell was greatly concerned over the paradox of lost fishermen dying of thirst when surrounded by an ocean of water. Actually, his research provided me many useful ideas."

"So, that's why Dad set you up here on Caretta. Not only would Parker Transworld save money, but it would make money with a super-efficient yet affordable apparatus."

"That's true. If I perfect this device, then Parker Transworld would be the first to benefit, but your father was most impressed by the possibilities for the masses. He had a philanthropic instinct mixed with hardheaded business sense."

"Yes, he did. Parker Transworld grew rapidly under his direction." She paused for a minute then returned her attention to Grant. "So, tell me. How is the research progressing?"

Grant hesitated as another image of Karen flashed through his mind. He reluctantly volunteered, "Very well, I believe. I may have it perfected in a year."

"Oh? I assumed you were closer."

"When you experiment, sometimes you have a breakthrough, sometimes you don't. I've made acceptable progress. Yet, I feel a bit uncomfortable promising anything sooner."

"I suppose it is hard to predict," Melanie mused. "I've never tried to create a new product all by myself."

"The individual aspect provides thrills, but a researcher always wonders if funds will be available to finish the project."

"Why are you concerned about funding?" she queried.

"Apparently, your brother doesn't share your father's feeling about this venture," Grant responded.

"Oh, probably not, but Ashley would never cut a person or project without good reason."

Grant let the comment slide, realizing he needed to discern what this brother-sister team might do now that they held the responsibility for the company and the island. All of his work over the past several months and his immediate future depended on their actions. Melanie's apparent enthusiasm for his project gave him hope. There was the possibility that she had enough influence over her brother to persuade him to continue the funding. Maybe she would be able to convince Ashley not only of the practical gains, but of the possible financial bonanza.

Framed in the kitchen window, Louisa continued to watch Melanie until she disappeared into Grant's lab. Quietly, she talked about the island's newest inhabitant with her husband, "She be a good girl, Jim."

Sprawled in a chair at the kitchen table, Jim sighed.

"I don' think we got to worry none," Louisa picked up where she left off. "Caretta's our home too. Miz Mellie won' ever make us leave."

Jim ran a large, gnarled-knuckled hand through his wiry, salt and pepper hair. "You be right. But, I seen lots o' harm comes from 'good' people."

Louisa nodded. "Lots more harm come from bad people though. I know you still feel de sting of Mistuh Courtland's father. Mastuh Edward was just plain differen' — differen' from his son and differen' from his father."

"Yeh, like our son be differen' from us."

"Well, yes an' no. Mastuh Edward was bad; our Jim ain't bad."

"I jus' hope Miz Mellie don' turn bad."

Returning her attention from her niece to the slick tourist magazine in her hand, Patrice burrowed comfortably into her chair and read an article about nearby Tybee Island. Adjusting her glasses down her nose, she shuddered as she looked at the photographs of what she considered congested traffic, garish shop signs, and tacky tourist clothes. Revolted, she wondered if Melanie's presence signaled the beginning of the end for her own island?

She leaned her head against the tall back of the chair and closed her eyes. She allowed the calm of what she loved best about the island to replace her anxiety. She imagined herself in a long, flowing dress of chiffon. Elegantly, she floated across the arched porch to greet guests queuing on the steps to Parker House....

And, the fifth observer?

* * *

3:00 p.m., Friday, April 29, 1988

Smoke hovered over the heads of the ten Indian warriors, seated inside the ring of oyster shells. With great ceremony, one stood, bowed, and picked up a large conch shell filled with a dark liquid. The warrior lifted the shell above his head and turned in a complete circle. Then, he tilted the shell and drained the yaupon holly tea into his mouth. He walked to a shallow pit, dug along the shell ring edge. Leaning over, he vomited. The cleansing ritual had begun.

"Excuse me, Patrice. I didn't realize you were in here."

Startled by the voice, the older woman uttered, "You dare interrupt a sacred ritual?" Then, seeing Melanie's puzzled expression as she stood at the library door, Patrice returned to the present, closed the old book resting on her lap. She whisked her eyeglasses off her face, took a breath, and replied, "Oh, it's you, Melanie. Come in, my dear."

Entering the paneled room, Melanie gazed around at the shelves filled with dark-colored volumes. She stopped at one wall to study old, framed charts.

"I'm curious about all the works stored here. When I was a child, I used to open the book covers, smell the musty pages, and wonder what mysteries they contained. I was never short on imagination," she gave a sheepish grin.

Patrice ventured a smile, "Actually, your childhood notions were quite accurate. There are countless adventures located within the walls of this room. Over the years, I've spent many a happy hour here, wandering in different times and spaces."

Melanie noticed a dreamlike quality drift over her aunt's face. Was it possible Patrice found more than curiosity satisfied here?

"Would you show me the works you find so fascinating, Patrice?"

"Are you serious?"

"Of course."

"Pardon my surprise. You're the first family member besides me to take any interest in a very long time." The flustered woman continued, then readjusted her glasses onto her face, "Let's see, where should you begin? Maybe you could examine the journals kept by your great-grandfather, Phillip Parker. They provide a lot of historical background," Patrice gestured to a shelf of brown, leather-bound books.

Melanie frowned. "I was under the impression you were the first Parker to actually live on the island. Until you came, I thought Parker House had always served as a vacation cottage. How could he have created so many journals?"

Patrice folded her hands over her book and sighed, "I doubt he planned a lengthy sojourn on Caretta. But, it was necessitated in order to regain his health. Back then, coming south was a popular remedy for maladies thought to be caused by the harsh climate of New England. I suspect those first months were lonely. I imagine he unearthed the history of this area, especially unusual events, to keep his sanity. He scrupulously recorded each detail in these journals. You'll see he found lots of fascinating items," she continued as she handed the old volume in her lap to Melanie. "Too, notice his excellent penmanship, characteristic of another age."

Melanie glanced over the yellowed pages written many years ago. The book opened to a section detailing Indian usage of the coastal islands around 1000 BC. As Patrice had indicated, the pages were covered with a fancy script.

"And, Great-Grandfather Phillip built this house, didn't he?"

"He most certainly did. He had an architect draw the plans to resemble a Spanish villa. Phillip so admired the Spanish and Moorish styles. He knew how to dream. It was your grandfather, my father, Edward who had the practical side. He bought the house in Savannah and turned this one into a vacation home."

Patrice continued gently, "You know, you remind me of your mother. She was a wonderful woman — a good match for Courtland and a marvelous mother to you and Ashley. Did she ever tell you how she selected your names?"

"No, tell me."

"She loved to read about this area, too. Her favorite book was Margaret Mitchell's *Gone with the Wind*. I believe she would have named you Rhett and Scarlett — if those two characters had been more law-abiding."

"Really?"

"Absolutely. But, your father tempered that bit of romanticism. So, you're Melanie and your brother is Ashley. Well, I'll leave you with the journals." Her aunt rose and walked regally to the door. Turning to Melanie, she smiled, "There's mention of pirates, buried treasures, smuggling, and kidnaping. It's a shame all the excitement has gone with the past."

After supper on this mild evening, Melanie asked Grant if he cared to take a stroll. His initial reluctance piqued her curiosity. Was he afraid to be alone with her? She hoped to put him at ease and draw out the man from behind his equipment. Silently, side by side, they walked along the road that ended at the dock.

"My favorite time of day and year," Grant exclaimed as he positioned his back against one of the large, weathered posts.

"Why year?" Melanie asked as she dangled her legs off the dock.

"Not too many insects," he replied.

"Hmm..., it is peaceful. And, not an automobile within hearing distance."

"I guess you would miss the sounds of cars and buses. Didn't you live in the city?"

"Yes, but I prefer the quiet life," Melanie answered. "How about you? Are you a city or country boy?"

"Outback, mate, like many Australians," Grant smiled. "Though we enjoy the good times offered by a crowd, most of us prefer the big, open spaces where livestock outnumber people."

"So, how did you get to the States?"

"There was a special graduate program offered at MIT. After school, came a wonderful job opportunity."

"Here on Caretta?"

"No, I met your father later. My first job was elsewhere." Grant slowed then halted his explanation. Once again the memory of that treachery engulfed the engineer.

Grant shifted positions against the piling post, stretching and flexing a bit. "Sorry, I'm stiff from paddling around the island this morning."

"Do you do that often?" Melanie questioned.

"As often as I can. Sometimes the research and sometimes the weather make getting out impossible."

After a moment of silence, Melanie ventured, "Have you found it difficult being here? Do you get homesick for Australia?"

"No, not really homesick. I have lots of acquaintances but no close family or friends. At school, I studied and partied. I excelled at both," he grinned. "Since then, it's been mainly work."

Grant wanted to add what he found difficult was American deviousness to the extent of winning at all costs instead of honestly competing. He wanted to be reassured by this friendly companion that she was different from Karen. Realizing there was no rational way to share these feelings, he changed the subject again. "Being an outsider, I've tried not to probe too much into personal affairs, but Patrice, Jim, and Louisa interest me. They're such an unlikely trio to live together on a small island. Yet, they do by choice. Why?"

"I'll try to explain," Melanie responded. "Aunt Patrice was engaged to be married when World War II broke out. Her fiancé died in a battle; she never recovered. The family island became her refuge. I realize that sounds spotty, but Patrice's choice was accepted, never debated by my parents."

"The island is definitely her life now," Grant observed.

"That's true for Jim and Louisa, too. They're part of what is called the Gullah or Geechee culture here in the sea islands. They're descendants of slaves, whose original African home was probably Angola. Supposedly, the word *Gullah* is a shortened form of the word *Angola*. Their language, stories, beliefs, social mannerisms, fishing and farming practices — all reflect African tradition merged with American slavery. Jim was born on the island; together they've raised a son here. I suppose they plan to die here."

"It's hard for me to imagine having such deep, strong roots to one piece of land. I guess I've moved around too much during my life. I imagine those three would do anything to preserve their home. That must make you feel comfortable as the owner."

"That's interesting. I haven't really considered myself as the owner of Caretta Island. That was always Mom and Dad — and Patrice. Now there is Ashley, too," Melanie concluded.

While she watched a group of wading birds, Melanie reflected on how she had always been at ease talking with her parents and, until immediately before the accident, her husband. Grant appeared to be relaxing. Perhaps she was going to be fortunate again, having someone like Grant living on the island.

When they were first married, she and Greg used to play a game with people they met, testing to see if they could handle Level One, Two, or Three conversations. Level One was to talk about the weather, sports, lightweight current events, or, as many people termed it, small talk. Level Two included travels and experiences, sharing personal insights on people and places. Level Three conversation delved into concepts without censorship, including the old taboos of religion, politics, and sex.

Melanie realized she would enjoy having a Level Three person in her life now. Could Grant fill that void? She hoped so.

CHAPTER 5

11:30 a.m., Sunday, May 1, 1988

"Ashley, what a surprise to hear your voice," Melanie spoke into the radio-telephone. "How's everything in New York?"

"No complaints. We're actually functioning quite well without you. I've always wondered how Pop felt as the big man. Now that I'm in charge, I'm really enjoying it."

"You always did relish power. I hope you're able to balance everything."

"Of course. How's the island these days?"

"Beautiful... and quiet. It's so peaceful compared to the city."

"Boring is more like it — stuck out there in the middle of nowhere. But, after all, you're the one who wanted seclusion."

"Yes, I did and, still, I think it's the best thing for me right now. Everyone here at Caretta has been extremely supportive."

"Speaking of Caretta, I've had a couple of talks with our lawyer, accountants, and tax people. I'm afraid the news about the island is not good for us," Ashley pronounced.

"What are they saying?"

"Caretta is viewed as an asset in the estate, just like money or cars or jewelry. That means the beneficiaries, you and me, must pay inheritance tax on it. The really bad news is that its assessed value will be determined by comparing it to other coastal real estate in the area — and that means it's worth millions. There are only preliminary figures available. But to keep the island as it is, we'll have to personally come up with several mill each."

"That seems unfair! Caretta is a relatively undeveloped barrier island. Why should it be taxed as a would-be resort?"

"Ask the IRS, not me."

Melanie gulped, "Can the company help with an advance or a loan?"

"No way. Parker Transworld is running in the black, but barely. I'm not sure of the exact numbers, but with all our expansion, I know our current cash flow can't support that kind of outlay in the near future."

"That's a lot of money, Ashley. We need to come up with a plan. Can you come to the island sometime soon to discuss possibilities? With some creative problem solving, we should be able to come up with some way we won't lose the island. After all this place holds a large chunk of our family history. It's part of us. Do you want to come here or should I fly up?" After a moment, she added, "Forget that idea. Right now, I can't take the city."

"OK, don't fly up. Work will be demanding between now and the end of our fiscal year. I'll come down when I can. In the meantime, perhaps you could be investigating some options for the island. A couple of years ago, there was this Savannah developer, Gardner was his name, who was interested in the island."

"Are you suggesting we sell out?"

"I don't know, Sis. You explore it. I do know a few million dollars is a lot for me. Since I've taken over, my ex-wife and her attorneys are really trying to take a bite out of my hide. Now that I've inherited the reins at Parker Transworld, they seem to think they can suck me dry. But, I have a surprise or two for them."

"Still, the future of Caretta is important. Think about options."

"Sure. Well, gotta run. Talk to you later."

Melanie wandered out on the porch and stared at the expanse of salt marsh. Where does one come up with several million in cash in a hurry?

* * *

As the stars peeked through the black silhouettes of the palms, Melanie was restless until, finally, sleep overtook her.

Melanie reached across the bucket seat to touch her husband's thigh. Greg rested his right hand lightly on hers as he turned his head briefly to smile at her. In the back seat of the BMW sedan, stuffed between her parents and buckled in his seat belt, sat their son Parker. He was looking through his newest book on his current favorite subject, dinosaurs.

"Look, Mom. Look how mean this one looks."

Melanie grinned at his repetitious nine-year-old vocabulary then agreed, "Tyrannosaurus was a great carnivore. Do you know what carnivore means?"

"Yeah. Me-at-eat-er," breathed her son.

Melanie shivered at his boyish delight. Her husband gently squeezed her fingers to physically relay: It's all right.

Her father and mother continued to turn the pages of the book while Parker read the scientific names to them.

"Bron-to-saur-us, P-ter-a-dac-tyl," he struggled with the unwieldy names.

"You're so smart, Parker," Melanie's mother lavished compliments on her grandson.

Melanie beamed as she watched her parents and child together.

She sensed rather than saw her husband tense and check the mirrors — left, right, and rear before rapidly repeating the sequence.

Melanie turned her attention to him and watched his mouth set in a grim straight line. A bead of sweat appeared on his brow. She felt the crashing of metal, heard the cracking of glass....

She woke.

The mosquito netting around the bed filtered the moonlight beaming through the bedroom window and created an unearthly aura. For a minute, Melanie imagined she was in the hospital — back in the room painted a sickly green where she had first learned her family had been killed in the car accident.

Melanie cried. She remembered the before and the after, but she couldn't detail the accident itself. All she knew was that she missed these people. Her life had been wrenched from her. Mentally exhausted from the horror of her remembrance, she fell back asleep.

Shortly after dawn, she awoke somewhat relieved. The psychiatrist had told her that, eventually, the numbness and unreality would fade away. She would be able to feel emotion again. At last, here at Caretta, it was beginning to happen.

Melanie understood she was establishing a new life for herself. She listed her accomplishments of the last few weeks: She had made all the arrangements to return to Caretta despite her brother's objections; she had made the trip; she had started an exercise program as the therapists had prescribed; she had met several new people; she had a pet to love and return her love. Too, there were other potential interests — the protection of Caretta and Grant's desalination project.

Feeling better about herself and her situation, Melanie threw off the bedcovers and stroked the now-alert cat before she parted the mosquito netting and rose to meet the new day.

* * *

9:00 a.m., Monday, May 2, 1988

Melanie heard a boat engine throb above the constant chittering of the birds and squirrels. Accompanied by Ali Cat, she walked to the creek and saw a vaguely familiar craft floating toward the dock. Now, who could that be? Who would be coming to the island unannounced? When she approached, the figure on deck waved at her as if he knew her.

The man was still fastening the ropes when Melanie reached the dock. The figure turned. She found herself face-to-face with Adam Gardner.

What interesting timing, Melanie reflected. First, Ashley mentions Adam during our phone conversation. Then, the handsome, self-assured, real-estate developer suddenly appears. Out loud she exclaimed warily, "Adam, what a surprise."

"Surprise? Remember: I said I'd come my next free sunny day. So here I am."

"On a Monday?"

"One advantage of being in charge," he grinned. "I hope you still want to see my development, The Hammock."

Though taken off-guard by this succession of events, Melanie couldn't concoct a rational reason to say no. Too, it was a gorgeous day. "Of course, I still want to see your project. I'm pleased you remembered. Let's walk up to the house and let Patrice and Louisa know where we're going."

While they walked, Adam observed Ali Cat shadowing them.

"That cat is smitten with you."

"He's become my constant companion, though I've noticed he never follows me into the woods. He must have met a hungry alligator or bobcat in there," Melanie observed with amusement.

"Speaking of jungles, how's your brother? How's he faring in New York without you?"

"He's managing. I didn't realize you knew Ashley."

"I met him two years ago when I was in New York and, of course, I've heard Susannah and Katherine Harris talk of him." Gesturing to the left, Adam asked, "What's this building?"

"That's Jim and Louisa's home. As you can see, the caretaker's cottage has touches of the Spanish influence, too."

As they walked on toward Parker House, Melanie wondered how frequent a visitor Adam Gardner had been to Caretta Island. She found it unusual that he was on a first-name basis with Patrice. Yet, he hadn't noticed the caretaker's cottage? Was Adam playing some kind of game with her? Was her aunt? And, he had mentioned Susannah and Katherine Harris. She understood Katherine was still Patrice's closest friend yet Melanie had seen neither of the Harrises for years.

When they reached the porch, Melanie called, "Louisa, Patrice, we have a guest."

Her aunt appeared almost immediately at the front door.

After customary greetings, Melanie explained, "Actually, I'm going to be Adam's guest at The Hammock today."

Just then Louisa stepped from the kitchen with a solemn air, assessing Adam before questioning Melanie, "Did you call, Miz Mellie?"

"Yes, Louisa. Would you pour Mr. Gardner a cup of coffee while I find my sunglasses and jacket?"

"Yez, Miz Mellie. Anythin' fo' you, Miz Patrice?"

"Coffee would be lovely, Louisa," replied the older woman. "Please serve it here on the porch."

When Louisa turned to go back into the kitchen, Adam exclaimed, "Ah, Louisa, I thoroughly enjoyed that southern dinner you fixed the other evening."

"Very good, Mistuh Gardner," tersely replied the still-solemn woman, not reacting to his comment.

Adam was surprised by her flat reaction to his compliment. He would have to put some planning into how to gain the housekeeper's confidence. He wondered how much influence she had over Patrice and Melanie.

"Please, make yourself comfortable, Adam," Patrice motioned to a chaise lounge on the screened porch. "And don't mind, Louisa. She is suspicious of strangers. You have to understand that she has spent most of her life on this island."

Adam nodded then settled onto the chaise. While he talked with Patrice, he admired the construction of the villa and its view of the grounds. Again, he found himself thrilling to the possibilities of its development.

He and Patrice were finishing their coffee when Melanie returned with her sunglasses and jacket. She commented, "I'm ready. Lead on." She found her mood rising to the unexpected occasion. After a week on the island, it would be pleasant to spend a few hours in different surroundings.

On the boat, Adam steered along the waterways leading to the busy marina at The Hammock. During the ride, he was attentive to Melanie and her questions. He pointed out various buoys and landmarks used for navigation.

At the marina, a tall weather-beaten man helped secure the lines and assisted Melanie onto the dock. "Do you have a moment, Adam?"

"Always, Mik, but first I'd like you to meet Melanie Evans from New York City. She's staying out on Caretta Island. I'm going to show her The Hammock." Turning to Melanie he said, "Melanie, meet Miklos Carras, The Hammock Harbormaster."

The three exchanged pleasantries then Adam and Mik conferred while Melanie surveyed the docked vessels with their unusual, often silly, names. She overheard occasional words and phrases about someone named Junior taking out Adam's boats. The harbormaster thought Junior was overusing his boating privileges. Adam assured Mik that Junior had permission to use the runabout or the yacht for his own personal business.

"Thanks for being so careful, Mik," Adam loudly thanked him.

Hurrying to Melanie's side, Adam apologized, "I'm sorry about the interruption. Business can intrude at the most inconvenient moments."

"It's perfectly fine, Adam. I've been busy admiring all these incredible boats."

"Yes, many of our property owners are avid water enthusiasts. They take great pride in their craft. I've found a quality marina is as big a selling point as a golf course, stable, airstrip, or tight security."

"The Hammock sounds as if it's your life."

"In a way, it is. Are you ready to see more?"

"That's why I'm here."

"We'll make this first visit short. I don't want to bore you."

The next hour went swiftly for Melanie as Adam gave her the guided tour of the large development. She'd seen many planned communities, but none with the attention to detail she was now witnessing. Viewing it through the eyes of its creator, she was gaining a new perspective. Many homes were in various stages of completion. All reflected the best in materials — cedar, cypress, or oak boards; copper, slate, or tile roofs. Meticulous landscaping highlighted the cabbage palms, oaks, and small freshwater ponds. Bike and foot paths cut through buffer areas of saw palmetto, flanking the marsh and creek banks.

"Where did you find so many buyers in Savannah?"

"Actually, most of our customers are retired or semi-retired executives from the Northeast. The climate and relaxed lifestyle appeal to them."

"How do you market to that group?"

Adam smiled, "That's right. Marketing is your field, isn't it? Then, you know the power of word-of-mouth advertising. In addition, we place ads in *The Wall Street Journal.*"

"Adam, from what I've seen, you've done a remarkable job."

"Thanks. It's coming along. I'm flattered you appreciate my work."

As Adam gauged Melanie's reactions to what she had seen at The Hammock, he decided she responded to visual stimuli. He probed by switching the subject, "Have you visited any art galleries since you've arrived in Savannah?"

"No, do you have a gallery here at The Hammock, too?"

"No, not yet, but I'm working on it." Taking her arm, he steered her toward a large building. "What I do have are rotating exhibits of regional artists in the clubhouse. A fairly new group called the Savannah College of Art and Design has energized the local scene. And, my favorite Savannah gallery owner, Yvonne Rogers, has assembled the current show of SCAD students. It will help me test the market here at The Hammock."

At the clubhouse, Adam confidently guided her through a series of handsomely decorated rooms until they reached a large room hung with watercolors, acrylics, and oils. There were beach scenes, lowcountry landscapes, portraits, abstracts, impressions of birds and a variety of sea creatures. A number of small sculptures completed the exhibit. All the works were originals. Obvious care had gone into the selection process forced by the limited display space.

They walked around the room and evaluated each work of art.

"Perhaps you would help me choose a painting for my house," Adam proposed.

"Oh, I'm no expert," Melanie protested, "though I'd be happy to give you my opinion."

"Thank you," mock-bowed Adam. "I have another idea, too. How about going to a polo match with me next Sunday? It's at Rose Hill over on Hilton Head Island."

Adam's invitation startled Melanie. She had enjoyed this short tour, but she had considered it as investigating possibilities for Caretta's future. This invitation, however, sounded like a date rather than a business appointment. She was anxious to keep the situation on a business footing. Tactfully she responded, "That's a lovely idea. Patrice would enjoy that, too."

Adam paused for a moment before he added, "Good idea. We can all look at the development on Hilton Head while we're there."

Melanie marveled at how quickly he adapted to a change in plans. Again she realized, this guy really is a smooth operator.

* * *

Several hours after Melanie and Adam's conversation and a few miles east of The Hammock, a freighter rolled gently on a hemisphere of black sea punctuated by occasional white caps. Above and around the freighter, yawned another dark sphere pricked with thousands of stars. Off to port, glowed the red and green running lights of a shrimp boat on an early morning trawl.

Two dark figures emerged on the shadowy deck. One sailor sauntered over to the rail and stared down into the black waters. No one else was about. A hurried motion was made to the other crewman, standing a few steps behind him. An object was pulled carefully through the open hatch. After a wary glance revealed no recent arrivals, they threw the buoy over the side. The rumble of the engines muffled the small splash. Silently, the two sailors vanished below.

Five minutes later, with the ship retreating in the distance, a small timer finished its countdown. On top of the floating object, an amber light began to flash an intermittent signal.

* * *

10:00 a.m., Thursday, May 5, 1988

After three weeks on the island, Melanie discerned that her body was adopting a new rhythm. Here life corresponded to sun, moon, winds, and tides rather than family concerns, business productivity, fluctuating exchange rates, and news flashes. This emerging pace produced a heightened awareness of basic feelings coupled with a removed sense of well-being — as if she were wrapped in a cocoon, monitoring her own life processes.

Today, however, she and Patrice were fulfilling a social obligation. Susannah Harris, a childhood playmate, and her mother, Katherine Harris who was Patrice's friend and confidante, were coming to a tea given by Patrice. Melanie felt as if she had to help entertain these distant acquaintances; the mitigating circumstance was that one visitor was her own age.

"I think I hear the boat. Does everything look acceptable?" Patrice asked as she flitted about nervously.

"Everything looks like a breath of spring," Melanie reassured her aunt. "Wildflowers are arranged in every room; the silver tea service is ready to pour." It's as if we're welcoming royalty. Melanie smiled and wondered how often her aunt indulged in the social pleasantry of a tea.

They waited on the porch for Jim to drive their two guests to the house — another Caretta formality, Melanie reflected. Appraising the approaching mother and daughter, Melanie viewed glittering but tasteful jewelry, coifed hair, understated make-up, and stylish clothing. It was obvious the two enjoyed a well-to-do lifestyle.

"Melanie, it's been too long!" Susannah called her greeting and waved. The sunlight refracted off a ring studding one of Susannah's fingers as she pushed her long, dyed-blonde hair off her shoulder.

Melanie beamed a smile in response as the two fashionable women alighted from the jeep and mounted the steps to Parker House. "So good to see both of you again," she welcomed them.

The four exchanged greetings, hugs, and kisses on each cheek in another customary opening ritual.

"I'm so pleased you could make it, Susannah. I know Melanie will enjoy talking to someone her own age," Patrice confided to Susannah.

"Melanie, you look so fine after the... uh... your misfortunate spell," Katherine lost her dignity momentarily due to the personal yet impersonal nature of her remarks.

"I'm doing quite well here. Thank you, Katherine," Melanie glossed over the situation, concluding the older woman meant to be kind, "Caretta has been good for me."

Rescuing the awkward moment, Patrice picked up the beat and offered, "There are refreshments prepared in the parlor. Shall we make ourselves comfortable?"

As they moved inside, Melanie experienced another outrageous, sarcastic moment — all this politeness and civility — how ridiculous!

The four women settled into facing loveseats; Melanie and Susannah occupied one side while Patrice and Katherine held the other. A long low table prepared with tea, sandwiches, and cookies separated them. Patrice poured the tea.

While they nibbled, conversation flitted from the boat trip to weather to social events in Savannah. Comments were made about Savannah and New York art galleries and historic buildings.

Susannah bent toward Melanie and whispered in her ear, "Let's get out of here. Mother and Patrice will talk like this all day, and we've got lots to catch up on. Let's head for the beach gazebo like we used to when we were kids."

"Good idea," Melanie whispered back. To the two older women, she announced, "Susannah and I are going down to the beach gazebo for a while. I'm sure you two have plenty to talk about without us."

"Yes, do," Katherine urged them.

"Do you want to take any food or drinks?" Patrice asked, still in her hostess role.

"No, we're fine," Melanie assured Patrice. "See you shortly."

The two former playmates piled into the jeep and breathed a sigh of relief as they cleared the grounds and gained the privacy of the woods.

"That scene takes me back a few years. It's as if I were a little girl again," chuckled Susannah "when men were gentlemen and ladies never let on how much they knew."

"Do you guess we'll act that way when we grow up?" Melanie wondered aloud.

"Never — at least, I hope not!" Susannah added.

The short trip to the gazebo allowed the intervening years to wash away. They relaxed under the sunshelter of the gray weathered-wood roof. Their perch above the sand dunes permitted an unobstructed view up and down the bright sunlit coast while allowing the light breeze to bring them a fresh, salty tang. Their conversation continued.

"You're looking marvelous, Susannah. Tell me about your life. It's been too many years since we've seen one another," Melanie began.

"We've both seen a lot of changes since those carefree girlish days. I'm divorced. As you know, I still live in little ol' Savannah, but I stay busy."

"You must have found something or somebody interesting to keep you here," Melanie probed.

"To tell the truth, the somebodies are few and far between. This sleepy town was only a hotbed of exciting men during the Civil War. Every now and then, there's an interesting diversion." She flushed slightly, giggled salaciously, "You've already met two of them. The Australian who stays out here caused some commotion. I've heard that the little redhead over at the Sea Island Institute got her hooks into him. And, then, there's Adam Gardner."

"Do you know a man named Adam Gardner?" Patrice asked Katherine Harris.

Taking a sip of her tea, Katherine replied, "Not that well, though Susannah and he date. They're friends — not romantically involved. Young people these days have such different ideas."

"Is he a good businessman?"

"He's bright. He's made a success of The Hammock project." A hell of a sight better than my late husband, she thought bitterly. "Why do you ask?"

"He's been so ingratiating these past few months. I...." Patrice searched for the appropriate terms. "I've wondered how much of his motivation comes from his good character and how much comes from his desire to develop Caretta."

"Caretta? It makes sense he might like to develop the island. As far as his character is concerned, he's probably as dependable as any other man," that means not dependable at all, in my book she concluded in her mind.

The interchange on the same subject continued at the gazebo.

"Oh, you know Adam?" Melanie asked, sensing Susannah more than knew him.

"Sure. Great looks, pleasant conversation, and often available. He's a good businessman, too." And an attentive lover, she smiled to herself. "We've worked together."

"You're in business? What are you doing?"

"Mostly fashion design. I've created a small company to produce high fashion apparel under the trademark Savvy."

"Tell me more about your business." Truly interested, Melanie pressed for details. "What kind of niche in the marketplace are you trying to fill?"

"I stay on the current wave of fashion, though I modify it slightly for my taste. Thanks to Adam, my manufacturing costs allow me to underprice the typical designer originals."

"It must be quite a task to stay up-to-date with the latest fashion trends."

"It is. I fly to New York weekly. After all, I can't use a Savannah address. Who'd buy designer clothes from a Southern firm? I do volunteer as a board member for SCAD, the Savannah College of Art and Design, to round out my resumé."

"And, you supervise the actual work of putting out the line?" Melanie asked.

"Not totally. I do the sketches and the patterns. The cutting and finishing are done all over Georgia and the Carolinas."

"You don't use a plant?"

"Too much overhead. It was Adam who helped me hire unemployed textile workers. Often these people are too old to land new jobs, so I hire them at an attractive rate."

"What about labor regulations?" Melanie questioned.

Susannah shrugged and tossed her long hair, "The workers are happy to find a paying job. The arrangement's a whole lot better than welfare."

"Susannah, you sound like a twentieth-century plantation owner," Melanie kidded.

"No, not me. The new slave bosses are in California and the Southwest. They make millions off the sweat of illegal aliens."

"I never realized that," responded Melanie.

"I've discovered we live in a highly competitive world. I've staked a small claim. In the process, I'm helping a lot more people than I'm hurting. It's exhilarating."

Susannah's explanation surprised Melanie. Her childhood playmate had grown up to be a formidable woman in many ways.

"This is one of my items." Susannah stood and paraded around the gazebo in her yellow dress, simple but daring in cut — each side seam slit to reveal her shapely thighs. "Like it?"

"It's stunning and you wear it beautifully," Melanie commented, admiring her companion's physical tone. In her mind, Melanie could hear Greg make favorable comments about Susannah's body. In their Olympic-style figure-rating system, Melanie heard him whisper his rating of almost ten. She knew he would not be as happy with her own current look. Not being too pleased with it herself, she renewed her determination to become more fit. To Susannah, she observed, "I see you work at staying in-shape, too."

"You remember how fat I was as a kid. Mercy! What a burden that was," came the reply as Susannah returned to the bench. "I still see fat every time I look in a mirror. That indelible image won't go away. So, free weights have become my passion. I've discovered I can keep my body looking like this if I work out five times a week. I've also found it pays off in many ways," Susannah smirked. The blonde realized as she was steering the conversation toward her favorite topic, sex, that it was not yet appropriate. She paused, "But, how about you? I heard you were in the hospital for weeks. Then, the loss.... Has your recovery this past year been difficult?"

Though she really didn't want to talk about that subject, Melanie sensed an obligation to explain to her old friend. "More than I can possibly share. The body has responded fine to therapy, but the mind.... It's the hidden wounds that are taking the longest to heal. Alone in New York, well.... Anyway, after a few weeks here, I feel one hundred per cent better."

"Give yourself time. You'll get stronger; you'll make it."

Melanie continued, "I feel I've traveled farther emotionally in the last several months than in my whole life. I don't know if that makes me any stronger."

"Do you have any plans for the immediate future?"

"None — other than deciding what to do about Caretta."

"What do you mean?"

"Whether to sell or develop or whatever."

"Why would you and Ashley want to sell the island?"

Melanie explained about the oppressive inheritance taxes.

"Lawd! That'll be a difficult decision." On a lighter note Susannah added, "At least, you can plan to join me for lunch in our little metropolis. I can show you some of the recent restorations in the historic district as well as new items from my Savvy line."

"Wonderful. Let's do it. And, speaking of trips to the city, why don't you look up my brother, Ashley, when you're in New York? "

"Ashley?" Susannah looked puzzled. "Ah, your older brother. I'm sorry to say that I don't have fond memories of him. He was always irritating us when we tried to play. How's he doing?"

"Pretty well, though he's still irritating at times. He was against my coming down here. His cure for everything is work. I'm sure glad I didn't listen to him." She paused. "He divorced his wife shortly before the accident. They're still going through the legal hassles. He says she's trying to bleed him. But, he would see giving her one dollar as bleeding." Melanie sighed, "Then, he had to handle all the family funeral arrangements plus take care of me for a while. All of that had to be emotionally trying. Of course, the accident threw a lot of business responsibilities on him. But, he's the type who focuses his attention on work to resolve his personal problems. If he doesn't sound too boring, give him a call — he deserves a little fun."

"Maybe I will look him up," Susannah grinned. "It might be interesting to see how the years have changed him."

The two younger women returned to the Big House. In less than an hour, the two guests reboarded their boat for the return trip to town.

"I must say Melanie looks worse for wear — so thin and pale," commented Katherine to her daughter.

"An immense loss extracts a hell of a price, doesn't it?" agreed Susannah. "However, I reckon she has a plan."

"Hmm... from what Patrice told me, the family faces several tough decisions. A lot of taxes must be paid when the estate is finally settled. Did you know Adam Gardner has been out to visit?"

"As a matter of fact, I did. He's no fool. Through the Parkers he may access a golden opportunity on that island."

"He wastes no time. I wonder if Melanie's plans involve him. I wouldn't let him stray too far, if I were you. Remember her mother, Margaret, took Courtland away from me."

Annoyed, Susannah replied, "Don't start that again, Mother. I'm not you. And, " she added, "I know what I'm doing."

CHAPTER 6

10:00 a.m., Saturday, May 7, 1988

As spring turned into summer, the sun warmed the island and its waters. Days lengthened; mosquitoes hatched; polliwogs frogged.

On some mornings, Grant joined Melanie whenever she jogged on the beach. Other days, when she wanted to be by herself, she pedaled the old bicycle with its balloon tires or rode the island horse, Derby. Grant accepted her need to be alone. On those occasions, he took out his kayak on the creek or around the island. Grant's sensitivity was an aspect Melanie appreciated.

Their bedrooms were across from each other so they were naturally aware of one another's routines. Too, being newer island residents and closer in age than the others, they shared day-to-day island events such as the birth of a fawn. Though she longed for more philosophical discussions, she was glad Grant was easy to get along with on the surface. Often their breakfasts or lunches coincided in Louisa's "come and get it when you're ready" kitchen. There they compared observations of the day. Dinner with Patrice was formal with conversation to match. After dinner came relaxed conversation on the porch or research in the library.

This morning, Melanie and Grant walked barefoot in the surf to cool-off after a run.

"What is it about a beach?" Melanie mused.

"You mean why are so many folks drawn to it?"

"Yes, it's like a return to the womb — soothing and comforting."

"Good point. Too, perhaps, it's because as we face the almost limitless expanse of water, we see few man-made objects. We hear only the sounds of the water. Society disappears. The basic elements engulf our senses. Or, perhaps, it's because we originated in the sea. It might even be a genetic memory."

"Spoken like a true scientist." While they waded, Melanie sensed the strange, pleasurable suction of the ocean, pulling wet sand from beneath her toes, "Look, it's got a pull even though it looks calm," she said with childish glee.

Grant grinned with equal pleasure. "The Atlantic may not be the most fearsome ocean, but it has its share of strong tides, currents, and undertows. On Caretta, it borrows sand from North Arm and deposits it at Tail End. Accretion — that's the scientific term — is one way the seas change the land. An ocean has strength, even when hidden under a mirror-smooth surface."

"Look at all these tiny shells burrowing into the sand," she pointed to the process happening at their feet. Thousands of coquina shells tinier than little fingernails, in multitudinous shades of gray, pink, and lavender were busy hiding themselves in the sand, wet from the last wave.

"Caretta is fortunate to have such an alive beach," Grant replied. "According to Fred Frazier, the Fish and Wildlife Warden, Caretta is one of the few remaining barrier islands where the endangered least terns and loggerhead turtles nest on the beach. Uncontrolled human intrusion has destroyed most nesting grounds. Fred claims this island shelters all of the animals known to live on the sea islands except for black bears, panthers, and wolves. Hunters must have exterminated them years ago. Humans tend to see predators as a threat. We forget they are important for balancing the environment."

"That's true. I've run across entries in the Caretta journals about hunting parties. They hunted ducks and deer for food. They shot any animals they considered threatening to their families. They just didn't know when to stop. All those animals are gone." Melanie continued, "I saw the warden out here last week. Does he come to the island often?"

"About once a week. He's studying the freshwater ponds near Tail End. He calls them a complete ecosystem. He's running counts on the different species living there over a year's period. Didn't your father authorize it?"

"Probably," Melanie replied as she stored away this piece of information. "How's your research coming along?"

"Smooth, but still no breakthroughs. In fact, I must stop by the laboratory before breakfast. See you later?"

Melanie nodded and Grant headed for his workshop.

As Melanie continued to walk along the edge of the gently rolling surf, she pondered Grant's reluctance to talk further about his research. She kept coming up against his continuing reserve. It made her slightly uncomfortable. She lectured herself: "Give him time." Perhaps, eventually, he would open up to her. Maybe it was because she was one of Caretta's owners and had influence over his project funding. Maybe Australians were simply more aloof. Besides, she reminded herself, he's an engineer, not a people-person. Meanwhile, she enjoyed these oceanside jogs and shared moments. She hoped he did, too.

Twenty minutes later, Melanie entered the coolness of the tabby house and headed for the shower. As the hot water streamed over her healthier body, she was momentarily pleased that her mind now wandered over other subjects, such as the Australian engineer. She no longer dwelled constantly on her loss. Other topics and interests were becoming more frequent.

* * *

That evening, Melanie read the family journals until the generators turned off the electricity for the night. Restless, she moved to the porch. Her mind spun with fragments from the fragile, age-yellowed pages. Stimulated by tales of the past on Caretta Island, she wanted to run down the paths of her imagination. Instead, she descended the porch steps to walk.

A light cloud cover left few stars to cut the darkness. Her eyes adjusted to the point where shadows were discernible. Surrounded by the unfamiliar, she chose the wider paths hugging the banks of the marsh and fringing the woods.

The chirring of the insects led by the noisy crickets set the tempo of her pace. In the distance she heard a piercing cry once, then again. Stopping, she strained to hear, wondering what animal made such a human noise? An exhilarating shiver ran through her.

When the sensation passed, she turned and headed for a cleared area on the marsh bank. Breathing steadily, she reclined on the grass slope and gazed at the heavens. Serenity enveloped her.

Searching for stars, the smell of the salt marsh penetrated her senses — salty and organic with decaying undertones. Others told her she would notice it less after a while. She hoped she would acclimate slowly. Everything about the island was more pleasant, more natural, than the chemical atmosphere of the city.

S-n-i-f-f. One long sniff then another sounded behind her head. A dry palmetto frond cracked as the creature moved. Adrenaline soared through Melanie's body. Totally alert, she cautiously sat up and turned to identify the animal. The blackness was absolute. She sensed, but did not see movement. She jumped to her feet, but the intruder exhibited no corresponding panic. Fear and suspicion took root and grew in the darkness. She saw the shape, about the size of a small dog, then a streak of white — a skunk.

Relief coursed through Melanie. It's only a skunk. Suddenly, she remembered: Skunks carry rabies in addition to their malodor. She made shooing noises and stomped her feet, trying to make the skunk change direction without activating its defense mechanism. Finally, in its own good time, the creature altered course.

A sigh escaped Melanie's chest as she watched the menace depart, still sniffing for edible morsels. One of her son's favorite plays on words flashed into her mind: "PU — that's two-thirds of a pun."

S-n-a-r-l. Melanie watched horrified as the skunk's striped tail straightened. She made out a set of glinting, yellow eyes and sharp, white teeth. A flick of this animal's tail revealed the ringed markings of a raccoon, disputing territory with the skunk. Holding her breath, she waited for the inevitable showdown. Seconds seemed like minutes. Eventually, both adversaries gave ground and continued foraging in the night.

Liberated, Melanie returned to the house. Calm crept into her consciousness. She laughed at her naiveté. Of course, she would have unexpected encounters with other island residents!

Thinking about the various island animals, Melanie strongly remembered her son who would have found tonight's experiences incredibly exciting. Her eyes filled with tears.

* * *

2:30 p.m., Sunday, May 8, 1988

Melanie lay on her bed and watched the ceiling fan go round and round. She tossed and turned under the weight of the oppressive air. The afternoon had become hot and humid, precursing summer. Patrice and Louisa recommended naps during the afternoon heat. Melanie found herself still adjusting to the island ways: generators for electricity that turned off at night, cumbersome communications equipment, no air conditioning — only paddle fans to move the breathless air. Although there were modern alternatives available, Patrice preferred the old ways.

Bored with lazing around in bed, Melanie decided to change into her swimsuit and spend the remainder of the afternoon on the beach. Perhaps there would be a breeze off the ocean to cool her. She liberally doused her exposed skin with insect repellent, grabbed her towel and suntan lotion, then, headed for the beach.

Walking along sandy Crossroad through the sundappled live oak, pine, and palmetto, she crossed the intersection of Backbone Road and continued on Crossroad to its terminus at the beach. It was a pleasant twenty-minute walk in the shade of the woods. The mosquitoes and sand flies swarmed, but the repellent kept them at bay.

At the end of the green tunnel created by the overhanging trees, Melanie saw the sea oats waving at her from Caretta's rounded dunes, suggesting the sought-after breeze. Walking carefully around the fragile plants, she emerged on the smooth beach. Sand dollars and channeled whelks punctuated wide gray sand. A couple of brown pelicans floated on even, regular waves. Sea gulls stood on one foot then another, eyeing her and a nude woman stretched out on the sand. A nude woman? It wasn't the naked female body that surprised her. It was seeing someone else on the island. Who was this adventurous interloper?

Trying to recall if anyone were visiting the island, a curious Melanie headed toward the redheaded figure.

The sun worshiper rolled over and caught a glimpse of Melanie. Slowly the redhead sat up and slipped into an oversize T-shirt, then waved.

Melanie returned the gesture.

"Hello, I'm Melanie Evans," she called.

"Rebecca Woody" replied the lightly-freckled woman. "Please, make yourself comfortable," she patted the sand alongside her.

Melanie smoothed out her towel and sat beside the now-covered woman.

"What brings you to Caretta?" inquired Rebecca.

"My brother and I own the island."

"But, the family name is Parker."

"Evans is my married name; Parker is my maiden name. What are you doing on the island?" parried Melanie.

"How embarrassing!" Rebecca swallowed then stated, "I'm the Loggerhead Project Director."

"Loggerhead Project? Oh, you mean the summer turtle research?"

"Yes. This is my third year in charge, though the Sea Island Institute has brought teams here for fifteen years."

"I remember now. Father gave the project the run of the beach during the sea turtles' laying season. He always had a soft spot for those huge creatures. When Ashley and I were children, he brought us to the beach one night to watch the turtles lay their eggs. Have they already started?"

"No. I just delivered equipment and supplies today. And, when I'm so close to this beach, I find it impossible to resist. It's so private — a swimsuit seems ridiculous. It feels so natural to lie naked on the beach. It renews my sense of connectedness with nature. Even during turtle tagging, I sun as often as my fair skin allows."

"Turtle tagging? That sounds like a game. What do you mean?" Melanie inquired.

"We put numbered plastic tags on their flippers," Rebecca replied seriously. "So do other teams on Wassaw and Little Cumberland as well as turtle projects all over the world. That way we can track the turtles' activities."

"All over the world?"

"Sure. There are six types of sea turtles. Besides our Atlantic loggerheads, there are the green, leatherback, olive Ridley, Kemp's Ridley, and hawksbill."

"Exactly what do you track?"

Rebecca screwed up her face as if she were reading a form, "How often and where a particular turtle nests. How big she is. What the weather conditions are when she lays — information like that."

"All that?"

"That and more. Will you be here long enough to join us one night?"

"Probably. My plans are indefinite but, I'm guessing, I'll be here for a couple of months."

"Great! I want to get to know you better. And, I really hope you'll join us for an occasional turtle tagging. We patrol the beach from sunset to sunrise from the end of May through mid-August. You'll see, we can use all the hands we can get."

"What do you do at the institute the rest of the year?"

Rebecca chuckled, "Too much. I help with the Gray's Reef Project. The reef is about fifteen miles offshore and it's one of the largest bottom reefs in the Atlantic. So, I keep busy studying its life forms and their adaptations, compiling and comparing research, then, raising funds for the sea turtle research and education program."

"Education program?"

"Yes, the one thing all the species of sea turtles have in common is man endangering their existence."

"What are we doing?" puzzled Melanie.

Again Rebecca screwed up her face then began ticking off reasons. "Of course, commercial fishermen with their trawling nets are the biggest killers. And, we destroy their nesting places by overdeveloping the coast. We kill them deliberately for their meat and for their shells. We kill them accidentally by throwing plastic bags over the sides of boats. You see, when the sun hits the plastic, the turtles recognize it as jellyfish, their favorite food. They swallow the bags and suffocate."

Rebecca paused, "I could talk all afternoon and night about sea turtles. Right now, though, I'd better catch the tide or you'll have an overnight guest. Then, you'd hear more than you ever wanted to know about turtles," she commented as she stepped into a pair of khaki shorts, then rolled up her bamboo mat. She held out her hand and said, "See you again soon."

Melanie shook the outstretched hand and replied, "I look forward to it, Rebecca."

Heading to the dock, Rebecca surmised Melanie must be the car wreck survivor. She's surprisingly attractive and she's certainly sharp. Thank goodness, she doesn't seem prudish. However, I'd better check with Grant about the best approach with her for continued use of the island. She pondered the fact that Grant was the only available man on the island. "And, a darn handsome one," she said aloud. Melanie had better not be Grant's type.

After Rebecca left, Melanie stretched on her towel in the afternoon sun. She rolled over and wiggled her toes in the sand. She had enjoyed the short encounter with the forthright Rebecca. She's right! There is no need for a swimsuit on this beach. Why am I wearing one? Melanie wiggled out of her suit. Exhilarated, she lay on her back, amazed at how delicious the sea breeze felt caressing her skin. I should have done this years ago. She fantasized what her staid aunt's reaction would be if she started running naked around the island. Probably, she would collapse in an epileptic fit. What about Louisa? What about Jim? She chuckled to herself. This summer might be more exciting than I ever imagined.

A gull landed in front of her and eyed her expectantly. Evenly, she returned its gaze while in her head she replayed the faces of people in recent months: Ashley, the doctors and hospital personnel, friends and co-workers, people here on the island and in Savannah. It was good to make new acquaintances who knew nothing about the accident, the recovery, and the misery. Once again she congratulated herself on making the decision to come here. She was pleased that Patrice seemed to be reaching out to her through the family journals. She relaxed, as she reviewed the current people in her life — Patrice, Louisa, Jim, Grant, Adam, Susannah, Rebecca....

Her thoughts drifted to Greg. Wouldn't it have been wonderful if we'd had the sense to do this together? She pictured herself and Greg together on Caretta's beach, holding hands and running naked along the water's edge. Stopping, Greg gently takes her into his strong arms; her firm breasts press comfortably against his chest. Gently he kisses her, whispers, "I love you, Melanie."

Smiling, she fell asleep.

A cool, late-afternoon ocean breeze woke Melanie. Dazed from her nap and pleasant dreams, it took her a few minutes to regain reality. Though not really wanting to leave, she shimmied into her swimsuit, shook the sand from her towel, scooped up her belongings, then strolled through the maritime forest to the Big House. She sighed with satisfaction as she settled into a rocker on the porch.

Louisa came out of the kitchen and beamed at her with approval. "I know dat comin' here do you good."

"Ah, Louisa, it's good to be alive — to feel the sun on my back and the sand between my toes." Although she wanted to share her sunbathing experience with Louisa, she sensed the large woman would not approve. Instead, she confided, "I just met an interesting woman with the Loggerhead Project."

"Becca's nice enough, but you take care. She put de mout' on you."

"Put de mout' on me?"

"Dat's a sea island expression. It means she has de power over people — she bewitch them with dat red hair — so you take care," warned Louisa.

"Why do you say that?"

"Jus' you be careful. Hear?"

* * *

In New York, a lean figure clad in black swung down the rope to the balcony of the Sutton Place co-op. He forced open the French doors and pushed the closed curtains far enough to one side to gain entrance.

He headed for a portrait of a man and boy hanging over the fireplace; the frame swung toward him, revealing a wall safe. He set a small plastic charge on the dial and impatiently waited for it to blow with its muffled "whoosh." The burglar pulled out the contents onto the floor and sifted through them in a purposeful fashion by the bright beam of his flashlight. He selected pieces of heirloom jewelry that he stuffed in his jacket pockets then zippered shut. Next he sat in the arm chair at the desk and worked systematically through each drawer.

The intruder moved down the hall to the master bedroom. Again he searched drawers; looked inside a jewelry box, woven baskets, and a flower vase; checked between the mattress and box springs. He walked through the rest of the rooms with an eye for hiding places. He opened cabinet doors, the refrigerator, and a toy box.

An approaching siren made him nervous. He knew he had set off no alarms; there were none. The downstairs guards provided the building security. Had a neighbor seen him enter or noticed the flashlight roving the walls? Cautious, he exited the luxurious cooperative apartment in the way he had arrived.

* * *

8:30 a.m., Monday, May 9, 1988

"Mrs. Evans?" the police detective inquired over the telephone.

"Yes, this is Melanie Evans," came the cautious reply.

"This is Detective Richard Stone of the New York City Police Department. Can you hear me? This connection sounds bad."

"I can hear you, Detective Stone. I'm talking on a radio-telephone. I control the sound transmission with a lever here; I have to anticipate when you're talking. It takes a little getting used to. How may I help you? Do you need information on the accident?"

"Accident? What accident, Mrs. Evans?"

Her mind froze. "You know. The car accident I was in last July. It killed my family."

"No," he paused. "No, I was calling about a break-in."

"A break-in? In my co-op?"

"Yes. A neighbor reported a suspicious noise last night. When we arrived, we found the wall safe blown open."

"What? Are you sure?" she queried as she rubbed her eyebrow.

"Yes, Mrs. Evans."

Who would want to break into her home and steal her possessions? She had always considered Sutton Place to be secure. Melanie felt violated — again. First, her family had been taken away from her, then, her purse had been snatched. And, now — a burglary? She almost missed the detective's comment.

"We're trying to determine what's missing."

"How do we do that? Do I need to fly back to New York?"

"No, I think we can handle it over the phone. Nothing appears disturbed except the safe. I've made an inventory of the contents. I can read it to you."

"That's not necessary. All we kept in the wall safe were my jewelry and any important papers to be transferred to the bank safe deposit box."

"I've got the estate papers prepared by your lawyer, Roger Morrison. He's the one who told me how to contact you. But, there's no jewelry."

"None?" Melanie swallowed. Most of the jewelry were pieces her father had given her mother. She knew they were insured for their value, but the attached memories were priceless. She held her breath and waited for the detective's answer.

"None. Can you describe the missing items?"

"Yes... or better yet, contact my brother, Ashley Parker at Parker Transworld. He can access my safe deposit box and give you copies of the appraisals which include photos for insurance purposes."

"Were these appraisals completed recently?"

"Yes. I inherited the majority of the pieces from my mother after her death. The insurance company insisted on current appraisals last year after I was released from the hospital."

"I see. Mrs. Evans, could you tell me a bit more about the car accident you mentioned?"

Melanie hesitated, "Well, it was almost ten months ago. And, I've never been able to remember the entire event. How would that help?"

"I never know. But, I like to investigate a family's background," the earnest voice replied.

"Why? The car wreck was just an accident, wasn't it?"

"Now, Mrs. Evans, I'm just being a detective. Asking questions gets to be a nasty habit. I didn't know about the car accident until you mentioned it. Can you tell me about it?"

"Not really. The date was July 22. After it happened, I was in a coma for more than six weeks. When I woke up, I remembered everything — but the wreck. All I can recall is the family riding down FDR Drive in our car," Melanie answered feebly, feeling a wave of helplessness wash over her.

"I can look up the accident report here. And, I'll call your brother about the insurance appraisals. You've been most helpful. If you recall something, please call me at this number. It's area code (212), then 799-NYPD. Ask for Detective Richard Stone."

"212-799-NYPD — Richard Stone," Melanie repeated. "I've got it, Detective Stone. And, if you learn anything important, would you please call me?"

"Absolutely. Thanks for your help, Mrs. Evans. Good-by for now."

"Thank you... I think. Good-by."

An unsettled Melanie returned the microphone to its place beside the speaker box. She stared at the pieces of communication equipment and digested the news she had received. In her short interval on the island, she had forgotten the daily crimes of the city. Vividly, she recalled the purse snatching. What if she had been at home during the burglary? Would she have been beaten? raped? worse? The urban jungle with its own version of brutality had reached out and touched her again, even here on peaceful Caretta Island.

"Melanie," Grant's voice intruded. "I couldn't help but overhear the conversation as I passed through the foyer. Might it be a good idea if you called the New York Police Department and verified the burglary? You never know, it might be some twisted bloke's idea of a joke."

"I guess it could be a joke." Contemplating who could be so cruel to her, Melanie picked up the microphone and called the operator. "Connect me with the New York City Police, please."

She heard the phone switch relays several times. Then, a voice chimed, "NYPD" against harried background noises.

"Detective Richard Stone, please."

"One moment."

Silence.

"Detective Richard Stone here," the same voice replied.

"Ah, yes, Detective Stone. This is Melanie Evans again... on Caretta Island... in Georgia."

"Yes, Mrs. Evans. Did you remember something else?"

"No. I simply wanted to verify your phone call... about the burglary... and the accident."

"I understand," the voice replied. She heard the sounds of papers being turned over. "I did call about the burglary. But, don't worry about what I asked about the accident. That was only my curious side. I guess I've watched too many TV detective shows and I'm addicted to detective novels. Sometimes, I even pretend I'm Sherlock Holmes," he sighed. "Please forget what I said, except for calling me in case you remember something to help solve the burglary."

"All right, I'll try to do that. Good-by again, Detective Stone."

"Good-by, Mrs. Evans." The voice disappeared.

Melanie exhaled and said to Grant, "I guess I'd better make a call to Ashley."

* * *

After the evening meal, Melanie rocked in an old wooden chair on the porch. Ali Cat purred in her lap. She stroked his soft fur while the insects buzzed lazily outside the screen. The air seemed hot and heavy — as if she could reach out and squeeze its moisture. A bold star penetrated the haze of the porch screen.

Patrice wandered out and took the neighboring rocking chair. The twosome rocked and thought, rocked and thought. Melanie reflected on the jarring call from New York then wondered what her aunt was thinking.

Patrice broke the silence, "Have you enjoyed reading the family journals?"

"Why, yes. As a matter of fact, I've gone through two volumes." Melanie had expected her aunt to awfulize about the burglary, to sympathize over her loss. Was Patrice denying an unpleasant event or was Patrice creating a diversion instead of bewailing the unchangeable? The surprised Melanie continued, "I find I must read them slowly. Great-Grandfather Phillip included so many places and events that are new to me."

The older woman sniffed, "It's nice to see someone of the younger generation interest themselves in worthwhile reading. A lot of scholarship and deliberation went into his writing."

Melanie started to react to the older woman's judgmental remark, but then quickly realized she was the first "younger" person to be around her aunt in years. "I suspect you're right. He may have started the journals as an intellectual challenge, but in places they sound a lot like self-analysis. It's as if the island's history gave him a new perspective on his own life and times."

"Yes, I agree with you, my dear. I find it fascinating that the word *journal* is simply a more acceptable term for diary. Diaries were for little girls to write down personal or romantic musings. Another term had to be used when grownups, especially men, did the same thing." Patrice's profile revealed nervousness with a hint of a sarcastic smile.

In her mind, Melanie played with the idea whether traits such as sarcasm could be inherited, "Whatever the term, Great-Grandfather Phillip has given me a new picture of this area. For one thing, I never appreciated how the islands served as a refuge. He found that over the centuries several Indian groups hunted and held religious ceremonies here. European sailors used these waters to avoid storms, though a shipwreck or two did happen. Pirates holed up here. It's intriguing that until the plantation era with its institution of slave labor, there were no permanent inhabitants on Caretta or the other sea islands."

"And, by my father's time," Patrice inserted, "the islands really began to be used and abused for selfish gain. Although I loved him, I never understood his journal entries. They're gibberish to me."

"You'll have to show me Edward's writing. I've not run across his notes yet."

"In due course, my dear," she paused. "What about you, Melanie? What is Caretta becoming to you?"

"It's too early to tell, Patrice." Melanie wondered what Patrice wanted to hear. With sudden clarity, she grasped how much the island must mean to Patrice, Louisa, and Jim. Here she was, lamenting the loss of a few pieces of jewelry. What must they be feeling about the potential loss of their home, their world? All of them must be keenly aware of the pending income tax problem. Melanie continued, "I feel as if things are coming together for me. Yet, something's still missing."

"Perhaps you can learn from Phillip's experience. You suggested he found valuable personal revelations while documenting the island's past. Maybe the same technique would work again."

"You mean finish the journals?" Melanie asked in disbelief.

"Exactly. The last hundred years have seen many changes — just ask Louisa and Jim. More than updating is needed; Phillip left gaps. This island has witnessed a wide variety of people trying to mesh themselves into the land. It's been trod by Indian moccasins, Spanish priests' sandals, boots of pirates and soldiers, the pumps of French and English aristocrats, not to mention the bare feet of slaves and well-shod heels of millionaires. By attempting to understand their attempts, you might uncover personal truths, too."

Melanie stared at the pulsing lightning bugs for several moments as she absorbed her aunt's allusion. Then she spoke in a steady tone, "That may be true. I don't know if researching and writing a journal can accomplish self-actualization. But, the project has merit."

"I'm so glad you'd consider it," Patrice sighed with relief. "Several times I've started myself. You know, I always fancied myself a bit like Fannie Butler or Margaret Mitchell."

"Really? Then let's work on it together. I'll ask Ashley to send us two notebook computers. We can record our personal observations and edit each other's findings until we feel we've got the essence of each place or event."

"You believe I can learn to use a computer at my age?"

"I'm positive. Once you learn how to use a word processing program, you'll never want to touch the typewriter again."

Melanie mused how her opinion of her aunt had changed in these few short weeks. She had arrived anticipating, even dreading, the possibility of dealing with a senile recluse. Instead, she was discovering a sharp-witted, slightly cynical, yet still-romantic woman who lived a quiet life by choice. Patrice was different from her own mother though she reminded Melanie of her. Perhaps it was because they held similar beliefs and were so close in age.

Patrice concluded, "Fine. I trust your opinion about computers." With a mysterious note, she added, "About Caretta, I know there's still a lot going on here that's hidden from most people's views."

CHAPTER 7

7:30 p.m., Wednesday, May 11, 1988

"Tell us about hoodoo and voodoo," urged Melanie.

"Dat's a tall, tall order, Miz Mellie," Jim replied.

"Tell us a small, small, small bit then," she continued, using what she knew to be a string of Gullah diminutives. "You know, I've always loved to hear about what makes good luck and bad luck."

On this warm evening, Louisa was cleaning up the kitchen while Jim, Grant, and Melanie gathered around the table and sipped coffee.

Dancing, storytelling, fishing, weaving nets and baskets, celebrating religious beliefs, making-do — Melanie never tired of listening to Louisa and Jim tell about the traditional sea island ways. Grant, too, enjoyed this sharing. Occasionally, he and Melanie spent their after-dinner time with Louisa and Jim in the kitchen, discussing sea island lore. Patrice, whose propriety demanded a certain distance between herself and her servants, found other diversions.

Grant interjected, "First, let me make sure I understand the difference between voodoo and hoodoo. Jim, last time, you said African ways blended with Catholicism to create voodoo while hoodoo grew from the other Christian denominations. Have I got it correct?"

"Actually dey grew in spite of dem," commented Louisa. "No priests or Baptis' preachers likes voodoo or hoodoo. Dey's jus' de beliefs of de black peoples mixed wid de white man's religions. Religion's importan' here. It gets peoples thru hard days an' hungry nights."

Melanie contemplated the truth in Louisa's words. In the past, sea island blacks had been enslaved on plantations. After they had gained their hard-fought freedom, they had sharecropped those same fields. All the while, the blacks had continued to live in a peaceful coexistence with the land and sea. Few had ever enjoyed success by white man's standards. Melanie had seen the lowcountry shanties on other islands and the mainland. As a high-rise condominium dweller, accustomed to every available service, she had wondered how the inhabitants survived.

"Dere's knots," Jim leaned back in his chair and began. "Dey tie knots in a rope with good thoughts and dey wears it aroun' de waist. It puts de mout' on evil. Or dey tie knots with bad thoughts and dey puts it under a person's porch. It makes dem bad luck."

"Dey say you scrub your floor, it bring good luck. But, I think, dat's jus' plain sanitary," Louisa chimed in as she joined them at the table.

"An' dere's all kinds of potions dey fix. Dey use herbs fo' causes an' cures."

"I give bloodroot to Jim fo' high blood pressure. Dat's not hoodoo — dat's medicine," Louisa explained.

Jim continued, "Sometimes dey use dirt or bones from a grave or a person's hair."

Louisa chortled, "Dey say if a woman wants a man, all she gotta do is mix 'er pubic hair in 'is coffee or Coke an' serve it to 'im." She poured more coffee into Grant's cup and said with emphasis, "Dis here coffee's fo' you, Grant."

They all laughed and Grant parried, "But, Louisa, I'm already in love with your cooking."

"Who says it's my hair?" Louisa calmly retorted.

Grant almost choked on his coffee, "Louisa! Are you playing matchmaker?" Between him and Melanie? He glanced at Melanie. He was beginning to appreciate the differences between her and the deceitful Karen. Com'on, man, you've got to let go of that experience! Though Melanie had worked in the corporate world, she seemed to have no need to exhibit power over another person or to indulge in one-upmanship. Too, he enjoyed her observations on natural events occurring on the island. They revealed a genuine curiosity. The only other woman in his life since Karen had been Rebecca. Her ambitions, however, kept him from forming an intimate relationship.

After they finished drinking their coffee, Louisa and Jim retired to their own house. Melanie and Grant moved to the screened porch and rocked in the cool night air.

Melanie speculated, "Some superstitions are based on common sense while others play on basic fear. Either way, they give you pause. They make you wonder who's actually in control of this universe, don't they?"

"Indeed. And, they're the basis for some ripping yarns." Grant stopped his rocking and turned toward Melanie. "Are Jim and Louisa's beliefs in hoodoo very strong?"

"I've wondered. People say for hoodoo to work, you really have to believe. I've heard its practice is still quite strong in the lowcountry. But with Jim and Louisa," she rocked for a minute, then, continued. "Well, I think Louisa is more into the AME Zion Church." She was silent for a while then asked, "What do you make of their sea island dialect?"

"I had to adjust to the swallowing of some ending consonants and the substituting of a 'd' sound for the hard 'th.' However, I find it's similar to other island cultures. Isolation seems to preserve an older version of a changing language as well as other customs. Don't forget. I grew up on a huge island — Australia."

"What a wonderful observation. I remember being struck by the melodious Elizabethan lilt in the speech of the people on Tangier Island when I visited there. That island's out in the middle of Chesapeake Bay."

Grant resumed rocking and continued, "Sometime, if I ever have the opportunity, I want to hear a storyteller spin some sea island tales. I understand the stories made their way from Africa and the Caribbean by word-of-mouth. Do Jim and Louisa know any storytellers?"

"Actually, they're both good storytellers. I understand they often perform for their grandchildren. Maybe if we ask, they'll include us the next time they create their island magic."

* * *

6:45 p.m., Friday, May 13, 1988

While she dressed, Melanie reflected on last weekend at the Rose Hill polo match. Adam had escorted her and Patrice to the event. He had been attentive to both, introducing them to many of his acquaintances. He had struck the proper attitude. When he had asked her to dinner, she had responded with a yes. Now, nearly a year after Greg's death, she was ready to date, but she was unsure of the man.

She surveyed her form in the mirror. Her hair had grown long enough to French braid. She enjoyed the lighter feel and sophisticated look of the off-the-shoulder style. The simple white dress accented her darkening tan. Touching-up her lipstick and grabbing a scarf, she was ready for dinner in Savannah.

After saying goodnight to Patrice and Louisa, Melanie headed toward the dock to watch the setting sun. Adam had promised to pick her up at sunset so she had several minutes to enjoy the spectacle that, once again, did not disappoint her with its grandeur.

The sun setting, ending another day, reminded her of a closing act in a play. With sudden clarity, she realized she was moving onto another stage. For almost a year, she had been saying good-by to the loved ones who had peopled her former life. They would always be loved. New experiences would never change that fact. It was time for her to accept their deaths and her regrets. She was beginning new scenes, involving new people in new relationships. She wondered how big a role Adam and Grant would play in the action. She wondered how big a role she wanted them to play. Was she ready for new, intimate relationships? Would she ever be ready? The idea revolted yet excited her. She had only loved one man.

A lone, white egret glided to a halt on the creek bank. The fiddler crabs scurried to get out of its way. As she observed the egret and crabs feed in the salt marsh, she allowed her mind to toy with the elemental concept of feeding. Animals went about the task, using long-established, efficient means. Humans had embellished the act far beyond a mere subsistence level. A simple necessity had evolved into elaborate rituals where providers created artful settings and meals, while consumers played games of status seeking, deal swinging, and sexual selling.

During her travels with Greg, they had joked about New York's gourmet pizzas and California's pink tofu. They were amused when the backcountry Cajun cuisine of the Louisiana bayous was elevated to gourmet snobbery. With "in-crowd" resignation, they had endured the trends of restaurants going in and out of style. She wondered how she would find these nuances implemented in a Southern coastal city. Would she enjoy discovering them with someone besides Greg?

Seeing the runabout swing around the curve in the channel, she forced her attention to her impending date. "I'm actually going on a date — that takes getting accustomed to all over again," she said aloud.

The boat floated into docking position. She sighted Adam dressed in a lightweight navy blazer over gray slacks, his hair tousled by the wind. He welcomed her on board, offering his hand to steady her climb over the rail, "Ready?"

"Ready!" she exclaimed, noticing his appreciative look when she stepped down to the deck. She felt girlish and womanly, all at the same moment — a nice feeling.

She tied the long, white scarf around her head and neck for the short voyage to Adam's private dock at The Hammock. The man and woman stood side-by-side behind the wheel watching the light recede from the pale-green marsh grasses. The boat sliced through the pastel, opalescent waters.

After Adam finished tying up the launch at The Hammock's marina, he led Melanie toward his Porsche and suggested, "How about a drink at the club?"

"Fine," agreed Melanie.

Adam drove them to The Hammock's clubhouse. In that short distance, Melanie was impressed with his careful driving of the Porsche — no exhibiting "Watch what I can do with this car, baby."

Adam made conversation as they were seated at a table on the deck with an expansive view of the marina lights to the left and the darkening golf course to the right. "I'm not up on the current drinks in New York, but I've created one that tastes better than it sounds. Care to try it?"

"Sure. I'm still searching for my favorite drink. What do you call it?"

"Susannah dubbed it the Adam Sour," he wrinkled his nose as a crisply-attired waiter in white coat and black trousers approached.

"Good evening, Mr. Gardner. Would you like something from the bar?"

"Yes, Lamont. We'll have two Adam Sours. By the way, how is Marvin doing with that broken arm?"

"Just like any eleven-year-old. He's trying everything possible to break it again, giving his parents a bad case of nerves," the waiter grinned.

"Tell him to be good if he wants another fishing trip any time soon."

"I'll do that. Be right back with your drinks."

Adam turned and commented, "The Hammock is a wonderful place to live. I've gotten to know all the people. I hope we'll have that opportunity, also, Melanie."

"Perhaps, we will," Melanie murmured, momentarily taken aback by his candor. She redirected the conversation, "Now tell me about your special drink."

"Wait and see if you can guess the flavors." Adam switched subjects, "How are you adapting to the pace of the island? It must be real slow after the city."

"It is. Time floats as if clocks were never invented. And, few decisions are required unlike my former frantic life in New York. My mind has relaxed. I walk. I jog the beach. I explore the island. All of that has brought me a greater feeling of harmony with nature — ancient beyond belief, vast beyond imagination. It has given me a fresh perspective on my problems. They're so little in comparison. Does that sound overly simplistic?"

"Quite honestly, it sounds refreshing. When I consider the pace of my past week, I covet what you've just described."

"Most satisfying to me," Melanie continued, "has been the total lack of desire to jump back into a hectic schedule."

The arrival of their drinks interrupted the conversation, but Melanie had sensed a moment of pleasure, putting her feelings into words. She was surprised to find the receiver of those remarks was Adam Gardner, the man she had considered a smooth operator.

"This is excellent," Melanie commented as she sipped the tall icy beverage.

"Guess the ingredients," Adam prompted.

"I wouldn't know where to start."

"Actually, it's a simple drink. A summer cooler made of grapefruit juice, seltzer, and Southern Comfort. Seems appropriate for this southern latitude, don't you agree?"

For the next hour, the couple enjoyed casual banter. Adam steered her to present-day topics, sometimes sensitive when a painful memory was touched. Melanie discovered a man who downplayed his working class origins and emphasized his determination to succeed at the highest possible levels. Along the way, he had developed a good sense of humor and impressive verbal fluency.

As they grew hungry, Adam suggested River's End for supper. He described the small restaurant with a captivating view of the Wilmington River, part of the Atlantic Intracoastal Waterway. Patrons arrived in boats or cars. On this beautiful evening, Adam suggested they travel by water.

During the boat trip, Melanie found herself impressed and immersed in Adam's monolog on the importance of waterways before highways. She learned about early American cities positioned on navigable rivers and protected by forts. He named Savannah's three fortresses, one engineered by Robert E. Lee. Adam hypothesized that population centers located elsewhere when transportation emphasized roads, then rails, then air corridors.

After tying the boat to the restaurant dock, Adam accompanied Melanie into a long, contemporary building of weathered wood and glass. With impetus provided by the superlative comments of gourmand Baron Roy Andries de Groot, the restaurant had become a regular meeting place for many of the region's prominent personalities. Though the South still favored elaborate parties in homes and memberships in private country clubs, social gatherings in public establishments were increasing in popularity.

Phrases of "Good to see you!" "How's it going?" greeted Adam as he guided Melanie among the numerous tables. She met a paper mill executive, a TV anchorwoman, a nuclear weapons expert, a banker, and other well-dressed individuals.

"What friendly people," Melanie observed to Adam as, finally, they sat down at their table.

"Is this your first exposure to the New South?" Adam inquired.

"I suppose it is, as an adult. I've heard the phrase 'New South' bantered about the past few years. But, I've never been sure exactly what it meant," she replied.

"The concept began as a journalist's quip, yet it has come to represent a new vitality. The old stereotype of a few wealthy plantation owners with everyone else either black slaves or white trash is being changed by educated, dynamic business leaders."

"It seems to me, there remain vestiges of the old, such as fundamentalist religion," Melanie countered. "I've heard one can't buy a bottle of wine in Savannah on Sunday."

"That's true. It takes time to change old ways. But, you'll see a lot of energy among these new policymakers."

Melanie thought before responding, "I grew up equating Southern tradition with a relaxed pace. No one seemed in a hurry. Overt greed was frowned upon. To me, that slower movement could allow a perspective needed for fostering a healthier relationship between man and his environment."

"You'll find debate on whether that relationship has been healthier or not. However, the slower pace may permit our current growth to benefit from past mistakes. You can see it happening in coastal development. Compare Tybee Island to Kiawah Island. On Tybee, what was once an enclave for the rich has mushroomed into a hodgepodge with little sensitivity to its location. On Kiawah Island, fragile areas have been protected and a well-thought-out plan has been carefully followed for the remainder. Hopefully, Tybee residents will wake up soon and protect what they've got."

Melanie responded, "What about the idea of no development on a barrier island? After all, isn't their purpose to serve as a buffer for the mainland? That's how the Indians treated them for thousands of years."

Adam paused before phrasing his answer. This woman was more aware than he had assumed. He proceeded carefully, "I maintain that meticulous planning allows most islands to serve many people while protecting the ecosystems. The real world forces such decisions. As you know, our tax system discourages individual ownership of large properties."

She shuddered. She sensed a crack in the foundation of her new existence. It had been almost a week since she had talked with Ashley about Caretta's future. Melanie reflected on the family lawyer's warning forthcoming inheritance tax liability. She knew a decision must be made in the next few months. She found it more than a coincidence that Adam brought up the subject now.

Adam correctly assessed her position and continued, "When you're ready, I could help your family design your island's future. Together we could construct a workable, aesthetically-pleasing solution that would be financially viable."

"That's quite a mouthful, Adam," she said sarcastically. Noticing him stiffen, she softened with, "I know from what I saw at The Hammock, you have an extensive background in real estate development. However, I'm not ready to deal with all those issues on Caretta." Melanie decided she would need to continue to be wary. It was strongly possible that he was not interested in her or her aunt's welfare. His eyes revealed he coveted Caretta, not for what it was, but for what it could be.

"I understand, Melanie. There's still time, though you must realize, decisions can't be put off too long." Silently, he knew he had achieved a point. His spirits soared high for the rest of the evening.

The meal was excellent and, as it progressed, their mood relaxed. The pair conversed on a variety of topics, Melanie finding him a more likable companion than she had first imagined. A kindling excitement filled an emotional void. Adam's physical aura intensified its effect, though she still questioned his motives.

The meal completed, they returned to the dock for the return boat ride to the island. An almost-full moon lit the calm evening; a soft breeze held down the biting insects. Adam kept the launch's speed low to savor every minute with his female companion.

Melanie found herself deriving pleasure from Adam's closeness. At one point, he steadied her and put his arm around her waist. She allowed herself to enjoy the contact.

Arrival at the island, the walk to the main house, and a casual goodnight kiss concluded a significant evening for the two — Melanie finding a missing part to her psyche, Adam feeling closer to developing the island.

* * *

9:00 a.m., Sunday, May 15, 1988

Above the noise of the rattling, dry palm branches, Melanie heard the engine sound of the expected boat in the tidal creek. The Sea Island Institute researchers were arriving on the high tide this morning.

A weather front was forcing cool, brisk breezes across the island. Grabbing a light jacket, Melanie and Ali Cat hurried to join Jim and Grant at the dock. There the salt marsh grasses splayed with the windgusts.

"Hello! Welcome to Caretta," Melanie shouted above the wind to the crew. Playing the Southern hostess, she felt obligated to meet Rebecca and her team, students from various colleges.

The researchers waved as a group, clustered in the rear of the boat with their duffel bags of clothes, ice chests of food, and additional crates of equipment. Melanie was looking forward to getting acquainted with them, especially Rebecca who was closest to her age.

When they disembarked, she introduced herself and the other islanders to the blue-jeaned, sweatshirted arrivals. "I'm Melanie Parker-Evans. This is Jim Johnson, the caretaker who knows the island better than anybody. And, this is Grant Yeats, another researcher — but in desalination not loggerheads — who lives and works here on the island. And, of course, I can't forget Ali Cat."

Melanie noted Grant hugging Rebecca, then shaking hands with the young black man. Of course, they know one another! They've been on the island the last few summers. What amazed her was that she experienced a small twinge of jealousy.

In turn, Rebecca performed her duties introducing the college students starting with the tallest. "Melanie, meet Daniel Jordan, my assistant. This is his third summer here on Caretta. He's a graduate student at Florida State, working on a master's degree in wildlife management."

The smiling, young black man offered his hand which Melanie shook. She liked his firm grip and warm smile. Daniel stood a little over six feet with a medium build; his eyes sparkled with enthusiasm.

"All of you, this is David Webster. David's going to be a sophomore at the University of Georgia. He claims he's interested in marine biology." Shorter than average and unsure of himself, David raised a pudgy but good-natured face toward Melanie.

"Hi!" David grinned.

"A Charlie Chaplain," sighed Rebecca.

"And, to even the male-female ratio, here's Lana Berg. Lana is a double major at Duke University — art and biology. I hope she'll enrich this summer's research report with a few drawings."

With brown hair and eyes, the pert teenager spoke in a cheerful voice, "It's a pleasure to meet all of you."

Melanie inhaled the youthful atmosphere. Impish David carried a slight load of baby fat he'd probably lose in the summer heat. Cute Lana possessed a fantastic figure. Add one sharp-looking assistant and vibrant project leader and the Caretta Island average age had dropped while its energy level had soared — not to mention the sex hormone scale.

Melanie laughed internally at her quasi-marketing observations and spoke to the new arrivals, "Now, I want Lana and David to meet the rest of us islanders. Louisa, Jim's wife, has homemade cocoa to warm you up after your wind-tossed crossing. She and my aunt, Patrice Parker, are waiting for us at the Big House."

Jim, Grant, and the researchers piled the jeep high with gear to make the first of several trips between the dock and Duck House, the old hunting lodge a mile south of Parker House. Here, in this rustic but serviceable dorm, the turtle taggers would sleep, cook and eat their meals, shower, read books, play cards, draw, write letters, and update their logbooks.

As Jim and Grant drove off with their cargo, Melanie herded the researchers toward the Parker House porch where Rebecca completed another round of introductions for the benefit of Patrice and Louisa.

"This house, this island — it's so breathtaking. How long has it been here?" questioned Lana.

"Several thousand years," David threw in, "...or did you mean the house?"

"Wise guy!" Lana punched him playfully on his bicep.

Patrice gave a thin smile to the students and replied, "The dwellings are over a hundred years old. They're notably well-built."

"They're not all that's well-built," muttered David under his breath, trying to figure out a method to get attention from Lana.

Patrice found David's boisterous youthfulness grating. Ignoring him, she continued, "The Parker family has attempted to disturb as little of the natural setting as possible. I know you will keep that in mind during your stay here."

"Indeed," interjected Daniel reflecting her serious, formal tone, "Caretta is one of the few pristine barrier islands left in this hemisphere. We feel fortunate to have the opportunity to be here."

Melanie wondered where Daniel had grown up. His speech showed no discernible dialect. He made an interesting contrast to old Jim. For that matter, Lana differed dramatically from Patrice. And, silly David? "Why, he's almost as immature as my nine-year-old son!" she thought. At this unexpected reminder of her now-dead son, she grabbed the back of the rocking chair. She struggled to collect herself.

One sure thing was that the island was going to be congested now. Was she going to enjoy sharing the space? "Come on, Melanie!" she counseled herself. "Let's make the most of this summer."

Conversation continued about the island's isolation, the beach, turtles, heat, bugs, and food as all munched on sugar cookies. Eager to organize camp and the first night's activities, Rebecca soon prodded her group into action.

"Thanks for the cocoa and cookies, Louisa," yelled the students as they shouldered their backpacks and hiked down Crossroad to Backbone Road and, finally, Duck House.

* * *

"Take care with these packages. This shipment is especially valuable."

"Wait a minute! Have you ever had a problem with the way I handle things?"

"No. It's just that there are twenty parcels today."

"Great. That should make unloading fun. I wish you'd remember this plane's not set up for cargo. There are only so many places I can safely stow the stuff."

"I know. I know. Tony will be there as usual for the pickup."

"He'd better be on time and fast. I've got important business of my own in the Big Apple."

"I bet. See you in a couple of days."

With its engines screaming, the small private plane lifted from the concrete runway, heading north.

CHAPTER 8

11:00 a.m., Tuesday, May 17, 1988

Even though her body craved the rush from a jog, Melanie knew only a fool would run in this swelter. The air was still and heavy with the humidity and smothering sweetness of jessamine, bay, and pine. Biking's a much better choice this morning, Melanie concluded. The bicycle would create its own breeze.

She grabbed her mountain bike with its wide, knobby tires and many gears. After enduring a few rides on the old bike with its balloon tires, Melanie had ordered this perfect contraption for the sandy island — though the dunes hardly qualified as mountains.

Slowly, Melanie pedaled through the woods up Backbone Road to the northern tip of the island where she walked the trail bike across the loose, dry sand of the cape until she reached damp, firm sand near the water. There she remounted and rode to the outlet that emptied the blue-gray lagoon into the channel. The green-gold marsh grasses stood tall; steeply eroded banks dropped into the lagoon. She viewed an occasional animal path through the swaying cordgrass.

On her bike, she ventured down one of the barely visible pathways. No person had walked this trail in a long time, if ever. Was she exploring new territory? First-hand, she was discovering the web of life, something she had never witnessed in her protected existence. The city environment had allowed few opportunities to wonder about nature. *National Geographic* specials on public television paled against this primary experience.

While she cycled, she drew parallels to her own personal growth. Just as spring was already changing to summer, one period of her life had ended; another was beginning. She could see the natural forces at work here on the island. She wished she could see the formative powers that would shape her future.

Melanie noticed other faint paths networking the field of grasses. She chose the branches that kept her closest to the edge of the lagoon. Her movement stirred numerous insects and an occasional ibis from repose as she encroached on their territory. There were lots of creatures, including alligators. It was a zoo without bars.

Before she reentered the shade of the dark forest and headed south on Backbone, she recalled Jim's caution, "Watch fo' ticks." She stopped to examine her legs and arms. The warm weather had hatched these pests; they waited in grasses and leaves for any warm-blooded host. Finding none, she forged on.

Sweat poured down every inch of her body, soaking her clothes. Intent on her decision to renew her physical condition, she pedaled faster.

The silence of the bicycle, combined with its speed, allowed her to approach unaware animals. Ahead she saw a red fox cross the path before it picked up the sound of the bike, flattened its ears, and disappeared into the safety of the brush.

Serenely, she rode through the flickering sunlight, filtered by the overhanging branches. The tranquillity of the island enveloped her. She felt as if she were in a cocoon, waiting for re-emergence into the world.

Suddenly, a high-pitched squeal split the air. A large shape loomed out of the undergrowth and lunged at her. Her bike slid on its side, dumping her on the pine needles. Jumping to her feet, she faced her attacker — a horse. Pawing the earth, flaring its nostrils, and whinnying nervously, it stared at her. Melanie stood riveted to her place; strained seconds passed. Finally, the stallion took her stationary position as an all-clear signal and turned away.

Wondering what prompted this aggressive behavior, Melanie continued to watch the animal. She had never experienced a horse's charge. Why? The bicycle? A previous attacker?

Keeping her vigil, Melanie caught sight of movement at its feet. Moving laterally for a better view, she saw another horse lying on the ground, birthing a foal. She smiled. The stallion was protecting his mare during this critical process. Mesmerized by the renewing spectacle of birth, she observed. Many minutes later, she quietly retrieved her bike and walked it away from the new parents; they had suffered enough for one day.

As she put distance between herself and the horses, her thoughts turned naturally to her own family. They were no longer around to protect her or be protected by her. Tears filled her eyes. She tumbled again into the black void of emptiness surrounding her.

Disappointed by her reaction, she pushed away the feeling of helplessness. "I've got to accept that for the rest of my life, things are going to happen that will remind me of Greg and Parker. I've got to understand that I'm in charge of how I remember them. I want those memories to be good, to be free of regret. And, I want a life."

She stood on the pedals as she pumped them vigorously, determined to be responsible for her newfound happiness.

* * *

6:00 a.m., Sunday, May 22, 1988

The tide reached its peak at 2:30 this May morning on Caretta. Nature's forces continued unwatched — eroding, building, taking, and giving. Left behind among the thousands of empty sea shells was one large carcass — wearing blue jeans and a T-shirt.

The early morning sky filled with a pink glow, heralding the sun's emergence. The sand sparkled as the waves receded, revealing the vast beach.

A small vehicle made its way down the strand, occasionally swinging toward the dunes and discharging one of its occupants.

"This ought to be number twenty-one," shouted the driver.

Lana looked around in the soft sand behind the dunes for the stake.

"Found it," she cried. "It looks OK. Let me drive it in; you see if it's tall enough." Lana straightened the stake then pounded the wood further into the sand.

The young, black male driver yelled, "That's fine. Let's keep going."

The college-age girl energetically bounced into the small motorized trike, similar to a golf cart. "Hey, Daniel, we're pretty quick. Maybe we can finish remarking the whole south end this morning."

"That would be nice. I've got several other items on the agenda that need to get done before the loggerheads start laying."

His perky helper commented with hope, "Gee, I thought this afternoon would be a good opportunity to grab some rays and work on a tan."

"Work at it long enough and maybe, just maybe, you'll get as dark as me," kidded Daniel.

They laughed as Daniel wheeled the trike toward the dunes, "See if you're as lucky finding number twenty-two."

He watched Lana's departing figure, showcased in tight shorts and a tanktop. "There's going to be plenty of summer romance on this beach," he mused. He'd already noticed appreciative looks at Lana from David and Grant.

A piercing scream shattered his musings. Jumping out of the vehicle, he ran to his turtle-tagging partner. Lana was breathing hard, holding both hands to her mouth, staring at the high tide mark. Her rigid stance revealed fright. Looking in the direction of her eyes, he saw the remains of a human body. On top, perched a turkey buzzard. It glared their way.

"Get out of here!" Daniel yelled as he clapped his hands.

The large bird flapped and soared to a nearby palm.

Putting his arm around the shivering Lana, he whispered, "There's nothing we can do now — absolutely nothing — except go report it."

Fifty-four-year-old Fred Frazier enjoyed his visits with the Australian engineer on Caretta. In fact, Fred loved visits with anyone, if there were good stories and ample reasons not to overwork on these warm days. In addition to his freshwater ecology research, Fred was in charge of enforcing the fish and game laws for this part of the coast. Dressed in camouflage fatigues, he covered his bald head with a matching baseball cap and kept a packet of Red Man chewing tobacco in his shirt pocket. He was outfitted for the job.

"So, how's the new mistress doin'? 'Skeeters botherin' her?"

Grant continued his work while talking with the warden. "Remember, mate, she owns this island. Actually, she's a jolly good sport. She rolls with the punches."

"New turtle crew settlin' in?"

"They're almost set up."

"You watch out for them young 'uns, boy. I know you must get a little horny out here, but some of them gals are real jail bait."

"There is one that's a ripper. But, you're right. She's young."

"I'd like to getta look at her."

Suddenly, the noise of a trike roaring full-out drew their attention. The instant Grant and Fred stepped outside the lab, Daniel slid the vehicle to a stop.

"Looks like you're going to get your chance to see her now," Grant nudged Fred.

Daniel stood up in the trike. He cupped his hands to his mouth and hollered over the windscreen at the two men, "There's a dead body on the beach!"

"What?" Grant looked at Daniel then Fred in disbelief.

"A dead body," Daniel gulped for air, "on the beach. It must have come in with the tide."

"Whereabout?" asked Fred as he shortened the distance between the two men and the loggerhead researchers.

"About halfway-down the south beach at marker twenty-two."

"Good grief!" Grant heaved a sigh and shook his head as he joined the group at the trike.

"Grant, why don't you jus' stay here and take care of the little lady," Fred drawled as he gave an appreciative glance at Lana, sitting in shock on the seat. "Me and this here gentleman will go have us a closer look."

This kind of incident was Fred's kind of action, more exciting than checking for valid permits. He pulled Daniel aside and spat a stream of thick, brown tobacco juice, "Before we take off, let me make a quick call to get permission to move the body. Meanwhile, see if you can find a large bag — one you can't see through so we don't have no hysterical women blubbering all over the place."

By the time the two men reached the corpse, the scavengers had been busy feasting. Shooing them away, Fred went to work, followed by a reluctant Daniel. Jagged holes of flesh testified to the vultures' attentions. The face was partially intact, revealing the remnants of a black mustache and thick black hair. Eyes were gone. A pale bloat of the body made the original skin tone a guess. The shredded clothing appeared to be blue jeans and a pullover shirt.

"I reckon we got us a sailor washed overboard, probably drunk. Kind of looks like a furriner. My guess is a Latino type," Fred summarized. His voice was steady, unemotional. His hunting background allowed rapid adaptation to the gruesome sight of ugly wounds.

Daniel, overcoming nausea, glanced at the body being scrutinized by the camouflage-dressed official. To his inexperienced eyes, the head looked as if it had been bashed-in. Attempting to focus, another wave of nausea forced him to direct his gaze to the pounding surf. He had dissected many animals in his school career, but this mutilated human body bothered him.

"Bring me that bag," Fred ordered as he stood up. "We might as well cart what's left of this character back to my boat. I'll drop it off so the taxpayers can pay for the burial. It's a shame the sharks didn't handle the matter for us. It would have saved us a lot of time and the state a lot of money."

Discussing possible food selections for the coming week, Melanie, Louisa, and Patrice were seated at the kitchen table. A well-planned list for groceries and other provisions was a necessity since there was no corner convenience store.

When a quieted Lana and somber Grant entered the kitchen, Grant politely interrupted the planning process, "Excuse us, ladies, there's been a shocking discovery on the beach."

"What's wrong, Grant?" asked a concerned Melanie.

"Lana and Daniel found a human body washed ashore. Fred Frazier and Daniel have gone to fetch it."

Patrice and Melanie uttered small gasps.

"We don' borrow trouble," intoned Louisa.

Everyone looked at each other uneasily.

At the sound of the returning trike, they hurried outside. Without Grant's prior warning, the three women would have assumed the two men were arriving from a beach cleanup expedition, which, in a sense, was exactly what they were doing.

Melanie stopped them with a wave of her arm, "What's going on?"

Fred looked quizzically at Daniel who leaned over and whispered, "Melanie Evans. She's the island's owner from New York City."

Fred nodded and turned to the approaching woman, "Nothing to worry yourself over, missy. There must have been an accident last night at sea. This here drunken sailor fell overboard. Unfortunately, the tide deposited him on your shore."

On another occasion, Melanie would have been outraged at being referred to as missy. She held her temper and asked, "Are you sure it's only a drowning?"

"Oh, yes. I've seen enough corpses to know what did 'em in. Naturally, I'll check it out with the sheriff and coroner."

Daniel wondered about the crushed skull, but concluded Fred was probably correct. Despite his callous attitude, Fred seemed to know what he was doing.

Melanie looked puzzled. "I didn't realize game wardens worked so closely with the law."

Fred shot back, "Now lady, I know you're from the big city, but out here, there're only so many officers spread over a large area. Since I patrol these islands anyway, the sheriff figures he gets better coverage with me as a part-time deputy. Now then," he turned to Daniel, "let's go ahead and load this body in my boat." He turned to Melanie and inquired, "Unless you have a problem with that."

"No, I appreciate your taking care of the matter."

"Happy to oblige," Fred now gave her a big smile. "Call on me any time you need help. Grant, can you give us a hand here?"

Melanie watched Daniel, Grant, and Fred lower the awkward cargo into the state Fish and Wildlife patrol boat, a small fishing skiff. She was uneasy as she watched the camouflage-uniformed man and bagged body leave. Was the wildlife officer handling this situation correctly? Were his surmisings accurate? Again, she wondered if her father had authorized his access to the island. Did events like this happen all the time on the coast? Was she over-reacting?

Fred muttered to himself as he pulled away, "Well, she's a purty one for a city folk, but she shor' has got a lot to learn." He chuckled to himself, "And, that young one! Whew! Bet that Aussie can't wait to score. Oh well, Fred, you better quit thinking about women and figure out how you're going to handle this corpse mess."

CHAPTER 9

6:45 p.m., Wednesday, May 25, 1988

Leaning against the dock posts, Daniel and Grant were swatting mosquitos while watching a spectacular sunset over the marsh. When Melanie arrived, she announced, "Jim and Louisa are ready, Grant."

"Do we need to take anything?"

"Only ourselves. Daniel, do you want to come? We've been invited to a storytelling. Louisa's promised her grandchildren a non-electronic adventure at her sister's place. It should be a real treat."

"I don't know," Daniel hesitated.

"Oh, come on," Melanie encouraged. "You've been working hard. And, you haven't started patrolling yet. Right?"

"True. But...."

Grant interrupted, "Besides, after finding that body, you deserve a diversion."

"And, you happen to be at the right place at the right time."

"OK," Daniel relented. "It'll be a new experience."

"For me, too," admitted Grant. He continued, "I understand Louisa will tell the story word-for-word the way she learned it from her parents, using the Gullah dialect. I wonder if it'll be one with a rabbit or a fox. Those tales became popular, even in Australia, especially after Walt Disney got a hold of them."

"Oh yeah, Br'er Rabbit and Br'er Fox," Daniel replied half-heartedly. Brightening, he recalled, "I once read somewhere that there are similar tales in almost every culture."

Louisa and Jim arrived just then. "Dis story differen'," grinned Jim. "Right, Louisa?"

"It shore is," Louisa chuckled.

The five stepped into the boat to make the trip along the twisting creeks. As the outboard motor strained to push its full load, Melanie's eyes kept returning to Grant's silhouette. The passage gave her a chance to reflect on their recent outing in Savannah.

First, they had wandered the Historic District where brick and stucco houses stood two to four stories tall; Victorian bric-a-brac decorated many gables, eaves, and balconies. Impressive staircases led to living rooms or business reception areas. Ironwork was abundant. The streets were paved in bricks; the spaces between streets and sidewalks were planted with ground covers, azaleas, live oaks, magnolias, and palms. Pigeons and bicycles found their way with ease among the slow-paced traffic.

Focusing on local eating opportunities, they had stood in line for many minutes to lunch at Mrs. Wilkes' Boarding House, a traditional haunt for advocates of all-you-can-eat Southern home cooking.

After the filling lunch, Grant had driven them to the restored railroad station that proclaimed the sign "Visitors Center." When they had entered the brick structure, a local artist's work had caught her eye. Walking around the framed and matted paintings, she had attempted to draw out Grant's opinions. "Look at these watercolors! Do you enjoy looking at artwork?"

"Yes and no. I know what I like and what I dislike. But, art is an area I want to know more about."

Melanie had admired his honest reply, reflecting on how many people feign competence in order to maintain an image.

Another incident that stuck in her mind had occurred as they had neared the information desk and had perused the numerous pamphlets and circulars promoting area attractions, restaurants, and inns. There had been so much to choose from to round out their day in town. Melanie had picked up a flyer on a restored cottage that contained a museum devoted to black history.

"Here's an area I want to investigate," she had said thumping the paper. "For years, our family has employed Jim and Louisa as servants. I accepted them as family. I knew they had a different background, but I never learned their entire story. Louisa is perceptive but not talkative. Jim tends to keep his mouth closed except when he believes it's absolutely necessary. Have you ever been to this museum?"

"No, let's pay it a visit. Is it open?"

"The hours aren't listed on the brochure," Melanie had puzzled.

"That's all right. We can get them at the Information Desk."

They had approached a plump, elderly lady who was sorting through packets of advertising materials. Her half-frame glasses rested on her nose and an attached chain looped around her neck.

"Yes, may I help you?"

"How late is the King-Tisdale Cottage open?" Grant had asked.

The older woman had glanced to both sides then leaned toward Grant. "You do know it's black?" she had questioned, her voice barely above a whisper.

"Yes."

"And, that it's in a black neighborhood?"

"Yes, we know that, too. Look, I promise we'll be careful," Grant had tried hard not to laugh at her imaginary fear.

Finally obtaining the requested information, they had retreated to the parking lot. Melanie had commented, "This is the New South?"

Grant had shaken his head, "I thought I had left that kind of attitude in Australia. I suppose it's everywhere. Obviously, she's from a different generation whose traditions die hard." He had paused, "Let's laugh it off. Are you ready for this unspeakable museum located in an unmentionable neighborhood?"

"I'm game. Let's risk it."

Only blocks away, the small cottage with its red roof and intricate white nautical wood trim proved a delightful find. Two rooms showcased a national artist's works while others had period furniture and displays of African artifacts. An attractive young woman guide warmed to their interest in the black heritage and provided information not in the displays.

Curious about the difficult period following the Civil War, Melanie had asked, "With the plantations in ruins, how did the former slaves survive?"

The guide had launched into her spiel, "Many local blacks — who were longshoremen or were related in various ways to shipping — moved North due to the depressed economy during Reconstruction. They were more fortunate than the many who found no work here. Slowly, small businesses grew on the fringes of white and black society.

For instance, the builder of this cottage ran a Presser Club, what we call a cleaners today. Thus, a typical slave function, laundry, was turned into a viable moneymaker."

"But, what about the island people?" Melanie had inquired.

"They continued to subsist off the sea and the land — what they caught and grew. The plantations of rice, indigo, and cotton had never made slaves prosperous, so the rural blacks did not see a dramatic change in their lives. However, there was widespread confusion after Sherman issued Field Order Fifteen," the guide had lectured.

"What was that? I've never heard of it," Melanie had admitted.

"The order set aside the sea islands as property to be owned by the freed blacks. Thousands of refugees came from all over Georgia for the free land. But, the hastily organized resettlement program dragged. When Lincoln was assassinated, the exiled white planters appealed to Andrew Johnson. That southern president overturned the order, allowing the planters to regain the land."

"That must have been a bloody mess," Grant had commented.

"Best characterized as an incredible amount of anguish and under-handed dealing. Government conspiracy continued through World War II. For example, valuable black-owned land was condemned for war use with the promise to return it later. After the war, it was simply auctioned off to the highest bidders — naturally, all whites. And, in recent history, rezoning the land and escalating the tax structure have forced blacks to sell — like at Hilton Head or Daufuskie. If one searches for reasons to be bitter, there are ample examples in the history of the coastal blacks."

"What about today's Sunbelt explosion? Are blacks benefitting from that economic burst?" Melanie had asked.

"I'm skeptical. Probably, the growth signals a new future for the region that may allow the past to die."

"So you see the Gullah culture dying?"

"Definitely. The remoteness of these islands and marshlands has succumbed to bridges, residential and commercial development. Combine those effects with the influence of television and mass communication. What we call the Gullah and Geechee lives will become memories in the next few years."

"Three hundred years changed in one generation — what a revolution," Melanie had found modern society's power more than a little unsettling.

"Let's hope your people will benefit this time," Grant had interjected.

The guide had smiled, "Let's hope. Here, our cause is to preserve the memory of the past that serves as a foundation of pride for the future. But even today, not all the doors are wide open."

Recalling the racist comments at the Visitors Center, both Grant and Melanie had nodded.

Emerging from the dimness of the cottage, Grant had suggested, "Shall we go to Forsythe Park to relax?"

Sitting on a bench in front of the large fountain, Melanie had analyzed the other park visitors: almost equal proportions of black and white, locals and tourists, complete with their cameras and maps.

"It's a pleasant park and it's definitely used."

"These squares are one of the signatures of the city. They provide a certain sense of serenity. This park is especially lovely when the azaleas bloom. At home, we'd call that a Bobby Dazzler."

"A Bobby Dazzler, huh?"

Soaking up the peaceful, sunny afternoon, Melanie had relaxed on the bench. She and Grant had continued to talk about the dichotomy of the black and white cultures; how the groups struggled with merging, melting, and mixing. The dying of the black sea island culture appeared swift and permanent to the woman from New York. To the man from "Down Under," the passing appeared similar to the Aborigine "solution."

The outboard motor slowed, prompting Melanie to return to the present. Jim was tying their boat next to another craft at a dilapidated dock. There were no other signs of human presence among the sweep of water, marsh grass, and live oak trees in a maritime forest.

"Dat's Jim Jr.'s boat," Louisa explained proudly. "He already brung de children."

In the dusk, the group followed Louisa down a narrow path through the dense jungle and emerged in front of a ramshackled wooden shanty.

The surrounding ground shone, bare of vegetation; the building looked old, barely able to stand.

Jim anticipated the younger group's reaction and explained, "De shanty's over a hundred years ol', but it's got de breath of life."

For Grant's benefit, Melanie interrupted. "You mean a house that's lived in is healthier than an empty one?"

"Dat's right," Jim grinned.

"Why so bare in front?" asked Grant. "There's so much vegetation everywhere else."

Jim smiled, "Dat's de meetin' place. It's always dirt — nice fo' peoples but not fo' creatures."

Melanie reflected on her preconceived notions about the shanties. She had always believed people lived this way because they didn't know any better. Now she was discovering there were actual, logical reasons for their choices.

Squeals of delight resounded through the clearing as the youngsters rushed from the house of their great-aunt to hug their grandparents. The two little girls had their hair plaited in cornrows; the little boy sported an Afro. All of them were dressed in Oshkosh overalls. The children were friendly to Melanie, Grant, and Daniel. Louisa's sister, a thinner version of Louisa, acknowledged their presence but maintained a distance.

Jim and Jim Jr. stood in the shadowy edge of the jungle overgrowth as the younger man prepared to leave, "Can't stay, Pop. Got a heavy weekend schedule."

"Your Mammy wanna see you, son."

"I know, I know. Don't start-up again. Denise and I both agree. It's better our family meets out here. We live a different life from you and Mom."

"Dere now. Sounds like you're ashamed of us."

"Hey, don't take offense. We're another generation with other types of friends and new opportunities. We won't let the old ways drag us down."

The old man sighed, "We wanna what's best fo' you. Fas' money usually mean trouble."

"Look, Pop, we're getting the things white folks like the Parkers have had for years. And, we're doing it without being a 'yassir, boss' nigger."

"Hold on a minute, boy! Neither your Mammy nor me has ever benna nigger. We've don hones' work and de Parkers have been better bosses dan dem big companies."

"Sure, Dad, sure."

"Jus' don' sell your soul, son," came the troubled warning. He knew a long preachy talk was destined to bounce off his son's ears as it had for years. A nagging suspicion stayed with Jim as he watched his son's departing figure. With sadness in his heart, he returned to the clearing.

The rising full moon cast eerie shadows as beams passed through low-hanging live oak branches tentacled with Spanish moss. Feeling the wind finger her hair, Melanie heard its voice sigh in the trees. She glanced at the mainly black faces reflecting the fire's orange glow. Louisa's three grandchildren turned toward the older woman; their sparkling brown eyes were eager with anticipation. Sitting beside Melanie and Grant, Daniel appeared uncomfortable in this family circle. Jim held his eyes partially closed and hummed to himself.

Louisa broke the silence by asking, "The night want fo' hear a story?"[1]

"Yes, yes," came the excited replies from the children. They loved their grandparents' stories.

Louisa slipped into her storytelling voice, "A woman had two children." She started slowly, creating a poetic rhythm, "And, e want fo' make a pie fo' she husband before e come home from de field. He bina plow."

Louisa paused, the listeners nodded, and she continued, "So she tell e children, say, 'I de go store fo' get sugar fo' make pie.' Tell em, say, 'Don't eat de three pear I leave on de table. I make pie out em when I de come back.'"

---

[1] Authors' Note: The following story appears verbatim as recorded by Patricia Jones-Jackson in **When Roots Die**, The University of Georgia Press, 1987. This traditional story reflects true Gullah speech; our adaptation of Jim and Louisa's dialog makes their conversation more readable.

Adjusting to Louisa's pronounced Gullah dialect, Melanie stifled her smile as one little boy whispered, "Uh oh."

"When she leave fo' go get sugar, de girl child de get hungry. E got hungry too much, man! So e gone and
- look on de pear
- look on de pear
- look on em
- look on em. Finally she get de pear and eat em. When de woman come home, look, see de pear ben gone."

Louisa looked at her grandson, "E ask e children, say, 'Who eat de pear I ben leave on de table heah?'

"The boy say, 'Sister, Mama, Sister. Sister ben eat em.'"

Turning to one of her granddaughters, Louisa said, "ask Sister, say, 'Who ben eat de pear, Sister?'

"Sister say, 'Brother, Mama, Brother. Brother ben eat em.'
"'Brother?'
"'Sister, Mama, Sister!'
"'Sister?'
"'Brother, Mama, Brother!'
"They
- go on
- go on
- go on
"de woman tell Sister, say, 'Sister, go lay head on de chop block out dere.'"

Melanie shook her head to stay alert.

"Sister gone and lay e head on de chop block out by de woodpile. By and by, de woman come and pick up de ax and
de chop Sister head off... and bury em in de onion patch.
Chop she leg... and bury em in de hen house.
Chop she arm... bury em in de barnyard.
Li bird ben see where e bury em."

The black night and the soft creature sounds coupled with the surreal visual images conjured by the storytelling. A shudder passed through the small group, "When de evening, de daddy come home and ask he wife, say, 'Where Sister?' Woman say, 'She over de other side de stay

with de grandma awhile.' By and by, de daddy ben go over de other side fo' get Sister. The grandma say, 'ain't see em.' So dey
- de look
- de look
- and de look fo' Sister. De woman tell em, say, 'Sister run away.'

"By and by, spring de come and time come fo' plant onion again. Woman grow em, get fine mess of em. One evening, dey bina eat supper and woman tell Brother, say, 'Go out dere in de onion patch and pull some onion fo' eat with de peas.' So Brother gone in de onion patch and de start fo' pull up onion. But when he de start fo' pull em, e yeddy somebody de sing:

Brother, Brother, Brother
Don't pull me hair
Know mama de kill me
Bout de three li pear

The boy ben so scare, e gone, run, tell e mother. De woman didn't believe de child. Tel em, say, 'Go out dere fo' get me some onion, boy!!!'"

Melanie glanced at Daniel. Intense interest was replacing his previous unease. Louisa continued, "The boy gone back and try fo' pull up onion again. He yeddy somebody de sing and de sing:

Brother, Brother, Brother
Don't pull me hair
Know mama de kill me
Bout de three li pear"

Louisa's voice was low and her body rocked, "So dis time de child de run, de cry, and e de holler. He daddy ask em, say, 'What ben de matter de you?' De child tell em what he de yeddy in de onion patch. So de daddy go fo' heself fo' see what Brother bina talk about. He get de onion patch, boot up fo' pull up onion, and he yeddy Sister de sing and de sing:

Daddy, Daddy, Daddy
Don't you pull me hair
Know mama de kill me
Bout de three li pear

"The man ben so bex, he go back in de house and ask he wife again. Ask em, say, 'What ben happen de Sister?' Woman say, 'I ain't know. You know she ben run away — long time now.' De man tell she, say, 'Go in onion patch and try fo' pull up onion.' De woman gone in de onion patch. E boot up, try fo' pull up onion. Soon e start fo' pull, e yeddy Sister de sing and de sing:

Mama, Mama, Mama
Don't you pull me hair
You know you kill me
Bout de three li pear

"The woman ben so scare, e run, run, run til e knock e head against a tree. Knock em and kill self.

"By and by, de li bird what see em all happen, e sit on de fence and sing de daddy where e find Sister bone. Say:

Look in de onion patch
Find e li head
Look in barnyard
Find e li leg
Look in hen house
Find e li arm
Po dog suck e bone"

Louisa paused then said, "The end of dat one!"

Melanie felt an involuntary chill pass through her body. The children breathed heavily, then stillness enveloped the group. No one spoke. All stared at the fire, absorbed in a trance.

"Ahhh..." broke the spell as a guttural sound rose above the wind's whistle. The young ones gasped and screamed; Melanie, Daniel, and Grant jumped. Louisa laughed as Jim, who had slipped away unnoticed, rejoined the group with, "Gotcha."

Laughter and relief touched even the adults. Melanie realized the children's story with its roots reaching back to the African continent was not so different from European fairy tales. It contained the fear of unthinkable, vivid violence and, of course, it supplied a moral. Louisa had told her story very well. So well, in fact, that Grant, Daniel, and she had trembled as if they were kids.

CHAPTER 10

7:00 p.m., Wednesday, June 1, 1988

As Melanie hurried along Backbone Road toward Duck House, she passed through patches of pitch-black darkness. Approaching the shadowy building, she heard the researchers loading their gear on their vehicles as they prepared for their night patrol.

She studied the two motorized trikes — three-wheeled carts, canopy-less, and lunar gray. They appeared to come from a futuristic Star Wars era. In the middle, between the front seat and the backward-facing, removable rear seat was a large flat area. Here the researchers had attached a big, wooden box to store their data sheets, tagging equipment, meter sticks, egg baskets, flashlights, jackets, coffee thermoses, and snacks.

Melanie laughed to see Derby, the only tame horse on the island, attempting to help himself to their food.

"Shoo-oo, Derby," commanded Melanie. She pushed the huge, brown animal's nose out of the equipment box. "I see Derby has discovered your presence on the island. He's always looking for a handout."

"Derby, don't be greedy," chided Lana. Turning to Melanie, she explained. "He's already eaten all our leftovers from dinner. But, you'd never know it."

A brisk Rebecca stepped out of Duck House. "Melanie, we're glad you're joining us tonight. You can ride with me on this trike," she gestured as she settled behind the driver's wheel. "David and I'll try to teach you everything we know about the loggerheads' nesting behavior."

"All right!" exclaimed an exuberant David as he bounded onto the rear seat of Rebecca's trike.

"I'm ready, too," replied Melanie as she climbed onto the front seat beside Rebecca.

"Daniel, you and Lana head south," continued Rebecca.

When the trike engines roared, Melanie was surprised at how loud they were. "Turtles must not hear very well," she yelled at Rebecca. "They react more to light. See, no headlights," she shouted back.

Jostling human and non-human cargo, the trikes bounced along the old hunting trail from Duck House to the beach. What a madcap caper — full of big bumps, loud noises, but no lights.

Once the trikes gained the beach, the ride became smooth. Daniel turned his trike south and Rebecca headed north.

The panorama assumed a supernatural quality this moonless night. The beach, the ocean, the waves, the sky, the clouds all took on various shades of gray. It was difficult to distinguish one object from another. Melanie wondered how she was expected to identify a turtle from a palm tree stump. The night was so dark they couldn't see and the engine noise was so loud they couldn't talk. They all strained their eyes for humpbacked shapes and for tracks resembling tank treads running across the sand.

Melanie shivered when they entered the stretch nicknamed Palmhenge. For approximately a half-mile, the width of the beach was strewn with stumps of palms and live oaks. Huge root systems of fallen live oak trees towered above the trike in spectral shapes while the palm trunks resembled giant pick-up-sticks. All lay helter-skelter, reminiscent of druidic ruins. The sea was chewing a chunk out of the island, toppling hundreds of large trees in the process.

Though the tide was going out, Rebecca had to back the trike out of pens created by the constantly changing locations of trunks, branches, and sea. Twisted roots formed gargoyles eyeing them and sinewy arms reaching for them. Palmhenge menaced all outsiders.

They worked their way through the maze toward North Arm. Once they rounded the cape and turned on a more westerly course, they left the protection of the trees. Wind picked up velocity; they reached for their jackets. Charcoal gray clouds chased silver gray ones across the sky.

Before stopping for a break, the researchers continued to the tidal creek dividing the main island from a small hammock and the surrounding marshland. Rebecca switched off the trike engine and the riders voiced their observations.

"What do you think of Palmhenge at night?" Rebecca prompted.

"That has to be one of the scariest places on earth," David encouraged Melanie to talk.

"I've never been so far up the beach after dark. It's really intimidating. How do you get through when the tide is high?" she asked.

"Depending on the moon, tides, and weather, we may not be able to find a way. In fact, sometimes we have to walk it," replied Rebecca. "David, pay close attention to the landmarks. I want everyone to be able to drive these trikes through Palmhenge."

"Sure thing, Rebecca," David replied. Squirming with curiosity, he asked, "Mrs. Evans, do you know any stories about pirates on Caretta?"

"I'd feel younger, David, if you called me Melanie." She giggled then continued, "I don't have any good tales about pirates. But, as a child, I remember hearing about bootleggers — they were called rumrunners around here. They used Caretta during Prohibition. It looks as if the island hides secrets even now, doesn't it?"

"Yeah," breathed David.

Melanie laughed ruefully, remembering a younger boy also enthralled with blood, guts, and adventure.

Rebecca interjected, "Anyone for stretching their legs before we start back?"

Negative responses prompted her to restart the trike for the return trip around North Arm. They were almost out of Palmhenge when Rebecca cut the engine. She pointed to two parallel tracks emerging from the water's edge and continuing to the high tide mark.

"Let's go! No lights until we're certain she's laying her eggs," Rebecca directed.

They crept toward the unaware sea creature, gasping in the heavy night air. When they came closer, they heard the soft sound of sand hitting sand. The female loggerhead turtle was preparing her nest, digging out the onion-shaped hollow with her rear flippers. She stopped excavating and the researchers held their breath. Had they spooked her or was she ready to lay her eggs? The researchers sighed with relief when they heard a soft plop followed steadily by others. Rebecca turned on her flashlight so all bore witness to the awesome 120 million-year-old regeneration process, a basic drive conducted under the cover of darkness.

In the golden glow of the flashlight, Melanie discerned the sand-covered creature among the reeds at the high water mark. Though it was laying eggs, it appeared sexless. Too, Melanie was struck by how small the head appeared in relation to the gargantuan shell. The turtle seemed so out of place.

"Let's get to work, gang," Rebecca said as she handed David the avalanche cord to drop into the hole. The heavy twine attached to a cork would enable them to relocate the eggs when the turtle had covered the nest. Rebecca handed Melanie the meter stick to measure the turtle's carapace.

Examination revealed this particular turtle was one meter long and had already been tagged; the tags remained in good condition. They recorded the reptile's size and tag numbers, sketched her crawl, stepped off the nest location to the nearest island meter indicator, and noted the weather conditions. All this data proved vital to the research project when it was computerized, compiled with other projects' findings, then analyzed.

None of the human activity deterred the turtle as she continued to lay her eggs. Her next task was to pack and smooth the sand in order to camouflage the nest from predators such as raccoons and ghost crabs. The need for the avalanche cord to mark the location became apparent. When the turtle finished the hiding process, the only clue to the exact location was the unburied end of the string.

The other research team arrived after completing its patrol of Caretta's Tail End. Together the five watched the loggerhead crawl to the sea before they set about the task of uncovering the eggs. David dug out the nest. Keeping the eggs level, Melanie counted and layered them in a utilitarian plastic bucket. This turtle had laid one hundred twenty-five eggs, an average lay according to Rebecca.

With care they placed the bucket in the equipment box and headed for the hatchery, located in the dunes between the ocean and Duck House. Here the researchers would keep an eye for hatchlings scheduled to emerge in approximately sixty days. Meanwhile, the eggs were safe from the ocean as well as the raccoons and crabs. Before laws were passed to protect the loggerhead turtle rookeries, many humans hunted nests for the treasured items. Believing in aphrodisiacal powers, people swallowed, scrambled, and baked the eggs.

"Well done, group," Rebecca complimented them. "Perhaps the next turtle will be a neophyte, one that's never been tagged. Then, Melanie, we can show you the tagging procedure."

"Let's go find us another female!" yelled David.

The others shook their heads or rolled their eyes at David, but all jumped onto the trikes. On this pass, Daniel and Lana drove north while Rebecca, Melanie, and David headed south. While they drove, Melanie reflected on the word neophyte. Minutes ago, she had witnessed a process unchanged from the primordial past. She, a representative of a species only one-hundredth as old, was the true neophyte.

The southern beach stretched forever. It grew wider and flatter in front of their eyes as the tide continued to recede.

When they reached Tail End, they took another break to relax their eyes and stretch their legs.

"Wow, I'm beginning to see things," said David.

"You, too?" inquired Melanie. She was relieved to learn she was not the only one beginning to hallucinate. "I'm seeing the big inflated balloons in the Macy's Thanksgiving Day parade. What are you seeing?"

"Viking boats," replied the teenager.

Rebecca addressed the night air, "It gives you a different perspective, doesn't it?"

Melanie commented, "And, how."

* * *

The twang of a country music song played as a backdrop to muffled conversations in the dimly lit, smoke-filled, waterfront lounge. High humidity intensified the cloying smells of stale beer and overripe fish. A handful of individuals occupied bar stools while several couples sat hidden in high-backed booths. In one of the booths with its red vinyl seats, a nearly inaudible, though intense, interchange was taking place.

"Murder was never a part of the bargain. What the hell got into you?"

"What was I supposed to do? Money flows in the right channels as long as there are no leaks. That greedy bastard wanted a cut. A slap on the wrist wasn't going to make him go away. So I plugged the leak, so to speak."

"How many other little 'leaks' do you figure are going to have to be plugged? I sure as hell wish you had weighted down the body or taken it further out to sea. Having it wash up on the island may have caused a problem."

"Sailing's pretty smooth as long as those new island inhabitants don't interfere."

"The island's my concern, not yours. And, everything's going to stay under control. No more dead bodies, you hear?"

* * *

10:30 p.m., Saturday, June 4, 1988

Melanie began her evening ritual of undressing for bed. She brushed her teeth and washed her face. Sitting down at the vanity table, she began to comb her hair. She was studying the sun's tanning effects on her face when Ali Cat jumped into her lap. His closeness and soft purr intruded on her introspective mood.

Stroking the cat's fur, she carried him across the room reassuring him, "You're a good cat, Ali. Such a close companion. So warm, so soft." When they reached the door, she opened it and pushed Ali Cat into the hall with a firm, "But tonight, I want to be by myself."

Melanie walked across the room and stood at the open window. A gentle breeze wafted through the screens and blew the sheer curtains and the diaphanous material of her gown. Her warm skin welcomed the moving air. She felt alive, a welcome feeling after all the months of numbness. After six weeks here on the island, she was finding renewal from exercising, eating Louisa's good cooking, sunbathing, and sharing new viewpoints offered by different people.

She analyzed the various people. Patrice, Louisa and Jim had been more supportive, more accepting than she had expected. They met her basic needs of food, clothing, and shelter. Yet, immense differences resulted from age and background. A gulf remained unbridged as if she were playing the child to their parenting. Now the youthful loggerhead researchers had arrived, bringing their uninhibited, unscarred lives and their unhidden desires. Contemplating desire, Melanie considered Grant. He was turning out to be someone with whom she enjoyed sharing day-to-day events. She found his viewpoints refreshing, especially his awareness of physical forces. She wished, however, he were more responsive to her emotional needs — like Adam Gardner. She found herself warming to this man and his obvious charms although she perceived he was paying attention to her for reasons yet to be totally revealed.

Personally, she felt more in-charge. She was getting stronger and making decisions. She vowed never to be a victim again — not to any purse snatcher or any others of his ilk — not if she had any input into the situation.

A cooling breeze softly kissed her body. She raised her arms and spread her legs to allow the breeze access. Suddenly, she felt sensual. She wanted Greg. It had been almost a year since she had experienced his touch. She craved his stroke on her arms, breasts, tummy, and legs. Looking down, she noticed her nipples were erect. Closing her eyes, she brought her right hand to her chest and caressed her breasts through the thin material of her gown.

With a whimper, Melanie bent double and pulled the gown over her head. Her hair billowed, electrically charged. Indeed, her whole body sensed a current surging through it. She dropped the gown to the floor and stood naked in the sea breeze.

Her hands pushed her hair from her face. Then she trailed her hands down her cheeks, throat, shoulders, and breasts. She fondled the breasts tentatively then assuredly. She closed her eyes and moaned with pleasure as she recalled her husband playing with her body. How she wished he were there to take her aching nipples between his lips, and to suck, lick, nibble them gently but firmly.

By instinct, Melanie jutted her hips forward. Her right hand caressed the smooth curves of her abdomen and thighs while the left hand continued to massage her nipples in an abandoned fashion. She ran the right hand through the blonde, curly mass of her pubic hair. The light pull of the hairs further charged her. She ran her fingers through the hairs again and again. Her legs grew weak from the almost-forgotten pleasure

She explored the wetness, the heat, and the pulse of her body. Her trembling hand began to search for the source. Rhythmically, she sought release from the throbbing urge that held her taut.

Her breath caught. Her mind flashed white. Her body shuddered in delight.

Leaving the gown on the floor, Melanie laid face down on the cool cotton sheets of the bed. When she had calmed, she allowed her mind to range over her ten years of marriage to Greg. She remembered their lovemaking — in beds, on the floor, in the shower, on a chaise lounge on the balcony, on a beach, against a tree in the woods.... At last, she could feel.

She wondered how much she could allow herself to feel again. Could she ever make love to another man? Did she want to open up to new possibilities, new pleasures, new pains? Was it too soon?

Physically satisfied, she fell asleep with the gentle sea breeze wafting over her. She slept more deeply than she had in almost a year.

CHAPTER 11

6:00 p.m., Wednesday, June 8, 1988

The heat from the charcoal pit swirled around the seated group devouring supper.

"Ain't this great? We've got just enough breeze to make the bugs tolerable and the smoke intolerable," cracked a grinning David. The college sophomore relished being the center of attention. While sitting on the marsh dock, a big hook and a lot of patience had paid off. He had caught tonight's meal — fresh shark.

Only Melanie and Lana had approached the cookout with hesitation. The rest of the researchers were familiar with the superb flavor of the grilled, muscular fish. Melanie relaxed among all the joking. She reflected that she and Grant were the elders of the gathering, a strange feeling for someone in her thirties. A pleasant surprise was the sense of camaraderie developing with the younger group.

Rebecca and Grant had plopped down side-by-side. As Melanie watched them, she wondered again how friendly the two were. Was there any truth to the rumored affair that Susannah had mentioned?

"So, what do ya'll think of shark?" Rebecca questioned Melanie and Lana.

"I'm amazed. It's so delicate in flavor," Melanie responded.

Lana chimed in brightly, "It's great!"

Daniel added, "In spite of its man-eating reputation, many more people eat the largest fish than vice-versa."

Melanie turned to Daniel, "Did you eat shark when you were growing up?"

The young black man paused before answering, "Yes, I guess we did. It's a fish caught near my home."

"What else did you eat?" Melanie continued.

"I guess, pretty much what everybody else eats — not so different from you."

She sensed from Daniel's curt tone that she had touched a nerve. "Daniel, I'm sorry if my question seemed rude."

"It's not so much that it's rude as.... Tell me — how often does someone ask you what you ate as a child? And, why the question at all? I don't want to be a stereotype."

"Stereotype?"

"You see, growing up black in the South sensitizes one to all that. Educated blacks face these preconceived attitudes on a daily basis. I've fought, maybe too hard, to try and escape them."

"What do you mean?"

"You asked what I ate. If I say I grew up on black-eyed peas, cornbread, ham hocks, and turnip greens, then many people immediately peg my whole life. In spite of my diet or my routines, I want to be an individual."

"I suppose I understand," Melanie mumbled then paused. "I've never had an experience quite like yours. I wonder what it was like for you. My only encounters with being prejudged were because of my name. You see, I was a Parker with an older brother who preceded me through private school. On many occasions, I felt all the teachers and other students had already made up their minds about me."

Daniel replied with relief in his voice, "You've had a small taste of how it can be. You wanted to be accepted as Melanie Parker; I want to be accepted as Daniel Jordan, a man who knows where he's been and where he's going."

"I'm still curious." She smiled and continued, "How did you feel the other night when Jim and Louisa were demonstrating the old storytelling tradition?"

"Proud. Confused. It was a powerful experience. I want to be true to my black heritage and, at the same time, I want to be respected for what I've become. I want to be measured by society's, and of course that means the white, yardstick. I'm not as at peace with this issue as I'd like to be."

Melanie was silent as she tried to frame the young man's dilemma in her own terms. Her past role as little rich girl had not been difficult by the world's standards. For the simple reason that she was a Parker, she had received many strokes for her grades, her looks, and her behavior. She had married her boyhood sweetheart. She'd never actually suffered until the traffic accident. Again, the emptiness overwhelmed her; tears stung her eyes. She forced herself to refocus onto her companion.

"It's like...," she cleared her throat and started again. "It's like getting one's balance, isn't it? You know, I'm looking for a balance, too. Suddenly I'm considered a widow — believe me, that's a scary term. Anyway, without my family, I'm unsure what role I'm supposed to play. As a woman, where do I fit in? I'm finding I can't simply discard my old life; I must examine it for what I liked. Yet, I must be open to new possibilities. I'm trying to be careful not to jump to the quick solution as the best answer."

Daniel nodded, "Yeah, I'd hate to replace one stereotype with another. You have to allow yourself space to create a new, strong life."

"OK, everybody, it's cleanup time," Rebecca's voice cut through the fireside chatter.

"Maybe we can talk more about this another time," suggested Daniel.

"I'd like that."

As the group pitched in with few murmurings, Melanie had a chance to speak to Rebecca.

"Rebecca, I've been thinking about last Friday. I wonder if perhaps I could work on one of the turtle tagging teams every Friday night."

"Gosh, are you serious? That'd be great. Then, I could let one of the regulars have time off. Want to start tonight?"

"Sure, why not?" Melanie offered.

"Wonderful. In fact, if you go out tonight, I can catch up on some paperwork."

The camp chores neared completion. David's high-pitched voice soared over the group, "Hey, everybody, we've got a few minutes. Whatta you say we play Botticelli?"

A chorus of groans and "Bottawhats?" echoed around the fire. Melanie looked to Rebecca for an explanation and caught a knowing glance pass between the redhead and Grant.

"Aw, come on. It's fun."

"All right, David," Grant pitched in. "Tell us how to play and maybe we'll give it a go."

"One person serves as the host and he — whoops — or she, has to think of a character who we all know. It can be anyone — a politician, a movie star, a sports hero. They can be dead or alive, just as long as he or she is well-known. The host tells everyone what letter of the alphabet the character's last name begins with.

"Next, everyone takes a turn and asks the host a classification question such as, 'If you were a color, what color would you be?' 'If you were a mode of transportation, what mode would you be?' Notice no direct 'are you' questions. The winner will be the first to guess the character from the clues. Any questions? OK, I'll start as the host. The letter is 'T.'"

Lana joined in, "I'll start the questions. If you were a fable, what fable would you be?"

David smiled and said, "The one about the hare and the tortoise."

Melanie went next, "What's your favorite sport?"

David rejoined, "Wrong kind of question. You have to phrase it 'If you were a sport, what sport would you be?'"

"I think I understand," replied Melanie and the game continued.

After several rounds of questions and answers plus a lot of good-natured laughing, the query: "If you were a movie, what movie would you be?" received the response: "Uh-oh. I can't tell you the title — it would give them away. I'll give you a hint though — they're in a cartoon."

Lana immediately hollered, "*Teenage Mutant Ninja Turtles!*"

A smiling David yelled, "You got it!"

While the early evening advanced, several additional rounds were played before time for the nightly turtle expedition. In the deepening shadows, more than once, Melanie had noticed several casual looks exchanged between Grant and Rebecca. She compared herself to the redhead. Who had the better body or personality? She caught herself thinking like a jealous schoolgirl, sizing up the competition. Acknowledging the silly, thrilly sensation, she laughed and leaned against the tree.

On the beach, Melanie and Lana saw the flashlights of the other team beyond the high tide mark near a palmetto stump. As she and Lana approached, David finished putting the last of the turtle eggs into the bucket.

"Wow! One hundred forty-seven eggs — that's the biggest nest yet," he exclaimed.

The two women noticed Daniel stepping off the turtle's tracks and sketching the pattern onto the research sheet.

"Hi!" he called. "Rebecca's sure going to be sorry she missed this one. Look how she crawled up to this log, then actually backed up and maneuvered around it. Now that's unusual. The nesting urge was so strong she overcame the normal retreat pattern."

It was easy to become captivated by David and Daniel's enthusiasm. Lana responded, "What can the girl team do?"

"Actually, it'd be great if you could bury the eggs at the hatchery. David and I saw another set of dry run tracks. We'd like to head south to see if she tries again."

"OK, Melanie?" asked Lana.

"Sure. David, give me that count again."

"One hundred forty-seven."

Melanie and Lana headed the trike and its precious cargo of reptilian eggs toward the protected nesting area built several meters beyond the highest water line. The hatchery construction was simple yet effective. The researchers had prepared an area several feet wide, then covered it with wire fencing. On the sides, they had sunk two-foot metal panels to deter any animal from digging. The fence itself was mounted on wooden frames. Lana and Melanie lifted one of the sections.

Once inside, Melanie used a post hole digger to excavate a hole the stretch of her arm. Then, she enlarged the bottom of the hole with a huge cockle shell so it simulated the loggerhead turtle's own bulbous hole. Without rotating the eggs, Lana redeposited them. Melanie verified the number for data purposes, and recorded it and the date on a metal flag to mark the nest's new location.

As the two women replaced the fence panel securing the hatchery, Melanie asked, "Do you know what happens when they hatch?"

"Well, it'll be a couple of months from now. I've been told that when the nest erupts, they bubble up to the surface. We'll gather them into the buckets and transport them near the water. There the hatchlings must crawl at least a short distance to the ocean so they can imprint the memory of Caretta's beach on their consciousness."

The two reboarded their little vehicle and resumed their patrol northward. They negotiated Palmhenge with ease, reaching North Arm. Lana cut off the trike's engine, leaving an engulfing silence broken by the smooth, rhythmic lap of the water. They stared at the brilliant blanket of stars overhead. The Milky Way cut across the middle of the heavens with an intensity Melanie had never witnessed. They watched one meteor, then, another streak across the star-encrusted blackness.

"It's awesome, isn't it?"

In the darkness, Melanie grinned at the teenager's enthusiasm. She responded, "It is incredible when you remove yourself from manmade lights. Add one relatively deserted island, waves, and.... You're right. It's awesome."

"What do you imagine that boat is doing?" the other questioned.

Melanie gazed at a darkened shape floating in the channel near the cape, "Probably a shrimper positioned for an early morning run."

"It's not the first time I've seen it. I think it's weird," prompted Lana.

"Are you sure it's the same boat?" asked Melanie.

"I can't be positive in the dark, but it's the same size and type. And, it's always in this general location."

"Hmm...."

"Maybe it's white slavers from South America — or plutonium smugglers from the Savannah River Plant." She noticed Melanie turn to stare at her, "I'm just kidding. But, it's fun to pretend out here when it's as quiet as it has been tonight."

"We haven't seen much action," agreed Melanie. "However, my creative powers can't change the boat from a shrimp trawler."

"It sure is fun to make up these things, though. But, I guess a shrimp boat is just a shrimp boat." Lana laughed, "Well, we can always stuff ourselves. Want some gorp?"

"Always."

While she munched on the peanut, raisin, and M&M mixture, Melanie stared at the boat's mysterious silhouette. She, too, had seen a similar vessel last Friday night. In an hour, after their next run down and up the beach, she would be curious to see if the boat were still there.

Back on patrol, the two rounded the cape and headed south when a noise built around them. The sound of the trike was obliterated. Melanie stopped the trike. They searched for the source. Coming straight down the coastline at a low altitude was the unmistakable silhouette of a helicopter with the raucous beating of its blades. It fanned a brilliant white searchlight in a random pattern along the black surface of the water.

"I wonder what they're looking for?" shouted Lana above the racket.

"Probably a lost fisherman or boat," suggested Melanie.

"Since they're this close to shore, I bet, they're trying to find drug smugglers."

"You have a great imagination," Melanie laughed. "At any rate, that searchlight will have spooked any turtle making a crawl. Let's hustle and see if we can catch one before she hits the surf."

An hour later when they returned to North Arm, the shrimp boat was gone.

CHAPTER 12

6:30 p.m., Thursday, June 16, 1988

Delicious aromas filled the dining room at Parker House on this Thursday evening.

"I must say, my dear Louisa, once again you have concocted a culinary masterpiece from home-grown ingredients. How do you do it?"

"Aw, Mistuh Grant, you do go on about things," responded the grinning housekeeper.

"It was excellent, Louisa. I've never eaten anything like it," added Melanie.

"Jus' crab an' rice an' some vegee-tahbles," Louisa replied. "It's like oysters an' rice bu' dere's nothin' finer dan oysters an' rice."

"Yes," Grant agreed. "If you stay until oyster season, you'll see what she means."

"Are these sea island recipes?" Melanie asked.

"I suppose so," Louisa answered. "I was raised on dese dishes. Dey's what you grew or gathered on de side. We dug oysters an' saved der juices. We added rice, onions, and peppers we grew. Den, we cooked dem all 'til de rice sucked up de flavors."

"Simple, yet delicious and satisfying," Patrice commented. "Louisa, tell Melanie and Grant about hush puppies."

"Oh, I know dey's heard dat tale."

"Tell us, Louisa," Grant prodded.

"Well, long befo' my time, lots o' corn grow'd. When der was a big fish fry, dey heated up de big pot of fat. De dogs went crazy at de smells an' howled up a storm. De cooks dropped de corn batter in de fat and gave it to de dogs sayin', 'hush, puppies.' One day among all, somebody tasted dem fried corn balls to see why de dogs liked 'em so much. Dat's why we eat hush puppies!"

"Great story! So, hush puppies are another sea island dish," Melanie observed.

Patrice concurred, "Corn was being used by the Guale Indians when the Spanish arrived. I read that the corn cobs recovered by archeologists on St. Helena Island were the original Mexican variety. Such a finding makes interesting speculation about the trade networks of the early Indians."

The sound of the radio-telephone interrupted the conversation.

Louisa bustled away to answer its summons.

"Miz Mellie, it's Mistuh Ashley fo' you," Louisa called.

While Melanie took the regular call from her brother, Louisa cleared the dining table and served dessert. Grant and Patrice waited to eat their last course until Melanie completed her call.

"And, how was Ashley?" Patrice asked.

"Fine, but busy. I tried to convince him to fly down here for a little rest and relaxation. He said he'd consider it."

Finishing his dessert, Grant excused himself to complete the installation of newly-arrived parts in the lab. Patrice and Melanie settled to work, using the new notebook computers in the library. Melanie referred to a journal about life on the islands before the Civil War.

The sun spread relentless rays across the land; a sweltering heat penetrated every pore of her skin. As she looked over the parched fields dotted with large white tufts of cotton, she sensed her own garments might suffocate her. The clothes, designed to protect females, created a prison.

She watched the glistening backs of the black men, working the crops and wearing nothing on their torsos but dark, sun-resistant skin. Once again, she felt distinctly out of place on this southern island.

A harsh voice penetrated her musing.

She watched, horrified, as the white overseer cracked his whip at an old man. The long pole used to cultivate the unique island cotton fell to the ground. "Pick up that pole!" the merciless voice yelled.

Troubled by her reverie, Melanie rejoined the twentieth century. Part of her yearned to be like Fanny Kemble Butler whose detailed descriptions of slavery in the Georgia lowlands had fanned the outcry against inhuman conditions. This British actress' journal had proved so effective in rousing public opinion, England dared not support the Confederacy's fight as originally planned.

Melanie had grown up believing in a Disney-like dream of life: eventually all would be just and fair. Reconciling those beliefs with her recent painful discoveries had shattered that simple dream. Fanny Butler's experiences freshened her resolve to continue her own growth.

Melanie glanced at her silent companion and wondered what Patrice was reading.

A glorious day as we begin to build a new town in this new land for the glory of Mother Spain. I cannot help but recall another bright sunny morning some forty-five years ago, in the Year of Our Lord 1520, when I was a young lad. Near this very spot on Saint Helena's Island, I was privileged to see Gordillo plant the Spanish flag. Now, as an old man, I return to help in the establishment of the first town in the New World.

"Patrice?" Melanie explored softly.

"Yes?" came the quiet reply as Patrice returned to the present.

"Where were you?"

"On an island north of here, St. Helena. I was part of the first permanent colony in North America," she offered without considering how the answer might be received.

In turn, Melanie contributed. "I was on a plantation as Fanny Butler. I experienced the suffering of the slaves as they toiled to produce the planter's cotton. I was refusing to accept what-was as what-had-to-be."

"Thank you for sharing, Melanie. It's been many years, far too many, since I've felt close enough to someone to share my fantasies," Patrice reflected with moist eyes.

Melanie realized that Patrice had chosen to wrap herself in a world of her own creation — gaining a broad view from the journals yet missing the day-to-day experiences of human interaction. Out loud Melanie said, "You know, in the past, my life was so structured and so hectic, I lost all perspective of how my life fit into the web of things — nature, history.... Now, on the island with the turtles and the journals, I'm gaining an understanding." Melanie paused and twisted a strand of her hair. "You know, it might be interesting for us to write a historical novel together. What do you think?"

"You mean like *Gone With The Wind?*"

Melanie chuckled, "I don't know if I'd visualize a bestseller. I'd simply consider it a great way to make the history of this place come alive."

The two women continued working in the comfort of the library. Neither needed to talk further. Finally, Patrice asked, "Will you show me once more how to boot or kick this little computer so I can write up some ideas?"

* * *

8:30 a.m., Saturday, June 18, 1988

Day after day, Melanie continued to explore the physical features of Caretta: ocean and beach, interdune meadow and maritime forest, freshwater lagoon and ponds, saltwater marsh and creek. Most days, she was eager to discover more about this island that was beginning to feel like a close friend. There were still some days when she had to will herself out the door, but her determination was paying off. On each excursion, her senses became attuned to the natural processes happening all around her — birth, growth, death, and decay.

In the evenings she enjoyed reading about or discussing the sea island past with Patrice or Jim, Louisa, and Grant. Those moments often triggered Melanie's memory of another place to visit. David's questions about pirates and Lana's comments about smugglers caused Melanie to wonder about former users of Caretta Island.

Last night, she had read one of Edward's cryptic notes, hinting at unusual activities on the island during the 1930s. She knew that during Prohibition, many sea islands had been used to cache rum from the Caribbean for eventual sale in the states. It seemed Edward knew that bootleggers had built a wooden lean-to located on a small hammock rising out of the swampy forestlands at the northwest tip of the island. A small waterway cut across Caretta creating the isolated spot, accessible only by water. This dense mound of shrubs and trees provided total concealment of the small structure.

This morning she approached Jim for fresh information. "Jim, I was reading in the journals about a rumrunners' hideaway on one of the hammocks."

"Who say dat?"

"My grandfather, Edward."

Jim shifted his weight and averted his eyes as he remembered Edward's escapades. Even after all these years, he still considered Edward a bad man. Was his spirit returning?

"Jim, all I want to know is if the hideaway's still standing or not. Is it?"

"Yez, Miz Mellie. Jim Jr. uses de hideaway fo' fishin'. He come every week. It's a getaway from his wife and de children."

"You and Louisa must love those regular visits."

"Sometimes he come see Louisa and me, but not offen. He too proud fo' his own good."

Melanie recalled her glimpse of the scowling Jim Jr. at the storytelling. He had ignored virtually everyone but his father, and he had appeared to pick a fight with him before disappearing. She wondered about the relationship between him and his parents.

"You wanna go dere?"

"There and to any other old structures in the hammocks," Melanie replied.

"Well, der's another Indian midden. It's not as big as Tail End's. You find more interestin' arrowheads and pots at Tail End," Jim responded.

Scratching his head, he continued, "And, dat same hammock has a rock foundation. Now dat's a differen' story."

Melanie waited for a second before prompting, "Can you tell me?"

"Dat house was owned by an edjucated black family before de Civil War. He was de son of a black woman and a rich white man. De man wanted de best fo' his child. He sent him to college up North and gave him dat land. De boy married a free woman and dey raised a daughter on dat little island. Dey black, but dey own slaves."

"I never knew blacks owned slaves, too," commented Melanie. "But, I am happy to hear of one white man who showed interest in the mulatto child he fathered. Insensitivity seems so common — not only man to his fellow man but man to his own flesh and blood. During the

Vietnam war, many American soldiers abandoned thousands of their Amerasian sons and daughters."

"Yassum, people can be bad. But, dey always think dey is right and all de other people is wrong. Dat never changes."

After a moment of reflection, Melanie turned to Jim, "I'd like to go find that foundation. Will you help me with the canoe?"

"Of course, Miz Mellie. You goin' by youself again?"

When they launched the canoe, the tidal creek was almost at full flood.

"Watch it now."

"I will," Melanie reassured Jim.

Melanie paddled with ease into the main channel. All around her, she could see various-sized hammocks poking their heads of pine, palm, and oak above the marsh grass. She directed her craft toward the one she guessed might hold the ruins of the homestead. When she saw a gradual bank, she headed the canoe into the shoreline. After gaining her footing on the slippery slope, she followed a raccoon path, noticing the brown, wilted condition of the plants. It had been weeks since the last rain, an unusual spring for the island. A thunderstorm would be welcome to revive the vegetation. While animal trails criss-crossed this little hammock, she discovered no features suggesting former human habitation.

At the next hammock-island, however, she spotted a large oak tree shading the broken foundation of a house. A remnant of a stone fireplace stood intact. With Jim's partial account still in her mind, Melanie pondered on this family's life. Had they been outcasts from society? Were they still alive when her great-grandfather bought Caretta? Were they mentioned in the Parker family journals?

Along another path leading to the creek, she discovered the small oyster shell ring or midden Jim had mentioned. To her untrained eye, it appeared to be an elevated mound. The meager remains of the refuse heap attested to the Guale Indians' use of the islands for hunting and ceremonial purposes. Had these natives created this midden during the same time span as the one at Tail End? How many people had used the island? How extensive was their culture?

Would she ever know the answers to all her questions?

With little effort, she continued along the narrow creek that led to the hammock at the northwest end of Caretta. Searching for signs of use of the secluded rumrunners' hideaway — the most recent remains of human occupation, Melanie floated around the hammock. Did Caretta hold secrets of more recent usage than Jim, Louisa, and Patrice knew? As she neared the muddy shore that had served as a boat landing for the rumrunners, she floated past banks of exposed reed roots testifying to the power of the tides.

Melanie saw recent prints in the pluff mud — imprints of the prow of another boat and footprints — perhaps those of Jim Jr. from his fishing trips? She looked again. More than one person had been here. Who else could be using the hideaway?

A small thicket of bamboo swayed in the wind. Beyond it, straight up-and-down trunks of pine trees formed the hiding place, barely discernible against the other trees of the hammock. Clear was the narrow path leading to it from the muddy landing. Melanie beached her canoe and followed the trail.

When she approached the sixty-plus-year-old structure, she noted new palmetto thatch on the roof. However, nothing else had been added, not even beer bottles or empty tin cans attesting to recent fishing trips.

An opening in the right side of the pine log structure formed the dark entrance. Melanie entered cautiously and allowed her eyes to adjust to the dimness, broken by scattered slats of sunlight filtering around the solid pine logs.

As she had expected, no one was there. A simple counter or sleeping platform jutted from the walls on three sides forming a u-shape. It was in good repair; a brace or two had been replaced. Fish nets and buoys hung from roof supports. Assorted crab pots were stacked neatly against the other wall. Stumps of palmetto served as seats. The interior, like the exterior, was scrupulously clean except for a dry dust that prickled her nose. If anything, the place seemed too neat to be used by fishermen. A sensation of something wrong seized her mind, but nothing appeared amiss.

Melanie stood there, rubbing her brow when, suddenly, she knew she had to get out of there. Yet, she didn't know why. Consciously swallowing her unexpected panic, she took another moment to look around the shack once again. She searched for any incongruous object but, she realized, she didn't know what she was looking for. *Maybe I'm making something out of nothing. There's nothing out of the ordinary inside or outside the shack.* But again, she was aware that she dare not stay any longer. Trying to control her growing sense of alarm, she hurried to the beached canoe.

Sweating from more than humid heat, she pushed off and jumped into the canoe. While she stroked against the swiftly retreating tide, the overwhelming, strange sensation evaporated. Working hard to move the canoe forward, the reality of physical exertion brought her down to earth. Really, there was nothing sinister in the hideaway. She decided that she was letting Lana's and David's wild imaginings affect her. The simple elation over her discoveries, however, stayed with her.

At the dock, Melanie tied up the canoe. Not seeing Jim, she went to look for him to help her stow away the boat. She found him in the old cemetery near his cottage. He was weeding and rearranging the whelk shells that covered his parents' graves.

As he assisted her with the canoe, Melanie shared the exciting details of her venture. Accenting the positive, she had found — on her own — the foundation, the midden, and the hideaway. She kept her forebodings to herself.

While they walked up the white shell road to Parker House, Melanie inquired about something Jim had said earlier, "Why doesn't Jim Jr. come see you and Louisa more often?"

"He says we work like slaves — Louisa in de Big House and me outside. He doesn' want to stay on de island — he doesn' want us to stay on de island."

"You mean he equates your jobs as housekeeper and caretaker to slave labor?"

"Yassum. He and his wife wanna big house, car, and flashy clothes. Dey do anythin' to get 'em. Dey criticize Louisa and me fo' stayin' here."

"Oh. Then why does he bring his children to the storytellings?"

"He wants de children to appreciate der roots," the older man replied.

Melanie reflected on the morals woven into the horror of the "Three Little Pear" story she had heard: Don't steal; Don't kill; Don't lie; Good wins out over evil. She could understand a parent wanting his children to have the benefit of such experiences.

"Because he thinks you and Louisa work like slaves, you meet at your sister's home for the storytellings?"

"My sister owns dat land and shanty. She makes her livin' off dat land and de sea. He believes if you own de land, den you not a slave."

"I see," Melanie said as she digested the importance of land ownership to many sea islanders. She wondered if it related to the chicanery the former slaves had endured again and again since the Civil War.

They approached the wide steps of the rear entry to Parker House. "Look at that, Jim!"

"What, Miz Mellie?"

"That — there — under the steps."

Jim picked up a piece of rope and studied a series of knots that ran its entire length.

Melanie asked, "What does it mean? Didn't you tell me that a knotted rope under a porch was a hoodoo hex? Does someone still practice hoodoo around here?"

Jim's eyes held a distinctly troubled look. For a few seconds he said nothing. Finally, he broke the silence with, "Don' you worry non'. I'll take care of it, Miz Mellie."

CHAPTER 13

8:15 p.m., Saturday, June 25, 1988

Splat! Splat! Splat!

Sultry weather bred biting flies, gnats, and mosquitoes. Unfortunately for Melanie, Patrice, and Grant, who had retired to the porch following dinner, the screen door had been left ajar and the bloodthirsty creatures awaited them. Rocking and relaxing on the porch was cut short by general consensus.

"They're too much for me. You young folks endure if you choose. I'm retreating to the library," commented Patrice as she began the exodus.

"I agree," Grant concurred. "I think I'll take cover, also. What's your pleasure, Melanie?"

"Go ahead. I'm going to head for the beach and see if there's any wind."

She watched him walk toward his workshop, considering his physique, lean and hard from his favorite pastimes of running and rowing. Annoying bites disrupted any additional observations. She hurried to the mountain bike for the short ride to the beach.

Darkness fell rapidly without an intervening twilight as she pedaled furiously through the forest. Though she was bombarded by insects, at least, they didn't have the chance to bite. Using a flashlight, she reached the softer sands of the interdune meadow and left the cycle there.

As soon as she hit the beach, a soft southeasterly breeze blew away the bugs. Sighing with relief, she turned into the gentle wind and strolled along the low tide line. Languid, lapping waves gave solace.

A line of clouds moved steadily toward the north obscuring then revealing the rising moon. Peeking between its covers, the full orb silvered the Atlantic then disappeared leaving dark gray, gurgling waters. A few rays glinted off the ocean surface then bright beams forced through another opening. The waves and sloughs of water reflected the full luminous lunar glow then dulled as clouds again scuttled across the face of the moon. The clouds turned the light show on then off; the waves varied the patterns as they riffled toward shore, broke into quicksilver, then rippled back into the ocean.

While she walked, the wind, clouds, moon, and waves formed a hypnotic mood. In the breaking waves, Melanie discerned pinpoints of phosphorescence created by small marine creatures. Never before had she been a part of such a night.

An unexpected flash of lightning fractured the night sky. Seconds later she heard distant rumbling thunder. The parched land needed rain. Remembering how fast a summer storm built, she hurried to her bicycle. Bright flashes and loud claps surrounded her.

When she approached the cut in the dunes, she noticed a faint orange glow to the south. It was too late for a parting shot from the sun. Her curiosity compelled her to return to the water's edge for a better view.

The source was on the island — fire!

Frantically, she ran to the bicycle and pedaled hard toward Parker House. Energy and panic surged through her body as the wavering flashlight marked her progress toward help. Melanie visualized runaway flames destroying the beautiful maritime forest and its inhabitants. She considered the possibility of an out-of-control fire engulfing the structures of the family compound.

The short ride seemed to take forever.

"Fire!" she screamed again and again as she entered the grounds of Parker House.

Grant, Patrice, Louisa, and Jim poured out of the house.

"Where?"

"At Tail End."

"How big?"

"Just started — walking the beach — not there then there," Melanie gasped, bending over out of breath.

Grant took charge.

"Louisa, take the bike and the flashlight. Wave down the turtle crews on the beach. Have them meet us on Backbone Road.

"Patrice, use the radio-telephone to contact Fred Frazier at Fish and Wildlife. See if he can round up some firefighters.

"Jim, Melanie, and I'll gather flashlights, shovels, axes — anything we can find."

Louisa, equipped with a flashlight, wobbled off on the bike. The cotton skirt covering her ample body flapped about the pedals. On another occasion, all would have laughed at the incongruous sight; tonight they didn't notice.

Patrice hurried into the house to the radio-telephone.

The other three scavenged house, workshop, and barn for useful equipment. Piling all in the island jeep, they tumbled in, too. Grant revved the engine, ground the gears into first, popped the clutch — almost spilling out his passengers. In a splattering of crushed sea shells, they jounced wildly along Crossroad then down Backbone.

"The wind's building and it's from the southeast," Grant shouted over the roar of the engine.

"Whadda we do? We don' have enough people or equipmen' to cut a real fire break," interjected Jim.

"True. Let's see how wide the fire is. Maybe we can contain it near the ponds."

The smell of acrid smoke filled their lungs. The orange glow grew brighter. Their ears picked up crashing sounds from the woods on both sides; their eyes saw shadows darting past.

"There go the deer. The smaller animals will be next. We'll have to watch out for snakes when we're clearing," Grant observed.

Melanie shivered at the idea of the reptiles crawling around the forest floor in the darkness. All the animals, including snakes, were escaping for their lives.

Crackling sounds exploded the heavy air. Falling limbs crashed to the ground. Twisted live oak trunks, dangling moss, and palm fronds silhouetted black against an orange inferno. A wind gust whipped the blaze. New flames flickered through the undergrowth on the left.

They neared the fire; Grant slowed the jeep.

"It's like hell," Grant observed as they clambered out. "Thank God, it hasn't gotten to the tops of the trees yet."

"Wind's buildin'," warned Jim.

"Where do we start?" coughed Melanie. Pungent smoke seared her lungs.

"I saw a trail about a hundred feet back," offered Grant. "Where does it lead, Jim?"

Jim looked through the nightmarish atmosphere, "Dat's an animal trace headin' down to Li'l Pond near de beach."

"That's good," said Grant. "Let's make it the firebreak."

They backed up the jeep and unloaded the equipment.

Behind them came the unmistakable sound of one of the trikes, moving fast. Waving his flashlight, Grant signaled the vehicle to a stop.

"Here's one team," Daniel called. "We walkie-talkied Rebecca and David. They're on their way from the North Arm. They'll approach from the beach on the other trike."

"What can we do?" cried Lana as she cut the small engine.

"Lana, you work the road and the first fifty feet of the trail. We need someone near the vehicles," instructed Grant as he handed out axes, shovels, and flashlights. "Cut any bridge you think the fire can use to jump across the trail — vines, Spanish moss, tree limbs. Then, clear the trail of pine needles, down to the sand. We need as wide a gap as possible. Without heavy equipment, it's going to be hard work.

"Jim, you take the next section of trail. Daniel can handle the next chunk. I'll take the part from there down to the pond. Melanie, you go from the pond to the beach. First, signal the other trike with the flashlight so they can help near the pond. Any questions?"

"Daniel, where be Louisa?" Jim asked.

"She took our walkie-talkie to the Big House. She'll let Rebecca know when help's on the way. She's making sandwiches for us. She says we'll need food for energy."

All nodded. It was time to work.

Lana started clearing a swath through the pine needles and live oak leaves on the road. The other four shouldered their tools; each carried an extra tool for Rebecca and David. They began the trek down the narrow trail. After a minute, Jim stopped. He handed Grant the extra ax then started clearing his section of the break.

The crackling, roaring sound of the encroaching fire filled the night and isolated each firefighter.

Daniel stopped at his assigned area, then Grant at his. Melanie continued with the extra tools. As she skirted the banks of the pond, she heard movement in the water among the nearby reeds — probably snakes or alligators. She shuddered and turned on her flashlight. Two red eyes confirmed the presence of at least one gator. She gulped, then hurried onto her assigned area.

The path narrowed on the seaward side of the pond so she began cutting a wider swath through the knee-high grasses. Progress was slow as she clumsily juggled tools and flashlight. She stopped when she sensed something touch her ankle and foot. Pointing the flashlight beam downward, she saw a black snake slither over her shoe.

Intent on reaching safety, the reptile paid her no attention.

Her composure and determination returned. Shining the light ahead every few feet, she continued slashing toward the dunes. When the growth thinned, she raced for the beach and waved her flashlight. Within a minute, she heard the other trike heading for her.

Switching off the trike, Rebecca asked, "Where are the others?"

"Creating a firebreak along a raccoon trail from here to Backbone. We need help in the thickest part on the other side of the pond," Melanie responded.

"Let's go!" shouted the ever-energetic David, ready for his first firefighting experience.

Using the precious tools, the three widened Melanie's hurried path. All pressed toward the forest area where the fire raged. Chopping, swinging, and shoveling, they steadily moved inland along the trail. Smoke burned their eyes and lungs.

When they worked their way into a small open area Rebecca called over her shoulder, "Melanie, you finish this area. David and I'll head for the others. It looks worse there."

"Fine," Melanie responded with an enthusiasm she didn't feel. Their departure meant, once again, she faced this raging nightmare in an isolated, lonely spot.

She set to work, throwing dead limbs, hacking vines, and blocking any other pathways for the flames. She felt the redness deepen, the heat intensify, the smoke thicken. A bolt of lightning followed by a deep clap of thunder caused her to look overhead. To her left, the fire had jumped to the top of a stand of pines. Trees burned like torches popping and roaring in the night's din. Branches wrapped in fire plunged from the crowns.

Melanie faced the frightening thought of being trapped by the fire. She was torn between saving herself and saving her friend, the island. Her hands ached from the relentless, unaccustomed use of the tools. The rapidly increasing heat caused sweat to pour from every pore. Each breath came harder and harder.

An orange glow enveloped her. Panic invaded her mind. She reversed her inland direction and hurried toward the beach. She must escape. Melanie stumbled through pockets of smoke and air, light and shadow, heat and coolness, deafening noise and deadly calm.

A loud crack sounded as if a heavy creature had stepped on a dry branch. She sensed movement. Sharp pain shot through her head before blackness engulfed her.

Grant discerned a figure working its way up the trail toward him.

"We can't stop it," came an exhausted voice.

Recognizing the smoke-smudged, sweat-runneled face of David, Grant sighed, "I'm afraid you're right. Where are Rebecca and Melanie?"

David motioned down the path, "That way. Where do we go from here?"

"I'll gather Melanie and Rebecca to the beach. You take off inland. Find Daniel, Jim, and Lana near the trike and jeep. Fall back to the hunting trail. Let's try to make another cut there. Don't let anyone get trapped."

"Got it!"

Moving down the trail, Grant reckoned the widened path would slow the fire's advance. The rumbling in the sky promised rain. He moved slowly, stamping out small flame patches where they had jumped the break. He noticed a brighter area ahead — too late. The fire had totally breached the firebreak.

Grant faced the decision of falling back or detouring around the hot spot. He considered Rebecca and Melanie. He chose the detour.

The heat became unbearable as Grant cut close to the raging fire. A fear of becoming disoriented and going in circles pounded in his brain.

He dodged a falling limb. When a flaming vine swung toward his face, he dived to the side.

Crawling on the ground, the cooler air revived him. An occasional unmistakable scent of sea air told him either the wind had shifted or he was around the worst part.

He saw the pond to his right. The fire had encircled part of the pond but was thwarted by the small body of water. Crouching close to the ground and breathing the fresher air, Grant continued his advance below the heavy smoke. Near the dunes, he glimpsed a figure and headed straight for it.

"Becca," he called when he got close enough to recognize her form. "Where's Melanie?"

"I haven't seen her. I thought she'd be by the trike, but she's not."

"MEL-A-NIE!" Grant shouted into the fire.

There was no human response to be heard above the noise of the blaze.

"Did you come down the trail?" he asked.

"Yes. The fire started to break over me, so I retreated down the path. If she were still fighting, I would have passed her. Maybe she's out on the beach."

"You check up and down the dunes. If you don't find her, take the trike north and join the others. They're regrouping to make another cut at the hunting trail. I'll follow the animal trace as far as I can."

The two parted. Grant returned to the wildfire he had escaped. Using his flashlight to augment the flickering now-red then-orange illumination, he scanned both sides of the trace. While he skirted the pond, the air filled with hot smoke. He struggled to keep going.

Passing a small depression, his flashlight revealed a dark shape — a body. He knelt down. It was Melanie. He bent closer and listened for her breath. She was breathing though unconscious.

Grant struggled to pick up Melanie's limp body, then, to carry her through the conflagration. Her dead weight made his already sore muscles scream; the soft sands shifted under his shuffling feet. He stumbled, caught his footing, and pressed onward. He was exhausted but determined to reach the protection of the dunes.

Placing his load down gently on the sandy slope, he surveyed her condition by flashlight. Smoke-blackened face, tangled hair, filthy clothes. Her chest rose and fell. She was alive. He relaxed and fell beside her.

Grant felt a splash of warm, wet rain on his upturned face. There was lightning and thunder over their heads then gusts of rain. Since there was no protection except the sand dune, he removed his shirt to shield their faces from the onslaught.

Melanie stirred.

Over the pounding of the rain stressed by sporadic thunder claps, Grant heard the hiss of steam. Nature would finish the job the handful of humans had begun.

Again, Melanie moved. With a shiver, she curled against Grant's bare chest. He put his arms around her and positioned his body to protect her from the deluge. He became acutely aware of her hair, face, and breath against his neck. She snuggled closer. Their two bodies became a tight refuge from the elements.

He heard Melanie moan. "Gre... Grant?" she inquired softly as she looked into his eyes.

"Everything's all right," he soothed her. "We're out of danger."

They squeezed each other in reassurance.

Minutes passed and the hug became an embrace. When Melanie tilted her head, their lips met. The gentle kiss became passionate, then, gentle again. Each caressed the other while the warm rain continued to fall.

Passion grew in the two lying so close together. Comforting strokes became sensuous. Melanie sensed his physical strength. Grant found his hands reaching for her breasts. Melanie felt herself rising on a tide of desire. Half-awake, she acted on instinct, swept by a current she could not control.

Each responded to the other's touches. He unbuttoned and unzipped her jeans, struggling to remove the clinging wet fabric. He stroked the silky smooth flesh of her abdomen and inner thighs. With trembling hands, she unfastened his pants, pushing them down and off his buttocks. Sighing, she explored the tautness, the hardness of his body. She urged him on top of her and between her parted legs. Hugging him tightly, almost desperately, she stroked his back. Sliding his hand under her shirt, he found her breast, pushed aside the thin material of the bra. He clutched the warm, moist mound and stroked the hard nipple. Instinctively, she guided Grant into the fiery heat of her inflamed body. Oblivious to the continuous pelts of the rain, their rhythms built. With an unleashed savageness, they coupled in the sand, celebrating their aliveness

The rain continued unabated for an hour before it tapered to a drizzle. Only when they heard the sound of a returning trike, did the two thoroughly soaked and sated firefighters pull on their wet clothes and venture toward the beach.

* * *

2:00 p.m., Sunday, June 26, 1988

The afternoon sun cut through the gray smoke cloud wisping around the south end of the island. Early that morning, Fred Frazier had arrived with several other men; they were stamping out isolated hot spots. Grant and Melanie took the jeep to check on their progress; both had eaten, bathed, and slept.

The ride south toward the crew had been awkwardly absent of conversation until Melanie asked, "How much damage did the fire cause?"

"I suspect several acres got scorched. You're lucky. The storm saved the island," responded Grant in a matter-of-fact tone.

Melanie observed the drawn, played-out features of his face and realized the extent of his exhaustion. He had taken control, given his all last night to save the island, its inhabitants, and his research.

What did he feel about their sexual encounter the night before? Their reaching out to one another now blurred with other memories of the frightening night. It had happened, hadn't it? Yes, she knew it had. The physical act with Grant had come naturally. They had faced death and found release from its grip in each other's arms.

As far as Melanie was concerned, she felt comfortable about their lovemaking. She was bothered only by the fact that she had made love to Grant without any romantic preliminaries. Grant was an attractive man. He had exhibited concern for her welfare ever since her arrival on the island. A mutual respect had developed. He was more sensitive yet less concerned with surface appearances than most men she had known. She enjoyed being around him, his natural curiosity, his approach to life. After their unexpected interlude the night before, now she hoped for an even deeper relationship. She felt that desire did not dishonor Greg's memory.

When they neared the devastated area, she viewed the blackened tree trunks sticking straight up into the air, giving off smoke like giant cigars. Smoldering clumps of brush oozed noxious vapors. Glowing embers dotted the gutted landscape.

The jeep slowed and turned toward a couple of soot-covered men, "G'day, Fred. How's it going?" inquired Grant.

"We've about got her whupped, you lazy Aussie," grinned the big man with his beer belly protruding from his fatigues. "But, I shore do like the way ya'll time thunderstorms."

"No argument there," Grant rejoined. "Where do you suppose it started?"

"What do you say we go have ourselves a look-see?"

"Hop in."

"Afternoon, ma'am," Fred touched his cap, acknowledging Melanie's presence.

"Good afternoon, Mr. Frazier. Thank you for helping us," Melanie responded.

"You may not be so thankful when the state sends you the bill."

"I'm thankful — for the storm and for your help," she assured him.

"The wind was from the southeast so let's head south on Backbone," suggested Grant.

The blackened area turned toward the sea. Melanie pointed, "I think it started over there and swept this way."

"Right you are, dearie," chimed Fred. "Let's walk, if ya'll are up to it."

The trio cut along the edge of the burned undergrowth. Soon they reached the remains of an ancient dune covered with the charred trunks of slash pine. From the small hill they observed the forest sweeping inland and marsh grasses fanning toward the ocean. Apparently the blaze had started atop the dune, then the prevailing wind had carried it rapidly into the dry woods.

"It must have been a lightning strike. One of these pine trees could have acted as a rod," commented Grant.

"Yep. This here little rise was jus' perfec' to attract a bolt," agreed Fred.

Looking about, Melanie queried, "What about the bent reeds over there? They look as if someone made their way from the beach to this dune."

"Probably an animal path, Melanie," responded Grant.

Suddenly, Grant's analytical side irritated her.

"And, I was knocked unconscious by a limb, right?"

"Of course, what else?" Grant asked in amazement, not understanding her sarcasm.

"I know all this is circumstantial. But, seeing this path, sensing someone, being hit over the head — something's not adding up," puzzled Melanie.

"Pardon me, but I reckon everyone's had a tough twenty-four hours. Sometimes, imagination gets kinda wild. That trail was made by an animal. You, missy, were knocked unconscious by a branch falling from a tree. The explanations are simple. There's nothing foul going on." A thick stream of tobacco juice shot from his mouth, landing in the damp sand of the dune. "We'll all think better in a day or two," soothed Fred in his drawl. "It won't be long before you'll be laughing at your hallucinations. Isn't that right, missy?" Looking her in the eye, he spat again.

Melanie felt furious. This man — these two men — were placating her like a hysterical schoolgirl. How had she even considered Grant as a lover? Any man, who would not defend her from the likes of a beastly man such as Fred Frazier, didn't deserve her love. And, if this obnoxious Georgia-cracker SOB with his bloated belly and ego... if he... if he calls me girlie or dearie or missy one more time, I'll... I'll.... Melanie stalked off, fuming at their insensitivity and better-than-thou attitude.

Forcing calm on herself, she hunted evidence to support her theory. As she searched, she realized she was looking for something left behind by an arsonist and a murderer. No wonder the men had reacted as they did. The idea did sound irrational. Yet....

The three returned to the jeep and drove to Parker House. Fred and Grant compared notes in the front while Melanie sat in the back. She analyzed the turn of events.

* * *

1:30 p.m., Monday, June 27, 1988

Adam was delighted with the message left with his answering service. That morning, Melanie had called to request that he come to the island as soon as possible. He cleared his calendar for the afternoon since the Caretta heiress was a high business priority — higher than any other priority. Too, to his surprise, he had discovered that he enjoyed her company. He was beginning to consider Melanie as more than just a way to gain control of Caretta. "Be careful, Adam! Don't let an attractive woman blind you from your true goals."

An agitated Melanie met him at the dock.

"I'm so glad you could come, Adam. Did you hear about the fire?"

"Fire? No! When?"

"Two nights ago. It started on the south end. We tried to control it, but it was so intense. Thank goodness, the thunderstorm saved the island from disaster."

"Are you OK?"

"Tired. But, I'm fine," Melanie tried to smile.

"Did anyone get hurt?"

"No," Melanie replied with hesitation, "maybe a few of the animals." She paused then asked, "Would you care to drive down and take a look?"

"Of course." Adam sensed something was bothering Melanie other than the fire. He waited for her to talk.

The ride south passed in silence. The scorched forest smelled of burnt wood and ash. Before Melanie stopped the jeep, they circled to a higher spot where the sea breeze made breathing easier.

"So, do you want to tell me what's troubling you?" Adam asked. "It must be more than what we're seeing."

"I'm afraid it may sound crazy."

"Try me. I'll give you my honest opinion."

"First, this dead body washed ashore a month ago. When it occurred, it appeared to be an unfortunate accident. But, now, I wonder. The body was whisked away, perhaps too conveniently."

"Who was responsible for that?"

"Fred Frazier. He happened to be out here. So, he said he'd take care of it."

"Fred's a wildlife officer. What's he doing handling drownings?"

"He says he's a deputy of the sheriff. And, there's more," Melanie warned Adam. "The researchers have been watching a shrimp boat anchor in the channel at unusual times. I'm guessing it's using the rumrunners' hideaway. Now, the fire and the blow."

"Blow?"

"I was knocked unconscious while cutting a fire break. If Grant hadn't found me, I wouldn't be here talking to you. Yesterday, when Grant, Fred, and I were looking for the origin of the fire, I found a path of bent marsh reeds. It leads to the dune where the fire started."

"So you think someone set the fire?"

"And, knocked me out. I know it sounds paranoid — at least, Grant and Fred thought so. But, there have been too many strange happenings this past month."

"What's important is that you made it through a close call. You say Grant found you, then, he and Fred believed you were imagining the cause?"

"Yes."

"So, what's the official cause listed for the fire?"

"Lightning strike, according to Fred," sighed Melanie.

Adam considered the implications, then asked, "Are Fred and Grant close friends?"

"I doubt it. They're so different from one another."

"Opposites come together, if they find mutual payoffs. You must examine who can benefit from your death or departure from the island."

"Adam, what a scary thought!" Melanie paused for a moment. "But, I've got to consider it. Can you stay a while?"

"No, I wish I could. But, I need to return to The Hammock," he replied regretfully.

While she drove Adam to the dock, she explored the shadowy ideas now out in the open. If she included the burglary of her co-op in New York, a lot had happened in a short time. Then, if the automobile wreck were not an accident, as the NYPD detective had asked.... Did she want to even consider that possibility? Was she becoming paranoid here on the island?

It was nice to have Adam here beside her. At least, he seriously considered her concerns, unlike the blowhard Fred and analytical Grant. Adam wasn't Greg. But, he was here, not in New York like Ashley. Adam was listening to her suspicions and helping her express her needs — obviously something Grant couldn't do. Adam's presence helped her feel less alone, less crazed.

When Adam prepared to board his boat, she caught his arm and asked, "Adam, tell me: Why are you spending all this time with me?"

He smiled broadly, "I think that answer is obvious."

They sensed Grant step onto the dock. He called, "Melanie, Patrice needs you at the house."

The two men watched Melanie leave in the jeep. As soon as she was out of earshot, Grant turned to Adam and challenged, "What are you doing here, Gardner?"

Adam took his hand off the boat starter and responded, "And, what business is it of yours, Yeats?"

"I don't like opportunistic bastards who take advantage of lonely, vulnerable women."

"Look, Aussie, at least I'm here for her. She called me. And, I listened to her — that's more than I can say for you. Now, if you'll excuse me, some of us have important work to do."

With that retort, Adam hit the starter and left Grant standing on the dock. Speechless, Grant wondered: "Is that con-artist correct? Does Melanie feel I'm not listening — that she can't talk to me?"

CHAPTER 14

Thursday, June 30, 1988

After the fire, Melanie roamed the island and noticed changes brought by the rain. Except for the burn area, nature had cast a green net over the land and the surrounding marshes. Transfigured from flat, crisp death to erect, lush life, the resurrection ferns carpeted outstretched live oak limbs. The tree ferns contrasted with the pink lichens patchworked on branches and trunks. New growth sprouted brave and bright near the fire-scorched woods.

Restorative processes began among the island inhabitants, too. A deer grazed contentedly on new grass. Ducks skittered on a full pond. A mud-slick mink, full of food, slipped through tall marsh grasses. Even the wild horses displayed a change — enjoying carefree gallops through the interdune meadow and in the surf.

The contrast caused Melanie to examine her personal concerns. Had someone wanted her to die during the forest fire or was the incident meant to be a warning? Did the mysterious shrimp boat have any connection with the dead sailor or the baffling fire? Had lightning caused the fire? What about the knotted rope? Had a branch fallen on her? Was she being irrational? Why was she not terrified? Actually, Melanie was beginning to feel indignant. Again, her stubbornness took hold of her emotions — maybe that streak was inherited along with sarcasm, she grimaced. As the fourth of July approached, Melanie worked hard to suppress all paranoia.

Patrice had suggested a clambake on the beach as a thank-you to the volunteer firefighters as well as a celebration of the holiday. At first, Melanie was unexcited. When she talked to others, however, she found them pleased with the idea. Even though it meant extra work for them, Louisa and Jim approved. Rebecca and her crew looked at it as a break from their tiring routine. Using his Australian lingo, Grant called it a barbie.

The advance preparations began. They planned the menu: clams, corn-on-the-cob, sweet potatoes, slaw, hush puppies, iced tea, and beer. The loggerhead researchers debated the purchase of fireworks since the bright flashes of light disturbed nesting turtles. Supplies were brought from the mainland. Louisa made her spicy, vinegary slaw.

* * *

4:00 p.m., Monday, July 4, 1988

Everyone gathered in the Parker House kitchen to load food into the jeep and trikes. They caravanned to the gazebo, overlooking the beach. Melanie, Grant, and the researchers were dressed in shorts, T-shirts, and old sneakers for raking the clams. Patrice wore ladylike slacks while Louisa wore one of her voluminous cotton dresses and Jim, his usual blue-cotton work pants and shirt. Fred Frazier had foregone his camouflage "uniform" for Bermuda shorts and an incongruous T-shirt proclaiming him to be a "Party Animal."

A lot of good-natured joking took place as everyone unloaded the vehicles. The firemen worked on starting a campfire while the women carried the food into the gazebo.

With the fire started, Jim instructed everyone on the fine art of clam raking: "You dig with dis here rake and put de clams in dis here pail." He divided the group into partners and set them off, up and down the wide, hot beach. Meanwhile, he settled down in the shade of the gazebo to keep an eye on the fire.

While the main course was being captured, Louisa and Patrice started preparing the foil-wrapped ears of corn and sweet potatoes for the campfire. The vegetables were buttered and seasoned with lots of black pepper.

Paired with Lana, Melanie walked in the hot sun along the expanse of wet sand and looked for telltale air bubbles. She asked, "Have you seen anything suspicious lately?"

"You mean, like the shrimp boat without lights or the helicopter with the searchlight?"

"Exactly," Melanie chuckled.

"By the way, Daniel told me you were right about the helicopter. It belongs to the Coast Guard. When we saw it that night, it was searching for a missing boat or, you know, the remains of a missing boat."

"That makes sense. What does he think about the shrimp boat?"

"He wonders about it, too. It just anchors there."

"Still?"

"Yeah."

"Hmm..., I see."

"Look at all these air bubbles. Let's dig here," pointed Lana.

After a half-hour, the sandy and sweaty clammers began returning to the gazebo with pails full of clams.

"Whew! Am I thirsty!" observed David. The others voiced similar groans, and the first gallons of iced tea and cold beer disappeared.

Refreshed, they rinsed mud off the clam shells in the surf. Jim supervised how much water to leave in each metal pail. Carefully, he placed the pails on a grate that he had positioned over the fire.

All gathered to watch the shells steam open.

Melanie cleared her throat and spoke, "I guess this is a good time as any for a speech."

"Aw right, everybody, take a seat and listen up. The little lady's got something to say," gregarious Fred's voice boomed over the group.

Melanie glared at Fred, disliking that he referred to her as "little lady." She tried not to show her irritation to the others as they settled down. She continued, "I want to thank each of you for fighting the fire last week. You helped save the island."

The self-proclaimed party animal emitted a series of whoops.

Melanie paused a moment, laughed, and shook her head. Then, she continued in a lighter tone of voice, "So, Patrice and I want you to eat all you can eat and..., uh, to have fun. Happy Independence Day, everyone!"

Rejoining the comfort of the seated group, Melanie realized, once again, she would never be an orator. She had hoped her speech would say more. To her, it had sounded too formal, too contrived. She had wanted to say something heartfelt to these volunteer firefighters.

More thanks and good wishes passed over the fire before they pulled the pails and foil-wrapped mounds of food from the coals. The feast was ready.

Pulling a clam from its shell and dipping it in melted butter, Lana tasted the succulent morsel. "Yummo! Clams are so tender this way, not leathery like those overcooked, fried guys."

"The taste is incomparable," agreed Patrice. "However, clambake is a misnomer when we've steamed open their shells."

Grant interjected, "Jolly good! This is the first time I've had sweet potatoes this way — sliced with onions, butter, and black pepper. Then, wrapped in foil and baked in the fire coals."

"Sea islan' cookin' — jus' sea islan' cookin'," Louisa acknowledged all the compliments.

Turning aside to Jim, Melanie commented, "Thanks for all your help today, Jim. Everything has turned out fine."

"My pleasure, Miz Mellie."

"By the way, have you found out anything about that knotted rope?"

"Nothin' yet," Jim replied.

"Knotted rope? Like in the hoodoo you told us about, Jim?" asked the within-earshot Grant.

Jim nodded his grizzled head.

"Where did you find the rope, Melanie?" questioned Grant.

"Under the back steps," she replied. Directing her gaze at Grant, she added, "It makes me wonder if someone is trying to harm me."

Grant struggled for a response.

Disappointed, Melanie turned away.

"Wow!" breathed David. "Fires, knotted ropes, hoodoo, rumrunners, and hideaways sure keep this place exciting!"

* * *

10:00 p.m., Tuesday, July 5, 1988

The turn of the conversation at the clambake caused Melanie's sublimated suspicions to resurface. This time, however, she resolved to do more than sit and wait for something else to happen. She decided to take action.

Sensing the hideaway played a part in the freakish events unfolding on the island, she decided to keep watch there during the night. Surreptitiously, she made her plans and packed a bag containing food, flashlight, and binoculars. She wanted no one to suspect her observation of the hideaway.

Melanie announced to Patrice, "I'm going paddling and stargazing tonight."

"I guess you're safe enough around the island. But, do me a favor and take this whistle, in case you need help. It's easy to get lost in the marsh."

Melanie accepted the whistle, "I'll be fine. But, I appreciate your concern. No need to wait up for me though."

As she added the Patrice-requested whistle to her bag, Melanie was amused at the mothering instinct of her aunt. Though a recluse by choice, Patrice possessed the soul of a caring person, usually hidden under the cloak of spinsterhood. Patrice's journey into her chosen role might prove interesting to trace.

Tonight, though, Melanie intended to play Nancy Drew. By herself, she loaded and launched the canoe. Stroking the water smoothly and quietly, she guided the canoe north along the tidal creek toward the hammock concealing the hideaway. She elected not to take the shortcut channel. Instead, by striking an outside passage, she remained hidden from anyone using the shelter. She beached the canoe and dragged the aluminum craft behind a clump of small saw palmettos.

Taking her bag, she walked to the highest point where she viewed both the channel and the inlet that created the north end of Caretta. From this vantage point, she saw the spot where the turtle patrols stopped for breaks, the small creek that split the hammock from the island, and the larger stream that meandered through the marsh joining the Wilmington River near the mainland. In the distance, the Atlantic appeared calm and quiet.

Melanie spotted the suspicious, dark, shrimp boat anchored in the large creek. She pulled out her binoculars and watched. She detected no sound or movement. The craft appeared abandoned or its crew slept.

She sat and watched. Minutes passed, but the scene remained the same. To stay awake, she identified constellations and looked for shooting stars. The southern sky no longer caused her to feel as if the earth had tipped on its axis; she felt at home under Caretta's stars — so nice after those years of city-living where the stars were rarely distinguishable.

Melanie was devouring the last of an apple when she heard the sound of a motor in the distance. It took several seconds before she isolated the source. When it grew louder, she identified the noise as a trike. Watching the beach, she made out the vehicle when it pulled into view and stopped. The lack of a moon kept visual details hidden. Soon, the engine cut off and she heard the voices of the two turtlers.

"Doesn't a night like this put you in a romantic mood?" a male voice floated over the water.

"Sorry, David. That line isn't going to work either."

Melanie chuckled as she heard Lana's unmistakable voice.

"It's only a matter of time before you appreciate what I'm offering," he countered.

"Maybe in a million years," Lana laughed.

"Well, what do you say if we fool our fearless leaders?"

"What do you have in mind?"

"Let's make some turtle tracks leading out of the surf to a mound of reeds at the high tide mark. Then, we'll hide and see how long it takes them to figure it out."

"I don't know..."

"What have we got to lose? Of course, if you prefer we could hang around here and make-out."

"OK, David. Let's go."

Melanie experienced a twinge of guilt at playing the role of eaves-dropper, but sound did carry on the water in the still night air. Soon Melanie heard the clatter of the trike fade away in the distance. At that moment, another male voice became audible.

"They're gone. Let's move."

Turning her attention to the dark boat, she strained to see a small dinghy inching away from the larger craft. The soft whine of an electric trolling motor and a tiny white wake were the only clues to its movement toward her position. She was sure the target of this secret mission was the rumrunners' hideaway. Quietly, she edged from her observation point and quickly moved toward the lean-to. She found a hiding place close enough for listening but obscured in the bamboo.

Minutes passed. The only audible sounds were the rasps of crickets and bellows of bull frogs. She waited for the intruders. Crack! Adrenaline pumping, Melanie jumped and turned her head. She stared into the black, but nothing had changed. Then, a scrape grated against the sand and mud. Though distant, she identified it as the noise of the dinghy's bow. Hollow footsteps resounded as the boat's occupants climbed from the boat to the shore.

Presently she sensed two people moving up the path. A strand of light alerted her that they had entered the shelter.

"The island's too damn crowded! I don't like so many people so close!"

"Com'on, stop your bellyaching. We've got a cargo that pays a hell of a lot better than fish. So, we've gotta take bigger risks."

"Yeah, it's high time we do something about all those people."

"Look, we've talked about all this before. The turtle crew comes every summer. And, we know how to predict them."

"What about that boat mark here a couple of weeks ago and those footprints? Someone's been here. I bet it's that nosy heiress."

"Don't you worry about her. You just do your job."

Cramped, Melanie shifted her weight from one foot to the other. The calf of her leg brushed a dry palmetto frond and caused it to rattle.

"Shhh..., did you hear something?"

Melanie heard a shuffle and then a flashlight beam scanned the bushes around her. She held her breath. Tiny beads of sweat popped out all over her skin; her heart pounded as if it were going to break through her chest. The bright ray of light passed back and forth above her head. After an interminable minute, it clicked off.

"You really gotta get a grip on your nerves."

"Shaddup. Let's get outta here."

The figures returned to the creek.

Shortly, Melanie heard the electric motor's whine. As the night noise returned to normal sounds, she rose cautiously from her hiding place. She backtracked to her earlier vantage point and watched the two forms tie the small dinghy to the large shrimp boat. She heard the engines fire. With a sigh of relief, she watched the boat move away. Soon, it was cloaked in a blanket of darkness.

Curiosity replaced her relief. Melanie walked into the hideaway to investigate. Inside, she snapped on her flashlight and splayed it around the interior. The table or sleeping platform, palmetto stump stools, the overhead fishing gear.... The only change seemed to be the fresh footprints. What was the key — something gone, something added? The interior seemed the same as she recalled from her daylight trip. Nothing appeared altered in the stark interior. Yet, the voices had talked about risk and valuable cargo.

A thunk on the roof broke the quiet. Melanie jumped. She clicked off the flashlight and hugged the side of the lean-to. Where could she hide? Scrabbling noises came through the thatch. Suddenly, a "whoo-whoo" screeched over her head. With relief, Melanie realized this intruder was a Great Horned Owl.

Turning on her light again, she examined more closely the footprints around the stumps. She stood on one stump and touched the nets. Nothing was wet. There was no indication of the shrimpers' activities. What were they doing here? What was she missing?

Finally, Melanie returned to the canoe with no tangible evidence but certain knowledge that a dangerous puzzle was forming: remote hideouts, risky cargo, set fires, threats on her life and, possibly, on others.

* * *

2:00 p.m., Wednesday, July 6, 1988

Grant hummed softly while he recorded the measurements of his solar collector. The night of the fire had revealed new aspects of the mistress of Caretta. He remembered her willingness to get dirty and work as hard as anyone to combat the blaze. Also, he relished their passion later in the dunes. He doubted whether the impetus to make love with him was as strong under everyday circumstances, especially when there was someone as handsome as Adam Gardner available. Too, he wondered, what did Melanie want from him? Karen had taught him about hidden agendas.

"So, there you are."

Startled, Grant turned to see Melanie watching him with hands on her hips.

"Melanie! You surprised me."

"I came to see if you're avoiding me." Melanie had missed their times together the past two weeks. Except for the clambake, Grant had immersed himself in his lab.

"Why would I do that? You know I enjoy your company."

"That's good to hear." Melanie paused. She wanted Grant to say more — about her, about them. How could she get beyond his fact-finding, logical demeanor? She stammered, "I thought you considered me someone with an overactive imagination."

"No, not at all."

"Good, because I want to check out something with you. Do you know where the rumrunners' hideaway is located?"

"Rumrunners?"

"A Prohibition term — for bootleggers."

"And, they had a hideaway around here?"

"Yes. It's a thatched lean-to."

Grant watched her curiously, "Right. That one out on the hammock near the top of the island?"

Melanie nodded and asked, "Have you noticed anything suspicious there? Like someone using it regularly?"

Grant stared at her, "No, I haven't, but Jim probably knows more than I do. You think there's something mysterious happening there?"

Melanie bristled at his tone but forged ahead, "I noticed it's been refurbished — new thatching, a replaced brace, a couple of stools, and fishing gear."

"Maybe Jim should put up a 'No Trespassing' sign and alert Fred."

"That's not what I mean. I'm looking for an explanation."

"To what?"

"I watched a dinghy motor ashore from that shrimp boat running without its lights. Two men came to the hideaway. I heard them talk about the risk of so many people on the island and their cargo being more valuable than fish."

"On the surface that does sound strange. But, we might figure out a logical explanation for it."

"Are you suggesting that I'm being illogical and that it's normal for two unidentified men to sneak around our property after dark?"

Grant, trying to use his most soothing voice, replied, "All I'm saying is: We must treat this situation like any other problem and search for a solution."

Melanie sensed her patience reach an end. His scientific approach with its apparent lack of excitement or interest bothered her. "Is there always a rational explanation for every act? What about us the night of the fire?"

"Oh, come on, Melanie. You know better than that."

"Do I?"

"We've established a good relationship. That evening presented a natural release."

"Is that all? A natural release? Well, I must say, Grant, you do put things in a pragmatic light," Melanie snapped as she stalked away.

Grant watched her departure and mentally reviewed the conversation. He concluded that he created more turbulence when he tried to avoid it.

Melanie cursed herself for letting her emotions control the last interchange. Grant could be so unreachable. During those moments, she needed more than what he offered. How she missed Greg!

When she walked into the dim coolness of the library, she realized she had not seen Ali Cat today. His pattern consisted of an early morning prowl around the grounds then a quick return to her side and the shade. Ali Cat was an independent but predictable animal. Where was he when she needed someone to stroke?

Checking with the others in the house, she discovered no one else had seen the cat. Her concern was higher than it would have been a few weeks ago. Too many other odd happenings had occurred.

CHAPTER 15

8:30 p.m., Friday, July 8, 1988

High offshore winds forced the tides higher than usual, making impossible any trike trips through Palmhenge. This evening, researchers patrolled on foot to North Arm; Lana and Melanie drew the first lot. By the light of the full moon, they criss-crossed the narrowing border of sand as they checked for signs of the gigantic loggerheads.

It was a relief to walk and talk instead of drive the trike with its incessant roar. While they trudged through the sand, Melanie questioned Lana about her goals and dreams. What were her personal expectations for the summer, for the Loggerhead Project, for college, for her career?

"You know, I had crazy ideas about this summer," Lana confided. "I imagined we researchers would engage in philosophical discussions about ecology, science — you know, life. And, I thought I would do a lot of drawing. Instead, we work, sleep, eat, and play pranks. Patrolling this beach from sunset to sunrise — almost nine hours a night, as you know — is hard work. We fall into bed at dawn. Then, it's too hot to sleep after eleven in the morning. We shower. We eat lunch. After we clean up the kitchen, we wash clothes, write home, and update our logs. Then, it's time to cook, or cleanup, and go to work again."

"Is this the first time you've ever cooked?"

"Yeah, Mom always did the cooking at home. At school, there was the cafeteria. All I ever had to do was get to the table and either eat or complain."

"Complain?" inquired Melanie.

"Yeah, you know. 'Yuck, mashed potatoes again!'" as she whined, drawling out the 'again' then she switched to a consternated voice and yelled, "Garlic?" Lana giggled. "I never knew I had it so good."

"How about your drawing?"

"I'm working on several pen and inks of the loggerheads for Rebecca to use in the final report. Rebecca's a good administrator. Sometimes, I know, she feels like she's a baby-sitter out here. But, we have been able to sneak away and sunbathe together."

"In the nude?"

"Shhh, one of the boys might hear you. It's hard enough shaking them as it is."

Melanie laughed. "What kind of jokes do you play on each another?"

"You know, things like short-sheeting someone's bed or stacking extra rolls of toilet tissue so they'll fall when the bathroom door opens all the way, serving formaldehyde-preserved hatchlings for dinner... stuff like that."

"Creating turtle tracks?"

"Yeah. Did you hear about that one? Rebecca and Daniel fell for it — hook, line, and sinker! It took them an hour to figure out it wasn't a turtle," Lana hooted.

"Speaking of pranks, have you seen Ali Cat?"

Lana was quiet for a moment as she mulled over the day. "No, not today. Why?"

"He's been gone all day — unusual for him."

Approaching Palmhenge, a wind whipped out of the northeast. Lana and Melanie shrugged into their jackets that had been tied loosely around their waists. Menacing, dark clouds moved across the sky and obliterated the array of stars as well as the rays of the moon.

The sudden darkness made it difficult to get through Palmhenge's tree trunks and root systems, often hidden in the waves of the rising tide. They tried walking above the high tide mark. The woods made that way even darker and tougher. Occasionally, one of them tripped over a root or sank knee-deep into reeds and pine needles. They resorted to turning on their flashlights in the darkest places, hoping no turtle would notice them, as they attempted to return to base, where Crossroad hit the beach.

A harsh cry rang in their ears. Looking up, they saw a silhouetted mass at the top of a dead palm.

"An osprey," Lana observed. "She's not pleased at us invading her territory. We'd better keep moving."

As they stumbled forward, Melanie spoke, "This must be what's called a 'Northeaster,' Lana. Look how high the tide is coming in — it's washing over the reeds. The wind's growing stronger and the temperature's dropping fast."

"Oh, no! It's going to be impossible to stay dry. Look how the waves are smashing against these roots," Lana wailed.

Even as she spoke, a wave dashed their feet with cold seawater and raindrops began to fall. Lana and Melanie pulled the strings tightening the hoods of their jackets about their faces.

Melanie motioned Lana to follow her to the edge of the woods. She turned on her flashlight to find a way to a nearby large live oak. They huddled against the big trunk; the tree sheltered them from the driving wind and rain.

The rain soaked through their jeans and sneakers. The cold wetness made them shiver. They jack-knifed their legs against their chests and sat close together.

"Let's talk about how hot it's been. Maybe that'll keep us warm," suggested Melanie.

"Yeah, I think, I'm adjusting to the heat. I stay inside working on the log or stuff like that until about four in the afternoon. It stays oppressive until then. That's when Rebecca and I swim or sunbathe. How about you?"

"It's not as big a change as you'd guess. You'd be amazed at how hot the pavement gets in New York City in the summer. There, everybody tries to stay in air-conditioned comfort. Now, living here without air conditioning has been different, to say the least — thank goodness for the paddle fans and the screen porch. Even the basic construction of Parker House allows air movement." Melanie rubbed her hands to stay warm and continued, "My biggest adjustment to the island has been learning to live without electricity after the generator turns off at nine."

"Yeah, we use kerosene lamps for reading on our nights off."

"Same here. My schedule, except for my Friday night expedition with you researchers, follows the sun more and more. I race nightfall to accomplish my lists of daily tasks. I'm learning to be realistic about what I can do in one day before 'lights out.'"

"Doesn't going out with us one night a week affect you?"

Melanie paused, wondering how much to share with the ebullient teenager. "It's had a euphoric effect. It may be because of the coma, then, the never-ending depression I experienced after the car accident. Anyway, the change feels good."

"Has it been very hard to learn to live without your family?" Lana asked quietly.

"Yes," Melanie replied slowly. "I was miserable in my co-op, that's an apartment I own in the city. Every object reminded me of my husband and son. That's why I came to Caretta. There are fewer reminders on the island since I'd never spent much time here with them, and it's been years since I had spent summers here with my parents and brother. It was difficult to leave New York because of my brother. The decision seemed healthful, however, so I stuck to it."

"To me, you handle everything so well. You're not ignoring your feelings. You're giving yourself the time it takes to recover from the deaths of people who meant a lot to you."

"I'm trying, Lana, and I've been getting lots of help."

"Melanie, may I ask you something?" the teenager continued.

"Sure," Melanie replied. She liked Lana and welcomed her confidences.

"I'm facing a situation I never even considered before now. I'm finding myself attracted to Daniel. He's such a likable guy. But, he's black and I'm white. And, our society — at least my family and friends — frown on black-white relationships. Out here, it seems so superficial, so judgmental. If anyone made the effort to know Daniel, he or she would like him, too."

Melanie had noticed Lana and Daniel together on occasion. Until this moment, however, she had not considered a budding romance. "Of course, anyone who knows Daniel likes him. But, you've run into that age-old problem: People judge other people by their skin color." Melanie paused and analyzed the situation. Lana seemed mature so Melanie asked, "What do you want to do about it?"

"I want to feel free to give myself time to get to know Daniel. You know, we're pretty removed from society here. It's an ideal place to find out how I feel about him and about prejudice, in general."

"That's sounds fine and, I think, you've touched on another part of your problem, Lana," Melanie continued gently.

"What do you mean?"

"You're young — your sexual hormones are at their peak. You're on a small island — a little like paradise — with only a few other people your age."

"Yeah, that's true. Isn't it?"

"Realizing those facts doesn't need to change your plan about giving yourself the opportunity to get to know Daniel and to examine your beliefs. That's a permission you give yourself. It's part of growing-up to question the beliefs handed down to you from your parents and teachers, to throw out the ones you find inapplicable, and to form your own values."

"You know, growing-up is confusing. I've been in an emotional turmoil the last couple of weeks trying to sort out my feelings and values. Now that I've made the decision to be open to a new experience, but actually do nothing, I feel a kind of peace."

"You're dealing with the power of your emotions. Isn't it amazing? It's our emotions that make the world a happy place or a terrible place. Reality is neither wonderful nor awful; our emotions make those distinctions. I've just learned that myself these past few months."

Lana looked at Melanie with surprise. "You know, you're right. Here we are sopping wet and cold, but it's OK. It really is."

"Yeah," said Melanie, "It's OK with me, too."

The storm continued unabated. The rhythmic sounds of the driving rain, crashing surf, soughing wind, and swaying branches lulled them to sleep.

"Li-SA. Mel-A-NIE. LI-sa. MEL-a-NIE," a wavering voice called.

The two women awoke from their light slumber.

"It sounds like Daniel," mumbled the groggy Lana. "He must be close, but his voice is coming from the woods, not the beach. Where can he be?"

"He must be on an old hunting road. Come on," the already standing Melanie offered Lana her hand, "I know the way."

The two sodden women lumbered up the beach through the tangle of roots, reeds, and waves.

The man's voice continued to call their names; the women trudged closer.

"Here. Here's where the old hunting road hits the beach," pointed Melanie as she peered into the maritime forest.

Lana had passed the place hundreds of times without recognizing it as an old road. The ocean had eroded the area, creating a drop-off from the road to the beach. The vegetation had reclaimed patches; grapevines hung across the opening; grasses and dewberries choked its path.

There stood Daniel in the middle of the overgrown road with the trike behind him.

Lana surged forward. "Daniel," she yelped with joy.

Daniel returned her feeling. He pushed toward them and hugged Lana. "Are you two OK?"

Lana nodded her head.

"How about you, Melanie?"

"We took shelter under an old live oak. It helped protect us from the wind and rain but, as you can see, we're soaked."

"This Northeaster blew up out of nowhere. Rebecca and David are already at Duck House. Let me take you on the trike."

Lana joined Daniel in the front; Melanie climbed onto the backward-facing rear seat.

Lana held the flashlight for Daniel so he could devote his full attention to driving the trike, pushing it to its limit along the seldom-used track. The light bounced up and down, right and left outlining forms and giving depth to the shades of greens and browns of the thick vegetation along the road.

Melanie glimpsed carved faces in gnarled tree trunks. Their mouths opened in incredulous circles as if they had never seen humans on such an adventure. Their twisted arms reached out to slow them; their glistening wet boas of Spanish moss dragged across them. She felt the occasional gossamer thread of spider web and wet slap of saw palmetto. Pockets of air smelled dank then fresh as they swept past swampy areas. The journey through the night became a carnival ride through a wet wonderland.

* * *

Saturday, July 9, 1988

By the time Melanie reached her bed, dawn was close. She had no trouble sleeping until the clock reached twelve noon and the thermometer hit ninety.

Descending to the kitchen, she sneaked behind Louisa and startled the older woman.

"Goodness, Miz Mellie, whatcha tryin' to do? Gimme a heart attack?"

"Sorry, Louisa."

"An' I worried about you out in dat storm," Louisa chided.

"It soaked us! Daniel rescued Lana and me as if he were a knight on a metallic gray trike," confided Melanie, figuring Louisa would like the romantic imagery.

Louisa ignored it and asked, "You wanna somethin' to eat?"

"Nothing much. It's already hot. Maybe fruit or cheese and crackers?"

"I'll bring dem to you in the library."

"Is Patrice there?"

"I think so."

"How about Ali Cat? Have you seen him?"

The large woman glanced at Melanie's feet, as if expecting to see the cat. "No, Miz Mellie. I haven't seen hide nor hair of dat cat dis mornin' — or yesterday. Dat's odd."

Melanie nodded and left the kitchen for the library.

Patrice looked up from the computer screen. She voiced motherly concerns over Melanie's being out in the storm. After reassuring her aunt of her safety, Melanie inquired about the still-missing Ali Cat. Now it was Patrice's turn to reassure Melanie that the cat would show up eventually.

Louisa brought in Melanie's tray of crackers and cheese with an apple. Melanie munched while she and Patrice worked on the journals, looking for novel ideas. "You know, Patrice, the more I discover about the history of the sea islands, the more I'm surprised at the gaps in courses I took in school."

"What have you been reading?"

"Details about the early Spanish settlements that were established over one hundred years before Jamestown. The Jesuits then the Franciscans established small missions all along this coast. Even the French Huguenots tried a settlement or two. I was taught the first European colony was Sir Walter Raleigh's Lost Colony, followed by Jamestown, then, Plymouth Rock."

"I suspect since England eventually bought, stole, or won most of the East Coast, a bias developed against Spain and France. Another possible reason for the sparse treatment, however, is that the writers and the publishers of school history textbooks lived in the Northeast. Some may be descended from those English settlers; they ignored a section of the country where they had no personal interest. Don't be shocked. Look at the usual one chapter given to the native Americans, the Indians."

"I guess, that's true," Melanie conceded. "You grow up, assuming what you're taught is the whole story. It's a surprise when you find there may be more to a tale than you were led to believe."

"Of course. Be thankful we have this wonderful research preserved in these volumes."

"I am. It's been an exciting few weeks for me. Not only am I learning about the island's past, but I'm helping research an ancient species and its role in a larger context. It's been a humbling, though rewarding, experience to realize the extent of my ignorance."

"Most people choose not to face their ignorance, Melanie. It frightens them. Any easily mastered, steady routine provides security, a comfortable situation."

"Yes, I've seen that drive for security, Patrice. It can produce blinders. It seems once people find a cozy niche or groove, it can evolve into a rut — even into a spiritual grave of narrowness from which there may be no escape."

"At my age when I look back, I realize, I've made several inhibiting choices. Yet, I've never regretted my decision to live on Caretta. I wonder what comes next."

"Don't worry, Patrice. We'll find a solution for you and for the island."

"I'm sure we will."

A soft purring and a rubbing against Melanie's leg distracted her from the conversation.

"Ali Cat! Where have you been, boy? I was concerned about you," Melanie spoke as she picked up the black cat and rubbed him behind his ears. "What's this you've caught on your flea collar?"

Melanie discovered a piece of paper taped to the plastic band. She unfolded and smoothed it with her hands, seeing words from magazines pasted on the sheet similar to ransom notes in movies. She read the message twice. Even the day's heat did not stop an involuntary chill from passing over her body.

CURIOSITY KILLS THE CAT!

CHAPTER 16

10:00 a.m., Sunday, July 10, 1988

"Miz Evans, can I have a minute?"

Melanie turned to the out-of-breath wildlife warden, "Certainly, Officer Frazier."

"I heard your little kitty cat has been collecting messages."

"Why, yes. But, who told you?"

"Grant. It's not a deep, dark secret, is it? It sounds more like a practical joke."

"You think it's a joke?"

"Shor' is a possibility. You got some young 'uns on that turtle crew."

Melanie paused before responding. "Perhaps David is immature enough. But, my intuition tells me that message was a warning."

"From who? Who could be trying to run you out of here?"

"I hadn't even considered someone might be trying to run me off the island."

From their vantage point near the dock, they both noticed a large craft rounding the curve of the channel. Fred concluded, "Well, think about it. Right now, I see, you've got a gentleman caller." He leered at her before ambling away.

Melanie thought, what a chauvinist! She shook her head in disgust and dismissed the encounter as she watched the yacht approach the dock.

"You look ravishing today, Melanie," called Adam.

"And, you sound like a rake, Adam! Let's cut the sweet talk and be off," she retorted. Still, she detected that Adam, the smooth talker with words designed to flatter, sounded sincere. She added, "By the way, your boat's a beauty."

"It's a forty-five-foot Bertram," Adam replied casually, without elaboration. He assumed that anyone living so near the water would be familiar with most types of water craft.

"Impressive," commented Melanie looking at the radar antenna and electronic devices covering the ship.

When he had helped her board the craft, Adam called to the tall, black man on the bridge, "Junior, do you remember Melanie?"

"My pleasure once again," the trim, middle-aged black man responded, touching his cap.

"Jim Jr.!" Melanie recognized Jim and Louisa's son. "I'm sorry I didn't recognize you when you picked me up at the airport. I guess I was still shaken up from the rough landing." She wondered why his parents had not told her that he worked for Adam Gardner. Were they ashamed for some reason? Indeed, Louisa's behavior bordered on being curt with Adam.

"No problem," Jim Jr. smiled and smoothed over the situation.

Adam interjected, "Junior's my number one captain and invaluable assistant in my business."

Melanie nodded, remembering past occasions when young Jim Jr., several years older than the Parker children, had resented the attention his parents had showered on Ashley and herself. She recalled Jim Jr.'s behavior at the storytelling and Jim Sr.'s explanation. Too, she called to mind the harbormaster's comments about Junior overusing Adam's boats. It appeared as if Jim Jr. had found quite a position with Adam.

With little effort, Jim Jr. steered the craft through the intricate waterways of the Georgia sea islands. The weather cooperated and they reached a smooth ocean surface. Calm water took on a blue cast reflecting the cerulean sky. The craft made its own breeze through the salt-scented air. Adam and Melanie relaxed in deck chairs, absorbing the sun and eating Southern vegetable sandwiches. Adam pointed out favorite coastal scenes. Well-trained by the area's fishing boats, gulls flocked and swooped around the stern.

Melanie was comfortable with Adam, even, soothed by his presence. She detected a sensuous undercurrent today that she hadn't felt before with him. She decided to go cautiously with the flow.

After an uneventful cruise, they approached Jekyll Island. Built at the turn of the century, the pier at Jekyll impressed new arrivals. Adam explained that during the heyday of the Jekyll Island Club, numerous yachts with tall masts and great sails tied up here, across from the millionaires' club. Members such as the Rockefellers, Morgans, Good-years, Goulds, Pulitzers, Vanderbilts, and Macys and their approved guests spent the winter in the mild climate. Families built elaborate cottages. Others stayed in the turreted clubhouse.

"Let's take the tour. There's no better way to learn about this opulent era of American history. It'll provide you a point of reference for any development on Caretta."

Melanie blanched at the mention of developing Caretta.

Slowly, they strolled across the lawns.

Melanie soaked in the rich atmosphere. Everywhere she looked, she saw gracious living. Dripping with Spanish moss, graceful live oaks studded rolling, green grass. Porches wrapped Victorian mansions. A terrace framed an Italian palazzo. They passed a gymnasium housing indoor tennis courts and arrived at the stables converted to a tram depot. Adam purchased their tickets and, as they waited for the next tour, they wandered through displays capturing Jekyll Island history.

The old photographs fascinated Melanie. Here were people in their lawn clothes — men in light-colored suits and women in long dresses with straw hats — playing croquet or relaxing with drinks. She learned the Federal Reserve Act, the foundation of the nation's monetary system, was drafted on Jekyll Island. The first transcontinental telephone call was placed from the island in 1915.

The movers and shakers who wintered on Jekyll had controlled one-sixth of the world's wealth. Their fun and games had ended during World War II when German submarines were spotted nearby. The island had evacuated within hours — and the families never returned. With the start of the federal income tax and the end of the war, properties were sold to the state of Georgia.

The tram tour transported Melanie, Adam, and other tourists to houses refurbished in the turn-of-the-century style. They walked among Aubusson carpets, velvet sofas and chairs, Tiffany lamps, and Ming vases that recreated a lifestyle never to exist on the Georgia island again. They visited the ecumenical chapel featuring a large Tiffany stained-glass window.

"Amazing, isn't it?" smiled Adam.

"More people must enjoy it now than then."

"Oh, definitely. Then, people had to be approved to stay on the island. What's more, they were limited to two weeks at the clubhouse. Absolutely no reporters were ever allowed."

"I never realized to what extent these islands were havens for the extremely wealthy."

"If you're interested in seeing more, we can boat over to Cumberland Island. The Carnegies owned that island and built several mansions there for the family. The main estate, Dungeness, burned. But, its ruins are still impressive. One of the children's dwellings, Plum Orchard, has been restored by the National Park Service, who now owns the island. It was rumored during Jimmy Carter's administration that Plum Orchard was going to be a presidential retreat. Anyway, it looks a lot like the White House."

While Jim Jr. guided the vessel toward Cumberland, Adam questioned Melanie about events on Caretta.

"Anything else unusual happen since the fire, Melanie?"

"As a matter of fact, yes. I simply refuse to be victimized any longer! I've decided to take an active role. I staked out the rumrunners' hideaway one night. I overheard two shrimpers from that suspicious boat without lights talk about a 'risky cargo.' Then, immediately after that night, Ali Cat was 'catnapped.' He showed up with a childish message taped to his collar."

"What was the message?"

"'Curiosity kills the cat' — can you believe it?"

"Doesn't that bother you?"

"It did at first. Then, I figured, the shrimpers were responsible for it. They must think I'm messing around their property instead of their trespassing on my property. Now, I'm curious about their 'risky cargo.'"

"You're an amazing woman, Melanie Parker Evans."

Within the hour, Adam's boat was gliding by Cumberland's shores. A herd of wild horses frolicked on the edge of the marsh. The chimneys of Dungeness pierced the air above the marshes and oyster flats.

"Let's go on to Plum Orchard. There will be fewer people there since the park service ferry puts the tourists off here at Dungeness Dock or at park headquarters near Sea Camp."

At Plum Orchard, they tied up the boat at the small dock and explored the exterior of the house. Peeking in windows, they viewed hand-stenciled wallpapers, tiled floors, a grand piano, and an indoor swimming pool. One porch sported a huge wooden swing. Melanie and Adam settled there and admired the grounds.

"Parker House blends into the sea island setting better with its Spanish architecture than this federalist look. Too, the grounds at Parker House are more lush than these," Adam observed. Tell me more about Caretta, Melanie."

"My great-grandfather Phillip Parker, who started Parker Shipping as it was called then, obtained the island after the Civil War as payment for an overdue debt. He built Parker House in the Spanish style he admired in the coastal area of Georgia and Florida. He spared no expense. I'm glad. It's still beautiful today, although subsequent Parkers have added amenities such as electricity, bathrooms, and closets.

As you know, I'm reading his and my grandfather's journals in the library. I'm learning about Caretta's history from them. Too, Patrice and I are trying to gather ideas for a possible novel. That's one reason I'm so interested in seeing other sea islands."

"What about your plans for Caretta? Have you and Ashley discussed ideas as you settle the estate?" Adam probed.

"As long as it's feasible, we'll keep Caretta in the family. Father, Ashley, Greg, and I made that decision two years ago when a Savannah developer made inquiries about building an exclusive resort on Caretta. Of course, the accident has created financial pressure."

"Melanie, that Savannah developer is me. And, I'm still interested in the island. I'd like to help you and the family when you consider change on the island. In fact, I can show you the plans my staff drew up for the resort. Then we can discuss other options your family has available. I've mentioned several ideas to Patrice. I believe she approves of restricted development as long as a family enclave remains on the island."

While she absorbed this information, Melanie contemplated all she had seen today and what she had read in the family journals. It seemed to her that even the designs of the wealthiest intruded on the barrier islands and their life forms. The islands had best served their purpose in the days of prehistory: a barrier to the mainland, protection for the salt marsh nurseries, and shelter to their indigenous creatures. "Perhaps we can talk about it later. At the moment, I'm famished. How about you?"

"Absolutely. I'll have Junior take us into Saint Simon's Sound near the Marshes of Glynn. Remember that Sidney Lanier poem? Meanwhile, I'll rustle up some grub in the galley."

The engine rumbles accompanied the raucous cries of the gulls as the large boat glided along the waterway. While Adam busied himself in the galley, Melanie relaxed in a deck chair, absorbing the last rays of sunshine and reflecting on her family. She hoped she was making the choices that they would have made under the same circumstances.

By the time Jim Jr. had dropped anchor and departed in the dinghy to fulfill his own plans in town, dinner was ready. Adam had pulled together an impromptu-appearing, though well-planned, meal.

The setting sun provided a golden glow as Adam produced a chilled bottle of Virginia's award-winning Prince Michel White Burgundy. A steaming casserole held center stage, flanked by a green garden salad with red onion rings and orange sections in a raspberry vinaigrette, and a bowl of buttered seashell pasta.

"Looks wonderful. What are we eating?"

"It's a Mediterranean dish — shrimp cooked in a spicy tomato sauce with lots of Feta cheese. I hope you'll like it."

"Gee, Adam, I had no idea you were so versatile. A gourmet cook as well as a real estate tycoon?"

"As a bachelor, I've found it in my best interest to cook. It always impresses the ladies," Adam responded with a good-natured wink as he lit two candles.

Melanie sensed the mood take a romantic turn. The wine warmed her skin. Adam's eyes sparkled in the flickering candlelight and his voice cast a soothing spell. His total attention riveted on her presence.

"Melanie, your range of interests astounds me. I try to keep up with current events and business happenings, but you're in tune with nature, history, and the arts as well. How did you capture such a wide field of vision?"

Melanie accepted the flattery, yet she questioned his sincerity. She told herself, I do question a lot — even more as an adult than I did as a child. To Adam, she replied, "You're seeing my curiosity. The schools and 'real world' never managed to take it away. If these past months have taught me anything, it's how to take several steps back — and look at life with more questions than ready-made answers. The experience has magnified my sense of wonder. Look at the lights behind you. An hour ago, it was a bridge, wharves, and ugly machinery. Now can you see the fairyland?"

"I'm afraid I've lost that perspective in all my goals and so-called achievements."

At the rail, the two stood side-by-side gazing across the dark water mirroring the sparkling lights. Adam slipped an arm around Melanie's waist and she leaned lightly against him.

"You're becoming a yachtswoman. Your hair has the clean, invigorating smell of sea-air," Adam murmured as his head touched hers.

"I have you to thank for that. Our voyage has been satisfying in many ways," she replied.

Adam looked into her eyes reflecting the night lights, tilted her head up with his hand, and kissed her. The kiss was short, but the embrace was long as the calm rocking of the boat provided pleasant sensations.

They kissed again.

Bites broke their concentration.

"What's that? Are you biting me?" Melanie asked.

Adam and she broke into laughter.

"Mosquitoes never occur in the movies. Shall we go below?" Adam commented between laughs.

"The sooner, the better."

He escorted her into the cabin, richly appointed in natural-finish woods. Every detail spoke quality. Her companion strove for the best in every endeavor — even to his hobbies. As she looked around her, she felt a selfish reaffirmation of her own worth through his desire for her as a sexual partner. Even before this cruise, she had sensed his interest. Now he had set the stage even to the point of Jim Jr. having business in town.

"So, Captain Gardner, what do you have in mind?"

This direct inquiry into his intentions caught Adam off-guard. Attempting a hasty rejoinder, he asked, "A quick game of Scrabble?" Then, he stopped and replied, "Melanie, I want to make love to you — carefully, slowly, totally."

Having considered this possibility earlier, Melanie was able to breathe, "Perhaps soon, Adam. I'm flattered. But tonight, let's just be friends."

"What?"

* * *

2:30 a.m., Saturday, July 16, 1988

Melanie sat on the rear seat of the moving trike, dragging her feet, making designs in the wet sand. Where her shoes hit the sand, small sparks of phosphorescence exploded against the dark background. Moving her feet, she created kaleidoscopic trails of light, reminiscent of comets trailing across the dark sky. Instead of looking for loggerhead turtles, she was thinking about Adam and Grant.

"Come forward a minute," Daniel turned and hollered above the engine clamor.

She scrambled over the equipment box and plopped down next to the graduate student.

"Look at the surf line. I believe Rebecca's team caught one."

Melanie observed the other trike parked on the beach and two figures clustered at water's edge. Daniel halted ten yards away and they watched the show. Lana and Rebecca had corralled a turtle reentering the waves. Now, they were faced with how to read her tags and measure her size.

"How about a little help here?" Rebecca yelled.

"What's wrong, boss? Ain't she cooperating?" Daniel responded in his most sarcastic tone.

"Thanks a lot, wise guy. She had a dry run. We barely caught her." Rebecca continued, struggling with the three-hundred-pound turtle.

"It looks like you'll have to flip her to study her," Daniel continued his goading.

"Are you going to help?"

"And, get all wet and nasty? Besides, I know you'd think I was being a male chauvinist to step in for the heavy work."

"Men!" came Rebecca's peeved reply.

The redhead slid her hands under the side of the carapace and jumped over its back, pulling the turtle with her in one motion, rolling the giant creature upside down. Her graceful move made the task look easy to upend a live object three times one's weight.

"Could you at least get the clipboard?" Rebecca shouted to Daniel.

"Yassuh, boss. My pleasure," came the good-natured answer.

While Melanie held the light and Lana struggled with the flippers, Rebecca called out the ID numbers from the tags and Daniel jotted them down. The turtle, however, did not appreciate the turn of events. With sudden fury and awesome power, she slung wet sand and water. The deluge continued as measurements were taken.

Hurrying, Rebecca expertly rolled the turtle upright. With a single lunge, the reptile gained enough depth to swim away from her captors.

The researchers laughed as they looked at each other's disheveled appearance.

"What an unhappy patient," Daniel noted.

"Next time, I would give her a chance to get away," Lana commented.

"Don't you dare," retorted Rebecca.

"It's a shame David missed her. She was one exciting female," Lana joked.

The four grew quiet standing on the sand, a starry night overhead, white froth visible on the crests of the black waves. The gentle whooshing of the water provided the only sound.

Lana sensed another presence on the deserted beach. She felt that something or someone was watching. A chill involuntarily passed through her. She glanced over her left shoulder and glimpsed a large, black shadow, moving closer and blocking the stars. Her scream split the calm night.

Melanie jumped as she turned toward Lana.

A huge object touched the college student. Sudden recognition caused laughter to erupt from all sides.

"Derby!" Lana croaked.

"You crazy horse," Rebecca cackled, "What are you doing out here? You scared the hell out of us."

"Perhaps, he heard all you females playing in the surf," chortled Daniel.

"And, like a typical male, he wanted to get in on the excitement," Melanie quipped.

"Or, like usual, he wanted to see if we have any food left," Lana managed to interject. She hoped her heart rate would soon return to normal.

"That's an idea. Gorp would taste great. I'll go get us some" Melanie turned toward the trike. As she left the group, she noticed Daniel enfold Lana in his arms.

Soon recovering her composure, Lana joined Melanie and Derby at the trike to find the gorp.

Meanwhile, Daniel and Rebecca compared notes.

"Did you notice the chunks missing out of that turtle's shell?" Daniel asked.

"Looked as if she'd had several run-ins with sharks," Rebecca responded.

"They reminded me of a lingering concern."

"What's that, Daniel?"

"About the dead body last month. That sailor's body had a bashed-in head. I mentioned it to Fred, but he acted as if it were nothing. Grant reacted the same way."

"What? You think the sailor was murdered?" gasped Rebecca.

"It's possible."

"Wow! I hadn't considered that." She paused. "To my knowledge, neither Grant nor Fred would hide a murder. Let's face it. The sea held that body in its power for hours — and you know what the sea can do."

"You're probably right. But, I'm still uneasy."

Melanie overheard bits of the conversation drift through the quiet night air. It was the first she had heard of the bashed-in skull, turning an accidental death into a possible murder.

* * *

10:00 p.m., Saturday, July 16, 1988

Another sultry night bore down on the island inhabitants. Sounds mirrored the heavy atmosphere. The crickets chirred in a slow rhythm. The owls hooted sporadically, as if it took too much effort. Melanie lay motionless on her bed. Even the absence of clothes didn't permit a cool position.

She focused on the men in her life, leaping backward a couple of years, then returning to the present. Her father, Greg, Grant, Adam — aspects of these men flooded her consciousness. Delineation blurred. Where did one end and another start?

With a sigh, she deliberately tried to put perspective on these relationships. What traces and influences had her father left etched on her life? Why had she enjoyed most of the time Greg and she had spent together? What did Grant and Adam offer?

Grant remained an enigma. He seemed close as they jogged, read the Caretta journals under Patrice's tutelage, or researched sea island history. Still, there was that hidden part or reserve that was more than isolated Australian breeding. A bad love affair? Punishing parents? Was this remoteness a symptom of a man who didn't know how to communicate emotion? Was he exhibiting that traditionally male flaw that resulted in floundering or stagnant relationships? The night of the fire revealed a passionate sexual partner. It was the only time he had held nothing back. Memories of that night contained dreamy qualities. His subsequent behavior shed no light on his feelings.

She vividly recalled the romantic evening with Adam. Together, they had danced the mating rituals leading up to that evening. He had brilliantly played his part of setting the stage complete with yacht, food, wine, plus flattering remarks; she had wanted to actively embrace the role of being swept off her feet. Adam was an intelligent, handsome, and surprisingly sympathetic companion. However, she sensed shadows behind the glitz. She discerned nothing sinister and, unlike Grant, the phantom parts seemed shallow. Perhaps a lower class childhood had left marks of shame that didn't fit Adam's cultivated image.

Neither man was Greg. Neither could become Greg. For the vast majority of her adult life, Greg had been by her side. She saw the unfinished business of their relationship that sadly would never be realized: the hours devoted to work instead of moments for personal self-discovery, the energy given to mundane activities rather than to understanding the world around them, the raising of Parker by accepted formulas instead of by wonder. Yet, the years with her adolescent sweetheart had been wonderful, on the whole. She was better prepared for the future, thanks to those loving moments. Since the accident, she had gained a heightened awareness of the fragility of life.

Her father had been the foundation of the family. With him as the rock, both she and Ashley were free to experiment and to make mistakes. Courtland's solid nature and broad experience had woven a strong, wide safety net, but he had wanted them to be perfect. Her brother had received the full brunt of this impossible goal. After all, he was the oldest and the male heir. She wished her father had required more specifics from them and less of a general expectation. If only he had made them work harder at small tasks and learn through little mistakes. Especially where she was concerned, he was a softy at heart — papa's little girl. Perhaps, because Courtland had made allowances for her sex, she felt more free to meet her own expectations than did Ashley.

Where did all these ramblings leave her? What did she need? She knew better than to find answers in another person. Simply finding a new mate would not make her feel whole again. Time was bringing changes — hopefully, positive changes. She could function as an independent person; that realization was growing. Adam and Grant might play roles in the process, but they had needs and desires, too. What did they want from her? She didn't feel strong enough to give much and, so far, they hadn't provided clear signals. Was Adam after a romantic fling — or an island? Did Grant seek anything other than occasional sex, no strings attached? How did she avoid becoming trapped in another person's problems until she became more confident in herself?

Melanie sighed, tossed, and turned in the sauna atmosphere of her bedroom. Life had complications, but she sensed joy in simply feeling again. She was regaining parts of herself that had disappeared that fateful day last July.

* * *

The trawlers rubbed against the wooden planks. Lines strained and creaked. The masts and tied nets created a skeletal image of bones and ribs against the night sky. A mixture of decaying fish and diesel fuel filled the nostrils of a figure hidden among the barrels scattered beside a shack on the dock. Hours ago, the last of the fishermen had secured their gear and departed, leaving the area to the ever-watchful gulls and pelicans.

The human observer wondered if the vigil would pay off tonight.

CHAPTER 17

4:00 p.m., Monday, July 18, 1988

Dressing minimally and avoiding movement, the turtle project team lounged around Duck House. Sweat glistened on their bodies. As the day's heat intensified, not a sliver of fresh air cut through the heavy atmosphere. Only biting flies and stinging gnats dared any activity in the afternoon smelter.

"Is every season so slow?" David asked no one in particular.

"Last year, we had tagged more turtles by this date. The number of nesting females handled by projects goes up and down each season. There's no discernible cycle or reason behind the swings. That's one of the reasons for our research," explained Rebecca.

"I wonder whether it's all worth it," whined Lana.

"What do you mean?" Rebecca shot back testily.

"I just question whether we're doing any good. There are so few of us trying to reverse the never-ending tide of people who want to build and settle on these rookeries. In the long-term, we all know who'll overcome."

"The good guys don't always lose," offered David.

"Take Caretta," continued Lana. "How long do you think the Parker family will keep it in its natural state now that the father is gone? You know, I bet Melanie can't pay the inheritance taxes without selling assets, which may be Caretta itself. She may not be able to afford to keep Caretta as a vacation retreat for herself or a retirement home for her aunt. Let's face it. It's prime real estate — easy to sell."

"She won't sell if I have anything to do with it," responded Rebecca intensely.

"How would you stop her?" Daniel entered the conversation.

"There are ways to apply pressure."

"I believe she's taken with that real estate smoothie, Adam Gardner. We all know what he'd do to this place. Maybe we can persuade Grant to show a little more romantic interest in her. He's good looking — or is that invading your territory?" Lana smiled sweetly at the director.

"Now wait a minute," Daniel spoke up quickly seeing the glower on Rebecca's face. "Let's make a few allowances for lousy sleep in this incredible heat. And, let's stick to subjects we can handle — such as our nature observations."

"Yeah, I have a concern," David expressed himself, relieved to change the subject from the personal issue. "In this project, we move all the loggerhead eggs to the hatchery for protection. Now, I don't know enough to criticize. But, I recall in one of my courses, the prof said man ought to do as little as possible to interfere with the natural process. What effect will the artificial hatchery have?"

"That's a good point," Daniel responded, supporting this less volatile topic. "One or two turtle projects have started to position protective cages around the nests wherever they occur. That way they disturb the pattern far less. What do you think, Rebecca?"

"At the last turtle conference, we had a discussion about the hatchery issue. One scientist hypothesized that the moving of nests to safe locations perpetuates bad genes. For example, a turtle who consistently nests too low on the beach might be doing so due to a defective gene. By saving her eggs, we may insure a whole new generation of low-nesters. Thus, our efforts weaken the genetic pool of the species. What we don't know about this multi-million-year-old egg- laying process is enormous. Naturally, it costs more to build and position single nest enclosures. Then, it creates the manpower problem of arriving at the scattered locations to help the hatchlings escape the ghost crabs. Our small project couldn't do it that way without much more in the way of resources."

"I'd like to know how the turtles find their way back to the same beach year after year, generation after generation. I get lost trying to find an exit off the interstate," grumbled Lana. "I doubt the turtles have big green signs to point the way."

"Like bird migration, whatever the navigational device employed, we stand to learn a lot," commented Daniel. "Researchers have hypothesized magnetic particles in the sand; others have assayed temperature and chemical variations such as manganite in the coastal waters. The miracle, as I see it, is that, whatever the method, it's being employed by a brain the size of a grape!"

Rebecca joined in, "There have been many superstitions about special turtle powers or rocks that attract turtles. Jack Rudloe covered those aspects in his book, *Time of the Turtle.* You know, if I could have one question answered, it would be: Where do sea turtles spend their early childhood? They seem to disappear."

"What do you say when someone challenges the idea of mankind trying to save any species?" David asked. "I read that over 95% of all species ever alive are now extinct. It has happened every day for eons."

Daniel grinned as he spoke, "We had a good session on that very topic in a seminar I took last semester. Our consensus relates to Rebecca's last comment. We humans are so ignorant of our home, the planet Earth. Our group decided humans need to take every precaution before we inadvertently wipe out what may be our salvation. Wouldn't it be ironic if we allowed, or encouraged, a species to die off — which, we discover later, possessed the cure to a disease such as AIDS or cancer? Or by manufacturing a chemical to get rid of a pest, we unleash a side-effect that is far more horrendous? That's what nearly happened with DDT."

"So, given that daily we see mankind trashing and harming this planet, do most humans act in this short-sighted manner because they're ignorant of the consequences or because they're stupid?" Rebecca asked. "Stupid, to me, means they actually know better. But, they refuse to take the time or they don't care or they're too greedy."

"Off that definition, I'd go with ignorance," Daniel answered.

"Stupidity," Lana said firmly. "You can't convince me all those college-educated engineers, business tycoons, and whoever aren't smart enough to know better. They simply don't care. Making money, creating jobs, and finishing a project always comes before conserving an animal or plant. Sustainable growth? Hogwash! They only care about their next quarter's profits. They never seem to consider future generations."

"I can't believe they're all so callous," said David.

"I maintain we're safer on the side of ignorance. At least it gives us a purpose: to educate. It gives us hope. Otherwise, we might as well give up and join the ranks of the non-caring," Daniel countered.

Rebecca added, "We can learn from the moves of the enemy who consistently wins again and again. A good general learns more in defeat than victory. Only a stupid one continues to use losing tactics."

"That gives me an idea, Rebecca," interjected Daniel. "I'm going to suggest to my black power buddies at school that they adopt the Confederate flag as their symbol. If it catches on, I wonder how long that hate-symbol will continue to fly over state capitals or ride around on redneck pick-up trucks."

The crew fell silent for a while as the sun turned the air a furnace red. David stirred first, "What's for supper?"

"Peanut butter," Rebecca answered.

"Not again," sighed Lana. "How about we go round up some crabs?"

"In this heat?" Daniel questioned.

"Peanut butter or crabs?" Lana rejoined.

"OK. Everybody up. It's a desperate moment," Rebecca concluded.

The four donned their mud-encrusted shoes, reserved for protecting their feet from oyster shells while treading in the gooey salt marsh. They spread out with chicken necks attached to fishing lines, enticing the blue crabs out of their watery homes. The buzzing of insects and the subsequent slapping of human hands provided the sound effects.

"Looks like a colony of 'gradygrits' over there," David shouted pointing to a group of great egrets.

"I saw marsh hens the other day — you know, the Clapper Rail. They make good eating," Daniel replied as the two men headed into the muck.

"Hey, boss, I'm sorry about that personal comment," Lana said in a conciliatory tone.

"No harm. We're too hot and uncomfortable to be rational," responded Rebecca.

"No hard feelings then?"

"None."

"That's good, 'cause here's mud in your eye," Lana whooped as she let fly a glob of wet slime that landed on top of the petite redhead.

"Why you!" Rebecca screamed as she let go of her line and scooped up a handful to toss at the teenager.

The two women were slinging mud at point-blank range. In a matter of minutes, both were soaked with their bodies now dark brown in color. The two men wandered over, attracted by the noise. David stared at Lana's breasts. Her erect nipples pointed through the wet tank top, clinging like a second skin to her body.

"And, what are you looking at?" Lana hollered as she aimed her next handful at the gaping David.

"Yeah, there's no room for spectators," joined in Rebecca as she threw a handful at Daniel.

Mud filled the air as Daniel and David joined in the cool, wet mudfight.

The foursome collapsed in howls of laughter.

"This is one hell of a way to cool off," Daniel commented as he wiped mud from his eyes.

"Now I know why pigs stay so filthy in the summer," David added.

"Speak for yourself," wisecracked Lana.

That comment prompted another flurry of mud.

After several minutes of lying on the creek bank to recover their breath, the four picked up their covered crab buckets and headed for the showers.

* * *

10:30 a.m., Wednesday, July 20, 1988

Miniature armies of fiddler crabs scooted back and forth across the brown-black flats of the salt marsh. The males waved and clicked their oversized pincers while females darted for the hole entrances to their dwellings. Melanie wondered at the creatures' sensitivity to movement and vibration. The slightest presence on the dock put them on alert. They reminded her of city dwellers scurrying about when viewed from a high vantage point. Today she was joining those milling crowds to lunch with Susannah Harris in the historic district of downtown Savannah.

She started the engine of the small craft and, using the chart highlighted by Jim, she headed for the city. Only after a lengthy discussion, had Jim conceded she was capable of piloting the boat. His advice had been peppered with many cautions. So, she allowed herself ample time to navigate the snakelike curves of the waterways that led her to the Savannah River. She knew tidal marsh estuaries deceived accomplished boaters so she paid close attention to the charts, buoys, and landmarks.

Gaining the Wilmington River, Melanie headed north toward Elba Island. When she neared the small land mass, she remembered one of her favorite childhood stories. For forty-four years in this unlikely location, a lone woman had made herself a worldwide legend. Florence Martus had greeted every ship that entered or departed Savannah, day or night. During daylight hours, she waved a handkerchief; after dark she signaled with a lantern. Sailors talked about her and carried her friendly message to ports far and wide. A Liberty Ship bore her name. Melanie contemplated the reaching out, the longing that drove both Florence and the crewmen to find a degree of fulfillment in her simple gestures.

Turning west at the intersection with the Savannah River, she motored into the wharf area of the city. At the riverfront, red brick and chipped plaster facades of old warehouses lined the banks. She tied the boat to a slip at the small dock in front of a modern hotel and started to explore the aging buildings.

Melanie strolled along the cobblestones, stepping carefully over the old railroad tracks embedded in the stone pavement. She sized up the shops, boutiques, and cafes now occupying the area. It's already moved from decay, past funky, and into trendy — similar to patterns of change found in other urban areas from Baltimore to San Francisco.

Since Parker Transworld used the port of Savannah on a regular basis, Melanie's father had instilled in his children an appreciation of the Savannah shipping history.

On the streetside of the warehouses, black iron ramps and walkways connected various levels of the tiered construction. Long ago, in the peak of shipping sea island cotton and lumber, this part of the port was given the name Factor's Walk. Here the men, known as factors, calculated the value of the incoming and outgoing goods.

Endangered

Melanie found the entrance to the restaurant where she was to meet Susannah. Maneuvering through the throngs of tourists and business people, she spotted Susannah across the crowded dining room.

When Melanie arrived at the table, Susannah commanded in her usual reckless, headlong manner, "Hold it! Let me see how the dress flatters you."

Melanie turned to show the fit of the jade-green linen dress Susannah had sent to her after Patrice's tea. "You have an excellent eye for estimating measurements as well as choosing flattering colors and lines, Susannah. I'm delighted with my Savvy original. Thank you."

"You're welcome, my dear. It's a trifle to raise your spirits. I must say you've already added some roundness to your curves plus a bit of tan to your fair skin."

As she settled into her seat, Melanie asked, "Have you ordered?"

"Just wine. For lunch, though, I like the crab cakes."

Seated among wooden barrels containing tall palms and peace lilies that softened the rough brick walls of the old warehouse, Melanie sipped her chilled glass of sauvignon blanc and analyzed the decor. Long colorful banners bearing British insignia hung from the high ceilings and muffled the noise; lights mounted in nautical and military hardware offered low light. Pewter plates and utensils accented the distressed-wood tables. All complemented the historic atmosphere of the restaurant in one of the old cotton exchanges along the Factor's Walk. Melanie wondered if the edifice dated back to General Oglethorpe's design for the city of Savannah.

A waiter dressed in a red mock-military uniform of a colonial British soldier appeared at Melanie's elbow.

"Has madame decided what she would like for lunch today?"

"Yes. I hear you offer delightful crab cakes."

"An excellent choice. And, you, mademoiselle?"

"The same — including more wine," Susannah smiled.

When the waiter left, Susannah commented, "Isn't it amazing how quickly men notice whether a woman is wearing a wedding band or not? And, speaking of men, how's Adam Gardner doing with you?"

Melanie almost choked on her drink. She had forgotten how direct and impulsive her childhood friend could be. Though more tactful,

Susannah still practiced the same wild abandon, trodding in places other people only considered.

"Actually, he's one of the reasons I wanted to lunch with you."

"Sounds promising. Tell me more," Susannah urged.

"I have more questions than items to report, Susannah," she chided gently.

"Oh. Am I being too pushy?"

"Only where Adam's concerned. One would guess you'd get a percentage if I married him," Melanie joked.

The waiter reappeared with Susannah's wine; she sampled it and nodded her approval. The waiter made a bow, leered suggestively at her, then turned on his heel.

Susannah gave a throaty chuckle, "Honestly, men can be so funny when it comes to sex or love." She sobered as she looked at Melanie. "I suppose all of us mix up those emotions at one time or another. So, what questions do you have about Adam Gardner?"

"How long have you known him?"

"Since I returned to Savannah — after my divorce."

"How well do you know him?"

"We've dated. We've provided one another a socially acceptable partner at dinner parties, benefits, that sort of occasion. And, he's given me excellent business advice. I believe I told you how he helped line up my labor force."

"Yes, you did. I know he's an exceptional businessman. The Hammock impresses anyone with that fact. What bothers me is his avoidance of talking about his life before he came to Savannah. It's as if he's hiding some dark secret. Has he ever talked to you about what he did before he came here?"

Susannah swirled the light golden liquid of her wine around the globe of her glass. "Not that I remember," she allowed.

Melanie observed, "The Hammock must have taken a lot of money to develop. I wonder how he made it."

"I know part of that answer. Good ol' daddy started the development — then called Harris Hammock. Real estate can be a house of cards. If one card falls, down come the rest. Daddy lost some of his financial backers because of cost overruns. Engineering the drainage in the marsh proved to be more complex and, consequently, more costly than Daddy estimated. Daddy had no reserves to allow for extensive errors. After other such financial debacles, no one trusted him enough to give him any additional backing. So, Daddy went bankrupt.

"What we Harrises have now was either in mother's name or my name and couldn't be touched by the courts — like my townhouse.

"Daddy committed suicide, though few people know that fact," Susannah sighed.

"Adam bought the land and the plan for a fraction of their cost. He arrived at the right place at the right time with the know-how and the polish to make the project a reality. Now, all the improvements have been completed. In addition, he shortened the name to The Hammock. So, he avoided any trace of a stigma.

"Never mention to mother that I told you about that mess," Susannah continued and swirled the wine in her glass. "She's still touchy about the situation. She pretends none of it ever happened."

"I'm so sorry about your father, Susannah. His death must have been a hard adjustment for you, too."

"Anyway, the subject is Adam, not Daddy. In answer to your question about Adam's past, I have to admit I know nothing beyond his Sir Galahad act with The Hammock. Perhaps you could make discreet inquiries about his financial underwriters and find specific details. My instincts, however, tell me he's a nice guy."

The waiter emerged with their plates of crab cakes, spinach salad, herbed rice, and a garnish of melon balls and strawberries.

"Anything else, ladies?"

"That's all for now. Thanks," Susannah dismissed the still-interested young man. Returning her attention to Melanie, Susannah asked, "So-o-o, what's keeping you away from Adam?"

"Actually, nothing. In fact, he was a big comfort after the fire. And, then we took a delightful boat trip to Jekyll and Cumberland," Melanie replied as she tried the rice. "Mmm, this rice is good."

"That's quite a trip," Susannah murmured.

"Yes, it was," Melanie agreed and met Susannah's inquisitive eyes.

"How bad was the fire? You mentioned Adam was a comfort," inquired Susannah.

"The rainstorm contained the fire to a few acres. I was lucky, very lucky. I was knocked out — either by a falling limb or by whoever started the fire. One of the researchers, Grant Yeats, saved me."

"WHAT? You think it was arson and attempted murder?" Susannah put down her fork and looked hard at Melanie.

"Possibly. At least, Adam considered the possibility instead of labeling me 'paranoid' as did Grant and Fred Frazier, the Fish and Wildlife Warden."

"I wouldn't worry too much about what Fred Frazier thinks. He's kind of a joke around here. He assumes he's more important than he is." She picked up her fork again and probed, "But, you suspect someone started the fire and knocked you out?"

"It's possible. There was a path of bent grasses all the way from the beach to the dune where the fire started. Too, if I were hit by a falling branch due to the fire, it would have been on-fire. I would have had burns. And, I have none. That gives me pause. But, what I can't figure is who would profit from my death?"

"That's a frightening thought. Let's talk about something less morbid." Susannah paused. "Did I tell you I took your advice and looked up your brother the last time I flew to New York?"

"Really? How is Ashley? I've heard nothing from him the last couple of weeks. He's busy with all the end-of-the-year details, so I didn't call him about the fire."

"Yes, he was involved with all that number-crunching mess. But, he did take me out to dinner at Four Seasons. You forgot to tell me he grew up to be good-looking."

"Yes, he is. Let me warn you that since his divorce, he fancies himself a playboy."

Susannah flipped her hair over her right shoulder and commented, "Hmm, I can vouch that he's quite satisfactory at that."

"Susannah!"

"Melanie?"

The two women laughed.

Susannah raised her wine glass in a toast, "To life and love!"

"To life — and love," Melanie responded.

Endangered

A short while later, Susannah excused herself and left the table. Melanie studied her wine glass and wondered if Susannah and Ashley had shared more than dinner. Looking in the direction her old friend had gone, she saw their handsome, young waiter. She saw Susannah standing close to him and slipping a business card into his hand.

* * *

8:00 p.m., Thursday, July 21, 1988

Quiet ruled most Thursday nights at Parker House. Patrice and Melanie used the evenings to research the journals. On occasion, Ashley placed a phone call to keep Melanie up-to-date on the happenings in New York. Sometimes Grant joined the women while they worked in the library. He would read passages they had found of interest. Then the three of them would hypothesize on how life was then. This rainy evening, Melanie and Patrice worked by themselves in the library.

"Patrice, I must make one small confession. I wondered about your rationale for staying so long in such an isolated place as Caretta. I tried to imagine what you did day after day except become completely bored and acquire a bad case of rock fever. After several months here, I see how limited my preconceptions were."

"Oh, Melanie, that's normal," Patrice laughed. She took off her glasses and studied Melanie. "How many of us ever understand what another does or feels? We become confused, even threatened, when others choose to spend their day distinctly different from how we spend ours." She paused then added, "I must say you're adjusting to island living."

"I've heard this option called 'simple' or 'more primitive,' even 'back-to-basics.' Those ideas fail to capture the true differences. I have time for my interests — more than I had in my busy executive existence. Life is complex in all its variety, but it's not nearly as confusing as man-made processes. I'm finding it far more thrilling to learn about the ancient loggerheads than to learn which method should be used in a market survey of potential customers. I'm enjoying this natural world of Caretta much more than the artificially created one of New York City."

"'But, what do you do all day?'" mimicked Patrice as she readjusted her glasses on her nose. "I've heard that question spoken to my face and behind my back so many times. At last, another soul appreciates the response."

Melanie grinned. "Yes, I was guilty of asking that question. I love finding the answer in a wondrous world far removed from city skyscrapers and suburban shopping malls."

"Oh, I hear the radio-telephone, Melanie. Would you answer it? It's probably Ashley."

Ashley sat back, cradling a brandy as he waited for the connection. His new power proved exhilarating. Still, he envied Melanie with time for the beach and relaxation. A burst of static filled his ear. Then, he heard Melanie's voice.

"Hello, Melanie! How's life at our private resort?"

Melanie smirked at the opening dig, typical of her older brother. For several exchanges, they conversed about current happenings and the weather. The steady rain patter against the window caused Melanie to request him to speak louder.

"Ashley, it's time for us to discuss Caretta's future. I know our tax extensions are running out. There are interested parties wondering what our decision will be."

"It is time. I'm almost finished with the year-end financial figures. Once they've gone to press, I'll be able to concentrate on that situation. I'll fly down to give us a chance to talk things over. Besides, a beach trip sounds rewarding."

"Good, Ashley. You'll enjoy meeting Grant and the turtle research crew. Plus, a change of pace will do you good. Has work been difficult?"

"Nothing out of the ordinary. I have a handle on everything. Well, I must go. See you in a couple of days."

Melanie reran the conversation, contemplating her sibling. His concern for her welfare since the accident had been the first indication of closeness he had exhibited in his adult life. Appearances indicated he was growing up — twenty years later than most people.

"It's quiet in here. Everyone all right?" Grant's voice broke through the stillness as he left his dripping rain gear on the porch and entered the house.

"Fine, Grant," Melanie greeted him and steered him toward the library. "I just finished talking with Ashley."

"How is Mr. Parker Transworld?"

"He's finishing up the company's year-end report and planning to fly here in a few days."

"Did he mention my research funding?"

"No. However, I'm sure he'll be interested in hearing how much progress you've made."

Grant guessed Ashley's interest would center around any commercial value from the project. He thought, "I'd better be ready with something or be ready to move on."

Overhearing the voices, Patrice wondered if her future would be determined for her or if Ashley would value her preferences.

In the kitchen, Louisa and Jim quietly discussed their opinion of young Ashley and questioned his intentions.

Melanie's question broke the pensive mood, "What are you chewing, Grant?"

"A leaf. I have a cold sore and this plant produces a mild numbing sensation. The old-timers call it the 'toothache tree.' According to Rebecca, its name is Zanthoxylum. But, it's commonly called Hercules Club."

"May I try it?"

"Of course."

Melanie sampled an offered green leaf, "Why, it's similar to Novocain. Where did you find it?"

"The bushes grow at Tail End, near the bluffs. Next time we're there, I'll show one to you."

Melanie sat down and looked at her two companions. Grant shared everyday discoveries; Patrice provided historical perspectives. One dealt with facts; the other lived with fantasy. After the announcement of Ashley's impending visit, Melanie sensed tension in both of them. Again, she felt the burden that she and her brother bore — the future of other peoples' lives.

CHAPTER 18

5:30 a.m., Saturday, July 23, 1988

Two exhausted turtlers stretched their arms, then, rubbed their eyes.

"Boy, am I glad to see morning. The last three hours seemed like forever," mumbled David.

"Thank goodness, it looks as if it's going to be a gorgeous day," Melanie responded. The sky reflected the first rays of sun. Oranges and reds streaked gray clouds, changing highlights to silver then gold.

"So, how did you like patrolling with me?" David asked.

"It was fun but, as you said, the last few passes went slowly — probably, because we found no turtles. The clock goes much faster with some action. What do you say we crank up the trike and head for bed?"

"I thought you'd never ask, ma'am."

"David, you're incorrigible!"

The youngster wheeled the trike around and drove south along the water's edge for the final swing down the beach. Searching for missed crawls but dreaming of sleep, Melanie and David sat like zombies, staring straight into the early-morning, pastel glow. The trike droned.

Even though she had been bored, she was glad she had elected to keep herself busy on the anniversary of her family's accident. Somehow, being around other people, especially young, alive people lessened the feeling of loss.

"Look! What do you suppose that is?" Melanie's voice broke the spell. She pointed toward the breakers.

"Looks like a float for a crab trap or a net. It must have broken loose. I guess we might as well retrieve it," David responded wearily.

He stopped the trike and the two waded to the floating object. It resembled a small squat rocket with a light mounted on its cone.

"I bet it's a buoy, though there are no markings on it," David observed as examined it. "It's lightweight and watertight."

"Shake it. See if anything rattles," Melanie suggested.

As David shook the buoy, a light clicked on and started blinking. While the intensity was less than brilliant, it was highly visible in the early dawn.

"I shook something up," David grinned.

"I suppose we could take it to Parker House and notify the Coast Guard so they can replace it."

The two wedged the wet buoy among their gear in the equipment box and restarted their trek toward Duck House. Perched on the vehicle, the blinking light gave the trike the appearance of a small plane taxiing down the beach. When they neared Palmhenge, the rumbling of a larger engine caught their attention.

"Look how close that shrimp trawler is to shore," David exclaimed.

"I've heard that shrimp boats get near the beach. But, I've never seen one this close," Melanie agreed.

While they watched the boat, two men weighed anchor, boarded a small dinghy, and headed straight toward them over the waves.

"You think they're in trouble?"

"We'll soon find out," answered Melanie.

As the two fishermen beached their small craft, they waved to the two researchers. The men trudged through the sand toward the waiting trike.

"We saw that flashing light on your vehicle and figured it might be what we've been searching for," one of the men called.

Melanie noticed the day-old beards and the dirty clothes. She wondered if she looked as rumpled after an all-night work detail. Then, she caught a whiff of the rancid smell of whiskey that turned her stomach.

"We found this object washed-up on the shore. What do you know about it?" she queried.

"Yeah, that's it. We use this-here type of float to mark our trawling grounds. The little light helps us spot 'em at night," the older man slurred.

"I've never heard of that technique," David interjected. "This buoy looks like a Coast Guard issue."

"It is."

"No way."

Both men had spoken simultaneously.

The older one glared at the younger before explaining, "What we mean is — it's salvage. We picked it up cheap then rigged it for our special use."

"Are you sure?"

"Just give it here, you little punk," the younger man spat.

"Stop! There's no reason to act ugly. We just want to make sure it's yours," Melanie explained.

"Look, lady. It's ours. Now hand it over so we can be on our way."

She turned and whispered to David, "What do you think?"

"Something smells fishy besides our two visitors."

"I'm with you. They're unsavory."

"Enough whispering! Give it here," the younger warned.

"We'll be back in a few minutes. We want to radio the Coast Guard."

"Get it, Joe!" one of the men shouted.

The men lunged toward the trike. David maneuvered it into gear and avoided their charge. Slowly, they outdistanced their pursuers.

Sput-sput-sput.

"We're running out of gas! Now what, Melanie?"

"Grab the buoy and run for Palmhenge. If we can make it into the dense area, perhaps we can lose them among the tree trunks."

As they started to run, they overheard, "We've got 'em now. Let's move. Without that buoy, our asses ain't worth a plug nickel."

David looked over his shoulder, then gasped, "The younger one's pulled a knife!"

Desperation marked the early morning foot race along the beach. All four were running for their lives.

When David and Melanie reached the edge of Palmhenge, they glanced over their shoulders. The two men were gaining ground. Melanie noticed David's labored breathing. Her wind was lasting, thanks to her exercise program. She took the buoy from David while they ran the tortuous, twisting route through the uprooted trees.

Melanie hopped over a small root system and ducked under a low hanging branch. "This way, David! Quick!"

"I'm trying, Melanie."

The sound of the men's feet hitting the sand obscured the beating of their hearts.

"Ouch! Dammit!" the younger fisherman roared as he clipped his head on a root from a toppled tree.

"Com'on! We've got 'em." The older man shouted, "Stop and give us that float! We ain't gonna hurt you as long as you give it back!"

"I can't run anymore," David panted.

"Look!" pointed Melanie. "It's Derby, come to the rescue — if we can reach him."

With their savior standing a hundred feet away, the two put on a small burst of speed. About halfway to the horse, Melanie tripped over a low-lying root and sprawled across the sand. The buoy rolled toward the breakers.

"Leave it, Melanie! We've got to reach Derby!" David screamed.

"They're gonna get away on that horse!"

The shout convinced Melanie to leave the buoy behind; they ran to the waiting animal. With no form but lots of adrenaline, they mounted the waiting horse and headed for the maritime woods. As Derby galloped, they clutched his mane for dear life.

Again they overheard the younger man ask the older one for direction. "Want me to go after 'em?"

"No chance of catchin' 'em on that flippin' horse. Besides, she dropped what we need. Let's get out of here."

"What if they report us?"

"We lay low for a while."

From the edge of the large live oaks, the two on horseback stopped and watched the shrimpers retrieve their dinghy and motor out to the trawler. As David and Melanie caught their breaths, the threat of immediate danger subsided. Melanie decided to leave David at Duck House. He and Rebecca could recover the abandoned trike. She continued to Parker House and the radio-telephone. As Derby trotted into the family compound, she encountered Grant on his way to his laboratory.

"Out for an early morning ride?" he called to her.

"Hardly. I just had a narrow escape."

An incredulous Grant ran to her and asked, "What?"

Endangered

Dismounting, Melanie began to recount the events of the past hour. Grant listened carefully. Noting her exhaustion, he suggested she get some sleep and allow him to handle the reporting. Wearily, she agreed.

* * *

4:30 p.m., Saturday, July 23, 1988

"Now you're mine," the grizzled face snarled as Melanie backed away.

She turned to run. His hand reached out and grabbed her arm. He pulled, and the sleeve of her elaborate silk dress ripped. She stumbled against the doorframe. She stared in horror at the bedraggled man with an unkempt reddish-brown beard and the unfamiliar uniform of a Spanish conquistador. As she spun out the door and ran, he lurched after her.

Under her feet, the shifting sand acted as weights tied to her ankles. She slogged up a dune and rolled down the other side. Scrambling, sandy grit entered her mouth; her breath came in short gasps. As she struggled to her feet, he was almost on top of her.

The sun's heat intensified. Sweat dripped into her eyes as she continued her flight. She felt his presence. There was no escape. A heavy hand landed on her shoulder and pushed her to the ground. He turned her over. As he lowered himself, she averted her eyes from his rotten-tooth grin....

Melanie sat up with a start and shook herself awake. The sun's brilliance on the light-colored sand caused her to squint as she looked around. "What a nightmare! Obviously, I fell asleep lying here on the beach," she reflected.

She lay back down to perform her own dream analysis. Chases, strange stories in the night, fires, journal entries — all had provided rich material for her subconscious.

"Still, why didn't I put up a real fight against that conquistador? No scream, no defense — I just ran. It reminds me of the purse snatching. I ran then, too. Though, then, I was giving chase. Maybe I'm being too hard on myself. At least, out of all those people, I was the one who took some action. I guess I'll just have to keep taking care of myself. Thank goodness, this experience was only a dream. Enough sun and daymares for one day!" she concluded.

She stood up and stared out to sea. The Atlantic resembled a giant lake on this perfectly still day. Waves were only inches tall and the surface was like turquoise glass. It almost looked Caribbean without the silt churned by the breakers. Melanie decided to take advantage of this rare calm for a swim. Besides, she spotted a school of dolphins not too far out.

She floated beneath the cloudless sky with a lazy kick or two every once in a while. The dolphins were only fifty feet from her. They rose and fell rhythmically as they played. She noticed another shape out of the corner of her eye. "Shark!" her mind screamed. Another part of her contained the panic. She took a closer look and recognized the unmistakable shape of a loggerhead turtle's shell. It was only a few yards away.

She quietly breast-stroked toward the mound. When she neared it, she could see flipper movement. Then, the turtle disappeared. She took a breath and went underwater, also. She could barely discern the turtle, swimming gracefully and parallel to her course. For a moment, she was tempted to get closer and maybe even grab a ride on the turtle's shell. Again, her rational mind stopped her — no mask, no snorkel, no scuba tank. Too, notice those jaws!

Breaking the surface, she savored her adventure — how exciting to get so close! The pure joy propelled her as she returned to her own element. On reaching the shore, she ran over to her sunning spot, rolled up her towel, and hurried toward the house. She wanted to share the experience with someone.

Crossing the hot sand, she heard an unidentifiable sound beyond a dune. She edged around to see a person bent over an object — Rebecca without clothes and a turtle on its back.

This turtle, however, wasn't moving. The redhead had broken open the carapace of the reptile and was pulling out the intestines.

Melanie choked on her own bile, but she resolved to watch the hideous process.

Again and again, Rebecca cut, extracted, examined, and discarded.

Melanie realized that this turtle might be the mate to the one she had seen swimming. Why else was it so close to shore during the day? Was it waiting patiently, but futilely, for its companion?

The research director turned and grabbed the sledgehammer that lay nearby. The nude Rebecca approached the turtle and swung the heavy mallet, striking the shell with full force. Again and again she swung, breaking the animal into pieces, fragments, then, pulp. Blood splattered the sand and the woman.

Melanie gasped for air. She stared at the sky and, then, looked again. There was a wild, crazed look on Rebecca's face. She continued to hammer away, though the target was completely unrecognizable; it was being ground into the sand. Finally, Rebecca stopped. Breathing heavily, she stared at the carnage. Blood and tissue clung to her body like an abstract painting. She turned and walked to the ocean to wash herself.

Melanie slipped away, unseen and shaken. What feelings or beliefs inside Rebecca had exploded into such a display of violence?

* * *

7:00 a.m., Tuesday, July 26, 1988

Louisa's gentle shaking brought Melanie from her deep sleep, "Miz Mellie, I'm sorry to wake you. Dere's a phone call fo' you. He says he's callin' from Porchagull."

Trying to clear away her grogginess, Melanie rubbed her eyes and stretched her arms over her head. A soft glow was illuminating her bedroom. "What time is it, Louisa?"

"Abou' seven, Miz Mellie."

"Goodness! A phone call from Portugal? So early in the day? Who'd want to talk...?" Melanie's thoughts spun out loud in the still air.

As she pulled on a light robe, her thoughts crystallized. A call from Portugal must involve Parker Transworld. The only person she knew well in the Lisbon Office was Emilio Balboa. He had started to work for the company before she was born. She and Ashley had made him an honorary uncle years ago. Her father had shown great confidence in Emilio; he had put all European operations under Emilio's control.

Running downstairs and reaching the radio-telephone, she depressed the talk lever and deliberately spoke louder than normal, "Emilio?"

"Melanie! I can hear you fine. We have an unusually good connection. Did I wake you?"

"Emilio, your call is a wonderful beginning to my day."

"Ah, Melanie, you're always most gracious. How are you feeling these days?"

"I'm feeling stronger now, thanks to being here on the island."

"Often you Americans are in too great a hurry. You've never realized the benefits of daily siestas and regular holidays. I'm glad you've let your psyche rejuvenate."

"Emilio, I hope, you're not going to tell me you've decided to retire or leave Parker Transworld in order to rejuvenate your psyche."

"Oh no, nothing like that," Emilio laughed. "Actually, I called to talk to Ashley. The New York Office gave me the information that he was at Caretta. However, since he has not yet arrived, I'll take this opportunity to talk with you about my concerns."

"What concerns, Emilio?"

"I've been studying the unofficial annual report. The branch managers receive a copy for review before publication. No one ever makes changes. But, it gives us a chance to compare our branch with others, come up with answers for the press, and so on. As I was examining the report, I was puzzled by a number of items."

"Well, finances were Greg's area. But, some competence may have rubbed off."

"If you prefer, I'll wait until Ashley arrives."

"No. Go ahead, Emilio. I'll share your concerns with Ashley when he gets here. Besides, maybe I know enough to shed some light on your questions."

"One recent personnel change surprised me. Kanjiro Fujiwara has quit the company. I met him only on a couple of occasions. But, from what your father and Greg said, he was not one to take off if the going got tough. I checked the Far Eastern financial section and found one division, SAF, losing a huge sum of money. Now, most branches have the same division types. But, I've never heard of this one. It made me wonder if there were a possibility of underhanded transactions occurring."

"I'm shocked, Emilio. As you said, Kanjiro Fujiwara was considered a major find for us. It's difficult to imagine him failing — or committing a dishonorable act," she added.

"That's my feeling, too. Thus, my concern with this mysterious division. I called accounting to determine what SAF means and was told it stands for Savannah Air Freight. With a base in Savannah, Georgia, it's an unusual holding for the Far Eastern branch."

"That's surprise number two, Emilio. I thought I knew everything Parker Transworld was doing in the States. I've never heard of Savannah Air Freight. To discover it's based here in Savannah, but assigned to the Far East is even more confusing. I'll check this out with Ashley."

"Thank you for listening to an old man, Melanie. I want to help. It's been difficult these past several months feeling like a bull too old to fight any longer and, as you say, being put out to pasture."

"I'm astonished. Father and Greg relied on your advice, Emilio. I'm sure any lowering of your input into company decisions must be due to confusion following the accident. I'll check on what's happening."

"Again, you're most gracious. Often an old man doesn't know when to quit and, if it's time, he needs to be told. Rest assured, day or night, I'm willing to help in any way. Parker Transworld is still my life."

"I know, Emilio. We wouldn't be where we are without you. Thank you for your call."

She concluded the call from the formerly unflappable executive. Short-circuited decision-making processes, unexplained personnel changes, and mercurial failures of strangely-assigned new divisions had been impossible a year ago.

CHAPTER 19

As he stood in the shower, needles of hot water prickled his back muscles. Clouds of steam penetrated his nose and eyes. He allowed himself to relax for the first time in what seemed ages.

Toweling himself dry, the tired man told himself, "One must keep priorities straight. Number one comes first!"

"Get your ass out here! I'm waiting!" a female voice demanded.

He opened the door and entered the bedroom. He met the glare of an impatient woman. Her irritation was obvious, but her body was more conspicuous. She was clothed alluringly in black stockings, a black satin garter belt, and a black leather vest tied with a cord between her full breasts. When he walked toward her, she stepped forward and slapped him across his face. Before he recovered, she followed with a backhanded slap that almost knocked him down. Again, she struck him, then, pushed him to the floor.

Slow to defend himself against her strong assault, he felt his wrists being bound above his head. He lay helpless on his back. The woman began a slow, rough handling of his nipples and genitals. Punishing yet laughing, she controlled him completely. Pain and arousal surged through his groin and brain. "She's wonderful!" he told himself.

* * *

9:00 a.m., Wednesday, July 27, 1988

"I'm relieved to see you. How was your run?" Patrice asked a sweat-drenched Melanie.

"Hot — as if I were running inside a pressure cooker! It's over ninety. And, it's still early!"

"You'd better be careful. Heatstroke can happen."

"I'm being cautious, Patrice." Melanie smiled at her aunt, "You said you were relieved to see me. Has something come up?"

"Dear me, yes. I do get sidetracked. Ashley called to say he's on his way. He wants someone to meet him at the airport. I can't locate Grant; he's off somewhere in his kayak."

"Don't fret. I'll call Adam. Perhaps he can spare Jim Jr., a car, and a boat for the trip."

Melanie made the connection with Adam who was pleased to be of service. Then, the household set about the putting on the finishing touches for Ashley's visit.

The thermometer hovered near the one-hundred-degree mark at three o'clock when the throaty sound of a diesel engine signaled Ashley's arrival. As usual, Jim brought visitor and luggage to the Big House.

Inside, Ashley and Melanie embraced; he complimented her tanned, refreshed appearance. A formal hello to Patrice, a warmer hug for Louisa, and a curt handshake with Grant concluded the greetings. Abruptly, Ashley announced he was heading upstairs to change into cooler clothes; Grant decided he'd head over to his workshop.

Later, the three family members were sipping Louisa's lemonade while rocking in the chairs on the porch.

"I hate to state the obvious, but this heat is plain unbelievable," Ashley commented.

"Worst part of the day," Melanie replied. "Occasionally we get late afternoon thunderstorms that cool down things. But, if the sun comes out, it creates a steam bath. Slows down the pace a bit."

"Actually, it's almost as bad in the city. But, there, we have air conditioning."

"No breaks at all, Ashley?"

"You're still perceptive. No, not many breaks. It's been harder than I imagined. But, I believe I'm getting the hang of being the 'big boss.' I hope so, 'cause I'm missing a lot of playtime."

"You always were the wild one," Melanie giggled. "It's refreshing to see a different side."

"You were straight enough for both of us. Someone had to provide the family with entertainment."

Patrice interjected, "It's certainly nice to see you've been able to shoulder the load."

Ashley responded, "It's satisfying."

"If you two will excuse me, I promised Louisa we'd go over the household details for the next few days."

"Certainly, Patrice. Call if you need any help," Melanie offered.

"The two of you seem to be getting along. How's it been living with our crazy aunt?"

"Actually, she's fascinating — far more complex than I'd presumed. Questions remain. But, your fears about her being crazy are totally unwarranted — happily I might add."

Ashley grinned, "Well, I'm glad it's been you, not me, here with her. However, you do look and sound better than when I last saw you."

"That conversation seems a hundred years ago. So much has happened in the past months and most of it for the better. I feel revitalized."

"So tell me about your experiences. You've mentioned the turtle team, the real-estate developer, and the engineer. Any romance?"

"Lots of new friends," Melanie laughed. "I hope you'll go out with the researchers one night on beach patrol."

"I'm a night person, but searching for reptiles has never been my idea of after-dark fun and games."

"The director is a cute, single redhead and then there's a college girl whose figure makes most males lose their composure."

"Hmm, maybe I will check out the situation," Ashley chuckled. "How about your male friends?"

"They've both been wonderful. Grant's an easy fellow to be around and Adam seems to be a class act."

"Hmm..., go for the class. You can get a dog who's easy to be around."

"Ah, the true romantic emerges," Melanie kidded.

"I'm going to go mix something more potent than lemonade. Care for anything?"

"Not right now. Thanks."

Ashley returned in a matter of minutes with a large martini. Staring out across the marsh he spoke, "Our legal people are pushing for a decision on the island."

"I've been giving it thought and, as you know, so has Adam Gardner. He says he's already contacted you about his interest. Since then, I believe, he's become intrigued. He's told me he would like to meet with the three of us to present his ideas."

"Sounds good. The three of us? Who's the third?"

"Why, Patrice, of course. Any decision involving the island's future must include her. After all, she's more involved with Caretta than any other Parker."

"I guess that's true," Ashley replied with a sigh. "Though it'd be easier to handle things between you and me."

"Oh, I almost forgot, Ashley. Emilio Balboa called yesterday to talk with you. But, he ended up talking with me."

"What in the world did Emilio want?"

"He had several concerns raised by the preliminary annual report. A new division, called SAF and located in Savannah but listed as part of the Far East branch, had shown a large loss this past year. Then, Kanjiro Fujiwara had left without any explanation to the other branch managers."

"Emilio is sticking his nose into areas where it doesn't belong."

"That's not fair, Ashley. He's conscientious and he cares about our company. I think he's justified in calling."

"He's an old hen, clucking about nonsense. The division is an experimental operation I put into place after years of being vetoed. It would have done well except that sneaky Jap bled the operation dry. I gave him the door. But, it was too late to turn around the figures. I figured Far East needed more action, so I set it up under them. The trial did reveal that yours truly, Ashley Parker, has spark and imagination."

Melanie puzzled, "It's hard to accept Kanjiro as dishonest. Actually, it's a shock."

"Welcome to the real world. Beneath the facades, there can be disappointing characters."

* * *

8:00 p.m., Thursday, July 28, 1988

The radio-telephone buzzed. Seated in the dining room, Patrice, Ashley, Melanie, and Grant heard Louisa answer its impatient summons.

"This is Detective Richard Stone with the New York Police Department. May I please speak to Mrs. Melanie Evans?" squawked the speaker box.

"Jus' one momen', suh," replied Louisa.

Melanie hurried from the dining room to the sitting room and the phone. "I heard. Thank you, Louisa."

"Detective Stone, this is Mrs. Evans. It's been a couple of months since we talked. Have there been new developments on the burglary?"

"No. Your brother itemized the stolen jewelry and furnished the insurance appraisals and photos. None of it has been fenced, to our knowledge. I'm calling to check on you — to see how you're doing."

"What a surprise! The New York Police Department must be better staffed than I thought for you to have time to check on my welfare."

"There's more to it than that, Mrs. Evans. You see, it's taken me this long to talk to all the officers who investigated the automobile wreck. It turns out that one of them, who was a rookie at the time, used to work on cars. Even though the vehicle was badly burned, it appeared to him that the brake line might have been partially cut. It was a detail he would have never noticed except the auto was upside down. The other officers convinced him that the damage was caused by the wreck," he paused. "So, I was sitting here at my desk, wondering if anything else unusual has happened to you."

"Oh, I see," Melanie responded woodenly, absorbing the impact of what he had told her.

"Well," he prompted her. "Has anything happened?"

"Uh..., yes."

"What?"

Trying to decide what all to tell the detective, Melanie began recounting the events. At first, she spoke in a halting voice. Then, an anger filled her. She wanted to catch whoever was responsible for the accident and the subsequent events. She began to pour out the details in machine-gun fashion. "A Latin American sailor's body washed ashore. I was knocked out during a forest fire that, I suspect, was set on purpose. There's a mysterious boat anchoring in the island channel without its lights and the crew's using the old rumrunners' hideaway. My cat disappeared then returned with a note reading 'Curiosity kills the cat.' Two shrimpers attacked me and one of the researchers to recover a blinking buoy -"

"Wait! Wait a moment! You're going too fast. Let's start at the top again. You say a dead Latin American sailor washed ashore?"

"Right."

"What did the local authorities say about that?"

"The authority is the Fish and Wildlife Warden. He says the sailor was drunk and fell off a freighter."

"How about the fire?"

"The Fish and Wildlife Warden surmises that heat lightning started the fire and a falling branch hit me."

"What is this man's name and how can I reach him?"

"Fred Frazier. Let's see," she stalled as she scanned the bulletin board behind the radio-telephone. "Ah, here's his number on Skidaway Island. The area code is 912. His office number is 234-5234."

"What happened next?"

"One of the loggerhead turtle researchers and I noticed a boat anchoring in the channel without lights — that means another boat could hit it."

"And?"

"I discovered the crewmen are using the old rumrunners' hideaway."

"Rumrunners?"

"During Prohibition."

"Oh," the detective digested the information. "And did you discover why the men are using the hideaway?"

"No."

"Then what?"

"My cat disappeared."

"Your cat?"

"Ali Cat, the island cat. He follows me almost everywhere. He disappeared — for over a day — then reappeared with a note around his collar."

"'Curiosity kills the cat'."

"Correct."

"That sounds threatening. How did you interpret it?"

"That the shrimpers didn't want me nosing around the hideaway, though Fred concluded it was just a practical joke."

"Whose hideaway is it?"

"It's on a hammock alongside Caretta. It's Parker property. But, the shrimpers may not know that."

"And, you say the shrimpers attacked you?"

"Me and one of the loggerhead turtle researchers."

"Are these shrimpers the ones who use the hideaway?"

"I think so. I spied on them one night and they sounded the same to me."

"OK. Who are all these researchers? Why are they on your island?"

"Because my father gave them permission to study the loggerhead turtles nesting on Caretta."

"Your father? I thought he was dead."

"He gave permission to the Sea Island Institute years ago. The researchers come every summer when the turtles lay their eggs."

"Why do you think one of the shrimpers attacked you? Was he after turtle eggs?"

"No. A researcher and I found a buoy washed up on the shore. When we picked it up, a light started to flash. The shrimpers wanted the buoy; they said it was part of their equipment."

"How did they attack you?"

"They chased us down the beach with a knife."

"What happened?"

"I dropped the buoy and they got it."

"Anything else?"

"No, that's all."

"Did you report the incident?"

"Grant reported it to the Fish and Wildlife Warden."

"How about the Coast Guard?"

"No. We debated calling them. Finally, we decided the shrimpers were drunk — and had lost their better judgment."

"Well, Mrs. Evans, your life on the island has been far from dull — slightly unusual, I would say. Let me see if I have all the people straight. There's you and your brother, Ashley Parker. There's the dead Latin American sailor — do you know his name?"

"No."

"There's Fred Frazier, the Fish and Wildlife Warden. Then there are the loggerhead turtle researchers. What are their names and where do they come from?"

"The Loggerhead Project is part of the Sea Island Institute. The project director is Rebecca Woody, that's W-o-o-d-y. Her assistant is a Florida State graduate student, Daniel Jordan. The other researchers are college students, David Webster from the University of Georgia and Lana Berg, that's B-e-r-g, from Duke."

"So, is that everyone on the island? Who's Grant?"

"He's another researcher — for desalination. His name is Grant Yeats. That's G-r-a-n-t Y-e-a-t-s. He's from Australia. Too, there's my aunt, the caretaker, and his wife who is the housekeeper."

"Can you give me the others' names, please?"

"Patrice Parker, Jim Johnson and his wife, Louisa. Patrice has lived on the island for thirty years. Jim was born on the island — his ancestors were slaves here. He married Louisa and brought her here to live."

"Slaves?"

"Yes. Before the Civil War his people were brought here from Angola to work on Caretta. Someone in their family has lived here ever since."

"That's unusual, isn't it?"

"Not in the sea islands. The black families tend to stick together, near their homeplace."

"You've given me a lot of information, Mrs. Evans. I'll be in touch. Good-by."

"Wh...," Melanie stammered, then she realized Detective Stone had already broken the connection.

Melanie turned to find Patrice, Ashley, and Grant staring at her.

* * *

In the car, Melanie reached across the console to touch her husband's leg, her signal to hold hands while he steered the car with his other hand. His right hand covered hers and he smiled at her. She felt his warm fingers squeeze and reassure her.

To better observe her son with her parents, she undid her seat belt. She turned in the seat and watched the three of them examine a new book.

Then, the bubble burst. The serenity was replaced by startling movements, screeching noises, and a flying sensation. There was no opportunity to grab onto her husband, child, or parents. She was being separated from them.

Melanie turned in bed. She entered the dream again. She wanted to recapture that feeling of love — between her and Greg, between them and their child, between their family and her parents....

She was in the BMW, seated beside Greg. In the rear seat, her parents flanked Parker. Parker was showing them how much he knew about dinosaurs. It was a precious moment. They were all content with their roles — happy to be there.

Melanie tried to hold onto the moment.

Her mind forced her to look at her husband and his last motions — his attempts to hold his family intact.

She remembered how his hand had tensed over hers before he had removed it to downshift the gears. She had heard the BMW whine in protest. She had turned to see his determined expression. She had watched his eyes, checking the traffic in the rear and side mirrors. Then, she had observed his right foot, pressing the brake pedal down again and again — all the way to the floor....

Melanie woke with a start. Detective Stone was correct. Someone had meddled with the brakes. She should be dead, too!

She pulled her nightgown tight about her body and sat huddled in misery in the center of her bed. Sensing her distress, Ali Cat cuddled close. The tears flowed as she realized someone had killed her family and, more than likely, had tried to kill her — again.

As she wiped the tears off her cheek with her hand, she heard a clicking noise. She noticed the door knob turning. She sat there horrified. Who was on the other side of the door and why? Was this another attempt on her life?

She separated the mosquito netting and jumped off the bed. She removed the globe off the kerosene lamp and hurried toward the slowly opening door. She raised the heavy glass lamp over her shoulder, ready to strike.

The figure entered tentatively.

"Melanie?" it inquired softly. "Are you all right?" Then more loudly, "Melanie! Where are you?"

Melanie shut the door.

The figure pivoted toward the door and her.

"Grant," Melanie breathed, recognizing him in the dim light, clothed only in his khaki shorts. "What are you doing here?"

"I heard you crying."

Melanie paused before she answered, calculating whether Grant could be involved in the murder plot. She lowered the lamp and answered, "You did. Detective Stone is correct about the brakes on the BMW. I dreamed about the accident. I saw Greg pumping the brake pedal again and again. I remember it all now."

"Oh, Melanie," he said as he embraced her, pulling her to his bare chest. "Melanie, Melanie," he repeated as he wiped the tears off her cheeks and pushed back stray strands of her hair.

Minutes passed as he held her close. Finally, he noticed the kerosene lamp in her hand. "I scared you, didn't I?"

Melanie nodded yes. She was too full of emotion to speak.

"Come. Let's set that lamp down and talk."

He took the lamp from her and placed it on the table beside her bed. He parted the mosquito netting and settled her on the side of the bed.

"You've had enough scares for one night, haven't you, love?"

His quiet, gentle voice soothed Melanie's jumbled spirits. He realized the shocks she had suffered this day: the news of the possibility of tampered brakes from the NYPD detective, then, the dream that confirmed this horrific knowledge.

He held her hand as she sat in a daze.

"Melanie?"

"Hmm...?"

"Do you want to talk about your dream and what it means?"

"I think it means someone is trying to kill me, Grant. What do you think?"

"I dare say you may be right," Grant phrased his reply with care.

"It's nice you believe me now."

"I never disbelieved you. The idea astounded me when you mentioned it at the fire. It's been in my mind ever since. However, you appeared to want to avoid me as well as the subject."

"Did I?"

"I thought so. Did you assume I took advantage of you, Melanie?"

She let out a long breath, "No, at the time, I felt our lovemaking was a natural reaction to the circumstances — a release — you know, kind of a celebration of still being alive after almost losing our lives and the island. That next morning, I realized, I wanted the act to mean something. Then, you and Fred made me so angry when you patronized me."

"Patronized you?"

"Yes, patronized me." Mimicking Fred's voice, Melanie continued. "'Everyone's had a tough twenty-four hours. Sometimes imagination gets kinda wild.'"

"Melanie, Fred said that — not me."

"I know, but you said nothing — as if you agreed with him."

"At that moment, I thought it best to get Fred off the island. I barely listened to his prattle. Afterward, you seemed more interested in spending your free time with Adam Gardner than with me. And, too, I had to come to grips with my feelings."

"Oh, Grant — "

"What's going on here?" demanded a voice from the doorway. Framed in the open doorway was the silhouette of Ashley Parker.

CHAPTER 20

8:00 a.m., Friday, July 29, 1988

Melanie ate, but the hearty breakfast settled uncomfortably in her stomach. Louisa had gone all out for Ashley's visit — fried country ham and eggs, red-eye gravy for the grits, and beaten biscuits with home-made dewberry preserves.

"About last night," began Ashley.

Melanie raised her eyebrows at him.

"I'm sorry if I interrupted anything between you and Grant. I —"

"You didn't —"

"Wait. Let me finish what I have to say. I was restless after the phone call from the NYPD. If only the detective had talked with me instead of you. Then, I could have gotten some information out of him. It seems to me that if someone did tamper with Greg's car and has made other attempts on your life here at the island, then, I'm in danger, too. I came to your room last night to find out why you hadn't told me about all these little happenings."

Melanie let out her breath. The conversation was as if she were re-experiencing another bad dream or a return to her childhood. Here was her big brother — around whom the world revolved — and here was she, little Melanie Parker Evans — to whom all these inconsequential events had occurred. Why hadn't she, the dumb dolt, called her super-smart brother?

Rubbing her brow, Melanie responded. "Ashley, you make it sound as if I'm guilty of a crime for not calling you. You had enough to consider without adding my suspicions. Besides, until Detective Stone called last night, there was no reason to connect what occurred in New York to what was going on here."

"Probably, Detective Stone is acting on a hunch. But, Melanie, you know I care about what's been happening to you. You can share all your concerns with me. Now tell me. How well do you know Grant Yeats?"

Attempting to determine where the conversation was headed and trying to decide how much Ashley needed to know about her personal relationships, Melanie paused before continuing. "Fairly well. We jog together. We've gone into Savannah together — eaten lunch, toured some sights. We've talked about his research, nature, and change on the island."

Ashley got up from the dining room table and peered through the lace curtains at the serene, sun-drenched grounds.

"What kind of man do you think he is?"

"What kind of man?" Melanie repeated his question.

Ashley turned from the window, stood next to the table, and faced Melanie. With exasperation in his voice, he uttered, "Yes, Melanie. Is the man capable of murder?"

* * *

2:00 p.m., Friday, July 29, 1988

Melanie wanted a few minutes to talk with Adam before he met with Ashley, Patrice, and her about the development potential of the island. While she walked to the dock to meet Adam's runabout, she contemplated Detective Stone's unsettling news. Again, she considered the question Adam had posed after the fire: Who might profit from her death?

She examined her trust level of the different people who surrounded her on the island. She had grown to appreciate Patrice and her pride in the island and its history. However, both Ashley and she stood in the way if Patrice wished to gain control of the island. In a way, Patrice had married the island thirty years ago. Had her fantasy life gotten out of hand? Would she kill to protect her "lover?"

Melanie loved Louisa and Jim despite their superstitious natures. Were they afraid for "their" island? Did they consider Caretta "heirs' land," the unwritten contract giving family rights to sections of property to sea island blacks? How far would they go to secure these supposed rights? Was "The Three Little Pear" story a thinly veiled warning? Was there a sacrificial element in hoodoo?

How about the researchers? The college students seemed too young and naive to be involved. Besides, there was no motive, no possible benefit — was there?

Daniel was older and this was his third summer here. Could he have set up Caretta as a drug drop? If so, where was he storing the goods and how did he plan to get them off the island? What was the connection to New York? Was that why her family had been killed? And, she had narrowly escaped twice? She dismissed the possibility. Just because Daniel was young and black, the media's favorite profile of a drug dealer, didn't make him one.

How about Rebecca? This was her third summer, too. Did Rebecca want more than Sea Island Institute access to the island? It was not in her best interest to jeopardize those rights. She's ambitious; she's single-minded where the turtles are concerned. Still, Melanie could not understand the grisly act of pounding the turtle to pulp. Melanie sighed. Let's face it. She'll go after what she wants, especially, if she's angry. Another unsettling thought was that Rebecca had been the closest person to her when she was knocked out the night of the fire.

Grant continued to be an enigma. Perhaps if Ashley had not interrupted them last night, she might have found what was concealed beneath that analytical layer that insulated him. It was the first occasion he had started to open up to her. She searched for a reason her death might provide Grant an opportunity — but an opportunity for what?

How about Adam? He definitely wanted the island. At least, he wanted to develop it. Again, she saw her death as a liability, not an asset, to Adam in his plan — the one he'd be presenting today.

Who or what was she overlooking?

"Hello!" shouted Adam. "Are you too deep in thought to help tie the lines?"

"Oh..., hello, Adam! Sure, I can do the lines. Throw me the rope."

She lashed the ropes to the cleats, securing the boat fore and aft.

Adam stepped onto the dock. "You look pale, Melanie. Are you OK? I can come back another time for this discussion, if you're not feeling well."

"I'm fine physically, Adam. However, I received a shocking phone call last night from the New York City police — from the detective who has been investigating the burglary in my co-op. Detective Stone phoned to say he theorizes someone could have messed with the brakes of our car and caused the accident a year ago. Then, I dreamed about the accident all over again. And, I think, he's correct," she finished emotionless.

"What? You're so calm! Have you and Ashley talked about this and what it means?"

"A little. He considers the detective to be an alarmist. He's really unhappy with the detective for calling me — instead of him."

"Hmm..., I can understand his protective tendencies. Come on. Let's head for the house. We'll talk while we walk."

As they walked, he continued, "I wish you would let me take you away from all this mess. Marry me and you'll never have another worry in your life."

Melanie came to a standstill, "That's quite a promise, Adam."

Adam faced her and placed his hands on her shoulders, "That's what I want for you."

"Marriage didn't protect me last time," Melanie observed bitterly. "I doubt it would protect me again. But, thanks for the offer, Adam."

"What? That's it? 'Thanks for the offer'?" an incredulous Adam blurted.

Melanie explained somberly, "Adam, your proposal comes out of the blue. Be patient. A lot's going on in my life. I need to absorb all the changes. I need to chart a new course, to put it in nautical terms."

Adam sighed, "I understand how it must seem to you. But, I've discovered I want you — forever. Remember that always. Will you, Melanie?"

"I promise." Melanie paused, then, implored, "Adam, please don't feel this is a slight. But, the meaning of the phone call has flooded my mind. It's really hard for me to think of anything else."

They turned and continued to walk toward the house.

"Are you sure you want me to do the presentation today?"

"Yes, you're prepared. You're here. Ashley's here, too. It may not be the best day for me. But, all of us need to hear your plan so we can make a decision about the island." She paused. "I just can't figure it. I've been over and over the people who have anything to do with the island.

The only obvious person to profit from my death is Ashley. And, although we don't always see eye-to-eye on decisions such as my stay here or other business matters, I know he loves me. There's got to be something else going on — something Ashley and I don't know about — on the island and in New York."

"Such as?"

"Something illegal — like running drugs or smuggling plutonium out of the country from the Savannah River Plant or..."

"Wow! When you start imagining, you think big, don't you?" interrupted Adam.

"And, you think small? I thought we were discussing future ideas for the island today."

"That's true. I do think big. And, I hope the rest of your family does as well."

The three Parkers and Adam Gardner gathered in the parlor for Adam's presentation. Adam presented his master plan that set aside a generous portion of the island for the Parker family. It provided another small section for Louisa and Jim Johnson and their heirs. It guaranteed beach access to the Sea Island Institute during the loggerhead turtle nesting season.

"I've tried to make everybody happy, Ashley. I've been listening to Patrice and Melanie about their concerns. Then, of course, I've talked with the Sea Island Institute and Jim Johnson, Jr. In fact, R. J. Reynolds set the precedent of leaving island property to descendants of its former slaves when he gave the bulk of Sapelo Island to the University of Georgia. The owners of Wassaw Island sold their island to the Nature Conservancy to protect its ecologies and kept a section of the island for their personal enjoyment. But, they received only a fraction of its true worth. Caretta Island is much too valuable a property to consider 'giving' it to a university or the Sea Island Institute. Besides, all these state-supported or nonprofit scientific groups need is the guaranteed access to the island.

"What I'm recommending with this master plan is the Parker family form a joint venture partnership with me to develop the island. We look at the island as a whole; we set aside the unique natural areas for all to observe and enjoy. Then, we carve out places for a few exclusive single family homes, townhouses, and a world-class, five-star resort. That way, we limit the number of people on the island."

Adam spread the master plan on the coffee table and used a pointer to direct their attention. He continued, "The facilities such as the marina, the golf course, swimming pool, and club house with dining facilities could be located on the sound as close as possible to the townhouses.

"To preserve as much vegetation and wildlife as possible, minimum roads would be cut. Old roads would be used wherever possible.

"What we need to do next is have disinterested, qualified parties appraise the island. Then, we decide how much of the island the family wants to keep for its own enjoyment and how much to sell to the partnership for development as well as for money to meet inheritance and income taxes. Ashley, when I called, you mentioned you would bring the Parker Transworld annual figures and the recommendations from your lawyer so that the family could evaluate the matter.

"At this point, I think, what is appropriate is that I answer any questions you have about the master plan. Then, I leave. That way, all of you can discuss Parker Transworld finances and your desires for Caraetta. Does that suit everyone?"

All three Parkers nodded, but remained silent.

Adam repeated, "Are there any questions?"

Patrice asked, "How much land can be set aside for the family compound?"

"Again, that's up to you and your financial picture. However, I visualize that this area," Adam pointed to the master plan map, "suits the marina. We could spin off the club house, swimming pool, and golf course near it. All of you would enjoy its proximity."

"That means the townhouses would be close to the Big House, doesn't it?" countered Melanie.

"They could be situated below the clubhouse. Perhaps, we could place the resort beachside, across from the clubhouse to use the golf course and swimming pool. Then, we could locate only single family houses above the family property."

"You speak in tentative terms, Adam," noted Ashley.

"Of course, we need to consider the recommendations of the surveyors, engineers, and architects. After their input, we make the final decisions."

"Absolutely. First priority must be to insure top dollar amounts," Ashley replied.

"How will people get to the island?" questioned Patrice.

"They could bring their own boats or take a small ferry run by the resort. For ecological purposes, it would be a good move to allow no personal cars. Guests could rent bicycles for a minimal fee similar to Mackinac Island in Michigan."

"Are we looking for full-time residents or vacationers? If people live here full-time, I think, they'll demand cars," pointed out Melanie.

"Probably, but that's part of the fine-tuning of the plan. Now, getting back to the concept, are there any other questions about the master plan?"

"What do you conceive will be the long-term effects on the island ecologies, such as the salt marsh, the freshwater ponds, the maritime forest, and the beach?" asked Patrice.

"As the developers, we will have to set aside those areas we want to protect. All of you have seen The Hammock at one time or another. There, such areas became buffer zones and common space."

The three were silent again.

"Let me leave the plan here with you for your discussions. You can call me at the office or at home with additional questions. Or, if you prefer, I can return at your convenience while Ashley is here. Just give me a call and let me know."

Melanie sank a bit in her chair as she contemplated what she was seeing and hearing. If she had her rathers, she realized, she wanted no additional development on the island — houses, townhomes, resort, golf course, marina — all were foreign to the natural beauty of the place.

"Adam, thank you for your presentation," said Patrice. "I believe I speak for all of us when I say how much we appreciate your efforts. We'll be in touch."

Melanie was surprised to hear Patrice close the meeting. In a way, she was pleased that Patrice was playing a stronger role in planning the future of the island. Melanie could not help but wonder what other surprises her aunt might have for her.

Ashley and Adam shook hands. Melanie got up and accompanied Adam to the front door. "Adam, that was a nice touch to consider deeding part of the island to Louisa and Jim and their family. And, it was appropriate to talk to the Sea Island Institute about their needs. Of course, the architect's renderings of the resort and marina are impressive. You've been busy. It gives us a lot to consider. I thank you."

"You're welcome, my lady. When do you and I see each other again? And, when do you think you'll have an answer for me?"

"How about if we plan a boat trip with Ashley and Susannah? I think they've been seeing each other when Susannah flies to New York. Would you enjoy that?"

"Fine. Perhaps we could boat up to Kiawah and look at the development there. It's one barrier island developed with sensitivity to the environment, similar to what we might do here on Caretta. How does that sound?"

"Delightful."

"And?" Adam prompted.

"It may sound odd. I kind of feel like one of those loggerhead turtles crawling up the beach to nest. I take time; I spook easily; I make elaborate preparations for my nest.... Right now, I need time, Adam."

They shared a light kiss and Melanie returned to the family discussion.

When she sat down again, Ashley reaffirmed, "The family needs to make a decision about Caretta. Here are the Parker Transworld preliminary annual figures for us, the sole stockholders. The figure of most concern, of course, is that bottom line."

He handed a copy of the Parker Transworld report to Melanie and to Patrice.

"The other figure of interest," he continued, "is not contained in the report. Our lawyer has supplied it. Morrison has written a letter outlining our tax responsibilities and his recommendations. Here's a copy of his letter."

Ashley distributed copies of Roger Morrison's letter, written on the legal office's linen stationery. Ashley allowed Melanie and Patrice a minute to read it.

"It's a lot to digest, I know. However, if you compare the figures, we need an additional 7.5 million dollars to pay the taxes."

"Ashley, do you know how Morrison came up with a tax value for the island?" asked Melanie.

"His research department made a comparative analysis based on recent sales of other island and oceanfront property."

"I see. And, the Parker Transworld report is a summary of each branch. Do you have the figures on each division within each branch?"

"Of course."

"Can I see the complete figures?"

"Sure, but I'll have to send them to you unless you're ready to come back to work."

A silence fell on the threesome.

Patrice ventured, "It's a relief to have a sensitive plan for change here on the island."

Louisa burst into the room without her usual knock. "Dere's a hurricane comin'!"

CHAPTER 21

5:00 p.m., Sunday, July 31, 1988

"I do hope Belinda stays out at sea," Patrice commented as she turned off the radio.

"What's the latest forecast?" Melanie asked as she entered the room.

"They're predicting a north to northeast course for the next twelve hours. If they're right, that places the storm center far above us. It will be the Carolinas' turn to start worrying."

Two days ago, tropical storm Belinda had matured into a full-fledged hurricane. Caretta's inhabitants, like all coastal dwellers, had been anxiously following the storm's progress.

"I'm relieved. I know I wasn't ready for a storm this season. I'll spread the news to the others. They'll have a better night, knowing we're out of the hurricane's path," Melanie said as she headed outside.

A smattering of wispy clouds marred an otherwise gorgeous starry night. It was hard to comprehend a large hurricane churning the ocean only a hundred miles east.

That night, sleep came easily to Melanie. But, it left as easily with the sound of high wind. Small fragments of live oak branches and dead palmetto fronds pelted the roof. Looking into the blackness, Melanie discerned pines and palms swaying wildly against a blanket of low, scurrying clouds. When she heard a trike coming toward the house, she slipped on a robe and rushed downstairs to the porch. Holding on tightly to her robe as the wind gusts tore around her, she watched Rebecca and Lana hop out and run to the porch.

"What's going on, Rebecca? The wind woke me."

"It's fierce on the beach. We came to see if we could raise NOAA on the radio-telephone."

Hustling inside, within minutes, the trio heard the worst possible news. Hurricane warnings were out. Fickle Belinda had decided to turn west. She was scheduled to broadside the coast in the next five hours. Caretta was dead center. The island must evacuate.

The women scattered. Rebecca walkie-talkied Daniel and David to return to Duck House for storm preparation. Melanie awakened all within the Parker House compound. They gathered to divide up the chores. Grant and Jim fastened the hurricane shutters. Melanie grabbed a flashlight and some rope. She tied down or carried inside all the porch furniture and plants. Patrice and Louisa battened down the interior while the researchers rendezvoused at Duck House to secure their area and pack the trikes with the necessary gear to take with them.

"Louisa, do you and Jim have a place to stay in Savannah?" Patrice asked.

"Yassum. I called my sister. She'll pick us up at de dock. Not de firs' time, you know."

"No, it's not. I hope we fare as well under Belinda as we have in the past," commented Patrice as she contemplated the island's impending inundation.

"De Lord works in mysterious ways. We be prepared."

When Melanie entered the house to relay the plan, Patrice asked, "Dear, do you have any ideas on a place for riding out this storm?"

"There's not enough room for us to stay with Ashley at the Parker Transworld office suite. Rebecca mentioned we could bunk with the rest at the Institute, but that wouldn't be very comfortable. I know we could stay with Susannah or Katherine Harris. You've stayed with Katherine before, haven't you?"

"Yes, but we'd have to split up — you with Susannah and me with Katherine."

"Let me call Adam. He might have an empty rental unit available at The Hammock. It would be the most comfortable and convenient place."

"Please try. At least there we wouldn't worry about being washed out to sea. And, these old bones aren't ready to sleep on any floor."

Melanie had to repeat her request twice to the sound-asleep Adam. Once he was awake, he offered to let them use the condo model. If she could estimate when she and Patrice might get off the island, he would meet them at the dock. Before he hung up his phone, he hurriedly thanked her for calling so he could alert The Hammock maintenance crews to prepare for the impending onslaught.

The loaded-down turtlers drove into the compound. The loggerhead researchers would be the first group to head for safety. Daniel offered to take Patrice, Louisa, or Grant with the crew in the institute's boat.

Louisa decided to wait for Jim. She said "I benna with 'dat Jim too long now."

Patrice simply said, "It'll be easier for Adam to make one trip to the dock to pick up Melanie and me."

Grant accepted the offer of the boat and of the institute's shelter.

The barometer continued to fall. The wind gusted at thirty-plus knots as the remaining group struggled to finish tasks. Occasional sheets of rain pelted down, making each job more difficult. The blackness slowly gave way to a dismal gray morning that allowed a better visual check on their progress. Louisa helped Melanie grab items missed during the night. Patrice filled the bathtubs with fresh water for use upon their return. Jim was fighting his way against the wind toward the main house when Melanie realized the storm was intensifying.

"Enough!" she cried. "Let's get to the dock! We've got to get out of here!"

* * *

Grant sat out the storm with Rebecca, Daniel, Lana, and David at the Sea Island Institute. The structure devoted most of its interior space to displays of sea island flora and fauna as well as human endeavors on the islands. Since the institute had few windows, the storm sounded worse without the visual reassurance that trees stood upright and other buildings remained erect.

Before the team had settled in, the power went out and they were plunged into total darkness. Rebecca checked the phone only to confirm it, too, was inoperative. Even the portable radio had been soaked in their hasty departure. They felt isolated.

To make the best of the situation, the researchers pulled their sleeping bags into various protected, interior rooms and decided to meet in one central location. Here, they set up a Coleman lantern for light and a portable stove to heat water for instant coffee and tea or to warm cans of beans. They sat around the stove as the hurricane played havoc on the land.

When they experienced the sudden quiet signaling the eye of the storm, they retold old and created new "Red Eye" stories, the tall tales of rogue alligators.

* * *

Patrice and Melanie settled into the two-bedroom townhouse that Adam had appropriated for their shelter. Coordinated with the current "in" colors by an interior decorator, the unit was fully furnished, including a large-screen color TV and a microwave.

"Shall we see if there's a weather channel tracking the storm?" Melanie asked.

"You mean there are TV channels for the weather?" Patrice's disbelief registered on her face.

"And, news, sports, kiddy shows, even pornographic movies — all beamed from satellite," Melanie laughed. "I'd forgotten how much one's spare time in a 'civilized' world revolves around the 'tube.'"

"By all means, let's indulge. I need to know what I've been missing."

* * *

The hurricane spent her force; Belinda blew her last breaths across the marsh grasses, pushing them to and fro. Splintered boards, sheets of plywood, and other debris littered the watery marsh where the grasses held sway. From the sentinel palms, an occasional dead frond broke and sailed with the wind. The rain fell — at times as if it were a sheet settling down, other times as if it were a plane of water plunging headfirst onto the ground and surrounding waters.

Behind the double-pane glass, hurricane partygoers watched the havoc subside. Soon it would be time to clean up after the storm wreckage, then, go on with life, as if hurricanes never happen. A last round of drinks was served. How soon we choose to forget.

In one corner, three people made quiet preparations.

"You go back to the island and we'll handle everything else here. OK?" one urged the other.

"OK. It's about three o'clock now — that's enough time to assess the damage before dark. I'll return by ten o'clock with my report," concluded the now-standing figure.

"Sounds good to me," said the first, rising. "I'm ready for that last drink. How about you?"

"Fine," replied the remaining seated person who turned to face the departing figure. "We'll make sure there's plenty of liquor left. That way, we can have a small celebration when you return."

"Very thoughtful. While the two of you stay high and dry, I'll go do the dirty work," concluded the one putting on a yellow mackintosh before leaving.

* * *

The shrimp boat fought its way, lumbering into the six-foot waves. The ship rolled dangerously from side to side as torrential rains lashed its deck. Inside the wheelhouse, two scruffy sailors struggled to maintain their balance on the heaving floor.

"My God, this baby's fierce! Let's hope we hold together until we reach the creek," the older man-in-charge commented as he scratched his graying, reddish-brown beard.

"Why couldn't we wait until it was past? We could still beat everybody back," whined the younger. "Let me have another swig."

"Go easy on that stuff. We've got work to do — and, I don't want you crapping out on me."

The fishing trawler labored along the storm-swollen river until, at last, the captain swung it into the tidal creek leading to the Caretta dock. The wind and, subsequently, the waves subsided in the protected area.

"Where are we going to anchor? We can't tie up at the dock."

"Get out the dinghy. We'll anchor at the usual place. No one's going to spot us there. We'll take the dinghy down the creek — as close as possible to the main house and beach it in the grasses. We may get a little wet, but it won't be too difficult," the older man ordered.

Within the hour, the two shrimpers had anchored their trawler and were pulling their small landing craft into a hiding place. Wearing yellow oilcloth slickers, they waded through ankle-deep mire left by the heavy rain and slogged to higher ground.

"The house is just beyond that grove of trees. Let's move! We need to be finished and in-place before anyone else arrives."

In short order, the two men arrived at Parker House. Using a crow bar, they forced their way through the locked front door. The younger man attacked the radio-telephone, smashing it more times than necessary to destroy it. Like a fury unleashed, he swung as if possessed. He continued around the sitting room, shattering a mirror and lamps. The older man took the instrument away.

"Feel bettah now?"

Panting and sweating, the younger man looked at him with a glazed stare, "Yeah! Yeah!"

"OK, there'll be no calls for help from here. Let's go find us a hiding place while we wait for them to return."

" Don't forget. You promised I'd get first crack at that broad. This is my chance to find out if a rich bitch makes a better lay then a poor bitch."

"I remember. But, man, I wonder about you sometimes."

The pair swaggered over to Grant's laboratory, broke open the door, and set up an observation post near the window. There, they reopened the bottle of whiskey and settled down to wait.

The captain looked at his young assistant. Sometimes Joe seemed full of fear; other times, he was just full of himself. He wasn't easy to predict — or to control. Now and then, the captain thought the young whippersnapper was crazed.

The captain took a drink of the burning liquor and reflected on his own position. He was glad to have this opportunity to make some money for a change. More and more government regulations on commercial fishing were making it difficult for fishermen with small fleets or, like himself, only one boat. He needed the money for his wife and children.

He hoped the Yankee heiress wouldn't put up much of a fight. He had little stomach for this kind of violence, but he recognized the message behind the knife impaled through the photographs of his wife and kids. He dared not fail. The players were ruthless — as the body of one dead Latin sailor proved.

He shook his head and told himself, "No one's going to interfere with this assignment — no one!"

CHAPTER 22

"Is that a knock on the door? Do you think Grant is back already?" inquired Lana.

Daniel remarked, "Hope he has good news about the storm's progress."

"Let's go see. I suppose the danger of any glass breaking has passed," commented Rebecca.

The group made their way through the institute to the plate glass front entrance. A mackintosh-covered figure peered through the double door.

"It's either Grant or a giant yellow canary," wisecracked David.

Rebecca unlocked the door and let in the dripping wet man.

"Did you find out anything?" asked Daniel.

"According to the weather station, the storm has turned into the Atlantic. It'll rain a tad longer. But, it's safe to go to the island. I need to check on my laboratory. Any of you want to go with me and check on your equipment at Duck House?"

"That's a good idea, Grant," approved Rebecca. She glanced at Daniel standing close to Lana. Then, she concluded, "I'll get my rain gear."

"Ah, I'd be happy to go, Rebecca. I'm going stir-crazy in here," offered David.

"Sorry. Director's prerogative — I'm ready to get out of here, too," she informed David.

"Why don't we all go?" continued David. "It would take less time to check everything, if everyone helped."

"No, David," Rebecca replied firmly. "I'm responsible for all of you. It's my job to check out the situation." She left the group standing in the entryway and retrieved her yellow slicker.

As she snapped the raincoat closed, she groaned to Grant. "I know we owe a big thanks to Charles Mackintosh who figured out how to waterproof material with rubber. You'd assume, however, that in the intervening two centuries, some designer would have figured out how to make this gear look sexier."

Grant laughed. "Come on, Becca, you look fine." To the group, he announced, "We'll return by sunset — maybe ten o'clock — at the latest. All right?"

"Sure, Grant. Have a really good time, you two," snidely commented Lana.

"Now ya'll don't have too good a time while I'm gone. Daniel, you're in charge," directed Rebecca. "Let's go, Grant."

They left the protection of the institute and entered the remnants of the hurricane.

"Which boat should we use?" asked Rebecca.

"Let's use the Caretta boat. It's steadier,"replied Grant. "Besides none of the family will be returning until tomorrow."

* * *

Patrice cautioned Melanie. "The island can wait until tomorrow morning. There's no reason for you to rush out there. Jim always closes up the house good and tight. It's weathered many a storm and the island has withstood many more. My dear, please, it's simply too dangerous — and there's really no need. Besides, the storm could regain force at sea and change direction again."

Melanie knew her aunt could be correct. She did not understand this driving force to return to the island. But, Adam was here — and he was offering to take her in his runabout.

"The weather station says the storm's on its way out to sea. Adam's a very careful boater. We're simply going to find out if we'll need any equipment or supplies to take to the island tomorrow in order to get it back to normal. We'll return before you know it. There's no reason to worry," she said giving her aunt a hug.

* * *

Susannah and Ashley arrived at The Hammock marina in her white Corvette. The tires splashed a wave of water across the parking lot as they squealed to a standstill.

"This is exciting — running out to the island at the tail end of the hurricane. It'll take a couple of minutes for Mik to authorize pulling the boat out of dry dock. I'm sure, he'll try to talk us out of going. You'll have to be patient."

"I'll make it worth his while — and ours," Ashley promised.

* * *

Adam steadied Melanie when she stepped onto the deck of the tossing runabout. Gusts of wind and rain whipped the surface as they prepared for the run to the island.

"Adam, look at those huge uprooted trees and the debris strewn everywhere. The Hammock is well-built. Yet, the wind damage has been substantial."

"Belinda has been forceful. But, we built to withstand her and any other hurricane. Underground wiring helps as does conservative engineering design. Our major work tomorrow will focus on repairing the projects under construction. The rest is mainly pick-up."

"This has been my first hurricane. The real thing's far more terrifying than TV coverage. The difference is in feeling the power of the wind and rain. I hope Caretta has fared well."

"We'll soon find out. The ride out will be a little rough, even though the weather's clearing rapidly."

While the boat struggled to make its way through the flooded salt marshes, Melanie reflected on the April day four months ago when Adam first ferried her to Caretta. She had crammed a lot of life into the short, intervening timespan. New people, fresh understandings, even, personal danger intertwined their strands into a new tapestry.

As they approached Tail End, her eagerness to return ebbed and gave way to nervous anticipation. What if the storm had created more havoc than all her imagining? Was she up to a major rebuilding task?

She noted birds wading and fishing in the marsh grasses as if there had been no storm. Focusing on the island proper, she viewed broken branches and an occasional toppled tree. When their winding route brought them close to the shore, she made out vast pools of standing water among the trees. She observed, "Of course, there's severe flooding on land, too — and not simply wind damage."

"Prepare yourself for a big mess in many areas," Adam interjected. "A storm acts like nature's gardener, pruning dead wood and thinning out weak growth. You'll see first-hand why Caretta is called a barrier island."

"The flooding has been my biggest surprise. I'd forgotten how low the land is. And, I hadn't realized how much rain a hurricane unleashes."

"You'll be astounded at the speed of recovery, too. It'll dry up rapidly. Even the fallen wood will blend into the landscape, disappearing without human intervention."

"I guess we'll be fine as long as the buildings didn't receive a direct hit from a toppling tree — or get blown away."

Walking from the dock past Jim and Louisa's house toward Parker House, Melanie and Adam were relieved to see only debris, no real damage to the structures. The yard was boggy as were the paths in and out of the area. Nearing the main house, Melanie noticed the front door left ajar.

"That's strange. I know we secured the door. How in the world did it blow open?"

When they started up the porch steps, the splintered remains of the jamb showed the forced entry by humans — not the wind.

"Stay on the porch, Melanie. Someone may be inside," Adam whispered as he firmly pushed her backwards with his arm.

Someone inside? Robbers? Looters on an island? In a hurricane? Her mind whirled.

Adam slipped inside the door, staying close to the walls, moving slowly and quietly, listening. The interior damage, isolated to the sitting room, was not the work of a professional burglar. The indiscriminate smashing surprised him. Were the two of them walking into a trap? He continued to listen.

Hearing nothing inside, Melanie stuck her head around the door. She looked into the sitting room and gasped, "Oh no! Who would do such a thing?"

Adam moved to her side and asked, "Is anything missing?"

"It's difficult to say. The radio-telephone is certainly inoperative." Her voice tightened, "Adam, could they still be on the island?"

CHAPTER 23

Peering out the laboratory window, the two shrimpers watched Adam and Melanie climb the porch steps of Parker House.

"Aw right! Let's go fix their boat before they try to hightail it out of here," the captain ordered.

Hustling to the dock, the two carried a stick of dynamite, a blasting cap, and wire. Upon gaining the wooden planking, the younger one hopped into the craft and wired the explosives to the starter.

"When do we take 'em? When do I get my chance with the broad?" the younger prodded.

"They're trapped now. There's no hurry. We'll jus' mosey toward the house," came the reply.

Cautiously, Adam and Melanie emerged from the Big House, looked around the grounds, then, turned onto the road leading to the dock.

"Let's stay calm. As soon as we board the boat, we'll go for help," Adam spoke in a low voice.

"You actually believe they're still around?"

"They smashed the only means of communication. To my way of thinking, that means trouble."

Their feelings of dread materialized in front of them. Two men blocked their way to the dock. Melanie recognized them as the two shrimpers who had chased her and David for the buoy. The older man was the Conquistador in her nightmare!

"Adam, those are the same men who came after the buoy!"

"Oh, God! Head for the jeep!"

The pair turned and ran for the garage where the jeep and trikes were stored during the storm. They reached the building ahead of their pursuers.

"Oh no! The keys to the jeep are in the house!" Melanie exclaimed.

"What about these carts? Can you drive one?"

"Sure. They aren't fast. But, they're better than running!"

Melanie hopped behind the wheel of one of the trikes and punched the electric starter. Popping the clutch, she spun the trike wildly out of the garage, almost running over the two shrimpers.

When Adam and Melanie bounced out of the clearing, water sprayed from the puddles. Bullets whistled past their heads.

"Try to keep down until we're out of range," Adam hollered above the scream of the small engine.

"No guns, Dummy!" the older man directed.

"What the hell! What difference does it make?" his partner retorted. "Now, whadda we do?" The younger man slammed his hand against the garage door.

"There's another one of them go-carts in here. Let's see if we can git 'er goin'."

After killing the engine once and jerking both of them around, the captain learned the basics well enough to head after the other trike.

Melanie sped along Crossroad as fast as the storm debris allowed. The immense flooding made driving treacherous. Often, she took the vehicle off the road and it crawled along ridges of higher ground in the forest. Several places, she dodged fallen trees. Always, her path headed toward the ocean. Upon reaching the mushy, foam-flecked beach, she opened up the trike all the way to its maximum speed.

"I hope we've managed to give them the slip," she shouted to Adam above the wind and the roar of the small engine. "What do you suggest we do now?"

He kept his gaze on the rear as he replied, "Head south. We'll hide until they give up."

Melanie attempted to grasp the turn of events. Were these guys robbers or what? The guns and shots suggested they were after her or Adam. Why?

Before she could get any farther with her thought processing, she heard Adam groan, "Damn! Here they come." He had spotted the other trike, wheeling out onto the beach several hundred yards behind.

As the two looked over their shoulders, they saw wisps of smoke as one man fired sporadic gunshots at them.

"It's too open out here!" Adam yelled. "They could get off a lucky shot. We've got to head inland."

"There's a hunting path in another quarter of a mile. We can try it. But, the flooding may have made it impassable."

"We'll have to take that chance. If we bog down, we jump and run for cover. They're not in the best of shape. Maybe we can lose them on foot," he exclaimed.

"We'd better get out of this rain gear. It makes us easy targets," Melanie added as she struggled out of her yellow slicker.

Melanie bounced the trike over the frontal dunes and into the interdune meadow. The hurricane had produced several sloughs that she avoided by running a slalom course. The vehicle careened wildly — slipping and sliding due to the lack of traction. She fought down her panic. Fortunately, the chase trike had even greater difficulty due to its inexperienced driver. Consequently, his helper failed to draw a good bead on his targets before the lead cart entered the woods.

"We can make Backbone now. Should we head south or north? It's probably a mile to the main compound," Melanie called out as she wrestled with the jolting trike.

"Let's go back to the dock. Maybe we can get to the boat or maybe someone else has arrived. If not, we can lead them in circles."

Turning on the north-south road, she added additional speed. But, they hadn't lost the shrimpers. On the straighter sections, they saw their pursuers.

"Oh, no!" Melanie commented. "Look ahead."

In front of them stretched a wide body of water left by the storm. Both ends of the shallow pond ended in dense undergrowth, preventing an easy way around the latest obstacle.

"Let's try to make it straight through! It's our only chance," Adam yelled as he checked both sides of the road.

"Hold on tight!" she screamed.

The small trike tried to become an amphibious craft. With less than ten feet of water remaining, the engine sputtered and died. A hasty punch on the starter proved fruitless — the motor had drowned.

"Jump and run," Adam roared, "before they get any closer!"

"Duck House is only a few hundred yards to our left. Let's head for it," Melanie cried.

The two splashed to firmer soil and ran as the second trike approached the water.

"We've got 'em now!" the driver exulted.

The second trike plowed into the huge puddle without slowing. The resulting cascades of water so effectively drenched the vehicle, it only reached the center before coughing and quitting.

"Damn! Damn!" the captain pounded the wheel. "Com'on. Let's go."

Melanie and Adam reached Duck House. They frantically searched for weapons, locating a filet knife and two boards to use as clubs. They heard crashing in the woods and hid.

When the two men entered the clearing to Duck House, they slowed their pace and methodically looked about them.

"We know you're in there!" one shouted toward the building. "Ya'll leave mighty clear tracks in this muck."

After several moments with no response, the captain turned to his helper and said, "You wanted your big chance. Well, here it is, tough guy. Go on in. I'll cover."

The younger one didn't hesitate. He smiled as he mounted the wooden steps and kicked open the door. Peering into the small front room of the hunting cabin, he saw nothing but stacks of the researchers' gear. When he entered, he waved his gun in all directions. His eyes darted left and right. Pausing in front of the opening that led to the bunk area, he yelled, "They're in the back! Get in here."

As he watched the captain start toward the cabin, Adam emerged from behind the gear and swung a board. A massive pain surged through the young man's head. Adam grabbed the falling sailor and wrenched the gun from his grasp. A shot exploded from the porch and the body went limp. Looking up, Adam saw the smoking muzzle of the captain's gun. His brain registered that the young man's body had shielded him. He'd better act fast.

Without taking time for careful aim, Adam pointed the wrested weapon, now in his hand, at the captain and fired. The sound resounded in the confines of the small room; gun smoke filled the air. The man grabbed at the left part of his upper chest; red blood oozed through his fingers. Scowling at Adam, he aimed and squeezed off another round.

From her hiding placed in the bunk room, Melanie couldn't see. She heard three shots, then, silence. What had happened? Where was Adam? Before she could move, she heard footsteps — reverberating on the wooden floor and coming toward her location.

Time slowed to a crawl.

As the footsteps drew nearer, she held her breath and flattened herself against the wall next to the opening. At last, a man staggered into the room. The build, the hair, the face, the smell — no, it couldn't be, but it was — here was the Conquistador! She hesitated another moment. Realizing this man had wounded or killed Adam and would do the same to her, she forced herself into action. She plunged the filet knife into the Conquistador's back.

As the man fell forward, she held onto the knife's handle, the blade covered with blood. He rolled over and glared at her. He raised the pistol clutched in his right hand and directed it squarely at her face. She was riveted by the look in his eyes. It was not wild or crazed nor was it glazed with pain; it was cold and calculated, the look of a man committed to murder. Terror swept through her. Click. The sound embedded into her consciousness. Click.

His vacant look changed to a sad, resigned stare. Melanie watched him for several moments until it became apparent he was no longer a threat. He was out of bullets.

"Why? Why are you trying to kill us?" her voice trembled.

"Orders. I follow orders," the hollow voice replied.

"Who? Who wants me dead? And, why?"

"You've been too nosy. Some people got real nervous."

She watched the man's eyes flutter, then, close as he slipped into unconsciousness, blood running from his chest and back. She couldn't make herself breathe or move. Then, she thought of Adam. She whirled into the next room. On the floor were two bodies. When she knelt next to Adam and turned him face-up, the obvious exploded in her brain — he's dead.

CHAPTER 24

The sturdy Caretta boat pushed through the swells and waves. Its two occupants huddled behind the wind screen and peered across the muddied gray bay and inundated marsh. At full-flood stage, it was difficult to see the channel.

"There's the creek. It's so swollen, it's hard to find," yelled Grant. "I'm glad I've seen this marsh after another big storm."

"Yeah, me too," rejoined Rebecca. "I hadn't visualized how the water would be everywhere. Do you think our equipment is still dry?"

"Probably. We may have to rent extra pumps to get the excess water out of some of the buildings. That's why we're here. We can determine if we need to be first in line tomorrow morning."

"Please," groaned Rebecca, "you know you're taking all the romance out of this outing. Why don't you leave me with some notions?"

"Notions? What kind?"

"Like you couldn't live without me after all."

"Becca, you know I cherish our friendship."

"Yeah, I suppose that's all it is," sighed Rebecca, "a good friendship. Though we've had a bunch of fun times together, haven't we?"

"Yes, we have. And, I'll remember them fondly when I'm back in Australia."

"You believe Ashley Parker's going to cut your research funding, don't you?"

"Yes, I do. From what I've overheard in telephone conversations, the Parkers are facing a whopping inheritance tax bill. They must run a really tight ship in the near future."

"I wish your research were closer to success." She paused before continuing, "I guess, that's the biggest difference between what you do and what I do. You reach a conclusion — one way or the other. My research goes on and on. Then, sometimes, I wonder if it makes any positive impact on the loggerheads' future. The troops had an argument about it the other day. It ended up in a mudsling. Did I tell you about it?"

"No. Sounds messy!"

"It was. But it was fun, too." Rebecca was silent for a minute then remarked, "I wish we knew Ashley Parker better so we'd know what to expect. Melanie's certainly been a willing and able helper this summer. Their father had a heart of gold. We might be wrong; Ashley might continue our projects."

"Ah, Becca. That's wishful thinking. If wishing made things happen...,"

"Look, Grant!" Rebecca interrupted. "There's a boat at the dock! It's Adam Gardner's runabout. I wonder what he's doing here?"

"I guess Melanie wanted to check on the island, too. She and Patrice were staying at one of his condos at The Hammock. They must have left as soon as the storm warning lifted."

"Does that bother you? Adam's interest in Melanie?"

"Shhh, Becca. Was that a gunshot?"

Rebecca and Grant listened intently. They heard two additional muffled reports.

"My God! What's going on?" cried Rebecca.

"Melanie suspects someone's been trying to kill her."

"Sounds like she's right! Let's hurry before it's too late!"

Grant throttled the boat engine, then, reversed it at the dock. Rebecca scuttled onto the boards. Grant threw her the ropes that she tied with a couple of quick, expert twists.

While they raced to the road, Rebecca gasped, "Where do you guess the shots came from? We barely heard them with the wind blowing out to sea. They must be further away than the family compound. Could Melanie be at Duck House?"

"Let's get the jeep out of the garage," pressed Grant. "I have a set of keys."

They hurried to the barn-like building with its doors standing wide open.

"They must have taken the trikes," Rebecca observed. She studied the wet ground intently, "Look at those tracks. Melanie was in a hurry to leave. And, the other driver was having a hard time with his trike.

I wonder who's chasing Melanie? Adam or somebody else? Do we follow the tracks or head for Duck House?"

"Let's follow as far as the cutoff to Duck House. Then, we'll decide," yelled Grant as he opened the jeep door.

Rebecca jumped into the jeep as Grant started the engine to back out of the cavernous building.

"Keep your eyes open for anything — Melanie, Adam, strangers, off-the-road trike tracks, anything!" Grant called.

"Absolutely!" Rebecca exclaimed as she glanced at the trail of tracks and searched the low-growing scrub. "The wind's still strong. There's a lot of movement."

"Do the best you can," encouraged Grant. "That's all both of us can do," he continued as he gunned the vehicle through a puddle and showered them with water. "Ugh, there's a lot of standing water, too. Sorry about that, luv."

"Just do the best you can, too!" retorted Rebecca, keeping her eyes glued to the roadsides as they sped along Crossroad.

As they approached the cutoff for Duck House, they had not seen anyone or heard any more shots.

"What do you think? Go to Duck House or follow the tracks?"

"Let's check out Duck House. The gunshots sounded as if they came from there," urged Rebecca. "It's only a short distance off the road."

"Agreed."

When they drove past a large flooded area and into the clearing around the lodge, they saw two empty trikes, but they heard no signs of life.

"This is eerie," commented Grant as he set the jeep brake.

"It's downright scary. Let's be careful. Shall we go in together or separately?"

"Let me go in first," said Grant. "Now I'm wishing we had taken the time to radio for help. You get into the driver's seat and keep the motor running — in case you need to get away fast. OK?"

"OK," breathed Rebecca. She crawled over the gear shift as he crept toward the front steps. She watched the doorway and windows, ready to yell a warning. But, she detected no movements inside the quiet lodge.

Grant gained the porch and stood to the side of the front door, listening. When he heard a low moan, he stepped into the dim interior.

While his eyes adjusted to the gloom, he saw two forms sprawled on the floor. He made his way to them. He squatted in the pools of blood surrounding them. To his surprise, one was the well-groomed, nicely dressed Adam Gardner. The other person was a scruffy young man, attired in dirty jeans, T-shirt, and yellow slicker. He checked their pulses. Neither man had one. Grant rocked on his heels, then, stood.

Again, he heard the moan. With caution, he made his way to the adjoining room where he saw another man sitting on the floor, leaning against a bunk bed. His hand attempted to staunch the flow of blood from his shoulder.

Approaching the man, Grant recognized him as a local shrimp boat captain. He had a grizzled, weather-beaten appearance. Grant moved closer.

The captain lifted his eyes to Grant, "She got away, Boss. But, I killed Gardner." His voice trailed away; his head drifted to his chest.

Grant leaned over the man and lifted his hand. There was a weak pulse at the wrist. The man had passed out from blood loss. Grant lowered him to the floor, placed a pillow from the bed under his head and checked his wounds. There was a gunshot in the left shoulder and a knife wound in the lower back. He picked up the man's gun and checked for bullets. The cartridge was empty. He took the gun, then, headed toward Rebecca and the jeep.

"What is it, Grant?" worried Rebecca, noting the steel-blue gun and Grant's grim, white face.

"Two dead, one wounded, and no Melanie."

"What is going on?" she asked, her eyes wide with disbelief.

"The shrimp boat captain mistook me for someone he called 'Boss.' He said that he killed Adam, but that Melanie got away."

"Who else is dead? You said two were dead."

"I'm guessing he's the deck hand from the trawler."

"Oh." Rebecca sat still, absorbing the grisly turn of events. Then, her authoritative side took charge, "Why don't you stay here to see if the captain regains consciousness and still assumes you're his boss. Maybe you can find out what's been happening. Let me take the jeep to Parker

House and call for help on the radio-telephone. Along the way, I'll keep my eyes open for Melanie. She's bound to head back to the house or the dock. Later, if the captain can withstand the ride to Parker House, bring him in one of the trikes. Otherwise, I'll return for both of you later. OK?"

"Fine. First let me make a quick check around the lodge to make certain Melanie's not wounded or hiding here."

The redhead hugged him, "Try not to worry about her, Grant. She's probably at Parker House, calling Fred Frazier, the Coast Guard, even, the NYPD SWAT Squad. Melanie's been through a lot. But, she's a spunky lady."

"Let's hope you're right," Grant sighed.

Rebecca watched him survey the area around the cabin. When he waved her on, she released the brake and shifted into gear.

Heading back the way they had come, Rebecca kept an eye trained for Melanie's blonde hair in the passing woods. As Rebecca was approaching the family compound, she caught a glimpse of Melanie, diving behind a clump of saw palmetto.

Rebecca stopped the vehicle in the middle of Crossroad and cupped her hands to project her voice. "Melanie, it's Rebecca. What's happening? Why are you hiding from me?"

All remained quiet except the wind creaking through the trees.

"Melanie, talk to me. I know you're there!" Rebecca got out of the jeep and started toward the saw palmetto.

Wet and muddy, Melanie stood and faced Rebecca, "Don't come any closer, Rebecca," she warned.

"Why, Melanie? I'm not going to hurt you."

"How can I believe you? I saw you butcher that turtle. You, the leader of a turtle research group!" Melanie stared at the woman, while her mind replayed the scene of carnage on the beach.

"Melanie, what are you talking about? I perform necropsies on every dead turtle I find. I have to discover how the poor creature died."

Filled with doubts at the explanation, Melanie challenged, "What I saw had nothing to do with scientific research. You were vicious and possessed."

"You saw me that day?" Rebecca felt mortified as she recalled the day from the viewpoint of an observer. She sighed. "You're right. What you witnessed had nothing to do with science," she admitted. "You see, Melanie, some people regard the shell of a sea turtle as a prize. They kill turtles for their shells. So, after a necropsy, I always break the shell to keep it from being sold." She grimaced as she continued, "But, when you saw me, I was releasing a whole lot of stored-up hostility toward those people and others who cannot see the results of their actions. I'm afraid I got carried away. I crushed that shell beyond all recognition"

Melanie listened and reflected, "Is this true? Can I trust Rebecca? She was the person working closest to me during the fire, too. I know she can wield a mean stick. But, did she knock me out?" Melanie searched Rebecca's eyes.

Rebecca shifted feet as she watched Melanie. "What can I say, Melanie? What can I do to make you believe me?" She started toward the other woman.

Melanie responded and hugged Rebecca. "Oh, Rebecca," she sobbed. "The shrimpers killed Adam — and they tried to kill me."

"Yeah, I know, Mel. It's over now," she comforted Melanie. "One shrimper is dead; the other's wounded. Let's go call for help. Come on. Get into the jeep."

"B-but," Melanie spluttered, "we c-can't."

"We can't what?" asked a confused Rebecca.

"W-we c-can't c-call for help. Th-they smashed the radio-telephone."

"Oh." Rebecca was quiet while she assimilated this latest news. "Then, I guess, I'll use the boat radio and go for help. Which boat is faster — the Caretta boat or Adam's runabout?"

"A-Adam's boat," hiccuped Melanie.

"Come on. Climb in. We'll get help one way or another," encouraged Rebecca as she assisted Melanie into the jeep. When she had settled the now docile woman, she drove the vehicle past Parker House to the dock.

"Mel, do you want to go with me or do you want to stay here and rest until help arrives?"

"I'll stay — at the house," replied Melanie, feeling drained of emotion and action.

"That's a good idea. You'll be fine now. Just try to relax. I'll be back with help in about an hour and a half. Do you have on a watch?"

Melanie showed Rebecca her wristwatch. "It's five-forty. That means you'll be here around seven-ten or seven-fifteen."

"Good girl," replied Rebecca as they got out and hurried to Adam's launch, bobbing in the rolling waters.

Melanie hugged Rebecca. "Thanks, Rebecca. Now you be careful out there."

Rebecca returned the hug, "I will. Now scat and try to get a little rest."

Melanie stayed long enough to throw Rebecca the ropes releasing the runabout from the dock. Then, while Rebecca studied the controls, Melanie walked wearily away.

Melanie stopped on the bank and waved to Rebecca. Her mind slowly churned up thoughts. "Really, why was Rebecca on the island now? Was she checking on... what? Had she come alone?"

Melanie recognized her mind was beginning to shift into overdrive. She forced herself to relax. She took several deep breaths. The storm has ended. The chase is over. The shrimpers are no longer threats.

"Wait a minute," Melanie speculated as she watched Rebecca. "Why is she leaving if the boat has a radio...?"

A deafening roar split the air.

To Melanie's horror, she saw the boat explode into flames.

CHAPTER 25

The explosion lit up the sky. Reverberations echoed in her ears as shock waves passed through her body. Melanie stared into the channel. Her eyes witnessed bits of burning debris, showering over the grasses and tidal creek, floating and creating another episode in this unabated nightmare. The carcass of the runabout cast a red-orange glow against the gray-brown water.

Tears coursed down her face as she thought of Rebecca. Watching the burning remains of Adam's boat, she realized the bomb had been intended for her and Adam! She had suggested Rebecca use a sabotaged craft! Why hadn't she considered a possible trap? After all, the shrimpers had been coming from the dock when she and Adam had left the house.

Shock and grief gave way to anger. Charged with adrenaline, she ran toward the water's edge. Scanning the littered surface, she saw a bright orange object, bobbing thirty to forty yards away.

It was Rebecca — as usual, prepared for anything. Even in a hurry, she had put on a life preserver. While Melanie waded through the mucky water, she anticipated what the remains might resemble. Could she take it? Could she do anything less?

Slipping, floundering, and paddling, Melanie struggled toward the body that floated with the current. She swam to catch up with it. Melanie grabbed hold of the life jacket and headed for the closest bank, dragging her load behind her. The Coast Guard approved life jacket had performed admirably, keeping the head out of the water. She saw small cuts lacing Rebecca's cheeks. Not much blood after an explosion, Melanie reflected grimly.

Struggling to maintain her balance on the slippery shore, she pulled and rolled the body out of the water. All Rebecca's limbs were intact. Recalling the lessons of a past CPR class, Melanie leaned over Rebecca's face and placed her cheek next to the victim's mouth. She sensed a faint breath! Calming herself, she held her position, concentrating on the body beneath her — breaths, shallow but unmistakable breaths.

Immediately, Melanie felt for a pulse, placing a finger along the carotid artery. There it was, faint but there. Reviewing her mental notes, she remembered with both pulse and breathing present, her sole duty was to monitor — and hope for help.

While she sat next to the research director, she untied the life preserver and insured nothing constricted Rebecca's breathing.

There were a few hours of daylight left. Would anyone else come before dark? Had Rebecca made radio contact? Had anyone heard or seen the boat explosion? She tried to plan what to do next. I must keep my senses. Hysteria only creates more problems.

Melanie looked around. A portion of the clearing around Parker House was visible; the dock was obscured. Rebecca was too close to death to risk dragging her to a better vantage point. She would have to listen for engines.

Fewer than fifteen minutes had elapsed when Melanie heard the drone of an outboard approach the dock area. It stopped. She watched Parker House to catch a glimpse of the new arrival. All was quiet. No one appeared. She was preparing to yell when she saw a trike arriving from Crossroad. It couldn't be the captain. He was too hurt to drive, wasn't he?

Her heart skipped several beats as she waited. It looked like Grant in the trike! "How and when had he gotten on the island?" As rapidly as Melanie phrased the questions, her mind answered them and triggered new questions. "How did he get to Duck House? He must have come with Rebecca using the Caretta boat. But if he had, why hadn't Rebecca mentioned him? And, where was he before, during, and after the explosion?"

While still sorting through this latest development, she received another shock. Walking across the clearing to meet Grant was Susannah! "Why was Susannah on the island?" While Melanie watched, the two entered the main house.

Puzzled, Melanie sat down again beside the unconscious form on the muddy bank. Susannah and Grant were in the house. Were they out here to help? Did she dare scream for attention? Are they the "nervous people" mentioned by the shrimper? What was going on? She diverted her anxiety by checking Rebecca's condition again — shallow breathing, faint pulse, no change — and waited.

* * *

Hearing the screen door slam in the distance, Melanie leapt to her feet. She saw the setting sun glint off Susannah's brassy-blonde hair as she stood in the clearing. Her childhood friend walked to the edge of the marsh, looking at the smoldering remains of Adam's boat.

Sticking to the shoreline, Susannah made her way closer and closer to Melanie's position. Melanie debated between calling and hiding. Too many shocks had occurred within the past few hours to trust anyone. Her dilemma resolved itself as Susannah caught sight of them.

Purposefully walking to their position, Susannah exclaimed, "Lawd, Melanie! What's going on?"

Melanie responded, "I wish I knew, Susannah. I wish I knew."

"Who is...? Lawd, it's Rebecca Woody! What happened to her? Is she dead?"

"Adam's boat exploded. But, she's alive — barely. She needs a doctor."

"Well, come on. Let's get to the house and grab a couple of blankets. Even though it's warm we can cut her risk to over-exposure and shock. Then, we'll figure out how to get her some medical assistance," Susannah ordered.

The idea made sense. Rebecca needed help. Reluctantly, Melanie agreed to return with Susannah to the house.

"You look as if you've been through a lot," Susannah remarked as she noted Melanie's wet hair and torn clothes. "Are you OK?"

Melanie grimaced, "I'm all right. But, I've pulled Rebecca out of the creek. And, there's been...," her voice trailed at the thought of the dead Adam. "But, Susannah, why are you here? What made you venture here after the hurricane?"

"I wanted to see how the island fared. I felt sure all of you had gotten off in time. But, I didn't know."

While the two entered the clearing in front of the house, Melanie noticed a body in the trike. She angled over to the vehicle with Susannah not far behind. The wounded captain was stretched across the rear seat. Grant must have brought him. She watched his chest rise and fall in short jerks.

Melanie's voice shook, "This is the man who tried to kill me. He shot Adam."

"Well then, we'll not worry about him. Let's go get the stuff for Rebecca," Susannah replied coldly.

"Help me," the prone figure whimpered.

"We can't leave him to die," responded Melanie flatly.

"And, why the hell not?" Susannah asked.

"But, Boss, you've got to help me! After all I've done..." the shrimper gasped.

"Boss?" Melanie said aloud. Her mind twirled. He called Susannah 'Boss'? Her childhood pal? Susannah had ordered the shrimpers to kill her and Adam?

"The man's delirious," Susannah interposed, "completely out of his mind. There's nothing we can do for him."

"Boss, help me! We were doing what you wanted."

A memory flashed through Melanie's mind. Louisa's story, "The Three Little Pear" concluded with the spirit of the dead sister, identifying her mother as the murderer. Here, the story was playing again with the captain calling the names. She voiced her conclusion, "Oh, no! You're here to make sure they did their job — not to insure we're safe. What are you involved in, Susannah?"

"You stupid little bitch! You've come to the wrong place at the wrong time! And, you've made it worse by sticking your nose where it doesn't belong!"

"You think you can get away with murder?"

"Who's going to stop me? You? Ha! The spoiled and pampered heiress? You, my dear, do not cause me to tremble with fear," spat Susannah.

Vivid memories of the purse-snatching bounded into Melanie's mind. Could she take care of herself now? She glanced beyond the fit blonde and noticed the unobstructed path to the dock and the two boats. She started to run, but Susannah stepped in her path, "You're going nowhere."

Susannah's strong hands grabbed Melanie's shoulders and pushed. Melanie knew she must get to the safety of the Caretta boat. Intuition controlled her actions. She slipped one leg behind Susannah's leg and shoved with all her might. The surprise move deposited Susannah on her rear.

Melanie sprinted. Susannah lunged for the fleeing legs. Melanie felt the hold tightening on her ankle and saw the ground rushing toward her face. Rolling on impact, she glared at the prone Susannah.

Without considering her strategy, Melanie forced Susannah onto her back, grabbed two handfuls of the woman's long hair, and knocked her head against the ground. Melanie surprised herself. Never before had she been involved in any fight — or ever dreamed of a fight, especially, with another woman. Now her moves came from a deep-core instinct to survive.

Susannah recovered her breath from the initial confrontation and drew into a ball. Melanie tried to leap on top of her opponent, but Susannah thrust her legs upward and kicked Melanie in the stomach.

Melanie staggered and Susannah got to her feet. They circled one another. Susannah leaned over and slapped Melanie on both cheeks. Through the stinging sensation, again, Melanie experienced the survival urge take its course. Momentarily, she recalled the loggerhead turtle who overcame obstacles to lay her eggs, assuring survival of her species. She remembered the jagged holes in another turtle's shell, attesting to shark attacks. That animal could survive. So, could she!

Susannah pushed her hair out of her eyes and stepped forward to deliver another strong slap. Seeing Susannah's arm extend, Melanie grabbed it, ducked underneath in a twisting motion, and shoved Susannah, throwing her onto her face. Rage exploded inside Melanie. "How could Susannah do it? How could she order someone to kill Adam — and me?" Melanie leapt onto the prone woman.

A surprised Susannah spluttered as Melanie knocked the air out of her. Melanie turned over the incapacitated woman and returned a volley of slaps.

A voice cut through the air, "That's enough. Move over here."

Melanie looked up and faced the familiar voice.

There stood her brother, Ashley, on the steps with a gun. And, the gun was pointed at her!

A breathless Susannah scrambled out from under Melanie. Getting to her feet, she glowered at Melanie, then, yanked her erect. "Let's go inside. Now!"

Melanie stared at the ground. Her mind reeled.

Susannah stepped in front of Melanie and brought her knee up hard between Melanie's legs, landing it squarely in the crotch. Melanie gasped and moved to protect herself with her hands. Susannah grabbed one hand and twisted it up behind Melanie's back. "I said — let's go into the house!" She forced Melanie forward.

In agony, Melanie stumbled toward the porch. She staggered, but managed to climb the steps. Susannah shoved her through the door and foyer into the dim parlor. Released, she took a deep breath as she looked around the room. Seated in one of the dining room chairs was Grant, his arms tied behind him! Relief, pain, shock, fear, exhaustion — all flooded her mind.

"Wake up! Wake up!"

But, the nightmare didn't fade.

"It looks as if you had a little trouble with Sis," Ashley remarked to Susannah.

"She puts up a better fight than you. I was beginning to enjoy myself."

"The two of you... What's going on?" Melanie struggled to understand.

"We've known each other for some time now, dear sister, personally and professionally."

"Professionally? The apparel business? You're involved with Savvy?" Melanie felt confused.

"Hardly clothes," Ashley snickered. "Remember that mysterious division, SAF, in the financial report. It really stands for Susannah's Air Freight, not Savannah Air Freight. And, by the way, it was highly profitable to us — though not to Parker Transworld."

"Wait a damn minute!" Susannah interrupted. "How much do you intend to tell her?"

"What does it matter, sweetheart? In a couple of hours the knowledge will go down with the ship."

"What do you mean?" Melanie asked.

Grant spoke up, "He means the two of us will die in a boat accident. We know too much."

"You're bright as well as good-looking," Susannah crooned. "Too bad I can't convince you to join us. I need a replacement for home entertainment. And, you have such muscle tone from all your kayaking," Susannah leered.

"So, the shrimpers are connected with you two?" Melanie ventured.

"Hired hands," Susannah replied. "Go ahead, Ashley. Tell your sister the whole story so she can see how clever you really are."

Ashley glared at his partner. Then, he turned to Melanie and began to explain. "SAF is a tax-free cash source. I arrange for special, high markup products to leave South America on one of Parker Transworld's freighters, heading for port in Savannah."

"Special products? You mean cocaine," Melanie accused.

"Marco de Costa has good contacts at the growing end and insures the shipment's safe loading. Since U. S. Customs has gotten tough, we drop the shipment in the Atlantic."

"Drop it overboard?" Suddenly, Melanie realized the purpose of the buoy. "The buoy!" she breathed.

"Yes, the buoy. Our shrimpers trawl the area to recover it. Then, they leave it in the old rumrunners' hideaway. I have our Grandfather Edward's journal notes to thank for that idea. It's just like the Roaring Twenties and the days of the bootleggers."

"No wonder I found nothing. The stuff's inside the float," Melanie commented.

"Our fisherman recovers the package and takes it to The Hammock airport."

"Who's the fisherman?" Grant asked. "I've never noticed anyone on a regular basis except Jim Jr."

"Smart, huh? No one questions a son, fishing around his parents' place. And, Hammock security never bothers Adam Gardner's personal assistant. At Adam's private airplane hanger, we cut the goods. Our special pilot takes off with the finished product for her 'buying trip' in the Big Apple."

Melanie was astonished, "I can't believe Adam didn't suspect. You were using his boat, dock, and airport."

Susannah laughed and answered, "He was one of our partners, you naive girl."

Melanie felt as if Susannah had slapped her again. Adam was a partner in this mess? She had been a fool. He had taken her in — totally.

"But, you killed him!"

"A simple business decision, Melanie," Ashley replied. "He balked at removing you as a roadblock. Since he knew all the details, we couldn't let him get in the way."

Melanie's bewilderment at Adam's role tempered a bit with his refusal to stoop to murder. Maybe his behavior toward her hadn't been a complete act. Maybe.... She'd never know. Obviously, she'd been wrong about Ashley.

"And, with you out of the way, Melanie, we can develop Caretta into a gold mine. We may have to find other drop points for the goods. But, that shouldn't prove too difficult. Ashley's screw-up a year ago opened lots of new enterprises," Susannah interjected.

"A year ago? The accident?" Melanie shuddered as she guessed the response. "You killed.... You bastard!" Melanie screamed as she launched herself at her brother.

"Whoa!" Susannah hollered as she grabbed hold of Melanie's shoulders and threw her into a chair. "You be sweet — or I'll play with you some more."

Ashley started to pace, "Actually, it was an accident. You see, your darling husband, Greg, was on to SAF. He had been doing some hush-hush investigating. I knew it was only a matter of time until he blew the whistle. So, I fixed the brakes on his BMW. But, he finished his meeting early and all five of you were in the car. It was only supposed to be him."

"Fortunately, Ashley's miscalculation gained him control of Parker Transworld. Soon, it'll be his alone," Susannah smirked.

"So, it was you who broke into my co-op — to find Greg's evidence. And, that's why he hadn't been acting like himself those last few months," Melanie spoke hoarsely.

"I knew you'd understand. While I was there, I figured I'd grab a few of the family jewels. After all, insurance money spends as well as any other kind."

Melanie sagged against the chair. Her only brother and her childhood friend were killers. Her family, a friend, and soon.... The hurt so engulfed and overwhelmed her, it prevented any further thinking about her own dangerous predicament.

Ashley waved his gun at Melanie, bringing her back to the present. "Untie your Aussie friend. You two have a date with the ocean."

As he finished speaking, a hard object pressed against Ashley's back and a low Southern voice drawled in his ear, "Now you jus' drop that cap pistol, boy. Drop it real slow so you don't get blown in half."

Ashley did as he was told. Lowering his hand, his gun was brusquely wrenched away. Glancing over his shoulder, he saw the grinning face of Fred Frazier.

"Who the hell are you?"

"The name's Frazier, boy. I'm normally Fish and Wildlife Warden. But, today, I'm Deputy Sheriff, fully empowered to take care of you and your sweetheart."

"Jim Jr.?" Ashley gasped as he caught sight of the black man standing to Fred's right.

"Junior here was along for the ride until he caught sight of what's left of Mr. Gardner's boat. Then, we had us a little talk with that hurt man right outside. Junior's had a change of heart."

Susannah walked up to Jim Jr. and asked, "What's he babbling about?"

"I didn't agree to murder, especially Adam's."

"Why you double-crossing, lousy nigger," she snarled.

Jim Jr. balled up his fist and buried it in the bottled blonde's midsection. Susannah doubled over and gasped for air.

"I've wanted to do that for a long, long time" he said with an air of satisfaction.

Melanie finished untying Grant and turned to Fred. "Rebecca Woody was hurt in the boat explosion. We need to get her to a hospital."

Fred nodded.

Grant asked, "What prompted you..."

"I've been suspicious ever since that body washed up a couple of months ago. When that forest fire was set, well, I..."

"Wait a minute! You acted as if I were crazy," Melanie sputtered.

"It was a feeling in my bones. If I was wrong, you'd be all riled up for no reason. After all, I knew you'd just been through a pretty horrible circumstance. I didn't see no use in scarin' you with no solid evidence."

Grant inquired, "What made you know something was happening today?"

"I'm gettin' to that. A Detective Stone from the New York Police called me. I guess you mentioned my name, ma'am," he nodded at Melanie.

Melanie confirmed his assumption. "I mentioned your lack of interest."

Fred smiled again, "Well, off and on, we had a couple more talks. He double-checked on the curious activities of a Mr. Ashley Parker. I investigated around the docks. Some of my buddies thought ol' Ian's fishing was fishy — s'cuse my punnin'."

"Hold it, Fred. Who's Ian?" Grant asked.

"Ian's the shrimp boat captain, lying out there in the cart. Anyway, it seems Ian and his buddy Li'l Joe were making extra runs. After those runs, they had no shrimp to sell to the packer. In spite of this bad luck, they were flashing a lot of cash. My break came after Detective Stone mentioned this here Ashley Parker. I checked the arriving vessels for Parker Transworld against Ian's poorly-timed runs. They matched perfectly."

"How about the connection with Adam?" Melanie winced as she posed the question.

"That took me a while to figure out. I knew they had to be smuggling something. And, I knew it couldn't come in on either a Parker ship or Ian's shrimp boat. Too many people would notice. I kept asking myself where there was a dock where no one would be checking. Also, I guessed the place needed a safe route to an airport or highway. The

Hammock fit the bill. So, I watched ol' Ian for a while. I saw him meet Junior in an out-of-the-way place."

"A payoff?" Grant questioned.

"I was guessing so. But, I couldn't prove it. Junior fitted. After all, The Hammock's security men dare not question the head man's assistant. Then, while the hurricane was blowing out, a buddy of mine called to tell me Ian was taking out his boat. I figured something was going on. I hightailed it over to The Hammock. When I got there, I found Adam had taken off with Melanie on board. I hunted down Junior. With the help of this little sidearm, we had a man-to-man talk."

"He scared you into cooperating?" Ashley questioned Jim Jr.

"No way, man. Fred and his gun just got my attention. That's all."

"While we talked, we heard an explosion out this way. Junior agreed to take a little boat ride to investigate. When we came into the creek, Junior identified what was left of Adam's boat. We coasted in from there."

"Seeing Mr. Gardner's boat shook me up," Jim Jr. offered. "Then, seeing Ian convinced me. I agreed to help with the business part of this arrangement. I even performed a hoodoo rope trick. But, killing Mr. Gardner.... Well, it doesn't take a genius to know who's going to be next."

"So, here we are," Fred concluded. "A helicopter is on the way to take Rebecca and Ian to the hospital. It'll be my honor to personally escort these two culprits to the hoosegow."

6:30 a.m., Monday, August 15, 1988

The powdery sand trembled. The grains moved once, twice, then inwardly collapsed. Surrounding this small dark sinkhole, several pairs of human eyes watched.

"They're on their way!" David exclaimed.

"Everyone got a pail?" asked Rebecca.

This August evening, the loggerhead researchers gathered at the hatchery and waited for the tiny loggerheads to appear, approximately two months after their eggs had been laid. Grant and Melanie joined them for the culminating event of the summer research.

"These sands have witnessed this ritual for hundreds of millions of years. I'm happy to be here — alive and safe — to witness this year's hatching," Melanie confided to her companions.

Grant added, "If this event doesn't give one pause, I fear, there's no hope for the future of any of us. We've certainly seen the results of short-term, greedy goals. It's time for us to prize the everyday miracles of life."

"I think, all of us have a new perspective on life," agreed the bandaged Rebecca.

The first brave turtlet launched himself into the night air. Scrambling up the soft sand, it headed instinctively for the brightest part of its surroundings — a flashlight strategically placed by Daniel. Another and another climbed out until the silver-dollar-size reptiles covered the sands. All scurried for the light.

"Gently but quickly," Rebecca instructed. "Let's capture them in the pails and transport them to the beach."

Minutes after the first emerged, over a hundred of the hatchlings were trapped in the plastic pails. The team walked their cargo from the hatchery, over the dunes, onto the beach. They stopped several yards above the surf.

"You first, Melanie. Now. you become a true turtler," Rebecca coached.

Melanie put down her pail and rolled it onto its side. Her load of baby loggerheads scrambled frantically for the white foam of the ocean. Millions of years had genetically trained the species to go for the bright bubbles. The humans had run interference past the raccoons and ghost crabs on the beach. Now, alone, the newborn faced schools of fish ranging in size to large sharks, feeding beyond the breakers.

A frenzy possessed the baby turtles. The strongest and luckiest might escape the predators until they reached hiding places among seaweed.

One by one, each researcher discharged more hatchlings. By performing the simple act of crawling, the babies produced another of the world's great unsolved mysteries. Moving along the sand, they imprinted the memory of this beach on their tiny brain. Fifteen or more years later, the adult female survivors would recall that memory and find their way across thousands of miles of ocean to Caretta Island.

Holding hands as they watched the conclusion of their summer-long efforts, the team felt close to nature and to one another. No one spoke. Gradually, one by one, they turned and wandered to the trikes. Rebecca, Grant, and Melanie stayed as Daniel, Lana, and David headed to Duck House.

"A new generation. I hope, in the future, mankind allows them to have a place to carry on this process," Rebecca commented with a sigh.

"Are you talking about the college students or the hatchlings?" Grant asked.

Rebecca smiled, "I was talking about the turtles. But, it applies to the researchers as well, doesn't it?"

"Either way, I know one small step is to have Caretta as a spot for study rather than exploitation. As far as stopping other short-sighted decisions, I resolve to speak out whenever I see any opportunity," Melanie commented.

"Wait a minute," Rebecca said. "What do you mean Caretta will be a place for study? I thought the inheritance taxes meant..."

"Before meeting all of you this evening, I talked with my lawyer, Roger Morrison. In one of his more impressive demonstrations of negotiating and arm-twisting, he has swung a brilliant future for the island," Melanie replied.

"What's going to happen?" Rebecca eagerly asked.

"Both of you know that the inheritance tax is substantial, since the island is valued at its current market rate. The taxes are in excess of seven million dollars. After Ashley's arrest, Roger and I talked about my preferences. Roger called friends all the way to the White House. He arranged a joint meeting with representatives of the Department of Interior, the Department of Justice, the IRS, and the White House."

"Some counselor you have there," Grant interjected.

"Isn't he? Anyway, one of his arguments involved using a little-known provision of the Comprehensive Crime Control Act, whereby land confiscated during a drug bust can be donated to other government agencies. Building from that basis, he emphasized to the White House the importance of the breakup of one of the largest drug rings on the East Coast. It has made excellent publicity for the war on drugs. So, Justice agreed to confiscate Ashley's half of the island if money could be found to 'buy' my half. Working with the budget allocations, a ten-million-dollar sum was discovered. The sum has been given to Interior to purchase my interest in Caretta as a wildlife preserve. Of course, seven million goes immediately to IRS for the inheritance taxes, so most of the money never leaves the government.

"The main house stays in the Parker-Evans family. I expect Patrice to stay there. The caretaker's cottage and the plot around it belong to Jim and Louisa and their family, never to be sold, only to be passed to future generations."

"That sounds most fair," Grant responded. "What about Jim Jr.?"

"In return for his giving evidence against Ashley and Susannah and for assisting Fred in the apprehension, a plea-bargain should get him a couple of years in prison — or less."

Rebecca continued to effuse, "And, Caretta a nature preserve! It's so fantastic, I can hardly believe it! What about the other three million?"

"I hope that aspect interests you and Grant. Duck House will become a research center. The three million will create the Gregory Parker Evans Research Endowment, named after my son. The interest from investments will fund studies for wildlife protection, ecological development, and resource engineering. In plain English, the fund will search for practical ways that mankind can advance without destroying the fragile parts of this planet. If there's one thing I've learned from reading the family journals, it's change can't be forced on the land or on people. As board chairperson, I am asking you, Rebecca, to become the administrative head and you, Grant, to serve as research coordinator."

The moonlight reflected tears, flowing down Rebecca's cheeks. Overcome, she hugged Melanie and walked silently down the beach.

Grant looked into Melanie's eyes as he answered, "I'm astounded, Melanie. Naturally, I accept the position. And, I thank you for it." He paused. "What about you? What about us?"

Melanie returned his warm gaze, "Grant, I want our friendship to continue — and to grow. You'll be busy here with the research center while I'm in New York reorganizing Parker Transworld. Because of the fund, we'll be in close communication. Let's give ourselves time to see what evolves."

"I accept that, too. When you came to Caretta, you reminded me of another woman. Meanwhile, I've learned to leave the past where it belongs and live in the present."

"To live in the present and to look forward to the future — working on projects we care about — it's a pretty good place to be, isn't it?"

Acknowledgments

In 1986, this book was inspired by a week of volunteer work. Nightly, we patrolled an island's beach for nesting loggerhead sea turtles. Daily, we fell in love with the island's environment and what was called "sea island culture."

Since we started traveling full-time in 1987, it took us a couple of years to research sea islands and loggerhead turtles. We gathered research at libraries in:
  Charlotte, NC
  Charleston, SC
  Savannah, GA
  Dade City, FL
  Gulf Shores, AL
  Galveston, TX

There were two books that left lasting impressions on us:
  When Roots Die by Patricia Jones-Jackson
  Time of the Turtle by Jack Rudloe

Experts were interviewed – sometimes in unexpected places:
  Cornelia Bailey, Georgia Department of Natural Resources
  Gwendolyn Dozier, Kings-Tisdale Cottage
  Robert Graham, Savannah Science Museum
  Charlotte Hope, South Carolina Department of Natural Resources
  Bobby Moulis, Savannah Science Museum
  Jon Streich, Georgia Department of Natural Resources
  Herbie Wright, Internal Revenue Service
  ? and ?, Naples, FL firefighters and AA members

Again, we thank acquaintances, friends, and family members who read our manuscript and offered suggestions. Some supplied lodging, too! In alphabetical order, they are:
  Laurene and Amory Bradford
  Deena and Bill Culp
  Pat and Dom Ferullo
  Jan and Jim Gambill
  Martha Glessing and Tam Beeler

Janet Gray
Barbara Jones
Victoria Joy (aka Julia Essig)
Cassandra and Patrick Kennedy
Sharon Mooney
Patti Peake
LeVan and John Paul Rogers
Sarah and Dana Ross
Barry Winningham

Other writers as well as English teachers shared their expertise:
Clara Alexander
Betty Carpenter
Dan Faris
Diana Gleasner
Betsy Goree
Mildred Barger Herschler
Mike Mooney
Jean Shula
Cathy Smith-Bowers
Gloria Underwood
Shirley Webb
Claire Wharton

Lastly but not leastly, we thank all the literary agents and publishing house editors who offered encouragement to finish this story:
Julian Bach
Linda Lee Barclay
Meredith Bernstein
Jacqueline Cantor
E. Stacy Creamer
Susan Rogers
Dawn Seferian
Jennifer Silverman
John Sterling
Alice Webster

The Authors

Mary Helen and Shuford Smith have published eight works of non-fiction. Their children's book, *ABC All-American Riddles*, was selected for a 2005 Children's Choice Award. *Endangered* is their first novel.

The Smiths live and work in Tryon, NC. See some of their articles and photographs on their website, www.livesimplywithstyle.com. Learn more about their wine list at www.winning-wines.com. Read background information on this book at www.endangeredthebook.com.

Made in the USA
Charleston, SC
09 October 2010